He was king of Valu... Valusia, a Valusia li........ ...g of bygone glory, but sti.. ....y land and the greatest of the Seven Empires. Valusia—Land of Dreams, the tribesmen named it, and sometimes it seemed to Kull that he moved in a dream. Strange to him were the intrigues of court and palace, army and people. All was like a masquerade, where men and women hid their real thoughts with a smooth mask. Yet the seizing of the throne had been easy—a bold snatching of opportunity, the swift whirl of swords, the slaying of a tyrant of whom men had wearied unto death, short, crafty plotting with ambitious statesmen out of favor at court—and Kull, wandering adventurer, Atlantean exile, had swept up to the dizzy heights of his dreams: he was lord of Valusia, king of kings. Yet now it seemed that the seizing was far easier than the keeping...

And now a strange feeling of dim unrest, of unreality, stole over him as of late it had been doing. Who was he, a straightforward man of the seas and the mountain, to rule a race strangely and terribly wise with the mysticisms of antiquity? An ancient race—

"I am Kull!" said he, flinging back his head as a lion flings back his mane. "I am Kull!"

Other Cosmos Books

SHADOW KINGDOMS

by

Robert E. Howard

COSMOS BOOKS

SHADOW KINGDOMS
July 2007

Published by

Dorchester Publishing Co., Inc.
200 Madison Avenue
New York, NY 10016

in collaboration with Wildside Press, LLC

Cover design by Garry Nurrish

Cover painting copyright © 2007 by Ken Kelly

Typeset by Swordsmith Productions

ISBN-13: 978-0-8439-5905-5
ISBN-10: 0-8439-5905-3

The name "Cosmos Books" and the Cosmos logo are the
property of Wildside Press, LLC.

Printed in the United States of America.

Contents

.

SHADOW KINGDOMS

The Lost Race

Weird Tales, January 1927

Cororuc glanced about him and hastened his pace. He
was no coward, but he did not like the place. Tall trees
rose all about, their sullen branches shutting out the
sunlight. The dim trail led in and out among them,
sometimes skirting the edge of a ravine, where
Cororuc could gaze down at the treetops beneath.
Occasionally, through a rift in the forest, he could see
away to the forbidding hills that hinted of the ranges
much farther to the west, that were the mountains of
Cornwall.

In those mountains the bandit chief, Buruc the
Cruel, was supposed to lurk, to descend upon such
victims as might pass that way. Cororuc shifted his
grip on his spear and quickened his step. His haste was
due not only to the menace of the outlaws, but also to
the fact that he wished once more to be in his native
land. He had been on a secret mission to the wild
Cornish tribesmen; and though he had been more or
less successful, he was impatient to be out of their
inhospitable country. It had been a long, wearisome
trip, and he still had nearly the whole of Britain to traverse. He threw a glance of aversion about him. He

longed for the pleasant woodlands, with scampering deer, and chirping birds, to which he was used. He longed for the tall white cliff, where the blue sea lapped merrily. The forest through which he was passing seemed uninhabited. There were no birds, no animals; nor had he seen a sign of human habitation.

His comrades still lingered at the savage court of the Cornish king, enjoying his crude hospitality, in no hurry to be away. But Cororuc was not content. So he had left them to follow at their leisure and had set out alone.

Rather a fine figure of a man was Cororuc. Some six feet in height, strongly though leanly built, he was, with gray eyes, a pure Briton but not a pure Celt, his long yellow hair revealing, in him as in all his race, a trace of Belgae.

He was clad in skillfully dressed deerskin, for the Celts had not yet perfected the coarse cloth which they made, and most of the race preferred the hides of deer.

He was armed with a long bow of yew wood, made with no especial skill but an efficient weapon; a long bronze broadsword, with a buckskin sheath; a long bronze dagger and a small, round shield, rimmed with a band of bronze and covered with tough buffalo hide. A crude bronze helmet was on his head. Faint devices were painted in woad on his arms and cheeks.

His beardless face was of the highest type of Briton, clear, straightforward, the shrewd, practical determination of the Nordic mingling with the reckless courage and dreamy artistry of the Celt.

So Cororuc trod the forest path, warily, ready to flee or fight, but preferring to do neither just then.

The trail led away from the ravine, disappearing around a great tree. And from the other side of the tree, Cororuc heard sounds of conflict. Gliding warily forward, and wondering whether he should see some of the elves and dwarfs that were reputed to haunt those woodlands, he peered around the great tree.

A few feet from him he saw a strange tableau. Backed against another tree stood a large wolf, at bay, blood trickling from gashes about his shoulder; while before him, crouching for a spring, the warrior saw a great panther. Cororuc wondered at the cause of the battle. Not often the lords of the forest met in warfare. And he was puzzled by the snarls of the great cat. Savage, blood-lusting, yet they held a strange note of fear; and the beast seemed hesitant to spring in.

Just why Cororuc chose to take the part of the wolf, he himself could not have said. Doubtless it was just the reckless chivalry of the Celt in him, an admiration for the dauntless attitude of the wolf against his far more powerful foe. Be that as it may, Cororuc, characteristically forgetting his bow and taking the more reckless course, drew his sword and leaped in front of the panther. But he had no chance to use it. The panther, whose nerve appeared to be already somewhat shaken, uttered a startled screech and disappeared among the trees so quickly that Cororuc wondered if he had really seen a panther. He turned to the wolf, wondering if it would leap upon him. It was watching him, half crouching; slowly it stepped away from the tree, and still watching him, backed away a few yards, then turned and made off with a strange shambling gait. As the warrior watched it vanish into the forest, an uncanny feeling came over him; he had seen many wolves, he had hunted them and had been hunted by them, but he had never seen such a wolf before.

He hesitated and then walked warily after the wolf, following the tracks that were plainly defined in the soft loam. He did not hasten, being merely content to follow the tracks. After a short distance, he stopped short, the hairs on his neck seeming to bristle. *Only the tracks of the hind feet showed: the wolf was walking erect.*

He glanced about him. There was no sound; the forest was silent. He felt an impulse to turn and put as much territory between him and the mystery as possible, but his Celtic curiosity would not allow it. He followed the trail. And then it ceased altogether. Beneath a great tree the tracks vanished. Cororuc felt the cold sweat on his forehead. What kind of place was that forest? Was he being led astray and eluded by some inhuman, supernatural monster of the woodlands, who sought to ensnare him? And Cororuc backed away, his sword lifted, his courage not allowing him to run, but greatly desiring to do so. And so he came again to the tree where he had first seen the wolf. The trail he had followed led away from it in another direction and Cororuc took it up, almost running in his haste to get out of the vicinity of a wolf who walked on two legs and then vanished in the air.

The trail wound about more tediously than ever, appearing and disappearing within a dozen feet, but it was well for Cororuc that it did, for thus he heard the voices of the men coming up the path before they saw him. He took to a tall tree that branched over the trail, lying close to the great bole, along a wide-flung branch.

Three men were coming down the forest path.

One was a big, burly fellow, vastly over six feet in height, with a long red beard and a great mop of red hair. In contrast, his eyes were a beady black. He was dressed in deerskins, and armed with a great sword.

Of the two others, one was a lanky, villainous-looking scoundrel, with only one eye, and the other was a small, wizened man, who squinted hideously with both beady eyes.

Cororuc knew them, by descriptions the Cornish-men had made between curses, and it was in his excite-ment to get a better view of the most villainous murderer in Britain that he slipped from the tree branch and plunged to the ground directly between them.

He was up on the instant, his sword out. He could expect no mercy; for he knew that the red-haired man was Buruc the Cruel, the scourge of Cornwall.

The bandit chief bellowed a foul curse and whipped out his great sword. He avoided the Briton's furious thrust by a swift backward leap and then the battle was on. Buruc rushed the warrior from the front, striving to beat him down by sheer weight; while the lanky, one-eyed villain slipped around, trying to get behind him. The smaller man had retreated to the edge of the forest. The fine art of the fence was unknown to those early swordsmen. It was hack, slash, stab, the full weight of the arm behind each blow. The terrific blows crashing on his shield beat Cororuc to the ground, and the lanky, one-eyed villain rushed in to finish him. Cororuc spun about without rising, cut the bandit's legs from under him and stabbed him as he fell, then threw himself to one side and to his feet, in time to avoid Buruc's sword. Again, driving his shield up to catch the bandit's sword in midair, he deflected it and whirled his own with all his power. Buruc's head flew from his shoulders.

Then Cororuc, turning, saw the wizened bandit scurry into the forest. He raced after him, but the fellow had disappeared among the trees. Knowing the uselessness of attempting to pursue him, Cororuc turned and raced down the trail. He did not know if there were more bandits in that direction, but he did know that if he expected to get out of the forest at all, he would have to do it swiftly. Without doubt the villain who had escaped would have all the other bandits out, and soon they would be beating the woodlands for him.

After running for some distance down the path and seeing no sign of any enemy, he stopped and climbed into the topmost branches of a tall tree that towered above its fellows.

On all sides he seemed surrounded by a leafy ocean. To the west he could see the hills he had avoided. To the north, far in the distance, other hills rose; to the south the forest ran, an unbroken sea. But to the east, far away, he could barely see the line that marked the thinning out of the forest into the fertile plains. Miles and miles away, he knew not how many, but it meant more pleasant travel, villages of men, people of his own race. He was surprized that he was able to see that far, but the tree in which he stood was a giant of its kind.

Before he started to descend, he glanced about

nearer at hand. He could trace the faintly marked line of the trail he had been following, running away into the east; and could make out other trails leading into it, or away from it. Then a glint caught his eye. He fixed his gaze on a glade some distance down the trail and saw, presently, a party of men enter and vanish. Here and there, on every trail, he caught glances of the glint of accouterments, the waving of foliage. So the squinting villain had already roused the bandits. They were all around him; he was virtually surrounded.

A faintly heard burst of savage yells, from back up the trail, startled him. So, they had already thrown a cordon about the place of the fight and had found him gone. Had he not fled swiftly, he would have been caught. He was outside the cordon, but the bandits were all about him. Swiftly he slipped from the tree and glided into the forest.

Then began the most exciting hunt Cororuc had ever engaged in; for he was the hunted and men were the hunters. Gliding, slipping from bush to bush and from tree to tree, now running swiftly, now crouching in a covert, Cororuc fled, ever eastward, not daring to turn back lest he be driven farther back into the forest. At times he was forced to turn his course; in fact, he very seldom fled in a straight course, yet always he managed to work farther eastward.

Sometimes he crouched in bushes or lay along some leafy branch, and saw bandits pass so close to him that he could have touched them. Once or twice they sighted him and he fled, bounding over logs and bushes, darting in and out among the trees; and always he eluded them.

It was in one of those headlong flights that he noticed he had entered a defile of small hills, of which he had been unaware, and looking back over his shoulder, saw that his pursuers had halted, within full sight. Without pausing to ruminate on so strange a thing, he darted around a great boulder, felt a vine or something catch his foot, and was thrown headlong. Simultaneously, something struck the youth's head, knocking him senseless.

When Cororuc recovered his senses, he found that he was bound, hand and foot. He was being borne along, over rough ground. He looked about him. Men carried him on their shoulders, but such men as he had never seen before. Scarce above four feet stood the tallest, and they were small of build and very dark of complexion. Their eyes were black; and most of them went stooped forward, as if from a lifetime spent in crouching and hiding; peering furtively on all sides. They were armed with small bows, arrows, spears and daggers, all pointed, not with crudely worked bronze but with flint and obsidian, of the finest workmanship. They were dressed in finely dressed hides of rabbits and other small animals, and a kind of coarse cloth; and many were tattooed from head to foot in ocher and woad. There were perhaps twenty in all. What sort of men were they? Cororuc had never seen the like.

They were going down a ravine, on both sides of which steep cliffs rose. Presently they seemed to come to a blank wall, where the ravine appeared to come to an abrupt stop. Here, at a word from one who seemed to be in command, they set the Briton down, and seizing hold of a large boulder, drew it to one side. A small cavern was exposed, seeming to vanish away into the earth; then the strange men picked up the Briton and moved forward.

Cororuc's hair bristled at the thought of being borne into that forbidding-looking cave. What manner of men were they? In all Britain and Alba, in Cornwall or Ireland, Cororuc had never seen such men. Small dwarfish men, who dwelt in the earth. Cold sweat broke out on the youth's forehead. Surely they were the malevolent dwarfs of whom the Cornish people had spoken, who dwelt in their caverns by day, and by night sallied forth to steal and burn dwellings, even slaying if the opportunity arose! You will hear of them, even today, if you journey in Cornwall.

The men, or elves, if such they were, bore him into the cavern, others entering and drawing the boulder back into place. For a moment all was darkness, and then torches began to glow, away off. And at a shout they moved on. Other men of the caves came forward, with the torches.

Cororuc looked about him. The torches shed a vague glow over the scene. Sometimes one, sometimes another wall of the cave showed for an instant, and the Briton was vaguely aware that they were covered with paintings, crudely done, yet with a certain skill his own race could not equal. But always the roof remained unseen. Cororuc knew that the seemingly small cavern had merged into a cave of surprizing size. Through the vague light of the torches the strange people moved, came and went, silently, like shadows of the dim past.

He felt the cords of thongs that bound his feet loosened. He was lifted upright.

"Walk straight ahead," said a voice, speaking the language of his own race, and he felt a spear point touch the back of his neck.

And straight ahead he walked, feeling his sandals scrape on the stone floor of the cave, until they came to a place where the floor tilted upward. The pitch was steep and the stone was so slippery that Cororuc could not have climbed it alone. But his captors pushed him, and pulled him, and he saw that long, strong vines were strung from somewhere at the top.

Those the strange men seized, and bracing their feet against the slippery ascent, went up swiftly. When their feet found level surface again, the cave made a turn, and Cororuc blundered out into a fire-lit scene that made him gasp.

The cave debouched into a cavern so vast as to be almost incredible. The mighty walls swept up into a great arched roof that vanished in the darkness. A level floor lay between, and through it flowed a river; an underground river. From under one wall it flowed to vanish silently under the other. An arched stone bridge, seemingly of natural make, spanned the current.

All around the walls of the great cavern, which was roughly circular, were smaller caves, and before each glowed a fire. Higher up were other caves, regularly arranged, tier on tier. Surely human men could not have built such a city.

In and out among the caves, on the level floor of the main cavern, people were going about what seemed daily tasks. Men were talking together and mending weapons, some were fishing from the river; women were replenishing fires, preparing garments; and altogether it might have been any other village in Britain, to judge from their occupations. But it all struck Cororuc as extremely unreal; the strange place, the small, silent people, going about their tasks, the river flowing silently through it all.

Then they became aware of the prisoner and flocked about him. There was none of the shouting, abuse and indignities, such as savages usually heap on their captives, as the small men drew about Cororuc, silently eying him with malevolent, wolfish stares. The warrior shuddered, in spite of himself.

But his captors pushed through the throng, driving the Briton before them. Close to the bank of the river, they stopped and drew away from around him.

Two great fires leaped and flickered in front of him and there was something between them. He focused his gaze and presently made out the object. A high stone seat, like a throne; and in it seated an aged man, with a long white beard, silent, motionless, but with black eyes that gleamed like a wolf's.

The ancient was clothed in some kind of a single, flowing garment. One claw-like hand rested on the seat near him, skinny, crooked fingers, with talons like a hawk's. The other hand was hidden among his garments.

The firelight danced and flickered; now the old man stood out clearly, his hooked, beak-like nose and long beard thrown into bold relief; now he seemed to recede until he was invisible to the gaze of the Briton, except for his glittering eyes.

"Speak, Briton!" The words came suddenly, strong, clear, without a hint of age. "Speak, what would ye say?"

Cororuc, taken aback, stammered and said, "Why, why—what manner people are you? Why have you taken me prisoner? Are you elves?"

"We are Picts," was the stern reply.

"Picts!" Cororuc had heard tales of those ancient people from the Gaelic Britons; some said that they still lurked in the hills of Siluria, but—

"I have fought Picts in Caledonia," the Briton protested; "they are short but massive and misshapen; not at all like you!"

"They are not true Picts," came the stern retort. "Look about you, Briton," with a wave of an arm, "you see the remnants of a vanishing race; a race that once ruled Britain from sea to sea."

The Briton stared, bewildered.

"Harken, Briton," the voice continued; "harken, barbarian, while I tell to you the tale of the lost race."

The firelight flickered and danced, throwing vague reflections on the towering walls and on the rushing, silent current.

The ancient's voice echoed through the mighty cavern.

"Our people came from the south. Over the islands, over the Inland Sea. Over the snow-topped mountains, where some remained, to slay any enemies who might follow. Down into the fertile plains we came. Over all the land we spread. We became wealthy and prosperous. Then two kings arose in the land, and he who conquered, drove out the conquered. So many of us made boats and set sail for the far-off cliffs that gleamed white in the sunlight. We found a fair land with fertile plains. We found a race of red-haired barbarians, who dwelt in caves. Mighty giants, of great bodies and small minds.

"We built our huts of wattle. We tilled the soil. We cleared the forest. We drove the red-haired giants back into the forest. Farther we drove them back until at last they fled to the mountains of the west and the mountains of the north. We were rich. We were prosperous.

"Then," and his voice thrilled with rage and hate, until it seemed to reverberate through the cavern, "then the Celts came. From the isles of the west, in their rude coracles they came. In the west they landed, but they were not satisfied with the west. They marched eastward and seized the fertile plains. We fought. They were stronger. They were fierce fighters and they were armed with weapons of bronze, whereas we had only weapons of flint.

"We were driven out. They enslaved us. They drove us into the forest. Some of us fled into the mountains of the west. Many fled into the mountains of the north. There they mingled with the red-haired giants we drove out so long ago, and became a race of monstrous dwarfs, losing all the arts of peace and gaining only the ability to fight.

"But some of us swore that we would never leave the land we had fought for. But the Celts pressed us. There were many, and more came. So we took to caverns, to ravines, to caves. We, who had always dwelt in huts that let in much light, who had always tilled the soil, we learned to dwell like beasts, in caves where no sunlight ever entered. Caves we found, of which this is the greatest; caves we made.

"You, Briton," the voice became a shriek and a long arm was outstretched in accusation, "you and your race! You have made a free, prosperous nation into a race of earth-rats! We who never fled, who dwelt in the air and the sunlight close by the sea where traders came, we must flee like hunted beasts and burrow like moles! But at night! Ah, then for our vengeance! Then we slip from our hiding places, ravines and caves, with torch and dagger! Look, Briton!"

And following the gesture, Cororuc saw a rounded post of some kind of very hard wood, set in a niche in the stone floor, close to the bank. The floor about the niche was charred as if by old fires.

Cororuc stared, uncomprehending. Indeed, he understood little of what had passed. That these people were even human, he was not at all certain. He had heard so much of them as "little people." Tales of their doings, their hatred of the race of man, and their maliciousness flocked back to him. Little he knew that he was gazing on one of the mysteries of the ages. That the tales which the ancient Gaels told of the Picts, already warped, would become even more warped from age to age, to result in tales of elves, dwarfs, trolls and fairies, at first accepted and then rejected, entire, by the race of men, just as the Neanderthal monsters resulted in tales of goblins and ogres. But of that Cororuc neither knew nor cared, and the ancient was speaking again.

"There, there, Briton," exulted he, pointing to the

post, "there you shall pay! A scant payment for the debt your race owes mine, but to the fullest of your extent."

The old man's exultation would have been fiendish, except for a certain high purpose in his face. He was sincere. He believed that he was only taking just vengeance; and he seemed like some great patriot for a mighty, lost cause.

"But I am a Briton!" stammered Cororuc. "It was not my people who drove your race into exile! They were Gaels, from Ireland. I am a Briton and my race came from Gallia only a hundred years ago. We conquered the Gaels and drove them into Erin, Wales and Caledonia, even as they drove your race."

"No matter!" The ancient chief was on his feet. "A Celt is a Celt. Briton, or Gael, it makes no difference. Had it not been Gael, it would have been Briton. Every Celt who falls into our hands must pay, be it warrior or woman, babe or king. Seize him and bind him to the post."

In an instant Cororuc was bound to the post, and he saw, with horror, the Picts piling firewood about his feet.

"And when you are sufficiently burned, Briton," said the ancient, "this dagger that has drunk the blood of a hundred Britons, shall quench its thirst in yours."

"But never have I harmed a Pict!" Cororuc gasped, struggling with his bonds.

"You pay, not for what you did, but for what your race has done," answered the ancient sternly. "Well do I remember the deeds of the Celts when first they landed on Britain—the shrieks of the slaughtered, the screams of ravished girls, the smokes of burning villages, the plundering."

Cororuc felt his short neck-hairs bristle. When first the Celts landed on Britain! That was over five hundred years ago!

And his Celtic curiosity would not let him keep still, even at the stake with the Picts preparing to light firewood piled about him.

"You could not remember that. That was ages ago."

The ancient looked at him somberly. "And I am age-old. In my youth I was a witch-finder, and an old woman witch cursed me as she writhed at the stake. She said I should live until the last child of the Pictish race had passed. That I should see the once mighty nation go down into oblivion and then—and only then—should I follow it. For she put upon me the curse of life everlasting."

Then his voice rose until it filled the cavern. "But the curse was nothing. Words can do no harm, can do nothing, to a man. I live. A hundred generations have I seen come and go, and yet another hundred. What is time? The sun rises and sets, and another day has passed into oblivion. Men watch the sun and set their lives by it. They league themselves on every hand with time. They count the minutes that race them into eternity. Man outlived the centuries ere he began to reckon time. Time is man-made. Eternity is the work of the gods. In this cavern there is no such thing as time. There are no stars, no sun. Without is time; within is eternity. We count not time. Nothing marks the speeding of the hours. The youths go forth. They see the sun, the stars. They reckon time. And they pass. I was a young man when I entered this cavern. I have never left it. As you reckon time, I may have dwelt here a thousand years; or an hour. When not banded by time, the soul, the mind, call it what you will, can conquer the body. And the wise men of the race, in my youth, knew more than the outer world will ever learn. When I feel that my body begins to weaken, I take the magic draft, that is known only to me, of all the world. It does not give immortality; that is the work of the mind alone; but it rebuilds the body. The race of Picts vanish; they fade like the snow on the mountain. And when the last is gone, this dagger shall free me from the world." Then in a swift change of tone, "Light the fagots!"

Cororuc's mind was fairly reeling. He did not in the least understand what he had just heard. He was positive that he was going mad; and what he saw the next minute assured him of it.

Through the throng came a wolf; and he knew that it was the wolf whom he had rescued from the panther close by the ravine in the forest!

Strange, how long ago and far away that seemed! Yes, it was the same wolf. That same strange, shambling gait. Then the thing stood erect and raised its front feet to its head. What nameless horror was that?

Then the wolf's head fell back, disclosing a man's face. The face of a Pict; one of the first "werewolves." The man stepped out of the wolfskin and strode forward, calling something. A Pict just starting to light the wood about the Briton's feet drew back the torch and hesitated.

The wolf-Pict stepped forward and began to speak

to the chief, using Celtic, evidently for the prisoner's benefit. Cororuc was surprized to hear so many speak his language, not reflecting upon its comparative simplicity, and the ability of the Picts.

"What is this?" asked the Pict who had played wolf. "A man is to be burned who should not be!"

"How?" exclaimed the old man fiercely, clutching his long beard. "Who are you to go against a custom of age-old antiquity?"

"I met a panther," answered the other, "and this Briton risked his life to save mine. Shall a Pict show ingratitude?"

And as the ancient hesitated, evidently pulled one way by his fanatical lust for revenge, and the other by his equally fierce racial pride, the Pict burst into a wild flight of oration, carried on in his own language. At last the ancient chief nodded.

"A Pict ever paid his debts," said he with impressive grandeur. "Never a Pict forgets. Unbind him. No Celt shall ever say that a Pict showed ingratitude."

Cororuc was released, and as, like a man in a daze, he tried to stammer his thanks, the chief waved them aside.

"A Pict never forgets a foe, ever remembers a friendly deed," he replied.

"Come," murmured his Pictish friend, tugging at the Celt's arm.

He led the way into a cave leading away from the main cavern. As they went, Cororuc looked back, to see the ancient chief seated upon his stone throne, his eyes gleaming as he seemed to gaze back through the lost glories of the ages; on each hand the fires leaped and flickered. A figure of grandeur, the king of a lost race.

On and on Cororuc's guide led him. And at last they emerged and the Briton saw the starlit sky above him.

"In that way is a village of your tribesmen," said the Pict, pointing, "where you will find a welcome until you wish to take up your journey anew."

And he pressed gifts on the Celt; gifts of garments of cloth and finely worked deerskin, beaded belts, a fine horn bow with arrows skillfully tipped with obsidian. Gifts of food. His own weapons were returned to him.

"But an instant," said the Briton, as the Pict turned to go. "I followed your tracks in the forest. They vanished." There was a question in his voice.

The Pict laughed softly. "I leaped into the branches of the tree. Had you looked up, you would have seen me. If ever you wish a friend, you will ever find one in Berula, chief among the Alban Picts."

He turned and vanished. And Cororuc strode through the moonlight toward the Celtic village.

The Song of the Bats

Weird Tales, May 1927

The dusk was on the mountain
And the stars were dim and frail
When the bats came flying, flying
From the river and the vale
To wheel against the twilight
And sing their witchy tale.

"We were kings of eld!" they chanted,
"Rulers of a world enchanted;
"Every nation of creation
"Owned our lordship over men.
"Diadems of power crowned us,
"Then rose Solomon to confound us,
"Flung his web of magic round us,
"In the forms of beasts he bound us,
"So our rule was broken then."

Whirling, wheeling into westward,
Fled they in their phantom flight;
Was it but a wing-beat music
Murmured through the star-gemmed night?
Or the singing of a ghost clan
Whispering of forgotten night?

The Ride of Falume

Weird Tales, October 1927

Falume of Spain rode forth amain when twi-
    light's crimson fell
To drink a toast with Bahram's ghost in the
    scarlet land of Hell.
His rowels clashed as swift he dashed along the
    flaming skies;
The sunset rade at his bridle braid and the moon
    was in his eyes.
The waves were green with an eery sheen over
    the hills of Thule
And the ripples beat to his horse's feet like a ser-
    pent in a pool.
On vampire wings the shadow things wheeled
    round and round his head,
Till he came at last to a kingdom vast in the Land
    of the Restless Dead.

They thronged about in a grisly rout, they caught
    at his silver rein;
"Avaunt, foul host! Tell Bahram's ghost Falume
    has come from Spain!"
Then flame-arrayed rose Bahram's shade: "What
    would ye have, Falume?"

"Ho, Bahram who on earth I slew where Tagus'
      waters boom,
Now though I shore your life of yore amid the
      burning West,
I ride to Hell to bid ye tell where I might ride to
      rest.
My beard is white and dim my sight and I would
      fain be gone.
Speak without guile: where lies the isle of mystic
      Avalon?"

"A league beyond the western wind, a mile
      beyond the moon,
Where the dim seas roar on an unknown shore
      and the drifting stars lie strewn:
The lotus buds there scent the woods where the
      quiet rivers gleam,
And king and knight in the mystic light the ages
      drowse and dream."
With sudden bound Falume wheeled round, he
      fled through the flying wrack
Till he came to the land of Spain with the sunset
      at his back.
"No dreams for me, but living free, red wine and
      battle's roar;
I breast the gales and I ride the trails until I ride
      no more.

The Riders of Babylon

Weird Tales, January 1928

The riders of Babylon clatter forth
Like the hawk-winged scourgers of Azrael
To the meadow-lands of the South and North
And the strong-walled cities of Israel.
They harry the men of the caravans,
They bring rare plunder across the sands
To deck the throne of the great god Baal.
But Babylon's king is a broken shell
And Babylon's queen is a sprite from Hell;
And men shall say, "Here Babylon fell,"
Ere Time has forgot the tale.

The riders of Babylon come and go
From Gaza's halls to the shores of Tyre;
They shake the world from the lands of snow
To the deserts, red in the sunset's fire;
Their horses swim in a sea of gore
And the tribes of the earth bow down before;
They have chained the seas where the
    Cretans sail.

But Babylon's sun shall set in blood;
Her towers shall sink in a crimson flood;
And men shall say, "Here Babylon stood,"
Ere Time forgot the tale.

The Dream Snake

Weird Tales, February 1928

The night was strangely still. As we sat upon the wide veranda, gazing out over the broad, shadowy lawns, the silence of the hour entered our spirits and for a long while no one spoke.

Then far across the dim mountains that fringed the eastern skyline, a faint haze began to glow, and presently a great golden moon came up, making a ghostly radiance over the land and etching boldly the dark clumps of shadows that were trees. A light breeze came whispering out of the east, and the unmowed grass swayed before it in long, sinuous waves, dimly visible in the moonlight; and from among the group upon the veranda there came a swift gasp, a sharp intake of breath that caused us all to turn and gaze.

Faming was leaning forward, clutching the arms of his chair, his face strange and pallid in the spectral light; a thin trickle of blood seeping from the lip in which he had set his teeth. Amazed, we looked at him, and suddenly he jerked about with a short, snarling laugh.

"There's no need of gawking at me like a flock of sheep!" he said irritably and stopped short. We sat bewildered, scarcely knowing what sort of reply to make, and suddenly he burst out again.

"Now I guess I'd better tell the whole thing or you'll be going off and putting me down as a lunatic. Don't interrupt me, any of you! I want to get this thing off my mind. You all know that I'm not a very imaginative man; but there's a thing, purely a figment of imagination, that has haunted me since babyhood. A dream!" he fairly cringed back in his chair as he muttered, "A dream! And God, what a dream! The first time—no, I can't remember the first time I ever dreamed it—I've been dreaming the hellish thing ever since I can remember. Now it's this way: there is a sort of bungalow, set upon a hill in the midst of wide grasslands—not unlike this estate; but this scene is in Africa. And I am living there with a sort of servant, a Hindoo. Just why I am there is never clear to my waking mind, though I am always aware of the reason in my dreams. As a man of a dream, I remember my past life (a life which in no way corresponds with my waking life), but when I am awake my subconscious mind fails to transmit these impressions. However, I think that I am a fugitive from justice and the Hindoo is also a fugitive. How the bungalow came to be there I can never remember, nor do I know in what part of Africa it is, though all these things are known to my dream self. But the bungalow is a small one of a very few rooms, and it situated upon the top of the hill, as I said There are no other hills about and the grasslands stretch to the horizon in every direction; knee-high in some places, waist-high in others.

"Now the dream always opens as I am coming up

the hill, just as the sun is beginning to set. I am carrying a broken rifle and I have been on a hunting trip; how the rifle was broken, and the full details of the trip, I clearly remember—dreaming. But never upon waking. It is just as if a curtain were suddenly raised and a drama began; or just as if I were suddenly transferred to another man's body and life, remembering past years of that life, and not cognizant of any other existence. And that is the hellish part of it! As you know, most of us, dreaming, are, at the back of our consciousness, aware that we are dreaming. No matter how horrible the dream may become, we know that it is a dream, and thus insanity or possible death is staved off. But in this particular dream, there is no such knowledge. I tell you it is so vivid, so complete in every detail, that I wonder sometimes if that is not my real existence and this a dream! But no; for then I should have been dead years ago.

"As I was saying, I come up the hill and the first thing I am cognizant of that it is out of the ordinary is a sort of track leading up the hill in an irregular way; that is, the grass is mashed down as if something heavy had been dragged over it. But I pay no especial attention to it, for I am thinking, with some irritation, that the broken rifle I carry is my only arm and that now I must forego hunting until I can send for another.

"You see, I remember thoughts and impressions of the dream itself, of the occurrences of the dream; it is the memories that the dream 'I' had, of that other dream existence that I can not remember. So. I come up the hill and enter the bungalow. The doors are open and the Hindoo is not there. But the main room is in confusion; chairs are broken, a table is overturned. The Hindoo's dagger is lying upon the floor, but there is no blood anywhere.

"Now, in my dreams, I never remember the other dreams, as sometimes one does. Always it is the first dream, the first time. I always experience the same sensations, in my dreams, with as vivid a force as the first time I ever dreamed. So. I am not able to understand this. The Hindoo is gone, but (thus I ruminate, standing in the center of the disordered room) what did away with him? Had it been a raiding party of Negroes they would have looted the bungalow and probably burned it. Had it been a lion, the place would have been smeared with blood. Then suddenly I remember the track I saw going up the hill, and a cold hand touches my spine; for instantly the whole thing is clear: the thing that came up from the grasslands and wrought havoc in the little bungalow could be naught else except a giant serpent. And as I think or the size of the spoor, cold sweat beads my forehead and the broken rifle shakes in my hand.

"Then I rush to the door in a wild panic, my only thought to make a dash for the coast. But the sun has set and dusk is stealing across the grasslands. And out there somewhere, lurking in the tall grass is that grisly thing—that horror. God!" The ejaculation broke from his lips with such feeling that all of us started, not realizing the tension we had reached. There was a second's silence, then he continued:

"So I bolt the doors and windows, light the lamp I have and take my stand in the middle of the room.

And I stand like a statue—waiting—listening. After a while the moon comes up and her haggard light drifts though the windows. And I stand still in the center of the room; the night is very still—something like this night; the breeze occasionally whispers through the grass, and each time I start and clench my hands until the nails bite into the flesh and the blood trickles down my wrists—and I stand there and wait and listen but it does not come that night!" The sentence came suddenly and explosively, and an involuntary sigh came from the rest; a relaxing of tension.

"I am determined, if I live the night through, to start for the coast early the next morning, taking my chance out there in the grim grasslands—with it. But with morning, I dare not. I do not know in which direction the monster went; and I dare not risk coming upon him in the open, unarmed as I am. So, as in a maze, I remain at the bungalow, and ever my eyes turn toward the sun, lurching relentless down the sky toward the horizon. Ah, God! if I could but halt the sun in the sky!"

The man was in the clutch of some terrific power; his words fairly leaped at us.

"Then the sun rocks down the sky and the long gray shadows come stalking across the grasslands. Dizzy with fear, I have bolted the doors and windows and lighted the lamp long before the last faint glow of twilight fades. The light from the windows may attract the monster, but I dare not stay in the dark. And again I take my stand in the center of the room—waiting."

There was a shuddersome halt. Then he continued,

barely above a whisper, moistening his lips: "'There is no knowing how long I stand there; Time has ceased to be and each second is an eon; each minute is an eternity, stretching into endless eternities. Then, God! but what is that?" He leaned forward, the moonlight etching his face into such a mask of horrified listening that each of us shivered and flung a hasty glance over our shoulders.

"Not the night breeze this time," he whispered. "Something makes the grasses swish-swish—as if a great, long, plaint weight were being dragged through them. Above the bungalow it swishes and then ceases—in front of the door; then the hinges creak— creak! The door begins to bulge inward—a small bit— then some more!" The man's arms were held in front of him, as if braced strongly against something, and his breath came in quick gasps. "And I know I should lean against the door and hold it shut, but I do not, I can not move. I stand there, like a sheep waiting to be slaughtered—but the door holds!" Again that sigh expressive of pent-up feeling.

He drew a shaky hand across his brow. "And all night I stand in the center of that room, as motionless as an image, except to turn slowly, as the swish-swish of the grass marks the fiend's course about the house. Ever I keep my eyes in the direction of the soft, sinister sound. Sometimes it ceases for an instant, or for several minutes, and then I stand scarcely breathing, for a horrible obsession has it that the serpent has in some way made entrance into the bungalow, and I start and whirl this way and that, frightfully fearful of making a noise, though I know not why, but ever with the feeling that the thing is at my back. Then the sounds commence again and I freeze motionless.

"Now here is the only time that my consciousness, which guides my waking hours, ever in any way pierces the veil of dreams. I am, in the dream, in no way conscious that it is a dream, but, in a detached sort of way, my other mind recognizes certain facts and passes them on to my sleeping—shall I say 'ego'? That is to say, my personality is for an instant truly dual and separate to an extent, as the right and left arms are separate, while making up parts in the same entity. My dreaming mind has no cognizance of my higher mind; for the time being the other mind is subordinated and the subconscious mind is in full control, to such an extent that it does not even recognize the existence of the other. But the conscious mind, now sleeping, is cognizant of dim thought-waves emanating from the dream mind. I know that I have not made this entirely clear, but the fact remains that I know that my mind, conscious and subconscious, is near to ruin. My obsession of fear, as I stand there in my dream, is that the serpent will raise itself and peer into the window at me. And I know, in my dream, that if this occurs I shall go insane. And so vivid is the impression imparted to my conscious, now sleeping mind that the thought-waves stir the dim seas of sleep, and somehow I can feel my sanity rocking as my sanity rocks in my dream. Back and forth it totters and sways until the motion takes on a physical aspect and I in my dream am swaying from side to side. Not always is the sensation the same, but I tell you, if that horror ever raises it terrible shape and leers at me, if I ever see the fearful thing in my dream, I shall become stark, wild insane." There was a restless movement among the rest.

"God! but what a prospect!" he muttered. "To be insane and forever dreaming that same dream, night and day! But there I stand, and centuries go by, but at last a dim gray light begins to steal through the windows, the swishing dies away in the distance and presently a red, haggard sun climbs the eastern sky. Then I turn about and gaze into a mirror—and my hair has become perfectly white. I stagger to the door and fling it wide. There is nothing in sight but a wide track leading away down the hill through the grasslands—in the opposite direction from that which I would take toward the coast. And with a shriek of maniacal laughter, I dash down the hill and race across the grasslands. I race until I drop from exhaustion, then I lie until I can stagger up and go on.

"All day I keep this up, with superhuman effort, spurred on by the horror behind me. And ever as I hurl myself forward on weakening legs, ever as I lie gasping for breath, I watch the sun with a terrible eagerness. How swiftly the sun travels when a man races it for life! A losing race it is, as I know when I watch the sun sinking toward the skyline, and the hills which I had to gain ere sundown seemingly as far away as ever."

His voice was lowered and instinctively we leaned toward him; he was gripping the chair arms and the blood was seeping from his lip.

"Then the sun sets and the shadows come and I stagger on and fall and rise and reel on again. And I laugh, laugh, laugh! Then I cease, for the moon comes up and throws the grasslands in ghostly and silvery relief. The light is white across the land, though the moon itself is like blood. And I look back the way I have come—and far—back"—all of us leaned farther toward him, our hair a-prickle; his voice came like a ghostly whisper—"far back—I—see—the—grass—waving. There is no breeze, but the tall grass parts and sways in the moonlight, in a narrow, sinuous line—far away, but nearing every instant." His voice died away.

Somebody broke the ensuing stillness: "And then—?"

"Then I awake. Never yet have I seen the foul monster. But that is the dream that haunts me, and from which I have wakened, in my childhood screaming, in my manhood in cold sweat. At irregular intervals I dream it, and each time, lately"—he hesitated and then went on—"each time lately, the thing has been getting closer—closer—the waving of the grass marks his progress and he nears me with each dream; and when he reaches me, then—"

He stopped short, then without a word rose abruptly and entered the house. The rest of us sat silent for awhile, then followed him, for it was late.

How long I slept I do not know, but I woke suddenly with the impression that somewhere in the house someone had laughed long, loud and hideously, as a maniac laughs. Starting up, wondering if I had been dreaming, I rushed from my room, just as a truly horrible shriek echoed through the house. The place was now alive with other people who had been awakened, and all of us rushed to Famings's room, whence the sounds had seemed to come.

Faming lay dead upon the floor, where it seemed he had fallen in some terrific struggle. There was no mark upon him, but his face was terribly distorted; as the face of a man who had been crushed by some super-human force—such as some gigantic snake.

The Hyena

Weird Tales, March 1928

From the time when I first saw Senecoza, the fetish-man, I distrusted him, and from vague distrust the idea eventually grew into hatred.

I was but newly come to the East Coast, new to African ways, somewhat inclined to follow my impulses, and possessed of a large amount of curiosity.

Because I came from Virginia, race instinct and prejudice were strong in me, and doubtless the feeling of inferiority which Senecoza constantly inspired in me had a great deal to do with my antipathy for him.

He was surprisingly tall, and leanly built. Six inches above six feet he stood, and so muscular was his spare frame that he weighed a good two hundred pounds. His weight seemed incredible when one looked at his lanky build, but he was all muscle—a lean, black giant. His features were not pure Negro. They more resembled Berber than Bantu, with the high, bulging forehead, thin nose and thin, straight lips. But his hair was as kinky as a Bushman's and his color was blacker even than the Masai. In fact, his glossy hide had a different hue from those of the native tribesmen, and I believe that he was of a different tribe.

It was seldom that we of the ranch saw him. Then without warning he would be among us, or we would see him striding through the shoulder-high grass of the veldt, sometimes alone, sometimes followed at a respectful distance by several of the wilder Masai, who bunched up at a distance from the buildings, grasping their spears nervously and eyeing everyone suspiciously. He would make his greetings with a courtly grace; his manner was deferentially courteous, but somehow it "rubbed me the wrong way," so to speak. I always had a vague feeling that the black was mocking us. He would stand before us, a naked bronze giant; make trade for a few simple articles, such as a copper kettle, beads or a trade musket; repeat words of some chief, and take his departure.

I did not like him. And being young and impetuous, I spoke my opinion to Ludtvik Strolvaus, a very distant relative, tenth cousin or suchlike, on whose trading-post ranch I was staying.

But Ludtvik chuckled in his blond beard and said that the fetish-man was all right.

"A power he is among the natives, true. They all fear him. But a friend he is to the whites. *Ja.*"

Ludtvik was long a resident on the East Coast; he knew natives and he knew the fat Australian cattle he raised, but he had little imagination.

The ranch buildings were in the midst of a stockade, on a kind of slope, overlooking countless miles on miles of the finest grazing land in Africa. The stockade was large, well suited for defense. Most of the thousand cattle could be driven inside in case of an uprising of the Masai. Ludtvik was inordinately proud of his cattle.

"One thousand now," he would tell me, his round face beaming, "one thousand now. But later, ah! Ten thousand and another ten thousand. This is a good beginning, but only a beginning. *Ja.*"

I must confess that I got little thrill out of the cattle. Natives herded and corralled them; all Ludtvik and I had to do was to ride about and give orders. That was the work he liked best, and I left it mostly to him.

My chief sport was in riding away across the veldt, alone or attended by a gun-bearer, with a rifle. Not that I ever bagged much game. In the first place I was an execrable marksman; I could hardly have hit an elephant at close range. In the second place, it seemed to me a shame to shoot so many things. A bush-antelope would bound up in front of me and race away, and I would sit watching him, admiring the slim, lithe figure, thrilled with the graceful beauty of the creature, my rifle lying idle across my saddle horn.

The native boy who served as my gun-bearer began to suspect that I was deliberately refraining from shooting, and he began in a covert way to throw sneering hints about my womanishness. I was young and valued even the opinion of a native; which is very foolish. His remarks stung my pride, and one day I hauled him off his horse and pounded him until he yelled for mercy. Thereafter my doings were not questioned.

But still I felt inferior when in the presence of the fetish-man. I could not get the other natives to talk about him. All I could get out of them was a scared rolling of the eyeballs, gesticulation indicative of fear, and vague information that the fetish-man dwelt among the tribes some distance in the interior. General opinion seemed to be that Senecoza was a good man to let alone.

One incident made the mystery about the fetish-man take on, it seemed, a rather sinister form.

In the mysterious way that news travels in Africa, and which white men so seldom hear of, we learned that Senecoza and a minor chief had had a falling out of some kind. It was vague and seemed to have no especial basis of fact. But shortly afterward that chief was found half-devoured by hyenas. That, in itself, was not unusual, but the fright with which the natives heard the news was. The chief was nothing to them; in fact he was something of a villain, but his killing seemed to inspire them with a fright that was little short of homicidal. When the black reaches a certain stage of fear, he is as dangerous as a cornered panther. The next time Senecoza called, they rose and fled en masse and did not return until he had taken his departure.

Between the fear of the blacks, the tearing to pieces of the chief by the hyenas, and the fetish-man, I seemed to sense vaguely a connection of some kind. But I could not grasp the intangible thought.

Not long thereafter, that thought was intensified by another incident. I had ridden far out on the veldt, accompanied by my servant. As we paused to rest our horses close to a kopje, I saw, upon the top, a hyena eyeing us. Rather surprised, for the beasts are not in the habit of thus boldly approaching man in the daytime, I raised my rifle and was taking a steady aim, for I always hated the things, when my servant caught my arm.

"No shoot, *bwana*! No shoot!" he exclaimed hastily, jabbering a great deal in his own language, with which I was not familiar.

"What's up?" I asked impatiently.

He kept on jabbering and pulling my arm, until I gathered that the hyena was a fetish-beast of some kind.

"Oh, all right," I conceded, lowering my rifle just as the hyena turned and sauntered out of sight.

Something about the lank, repulsive beast and his shambling yet gracefully lithe walk struck my sense of humor with a ludicrous comparison.

Laughing, I pointed toward the beast and said, "That fellow looks like a hyena-imitation of Senecoza, the fetish-man." My simple statement seemed to throw the native into a more abject fear than ever.

He turned his pony and dashed off in the general direction of the ranch, looking back at me with a scared face.

I followed, annoyed. And as I rode I pondered. Hyenas, a fetish-man, a chief torn to pieces, a country-side of natives in fear; what was the connection? I puzzled and puzzled, but I was new to Africa; I was young and impatient, and presently with a shrug of annoyance I discarded the whole problem.

The next time Senecoza came to the ranch, he managed to stop directly in front of me. For a fleeting instant his glittering eyes looked into mine. And in spite of myself, I shuddered and stepped back, involuntarily, feeling much as a man feels who looks unaware into the eyes of a serpent. There was nothing tangible, nothing on which I could base a quarrel, but there was a distinct threat. Before my Nordic pugnacity could reassert itself, he was gone. I said nothing. But I knew that Senecoza hated me for some reason and that he plotted my killing. Why, I did not know.

As for me, my distrust grew into bewildered rage, which in turn became hate.

And then Ellen Farel came to the ranch. Why she should choose a trading-ranch in East Africa for a place to rest from the society life of New York, I do not know. Africa is no place for a woman. That is what Ludtvik, also a cousin of hers, told her, but he was overjoyed to see her. As for me, girls never interested me much; usually I felt like a fool in their presence and was glad to be out. But there were few whites in the vicinity and I tired of the company of Ludtvik.

Ellen was standing on the wide veranda when I first saw her, a slim, pretty young thing, with rosy cheeks and hair like gold and large gray eyes. She was surprisingly winsome in her costume of riding-breeches, puttees, jacket and light helmet.

I felt extremely awkward, dusty and stupid as I sat on my wiry African pony and stared at her.

She saw a stocky youth of medium height, with sandy hair, eyes in which a kind of gray predominated; an ordinary, unhandsome youth, clad in dusty riding-clothes and a cartridge belt on one side of which was slung an ancient Colt of big caliber, and on the other a long, wicked hunting-knife.

I dismounted, and she came forward, hand outstretched.

"I'm Ellen," she said, "and I know you're Steve. Cousin Ludtvik has been telling me about you."

I shook hands, surprised at the thrill the mere touch of her hand gave me.

She was enthusiastic about the ranch. She was enthusiastic about everything. Seldom have I seen anyone who had more vigor and vim, more enjoyment of everything done. She fairly scintillated with mirth and gaiety.

Ludtvik gave her the best horse on the place, and we rode much about the ranch and over the veldt.

The blacks interested her much. They were afraid of her, not being used to white women. She would have been off her horse and playing with the pickaninnies if I had let her. She couldn't understand why she should treat the black people as dust beneath her feet. We had long arguments about it. I could not convince her, so I told her bluntly that she didn't know anything about it and she must do as I told her.

She pouted her pretty lips and called me a tyrant, and then was off over the veldt like an antelope, laughing at me over her shoulder, her hair blowing free in the breeze.

Tyrant! I was her slave from the first. Somehow the idea of becoming a lover never enter my mind. It was not the fact that she was several years older than I, or that she had a sweetheart (several of them, I think) back in New York. Simply, I worshipped her; her presence intoxicated me, and I could think of no more enjoyable existence than serving her as a devoted slave.

I was mending a saddle one day when she came running in.

"Oh, Steve!" she called; "there's the most romantic-looking savage! Come quick and tell me what his name is."

She led me out of the veranda.

"There he is," she said, naively pointing. Arms folded, haughty head thrown back, stood Senecoza.

Ludtvik who was talking to him, paid no attention to the girl until he had completed his business with the fetish-man; and then, turning, he took her arm and they went into the house together.

Again I was face to face with the savage; but this time he was not looking at me. With a rage amounting almost to madness, I saw that he was gazing after the girl. There was an expression in his serpentlike eyes—

On the instant my gun was out and leveled. My hand shook like a leaf with the intensity of my fury. Surely I must shoot Senecoza down like the snake he was, shoot him down and riddle him, shoot him into a shredded heap!

The fleeting expression left his eyes and they were fixed on me. Detached they seemed, inhuman in their sardonic calm. And I could not pull the trigger.

For a moment we stood, and then he turned and strode away, a magnificent figure, while I glared after him and snarled with helpless fury.

I sat down on the veranda. What a man of mystery was that savage! What strange power did he possess? Was I right, I wondered, in interpreting the fleeting expression as he gazed after the girl? It seemed to me, in my youth and folly, incredible that a black man, no matter what his rank, should look at a white woman as he did. Most astonishing of all, why could I not shoot him down?

I started as a hand touched my arm.

"What are thinking about, Steve?" asked Ellen, laughing. Then before I could say anything, "Wasn't that chief, or whatever he was, a fine specimen of a savage? He invited us to come to his kraal; is that what you call it? It's away off in the veldt somewhere, and we're going."

"No!" I exclaimed violently, springing up.

"Why Steve," she gasped recoiling, "how rude! He's a perfect gentleman, isn't he, Cousin Ludtvik?"

"*Ja*," nodded Ludtvik, placidly, "we go to his kraal sometime soon, maybe. A strong chief, that savage. His chief has perhaps good trade."

"No!" I repeated furiously. "*I'll* go if somebody has to! Ellen's not going near that beast!"

"Well, that's nice!" remarked Ellen, somewhat indignantly. "I guess you're my boss, mister man?"

With all her sweetness, she had a mind of her own. In spite of all I could do, they arranged to go to the fetish-man's village the next day.

That night the girl came out to me, where I sat on the veranda in the moonlight, and she sat down on the arm of my chair.

"You're not angry at me, are you, Steve?" she said, wistfully, putting her arm around my shoulders. "Not mad, are you?"

Mad? Yes, maddened by the touch of her soft body—such mad devotion as a slave feels. I wanted to grovel in the dust at her feet and kiss her dainty shoes.

Will women never learn the effect they have on men?

I took her hand hesitantly and pressed it to my lips. I think she must have sensed some of my devotion.

"Dear Steve," she murmured, and the words were like a caress, "come, let's walk in the moonlight."

We walked outside the stockade. I should have known better, for I had no weapon but the big Turkish dagger I carried and used for a hunting-knife, but she wished to.

"Tell me about this Senecoza," she asked, and I welcomed the opportunity. And then I thought: what could I tell her? That hyenas had eaten a small chief of the Masai? That the natives feared the fetish-man? That he had looked at her?

And then the girl screamed as out of the tall grass leaped a vague shape, half-seen in the moonlight.

I felt a heavy, hairy form crash against my shoulders; keen fangs ripped my upflung arm. I went to the earth, fighting with frenzied horror. My jacket was slit to ribbons and the fangs were at my throat before I found and drew my knife and stabbed, blindly and savagely. I felt my blade rip into my foe, and then, like a shadow, it was gone. I staggered to my feet, somewhat shaken. The girl caught and steadied me.

"What was it?" she gasped, leading me toward the stockade.

"A hyena," I answered. "I could tell by the scent. But I never heard of one attacking like that."

She shuddered. Later on, after my torn arm had been bandaged, she came close to me and said in a wondrously subdued voice, "Steve, I've decided not to go to the village, if you don't want me to."

After the wounds on my arm had become scars Ellen and I resumed our rides, as might be expected. One day we had wandered rather far out on the veldt, and she challenged me to a race. Her horse easily distanced mine, and she stopped and waited for me, laughing.

She had stopped on a sort of kopje, and she pointed to a clump of trees some distance away.

"Trees!" she said gleefully. "Let's ride down there. There are so few trees on the veldt."

And she dashed away. I followed some instinctive caution, loosening my pistol in its holster, and, drawing my knife, I thrust it down in my boot so that it was entirely concealed.

We were perhaps halfway to the trees when from the tall grass about us leaped Senecoza and some twenty warriors.

One seized the girl's bridle and the others rushed me. The one who caught at Ellen went down with a bullet between his eyes, and another crumpled at my second shot. Then a thrown war-club hurled me from the saddle, half-senseless, and as the blacks closed in on me I saw Ellen's horse, driven frantic by the prick of a carelessly handled spear, scream and rear, scattering the blacks who held her, and dash away at headlong speed, the bit in her teeth.

I saw Senecoza leap on my horse and give chase, flinging a savage command over his shoulder; and both vanished over the kopje.

The warriors bound me hand and foot and carried me into the trees. A hut stood among them—a native hut of thatch and bark. Somehow the sight of it set me shuddering. It seemed to lurk, repellent and indescribably malevolent amongst the trees; to hint of horrid and obscene rites; of voodoo.

I know not why it is, but the sight of a native hut, alone and hidden, far from a village or tribe, always has to me a suggestion of nameless horror. Perhaps that is because only a black who is crazed or one who is so criminal that he has been exiled by his tribe will dwell that way.

In front of the hut they threw me down.

"When Senecoza returns with the girl," said they, "you will enter." And they laughed like fiends. Then, leaving one black to see that I did not escape, they left.

The black who remained kicked me viciously; he was a bestial-looking Negro, armed with a trade-musket.

"They go to kill white men, fool!" he mocked me. "They go to the ranches and trading-posts, first to that fool of an Englishman." Meaning Smith, the owner of a neighboring ranch.

And he went on giving details. Senecoza had made the plot, he boasted. They would chase all the white men to the coast.

"Senecoza is more than a man," he boasted. "You shall see, white man," lowering his voice and glancing about him, from beneath his low, beetling brows; "you shall see the magic of Senecoza." And he grinned, disclosing teeth filed to points.

"Cannibal!" I ejaculated, involuntarily. "A Masai?"

"No," he answered. "A man of Senecoza."

"Who will kill no white men," I jeered.

He scowled savagely. "I will kill you, white man."

"You dare not."

"That is true," he admitted, and added angrily, "Senecoza will kill you himself."

And meantime Ellen was riding like mad, gaining on the fetish-man, but unable to ride toward the ranch, for he had gotten between and was forcing her steadily out upon the veldt.

The black unfastened my bonds. His line of reasoning was easy to see; absurdly easy. He could not kill a prisoner of the fetish-man, but he could kill him to prevent his escape. And he was maddened with the blood-lust. Stepping back, he half-raised his trade-musket, watching me as a snake watches a rabbit.

It must have been about that time, as she afterward told me, that Ellen's horse stumbled and threw her. Before she could rise, the black had leaped from his horse and seized her in his arms. She screamed and fought, but he gripped her, held her helpless and laughed at her. Tearing her jacket to pieces, he bound her arms and legs, remounted and started back, carrying the half-fainting girl in front of him.

Back in front of the hut I rose slowly. I rubbed my arms where the ropes had been, moved a little closer to the black, stretched, stooped and rubbed my legs; then with a catlike bound I was on him, my knife flashing from my boot. The trade-musket crashed and the charge whizzed above my head as I knocked up the barrel and closed with him. Hand to hand, I would have been no match for the black giant; but I had the knife. Clinched close together we were too close for him to use the trade-musket for a club. He wasted time trying to do that, and with a desperate effort I threw him off his balance and drove the dagger to the hilt in his black chest.

I wrenched it out again; I had no other weapon, for I could find no more ammunition for the trade-musket.

I had no idea which way Ellen had fled. I assumed she had gone toward the ranch, and in that direction I took my way. Smith must be warned. The warriors were far ahead of me. Even then they might be creeping up about the unsuspecting ranch.

I had not covered a fourth of the distance, when a drumming of hoofs behind me caused me to turn my head. Ellen's horse was thundering toward me, riderless. I caught her as she raced past me, and managed to stop her. The story was plain. The girl had either reached a place of safety and had turned the horse loose, or what was much more likely, had been captured, the horse escaping and fleeing toward the ranch, as a horse will do. I gripped the saddle, torn with indecision. Finally I leaped on the horse and sent her flying toward Smith's ranch. It was not many miles; Smith must not be massacred by those black devils, and I must find a gun if I escaped to rescue the girl from Senecoza.

A half-mile from Smith's I overtook the raiders and went through them like drifting smoke. The workers at Smith's place were startled by a wild-riding horseman charging headlong into the stockade, shouting, "Masai! Masai! A raid, you fools!" snatching a gun and flying out again.

So when the savages arrived they found everybody

ready for them, and they got such a warm reception that after one attempt they turned tail and fled back across the veldt.

And I was riding as I never rode before. The mare was almost exhausted, but I pushed her mercilessly. On, on!

I aimed for the only place I knew likely. The hut among the trees. I assumed that the fetish-man would return there.

And long before the hut came into sight, a horseman dashed from the grass, going at right angles to my course, and our horses, colliding, sent both tired animals to the ground.

"Steve!" It was a cry of joy mingled with fear. Ellen lay, tied hand and foot, gazing up at me wildly as I regained my feet.

Senecoza came with a rush, his long knife flashing in the sunlight. Back and forth we fought—slash, ward and parry, my ferocity and agility matching his savagery and skill.

A terrific lunge which he aimed at me, I caught on my point, laying his arm open, and then with a quick engage and wrench, disarmed him. But before I could use my advantage, he sprang away into the grass and vanished.

I caught up the girl, slashing her bonds, and she clung to me, poor child, until I lifted her and carried her toward the horses. But we were not yet through with Senecoza. He must have had a rifle cached away somewhere in the bush, for the first I knew of him was when a bullet spat within a foot above my head.

I caught at the bridles, and then I saw that the mare

had done all she could, temporarily. She was exhausted. I swung Ellen up on the horse.

"Ride for our ranch," I ordered her. "The raiders are out, but you can get through. Ride low and ride fast!"

"But you, Steve!"

"Go, go!" I ordered, swinging her horse around and starting it. She dashed away, looking at me wistfully over her shoulder. Then I snatched the rifle and a handful of cartridges I had gotten at Smith's, and took to the bush. And through the hot African day, Senecoza and I played a game of hide-and-seek. Crawling, slipping in and out of the scanty veldt-bushes, crouching in the tall grass, we traded shots back and forth. A movement of the grass, a snapping twig, the rasp of grass-blades, and a bullet came questing, another answering it.

I had but a few cartridges and I fired carefully, but presently I pushed my one remaining cartridge into the rifle—a big, six-bore, single-barrel breech-loader, for I had not had time to pick when I snatched it up.

I crouched in my covert and watched for the black to betray himself by a careless movement. Not a sound, not a whisper among the grasses. Away off over the veldt a hyena sounded his fiendish laugh and another answered, closer at hand. The cold sweat broke out on my brow.

What was that? A drumming of many horses' hoofs! Raiders returning? I ventured a look and could have shouted for joy. At least twenty men were sweeping toward me, white men and ranch-boys, and ahead of them all rode Ellen! They were still some distance away. I darted behind a tall bush and rose, waving my hand to attract their attention.

They shouted and pointed to something beyond me. I whirled and saw, some thirty yards away, a huge hyena slinking toward me, rapidly. I glanced carefully across the veldt. Somewhere out there, hidden by the billowing grasses, lurked Senecoza. A shot would betray to him my position—and I had but one cartridge. The rescue party was still out of range.

I looked again at the hyena. He was still rushing toward me. There was no doubt as to his intentions. His eyes glittered like a fiend's from Hell, and a scar on his shoulder showed him to be the same beast that had once before attacked me. Then a kind of horror took hold of me, and resting the old elephant rifle over my elbow, I sent my last bullet crashing through the bestial thing. With a scream that seemed to have a horribly human note in it, the hyena turned and fled back into the bush, reeling as it ran.

And the rescue party swept up around me.

A fusillade of bullets crashed through the bush from which Senecoza had sent his last shot. There was no reply.

"Ve hunt ter snake down," quoth Cousin Ludtvik, his Boer accent increasing with his excitement. And we scattered through the veldt in a skirmish line, combing every inch of it warily.

Not a trace of the fetish-man did we find. A rifle we found, empty, with empty shells scattered about, and (which was very strange) *hyena tracks leading away from the rifle.*

I felt the short hairs of my neck bristle with intangible horror. We looked at each other, and said not a word, as with a tacit agreement we took up the trail of the hyena.

We followed it as it wound in and out in the shoulder-high grass, showing how it had slipped up on me, stalking me as a tiger stalks its victim. We struck the trail the thing had made, returning to the bush after I had shot it. Splashes of blood marked the way it had taken. We followed.

"It leads toward the fetish-hut," muttered an Englishman. "Here, sirs, is a damnable mystery."

And Cousin Ludtvik ordered Ellen to stay back, leaving two men with her.

We followed the trail over the kopje and into the clump of trees. Straight to the door of the hut it led. We circled the hut cautiously, but no tracks led away. It was inside the hut. Rifles ready, we forced the rude door.

No tracks led away from the hut and no tracks led to it except the tracks of the hyena. Yet there was no hyena within that hut; and on the dirt floor, a bullet through his black breast, lay Senecoza, the fetish-man.

The Gates of Nineveh

Weird Tales, July 1928

These are the gates of Nineveh; here
   Sargon came when his wars were won,
Gazed at the turrets looming clear,
   Boldly etched in the morning sun.

Down from his chariot Sargon came,
   Tossed his helmet upon the sand,
Dropped his sword with its blade like flame,
   Stroked his beard with his empty hand.

"Towers are flaunting their banners red,
   The people greet me with song and mirth,
But a weird is on me," Sargon said,
   "And I see the end of the tribes of earth.

"Cities crumble, and chariots rust—
   I see through a fog that is strange and gray—
All kingly things fade back to the dust,
   Even the gates of Nineveh."

Red Shadows

Weird Tales, August 1928

1. The Coming of Solomon

The moonlight shimmered hazily, making silvery mists of illusion among the shadowy trees. A faint breeze whispered down the valley, bearing a shadow that was not of the moon-mist. A faint scent of smoke was apparent.

The man whose long, swinging strides, unhurried yet unswerving, had carried him for many a mile since sunrise, stopped suddenly. A movement in the trees had caught his attention, and he moved silently toward the shadows, a hand resting lightly on the hilt of his long, slim rapier.

Warily he advanced, his eyes striving to pierce the darkness that brooded under the trees. This was a wild and menacing country; death might be lurking under those trees. Then his hand fell away from the hilt and he leaned forward. Death indeed was there, but not in such shape as might cause him fear.

"The fires of Hades!" he murmured. "A girl! What has harmed you, child? Be not afraid of me."

The girl looked up at him, her face like a dim white rose in the dark.

"You—who are—you?" her words came in gasps.

"Naught but a wanderer, a landless man, but a friend to all in need." The gentle voice sounded somehow incongruous, coming from the man.

The girl sought to prop herself up on her elbow, and instantly he knelt and raised her to a sitting position, her head resting against his shoulder. His hand touched her breast and came away red and wet.

"Tell me." His voice was soft, soothing, as one speaks to a babe.

"Le Loup," she gasped, her voice swiftly growing weaker. "He and his men—descended upon our village—a mile up the valley. They robbed—slew—burned—"

"That, then, was the smoke I scented," muttered the man. "Go on, child."

"I ran. He, the Wolf, pursued me—and—caught me—" The words died away in a shuddering silence.

"I understand, child. Then—?"

"Then—he—he—stabbed me—with his dagger—oh, blessed saints!—mercy—"

Suddenly the slim form went limp. The man eased her to the earth, and touched her brow lightly.

"Dead!" he muttered.

Slowly he rose, mechanically wiping his hands upon his cloak. A dark scowl had settled on his somber brow. Yet he made no wild, reckless vow, swore no oath by saints or devils.

"Men shall die for this," he said coldly.

2. The Lair of the Wolf

"You are a fool!" The words came in a cold snarl that curdled the hearer's blood.

He who had just been named a fool lowered his eyes sullenly without answer.

"You and all the others I lead!" The speaker leaned forward, his fist pounding emphasis on the rude table between them. He was a tall, rangy-built man, supple as a leopard and with a lean, cruel, predatory face. His eyes danced and glittered with a kind of reckless mockery.

The fellow spoken to replied sullenly, "This Solomon Kane is a demon from Hell, I tell you."

"Faugh! Dolt! He is a man—who will die from a pistol ball or a sword thrust."

"So thought Jean, Juan and La Costa," answered the other grimly. "Where are they? Ask the mountain wolves that tore the flesh from their dead bones. Where does this Kane hide? We have searched the mountains and the valleys for leagues, and we have found no trace. I tell you, Le Loup, he comes up from Hell. I knew no good would come from hanging that friar a moon ago."

The Wolf strummed impatiently upon the table. His keen face, despite lines of wild living and dissipation, was the face of a thinker. The superstitions of his followers affected him not at all.

"Faugh! I say again. The fellow has found some

cavern or secret vale of which we do not know where he hides in the day."

"And at night he sallies forth and slays us," gloomily commented the other. "He hunts us down as a wolf hunts deer—by God, Le Loup, you name yourself Wolf but I think you have met at last a fiercer and more crafty wolf than yourself! The first we know of this man is when we find Jean, the most desperate bandit unhung, nailed to a tree with his own dagger through his breast, and the letters S.L.K. carved upon his dead cheeks. Then the Spaniard Juan is struck down, and after we find him he lives long enough to tell us that the slayer is an Englishman, Solomon Kane, who has sworn to destroy our entire band! What then? La Costa, a swordsman second only to yourself, goes forth swearing to meet this Kane. By the demons of perdition, it seems he met him! For we found his sword-pierced corpse upon a cliff. What now? Are we all to fall before this English fiend?"

"True, our best men have been done to death by him," mused the bandit chief. "Soon the rest return from that little trip to the hermit's; then we shall see. Kane can not hide forever. Then—ha, what was that?"

The two turned swiftly as a shadow fell across the table. Into the entrance of the cave that formed the bandit lair, a man staggered. His eyes were wide and staring; he reeled on buckling legs, and a dark red stain dyed his tunic. He came a few tottering steps forward, then pitched across the table, sliding off onto the floor.

"Hell's devils!" cursed the Wolf, hauling him

upright and propping him in a chair. "Where are the rest, curse you?"

"Dead! All dead!"

"How? Satan's curses on you, speak!" The Wolf shook the man savagely, the other bandit gazing on in wide-eyed horror.

"We reached the hermit's hut just as the moon rose," the man muttered. "I stayed outside—to watch—the others went in—to torture the hermit—to make him reveal—the hiding-place—of his gold."

"Yes, yes! Then what?" The Wolf was raging with impatience.

"Then the world turned red—the hut went up in a roar and a red rain flooded the valley—through it I saw—the hermit and a tall man clad all in black— coming from the trees—"

"Solomon Kane!" gasped the bandit. "I knew it! I—"

"Silence, fool!" snarled the chief. "Go on!"

"I fled—Kane pursued—wounded me—but I outran—him—got—here—first—"

The man slumped forward on the table.

"Saints and devils!" raged the Wolf. "What does he look like, this Kane?"

"Like—Satan—"

The voice trailed off in silence. The dead man slid from the table to lie in a red heap upon the floor.

"Like Satan!" babbled the other bandit. "I told you! 'Tis the Horned One himself! I tell you—"

He ceased as a frightened face peered in at the cave entrance.

"Kane?"

"Aye." The Wolf was too much at sea to lie. "Keep close watch, La Mon; in a moment the Rat and I will join you."

The face withdrew and Le Loup turned to the other.

"This ends the band," said he. "You, I, and that thief La Mon are all that are left. What would you suggest?"

The Rat's pallid lips barely formed the word: "Flight!"

"You are right. Let us take the gems and gold from the chests and flee, using the secret passageway."

"And La Mon?"

"He can watch until we are ready to flee. Then— why divide the treasure three ways?"

A faint smile touched the Rat's malevolent features. Then a sudden thought smote him.

"He," indicating the corpse on the floor, "said, 'I got here first.' Does that mean Kane was pursuing him here?" And as the Wolf nodded impatiently the other turned to the chests with chattering haste.

The flickering candle on the rough table lighted up a strange and wild scene. The light, uncertain and dancing, gleamed redly in the slowly widening lake of blood in which the dead man lay; it danced upon the heaps of gems and coins emptied hastily upon the floor from the brass-bound chests that ranged the walls; and it glittered in the eyes of the Wolf with the same gleam which sparkled from his sheathed dagger.

The chests were empty, their treasure lying in a shimmering mass upon the bloodstained floor. The Wolf stopped and listened. Outside was silence. There was no moon, and Le Loup's keen imagination pictured the dark slayer, Solomon Kane, gliding through the blackness, a shadow among shadows. He grinned crookedly; this time the Englishman would be foiled.

"There is a chest yet unopened," said he, pointing.

The Rat, with a muttered exclamation of surprize, bent over the chest indicated. With a single, catlike motion, the Wolf sprang upon him, sheathing his dagger to the hilt in the Rat's back, between the shoulders. The Rat sagged to the floor without a sound.

"Why divide the treasure two ways?" murmured Le Loup, wiping his blade upon the dead man's doublet. "Now for La Mon."

He stepped toward the door; then stopped and shrank back.

At first he thought that it was the shadow of a man who stood in the entrance; then he saw that it was a man himself, though so dark and still he stood that a fantastic semblance of shadow was lent him by the guttering candle.

A tall man, as tall as Le Loup he was, clad in black from head to foot, in plain, close-fitting garments that somehow suited the somber face. Long arms and broad shoulders betokened the swordsman, as plainly as the long rapier in his hand. The features of the man were saturnine and gloomy. A kind of dark pallor lent him a ghostly appearance in the uncertain light, an effect heightened by the satanic darkness of his lowering brows. Eyes, large, deep-set and unblinking, fixed their gaze upon the bandit, and looking into them, Le Loup was unable to decide what color they were. Strangely, the mephistophelean trend of the lower features was offset by a high, broad forehead, though this was partly hidden by a featherless hat.

That forehead marked the dreamer, the idealist, the introvert, just as the eyes and the thin, straight nose betrayed the fanatic. An observer would have been struck by the eyes of the two men who stood there, facing each other. Eyes of both betokened untold deeps of power, but there the resemblance ceased.

The eyes of the bandit were hard, almost opaque, with a curious scintillant shallowness that reflected a thousand changing lights and gleams, like some strange gem; there was mockery in those eyes, cruelty and recklessness.

The eyes of the man in black, on the other hand, deep-set and staring from under prominent brows, were cold but deep; gazing into them, one had the impression of looking into countless fathoms of ice.

Now the eyes clashed, and the Wolf, who was used to being feared, felt a strange coolness on his spine. The sensation was new to him—a new thrill to one who lived for thrills, and he laughed suddenly.

"You are Solomon Kane, I suppose?" he asked, managing to make his question sound politely incurious.

"I am Solomon Kane." The voice was resonant and powerful. "Are you prepared to meet your God?"

"Why, *Monsieur*," Le Loup answered, bowing, "I assure you I am as ready as I ever will be. I might ask *Monsieur* the same question."

"No doubt I stated my inquiry wrongly," Kane said grimly. "I will change it: Are you prepared to meet your master, the Devil?"

"As to that, *Monsieur*"—Le Loup examined his finger nails with elaborate unconcern—"I must say that I can at present render a most satisfactory account to his Horned Excellency, though really I have no intention of so doing—for a while at least."

Le Loup did not wonder as to the fate of La Mon; Kane's presence in the cave was sufficient answer that did not need the trace of blood on his rapier to verify it.

"What I wish to know, *Monsieur*," said the bandit, "is why in the Devil's name have you harassed my band as you have, and how did you destroy that last set of fools?"

"Your last question is easily answered, sir," Kane replied. "I myself had the tale spread that the hermit possessed a store of gold, knowing that would draw your scum as carrion draws vultures. For days and nights I have watched the hut, and tonight, when I saw your villains coming, I warned the hermit, and together we went among the trees back of the hut. Then, when the rogues were inside, I struck flint and steel to the train I had laid, and flame ran through the trees like a red snake until it reached the powder I had placed beneath the hut floor. Then the hut and thirteen sinners went to Hell in a great roar of flame and smoke. True, one escaped, but him I had slain in the forest had not I stumbled and fallen upon a broken root, which gave him time to elude me."

"*Monsieur*," said Le Loup with another low bow, "I grant you the admiration I must needs bestow on a brave and shrewd foeman. Yet tell me this: Why have you followed me as a wolf follows deer?"

"Some moons ago," said Kane, his frown becoming more menacing, "you and your fiends raided a small village down the valley. You know the details better than I. There was a girl there, a mere child, who, hoping to escape your lust, fled up the valley; but you, you jackal of Hell, you caught her and left her, violated and dying. I found her there, and above her dead form I made up my mind to hunt you down and kill you."

"H'm," mused the Wolf. "Yes, I remember the wench. *Mon Dieu*, so the softer sentiments enter into the affair! *Monsieur*, I had not thought you an amorous man; be not jealous, good fellow, there are many more wenches."

"Le Loup, take care!" Kane exclaimed, a terrible menace in his voice, "I have never yet done a man to death by torture, but by God, sir, you tempt me!"

The tone, and more especially the unexpected oath, coming as it did from Kane, slightly sobered Le Loup; his eyes narrowed and his hand moved toward his rapier. The air was tense for an instant; then the Wolf relaxed elaborately.

"Who was the girl?" he asked idly. "Your wife?"

"I never saw her before," answered Kane.

"*Nom d'un nom!*" swore the bandit. "What sort of a man are you, *Monsieur*, who takes up a feud of this sort merely to avenge a wench unknown to you?"

"That, sir, is my own affair; it is sufficient that I do so."

Kane could not have explained, even to himself, nor did he ever seek an explanation within himself. A true fanatic, his promptings were reasons enough for his actions.

"You are right, *Monsieur*." Le Loup was sparring now for time; casually he edged backward inch by inch, with such consummate acting skill that he aroused no suspicion even in the hawk who watched him. "*Monsieur*," said he, "possibly you will say that you are merely a noble cavalier, wandering about like a true Galahad, protecting the weaker; but you and I know different. There on the floor is the equivalent to an emperor's ransom. Let us divide it peaceably; then if you like not my company, why—*nom d'un nom!*— we can go our separate ways."

Kane leaned forward, a terrible brooding threat growing in his cold eyes. He seemed like a great condor about to launch himself upon his victim.

"Sir, do you assume me to be as great a villain as yourself?"

Suddenly Le Loup threw back his head, his eyes dancing and leaping with a wild mockery and a kind of insane recklessness. His shout of laughter sent the echoes flying.

"Gods of Hell! No, you fool, I do not class you with myself! *Mon Dieu, Monsieur* Kane, you have a task indeed if you intend to avenge all the wenches who have known my favors!"

"Shades of death! Shall I waste time in parleying with this base scoundrel!" Kane snarled in a voice suddenly blood-thirsting, and his lean frame flashed forward like a bent bow suddenly released.

At the same instant Le Loup with a wild laugh bounded backward with a movement as swift as Kane's. His timing was perfect; his back-flung hands struck the table and hurled it aside, plunging the cave into darkness as the candle toppled and went out.

Kane's rapier sang like an arrow in the dark as he thrust blindly and ferociously.

"*Adieu, Monsieur* Galahad!" The taunt came from somewhere in front of him, but Kane, plunging toward the sound with the savage fury of baffled wrath, caromed against a blank wall that did not yield to his blow. From somewhere seemed to come an echo of a mocking laugh.

Kane whirled, eyes fixed on the dimly outlined entrance, thinking his foe would try to slip past him and out of the cave; but no form bulked there, and when his groping hands found the candle and lighted it, the cave was empty, save for himself and the dead men on the floor.

3. The Chant of the Drums

Across the dusky waters the whisper came: boom, boom, boom!—a sullen reiteration. Far away and more faintly sounded a whisper of different timbre: thrum, throom, thrum! Back and forth went the vibrations as the throbbing drums spoke to each other. What tales did they carry? What monstrous secrets whispered across the sullen, shadowy reaches of the unmapped jungle?

"This, you are sure, is the bay where the Spanish ship put in?"

"Yes, *Senhor*; the Negro swears this is the bay where the white man left the ship alone and went into the jungle."

Kane nodded grimly.

"Then put me ashore here, alone. Wait seven days; then if I have not returned and if you have no word of me, set sail wherever you will."

"Yes, *Senhor*."

The waves slapped lazily against the sides of the boat that carried Kane ashore. The village that he sought was on the river bank but set back from the bay shore, the jungle hiding it from sight of the ship.

Kane had adopted what seemed the most hazardous course, that of going ashore by night, for the reason that he knew, if the man he sought were in the village, he would never reach it by day. As it was, he was taking a most desperate chance in daring the nighttime jungle, but all his life he had been used to taking desperate chances. Now he gambled his life upon the slim chance of gaining the Negro village under cover of darkness and unknown to the villagers.

At the beach he left the boat with a few muttered commands, and as the rowers put back to the ship which lay anchored some distance out in the bay, he turned and engulfed himself in the blackness of the jungle. Sword in one hand, dagger in the other, he stole forward, seeking to keep pointed in the direction from which the drums still muttered and grumbled.

He went with the stealth and easy movement of a leopard, feeling his way cautiously, every nerve alert and straining, but the way was not easy. Vines tripped him and slapped him in the face, impeding his progress; he was forced to grope his way between the huge boles of towering trees, and all through the underbrush about him sounded vague and menacing rustlings and shadows of movement. Thrice his foot touched something that moved beneath it and writhed away, and once he glimpsed the baleful glimmer of feline eyes among the trees. They vanished, however, as he advanced.

Thrum, thrum, thrum, came the ceaseless monotone of the drums: war and death (they said); blood and lust; human sacrifice and human feast! The soul of Africa (said the drums); the spirit of the jungle; the chant of the gods of outer darkness, the gods that roar and gibber, the gods men knew when dawns were young, beast-eyed, gaping-mouthed, huge-bellied, bloody-handed, the Black Gods (sang the drums).

All this and more the drums roared and bellowed to Kane as he worked his way through the forest. Somewhere in his soul a responsive chord was smitten and answered. You too are of the night (sang the drums); there is the strength of darkness, the strength of the primitive in you; come back down the ages; let us teach you, let us teach you (chanted the drums).

Kane stepped out of the thick jungle and came upon a plainly defined trail. Beyond through the trees came the gleam of the village fires, flames glowing through the palisades. Kane walked down the trail swiftly.

He went silently and warily, sword extended in front of him, eyes straining to catch any hint of movement in the darkness ahead, for the trees loomed like sullen giants on each hand; sometimes their great branches intertwined above the trail and he could see only a slight way ahead of him.

Like a dark ghost he moved along the shadowed trail; alertly he stared and harkened; yet no warning came first to him, as a great, vague bulk rose up out of the shadows and struck him down, silently.

4. The Black God

Thrum, thrum, thrum! Somewhere, with deadening monotony, a cadence was repeated, over and over, bearing out the same theme: "Fool—fool—fool!" Now it was far away, now he could stretch out his hand and almost reach it. Now it merged with the throbbing in his head until the two vibrations were as one: "Fool—fool—fool—fool—"

The fogs faded and vanished. Kane sought to raise his hand to his head, but found that he was bound hand and foot. He lay on the floor of a hut—alone? He twisted about to view the place. No, two eyes glimmered at him from the darkness. Now a form took shape, and Kane, still mazed, believed that he looked on the man who had struck him unconscious. Yet no; this man could never strike such a blow. He was lean, withered and wrinkled. The only thing that seemed alive about him were his eyes, and they seemed like the eyes of a snake.

The man squatted on the floor of the hut, near the doorway, naked save for a loin-cloth and the usual paraphernalia of bracelets, anklets and armlets. Weird fetishes of ivory, bone and hide, animal and human, adorned his arms and legs. Suddenly and unexpectedly he spoke in English.

"Ha, you wake, white man? Why you come here, eh?"

Kane asked the inevitable question, following the habit of the Caucasian.

"You speak my language—how is that?"

The black man grinned.

"I slave—long time, me boy. Me, N'Longa, ju-ju man, me, great fetish. No black man like me! You white man, you hunt brother?"

Kane snarled. "I! Brother! I seek a man, yes."

The Negro nodded. "Maybe so you find um, eh?"

"He dies!"

Again the Negro grinned. "Me pow'rful ju-ju man," he announced apropos of nothing. He bent closer. "White man you hunt, eyes like a leopard, eh? Yes? Ha! ha! ha! ha! Listen, white man: man-with-eyes-of-a-leopard, he and Chief Songa make pow'rful palaver; they blood brothers now. Say nothing, I help you; you help me, eh?"

"Why should you help me?" asked Kane suspiciously.

The ju-ju man bent closer and whispered, "White man Songa's right-hand man; Songa more pow'rful than N'Longa. White man mighty ju-ju! N'Longa's white brother kill man-with-eyes-of-a-leopard, be blood brother to N'Longa, N'Longa be more pow'rful than Songa; palaver set."

And like a dusky ghost he floated out of the hut so swiftly that Kane was not sure but that the whole affair was a dream.

Without, Kane could see the flare of fires. The drums were still booming, but close at hand the tones merged and mingled, and the impulse-producing vibrations were lost. All seemed a barbaric clamor without rhyme or reason, yet there was an undertone of mockery there, savage and gloating. "Lies," thought Kane, his mind still swimming, "jungle lies like jungle women that lure a man to his doom."

Two warriors entered the hut—black giants, hideous with paint and armed with crude spears. They lifted the white man and carried him out of the hut. They bore him across an open space, leaned him upright against a post and bound him there. About him, behind him and to the side, a great semicircle of black faces leered and faded in the firelight as the flames leaped and sank. There in front of him loomed a shape hideous and obscene—a black, formless thing, a grotesque parody of the human. Still, brooding, bloodstained, like the formless soul of Africa, the horror, the Black God.

And in front and to each side, upon roughly carven thrones of teakwood, sat two men. He who sat upon the right was a black man, huge, ungainly, a gigantic and unlovely mass of dusky flesh and muscles. Small, hoglike eyes blinked out over sin-marked cheeks; huge, flabby red lips pursed in fleshly haughtiness.

The other—

"Ah, *Monsieur*, we meet again." The speaker was far from being the debonair villain who had taunted Kane in the cavern among the mountains. His clothes were rags; there were more lines in his face; he had sunk lower in the years that had passed. Yet his eyes still gleamed and danced with their old recklessness and his voice held the same mocking timbre.

"The last time I heard that accursed voice," said

Kane calmly, "was in a cave, in darkness, whence you fled like a hunted rat."

"Aye, under different conditions," answered Le Loup imperturbably. "What did you do after blundering about like an elephant in the dark?"

Kane hesitated, then: "I left the mountain—"

"By the front entrance? Yes? I might have known you were too stupid to find the secret door. Hoofs of the Devil, had you thrust against the chest with the golden lock, which stood against the wall, the door had opened to you and revealed the secret passageway through which I went."

"I traced you to the nearest port and there took ship and followed you to Italy, where I found you had gone."

"Aye, by the saints, you nearly cornered me in Florence. Ho! ho! ho! I was climbing through a back window while *Monsieur* Galahad was battering down the front door of the tavern. And had your horse not gone lame, you would have caught up with me on the road to Rome. Again, the ship on which I left Spain had barely put out to sea when *Monsieur* Galahad rides up to the wharfs. Why have you followed me like this? I do not understand."

"Because you are a rogue whom it is my destiny to kill," answered Kane coldly. He did not understand. All his life he had roamed about the world aiding the weak and fighting oppression, he neither knew nor questioned why. That was his obsession, his driving force of life. Cruelty and tyranny to the weak sent a red blaze of fury, fierce and lasting, through his soul. When the full flame of his hatred was wakened and loosed, there was no rest for him until his vengeance had been fulfilled to the uttermost. If he thought of it at all, he considered himself a fulfiller of God's judgment, a vessel of wrath to be emptied upon the souls of the unrighteous. Yet in the full sense of the word Solomon Kane was not wholly a Puritan, though he thought of himself as such.

Le Loup shrugged his shoulders. "I could understand had I wronged you personally. *Mon Dieu!* I, too, would follow an enemy across the world, but, though I would have joyfully slain and robbed you, I never heard of you until you declared war on me."

Kane was silent, his still fury overcoming him. Though he did not realize it, the Wolf was more than merely an enemy to him; the bandit symbolized, to Kane, all the things against which the Puritan had fought all his life: cruelty, outrage, oppression and tyranny.

Le Loup broke in on his vengeful meditations. "What did you do with the treasure, which—gods of Hades!—took me years to accumulate? Devil take it, I had time only to snatch a handful of coins and trinkets as I ran."

"I took such as I needed to hunt you down. The rest I gave to the villages which you had looted."

"Saints and the devil!" swore Le Loup. "*Monsieur*, you are the greatest fool I have yet met. To throw that vast treasure—by Satan, I rage to think of it in the hands of base peasants, vile villagers! Yet, ho! ho! ho! ho! they will steal, and kill each other for it! That is human nature."

"Yes, damn you!" flamed Kane suddenly, showing

that his conscience had not been at rest. "Doubtless they will, being fools. Yet what could I do? Had I left it there, people might have starved and gone naked for lack of it. More, it would have been found, and theft and slaughter would have followed anyway. You are to blame, for had this treasure been left with its rightful owners, no such trouble would have ensued."

The Wolf grinned without reply. Kane not being a profane man, his rare curses had double effect and always startled his hearers, no matter how vicious or hardened they might be.

It was Kane who spoke next. "Why have you fled from me across the world? You do not really fear me."

"No, you are right. Really I do not know; perhaps flight is a habit which is difficult to break. I made my mistake when I did not kill you that night in the mountains. I am sure I could kill you in a fair fight, yet I have never even, ere now, sought to ambush you. Somehow I have not had a liking to meet you, *Monsieur*—a whim of mine, a mere whim. Then— *mon Dieu!*—mayhap I have enjoyed a new sensation—and I had thought that I had exhausted the thrills of life. And then, a man must either be the hunter or the hunted. Until now, *Monsieur*, I was the hunted, but I grew weary of the role—I thought I had thrown you off the trail."

"A Negro slave, brought from this vicinity, told a Portugal ship captain of a white man who landed from a Spanish ship and went into the jungle. I heard of it and hired the ship, paying the captain to bring me here."

"*Monsieur*, I admire you for your attempt, but you must admire me, too! Alone I came into this village, and alone among savages and cannibals I—with some slight knowledge of the language learned from a slave aboard ship—I gained the confidence of King Songa and supplanted that mummer, N'Longa. I am a braver man than you, *Monsieur*, for I had no ship to retreat to, and a ship is waiting for you."

"I admire your courage," said Kane, "but you are content to rule amongst cannibals—you the blackest soul of them all. I intend to return to my own people when I have slain you."

"Your confidence would be admirable were it not amusing. Ho, Gulka!"

A giant Negro stalked into the space between them. He was the hugest man that Kane had ever seen, though he moved with catlike ease and suppleness. His arms and legs were like trees, and the great, sinuous muscles rippled with each motion. His apelike head was set squarely between gigantic shoulders. His great, dusky hands were like the talons of an ape, and his brow slanted back from above bestial eyes. Flat nose and great, thick red lips completed this picture of primitive, lustful savagery.

"That is Gulka, the gorilla-slayer," said Le Loup. "He it was who lay in wait beside the trail and smote you down. You are like a wolf, yourself, *Monsieur* Kane, but since your ship hove in sight you have been watched by many eyes, and had you had all the powers of a leopard, you had not seen Gulka nor heard him. He hunts the most terrible and crafty of all beasts, in their native forests, far to the north, the beasts-who-walk-like-men—as that one, whom he slew some days since."

Kane, following Le Loup's fingers, made out a curious, manlike thing, dangling from a roof-pole of a hut. A jagged end thrust through the thing's body held it there. Kane could scarcely distinguish its characteristics by the firelight, but there was a weird, human-like semblance about the hideous, hairy thing.

"A female gorilla that Gulka slew and brought to the village," said Le Loup.

The giant black slouched close to Kane and stared into the white man's eyes. Kane returned his gaze somberly, and presently the Negro's eyes dropped sullenly and he slouched back a few paces. The look in the Puritan's grim eyes had pierced the primitive hazes of the gorilla-slayer's soul, and for the first time in his life he felt fear. To throw this off, he tossed a challenging look about; then, with unexpected animalness, he struck his huge chest resoundingly, grinned cavernously and flexed his mighty arms. No one spoke. Primordial bestiality had the stage, and the more highly developed types looked on with various feelings of amusement, tolerance or contempt.

Gulka glanced furtively at Kane to see if the white man was watching him, then with a sudden beastly roar, plunged forward and dragged a man from the semicircle. While the trembling victim screeched for mercy, the giant hurled him upon the crude altar before the shadowy idol. A spear rose and flashed, and the screeching ceased. The Black God looked on, his monstrous features seeming to leer in the flickering firelight. He had drunk; was the Black God pleased with the draft—with the sacrifice?

Gulka stalked back, and stopping before Kane,

flourished the bloody spear before the white man's face.

Le Loup laughed. Then suddenly N'Longa appeared. He came from nowhere in particular; suddenly he was standing there, beside the post to which Kane was bound. A lifetime of study of the art of illusion had given the ju-ju man a highly technical knowledge of appearing and disappearing—which after all, consisted only in timing the audience's attention.

He waved Gulka aside with a grand gesture, and the gorilla-man slunk back, apparently to get out of N'Longa's gaze—then with incredible swiftness he turned and struck the ju-ju man a terrific blow upon the side of the head with his open hand. N'Longa went down like a felled ox, and in an instant he had been seized and bound to a post close to Kane. An uncertain murmuring rose from the Negroes, which died out as King Songa stared angrily toward them.

Le Loup leaned back upon his throne and laughed uproariously.

"The trail ends here, *Monsieur* Galahad. That ancient fool thought I did not know of his plotting! I was hiding outside the hut and heard the interesting conversation you two had. Ha! ha! ha! ha! The Black God must drink, *Monsieur*, but I have persuaded Songa to have you two burnt; that will be much more enjoyable, though we shall have to forego the usual feast, I fear. For after the fires are lit about your feet the devil himself could not keep your carcasses from becoming charred frames of bone."

Songa shouted something imperiously, and blacks came bearing wood, which they piled about the feet of

N'Longa and Kane. The ju-ju man had recovered consciousness, and he now shouted something in his native language. Again the murmuring arose among the shadowy throng. Songa snarled something in reply.

Kane gazed at the scene almost impersonally. Again, somewhere in his soul, dim primal deeps were stirring, age-old thought memories, veiled in the fogs of lost eons. He had been here before, thought Kane; he knew all this of old—the lurid flames beating back the sullen night, the bestial faces leering expectantly, and the god, the Black God, there in the shadows! Always the Black God, brooding back in the shadows. He had known the shouts, the frenzied chant of the worshipers, back there in the gray dawn of the world, the speech of the bellowing drums, the singing priests, the repellent, inflaming, all-pervading scent of freshly spilt blood. All this have I known, somewhere, sometime, thought Kane; now I am the main actor—

He became aware that someone was speaking to him through the roar of the drums; he had not realized that the drums had begun to boom again. The speaker was N'Longa:

"Me pow'rful ju-ju man! Watch now: I work mighty magic. Songa!" His voice rose in a screech that drowned out the wildly clamoring drums.

Songa grinned at the words N'Longa screamed at him. The chant of the drums now had dropped to a low, sinister monotone and Kane plainly heard Le Loup when he spoke:

"N'Longa says that he will now work that magic which it is death to speak, even. Never before has it been worked in the sight of living men; it is the name-less ju-ju magic. Watch closely, *Monsieur*; possibly we shall be further amused." The Wolf laughed lightly and sardonically.

A black man stooped, applying a torch to the wood about Kane's feet. Tiny jets of flame began to leap up and catch. Another bent to do the same with N'Longa, then hesitated. The ju-ju man sagged in his bonds; his head drooped upon his chest. He seemed dying.

Le Loup leaned forward, cursing, "Feet of the Devil! Is the scoundrel about to cheat us of our plea-sure of seeing him writhe in the flames?"

The warrior gingerly touched the wizard and said something in his own language.

Le Loup laughed: "He died of fright. A great wizard, by the—"

His voice trailed off suddenly. The drums stopped as if the drummers had fallen dead simultaneously. Silence dropped like a fog upon the village and in the stillness Kane heard only the sharp crackle of the flames whose heat he was beginning to feel.

All eyes were turned upon the dead man upon the altar, *for the corpse had begun to move!*

First a twitching of a hand, then an aimless motion of an arm, a motion which gradually spread over the body and limbs. Slowly, with blind, uncertain ges-tures, the dead man turned upon his side, the trailing limbs found the earth. Then, horribly like something being born, like some frightful reptilian thing bursting the shell of non-existence, the corpse tottered and reared upright, standing on legs wide apart and stiffly braced, arms still making useless, infantile motions.

Utter silence, save somewhere a man's quick breath sounded loud in the stillness.

Kane stared, for the first time in his life smitten speechless and thoughtless. To his Puritan mind this was Satan's hand manifested.

Le Loup sat on his throne, eyes wide and staring, hand still half-raised in the careless gesture he was making when frozen into silence by the unbelievable sight. Songa sat beside him, mouth and eyes wide open, fingers making curious jerky motions upon the carved arms of the throne.

Now the corpse was upright, swaying on stiltlike legs, body tilting far back until the sightless eyes seemed to stare straight into the red moon that was just rising over the black jungle. The thing tottered uncertainly in a wide, erratic half-circle, arms flung out grotesquely as if in balance, then swayed about to face the two thrones—and the Black God. A burning twig at Kane's feet cracked like the crash of a cannon in the tense silence. The horror thrust forth a black foot—it took a wavering step—another. Then with stiff, jerky and automatonlike steps, legs straddled far apart, the dead man came toward the two who sat in speechless horror to each side of the Black God.

"Ah-h-h!" from somewhere came the explosive sigh, from that shadowy semicircle where crouched the terror-fascinated worshipers. Straight on stalked the grim specter. Now it was within three strides of the thrones, and Le Loup, faced by fear for the first time in his bloody life, cringed back in his chair; while Songa, with a superhuman effort breaking the chains of horror that held him helpless, shattered the night with a wild scream and, springing to his feet, lifted a spear, shrieking and gibbering in wild menace. Then as the ghastly thing halted not its frightful advance, he hurled the spear with all the power of his great, black muscles, and the spear tore through the dead man's breast with a rending of flesh and bone. Not an instant halted the thing—for the dead die not—and Songa the king stood frozen, arms outstretched as if to fend off the terror.

An instant they stood so, leaping firelight and eery moonlight etching the scene forever in the minds of the beholders. The changeless staring eyes of the corpse looked full into the bulging eyes of Songa, where were reflected all the hells of horror. Then with a jerky motion the arms of the thing went out and up. The dead hands fell on Songa's shoulders. At the first touch, the king seemed to shrink and shrivel, and with a scream that was to haunt the dreams of every watcher through all the rest of time, Songa crumpled and fell, and the dead man reeled stiffly and fell with him. Motionless lay the two at the feet of the Black God, and to Kane's dazed mind it seemed that the idol's great, inhuman eyes were fixed upon them with terrible, still laughter.

At the instant of the king's fall, a great shout went up from the blacks, and Kane, with a clarity lent his subconscious mind by the depths of his hate, looked for Le Loup and saw him spring from his throne and vanish in the darkness. Then vision was blurred by a rush of black figures who swept into the space before the god. Feet knocked aside the blazing brands whose heat Kane had forgotten, and dusky hands freed him;

others loosed the wizard's body and laid it upon the earth. Kane dimly understood that the blacks believed this thing to be the work of N'Longa, and that they connected the vengeance of the wizard with himself. He bent, laid a hand on the ju-ju man's shoulder. No doubt of it: he was dead, the flesh was already cold. He glanced at the other corpses. Songa was dead, too, and the thing that had slain him lay now without movement.

Kane started to rise, then halted. Was he dreaming, or did he really feel a sudden warmth in the dead flesh he touched? Mind reeling, he again bent over the wizard's body, and slowly he felt warmness steal over the limbs and the blood begin to flow sluggishly through the veins again.

Then N'Longa opened his eyes and stared up into Kane's, with the blank expression of a new-born babe. Kane watched, flesh crawling, and saw the knowing, reptilian glitter come back, saw the wizard's thick lips part in a wide grin. N'Longa sat up, and a strange chant arose from the Negroes.

Kane looked about. The blacks were all kneeling, swaying their bodies to and fro, and in their shouts Kane caught the word, "N'Longa!" repeated over and over in a kind of fearsomely ecstatic refrain of terror and worship. As the wizard rose, they all fell prostrate.

N'Longa nodded, as if in satisfaction.

"Great ju-ju—great fetish, me!" he announced to Kane. "You see? My ghost go out—kill Songa—come back to me! Great magic! Great fetish, me!"

Kane glanced at the Black God looming back in the

shadows, at N'Longa, who now flung out his arms toward the idol as if in invocation.

I am everlasting (Kane thought the Black God said); I drink, no matter who rules; chiefs, slayers, wizards, they pass like the ghosts of dead men through the gray jungle; I stand, I rule; I am the soul of the jungle (said the Black God).

Suddenly Kane came back from the illusory mists in which he had been wandering. "The white man! Which way did he flee?"

N'Longa shouted something. A score of dusky hands pointed; from somewhere Kane's rapier was thrust out to him. The fogs faded and vanished; again he was the avenger, the scourge of the unrighteous; with the sudden volcanic speed of a tiger he snatched the sword and was gone.

5. The End of the Red Trail

Limbs and vines slapped against Kane's face. The oppressive steam of the tropic night rose like mist about him. The moon, now floating high above the jungle, limned the black shadows in its white glow and patterned the jungle floor in grotesque designs. Kane knew not if the man he sought was ahead of him, but broken limbs and trampled underbrush showed that some man had gone that way, some man who fled in haste, nor halted to pick his way. Kane followed these signs unswervingly. Believing in the justice of his vengeance, he did not doubt that the dim beings who rule men's destinies would finally bring him face to face with Le Loup.

Behind him the drums boomed and muttered. What a tale they had to tell this night of the triumph of N'Longa, the death of the black king, the overthrow of the white-man-with-eyes-like-a-leopard, and a more darksome tale, a tale to be whispered in low, muttering vibrations: the nameless ju-ju.

Was he dreaming? Kane wondered as he hurried on. Was all this part of some foul magic? He had seen a dead man rise and slay and die again; he had seen a man die and come to life again. Did N'Longa in truth send his ghost, his soul, his life essence forth into the void, dominating a corpse to do his will? Aye, N'Longa died a real death there, bound to the torture stake, and he who lay dead on the altar rose and did as N'Longa would have done had he been free. Then, the unseen force animating the dead man fading, N'Longa had lived again.

Yes, Kane thought, he must admit it as a fact. Somewhere in the darksome reaches of jungle and river, N'Longa had stumbled upon the Secret—the Secret of controlling life and death, of overcoming the shackles and limitations of the flesh. How had this dark wisdom, born in the black and blood-stained shadows of this grim land, been given to the wizard? What sacrifice had been so pleasing to the Black Gods, what ritual so monstrous, as to make them give up the knowledge of this magic? And what thoughtless, time-less journeys had N'Longa taken, when he chose to send his ego, his ghost, through the far, misty coun-tries, reached only by death?

There is wisdom in the shadows (brooded the

drums), wisdom and magic; go into the darkness for wisdom; ancient magic shuns the light; we remember the lost ages (whispered the drums), ere man became wise and foolish; we remember the beast gods—the serpent gods and the ape gods and the nameless, the Black Gods, they who drank blood and whose voices roared through the shadowy hills, who feasted and lusted. The secrets of life and of death are theirs; we remember, we remember (sang the drums).

Kane heard them as he hastened on. The tale they told to the feathered black warriors farther up the river, he could not translate; but they spoke to him in their own way, and that language was deeper, more basic.

The moon, high in the dark blue skies, lighted his way and gave him a clear vision as he came out at last into a glade and saw Le Loup standing there. The Wolf's naked blade was a long gleam of silver in the moon, and he stood with shoulders thrown back, the old, defiant smile still on his face.

"A long trail, *Monsieur*," said he. "It began in the mountains of France; it ends in an African jungle. I have wearied of the game at last, *Monsieur*—and you die. I had not fled from the village, even, save that—I admit it freely—that damnable witchcraft of N'Longa's shook my nerves. More, I saw that the whole tribe would turn against me."

Kane advanced warily, wondering what dim, forgotten tinge of chivalry in the bandit's soul had caused him thus to take his chance in the open. He half-suspected treachery, but his keen eyes could detect no shadow of movement in the jungle on either side of the glade.

"*Monsieur*, on guard!" Le Loup's voice was crisp. "Time that we ended this fool's dance about the world. Here we are alone."

The men were now within reach of each other, and Le Loup, in the midst of his sentence, suddenly plunged forward with the speed of light, thrusting viciously. A slower man had died there, but Kane parried and sent his own blade in a silver streak that slit Le Loup's tunic as the Wolf bounded backward. Le Loup admitted the failure of his trick with a wild laugh and came in with the breath-taking speed and fury of a tiger, his blade making a white fan of steel about him.

Rapier clashed on rapier as the two swordsmen fought. They were fire and ice opposed. Le Loup fought wildly but craftily, leaving no openings, taking advantage of every opportunity. He was a living flame, bounding back, leaping in, feinting, thrusting, warding, striking—laughing like a wild man, taunting and cursing.

Kane's skill was cold, calculating, scintillant. He made no waste movement, no motion not absolutely necessary. He seemed to devote more time and effort toward defense than did Le Loup, yet there was no hesitancy in his attack, and when he thrust, his blade shot out with the speed of a striking snake.

There was little to choose between the men as to height, strength and reach. Le Loup was the swifter by a scant, flashing margin, but Kane's skill reached a finer point of perfection. The Wolf's fencing was fiery, dynamic, like the blast from a furnace. Kane was more steady—less the instinctive, more the thinking fighter, though he, too, was a born slayer, with the coordination that only a natural fighter possessed.

Thrust, parry, a feint, a sudden whirl of blades—

"Ha!" the Wolf sent up a shout of ferocious laughter as the blood started from a cut on Kane's cheek. As if the sight drove him to further fury, he attacked like the beast men named him. Kane was forced back before that blood-lusting onslaught, but the Puritan's expression did not alter.

Minutes flew by; the clang and clash of steel did not diminish. Now they stood squarely in the center of the glade, Le Loup untouched, Kane's garments red with the blood that oozed from wounds on cheek, breast, arm and thigh. The Wolf grinned savagely and mockingly in the moonlight, but he had begun to doubt.

His breath came hissing fast and his arm began to weary; who was this man of steel and ice who never seemed to weaken? Le Loup knew that the wounds he had inflicted on Kane were not deep, but even so, the steady flow of blood should have sapped some of the man's strength and speed by this time. But if Kane felt the ebb of his powers, it did not show. His brooding countenance did not change in expression, and he pressed the fight with as much cold fury as at the beginning.

Le Loup felt his might fading, and with one last desperate effort he rallied all his fury and strength into a single plunge. A sudden, unexpected attack too wild and swift for the eye to follow, a dynamic burst of speed and fury no man could have withstood, and Solomon Kane reeled for the first time as he felt cold steel tear through his body. He reeled back, and Le

Loup, with a wild shout, plunged after him, his reddened sword free, a gasping taunt on his lips.

Kane's sword, backed by the force of desperation, met Le Loup's in midair; met, held and wrenched. The Wolf's yell of triumph died on his lips as his sword flew singing from his hand.

For a fleeting instant he stopped short, arms flung wide as a crucifix, and Kane heard his wild, mocking laughter peal forth for the last time, as the Englishman's rapier made a silver line in the moonlight.

Far away came the mutter of the drums. Kane mechanically cleansed his sword on his tattered garments. The trail ended here, and Kane was conscious of a strange feeling of futility. He always felt that, after he had killed a foe. Somehow it always seemed that no real good had been wrought; as if the foe had, after all, escaped his just vengeance.

With a shrug of his shoulders Kane turned his attention to his bodily needs. Now that the heat of battle had passed, he began to feel weak and faint from the loss of blood. That last thrust had been close; had he not managed to avoid its full point by a twist of his body, the blade had transfixed him. As it was, the sword had struck glancingly, plowed along his ribs and sunk deep in the muscles beneath the shoulder blade, inflicting a long, shallow wound.

Kane looked about him and saw that a small stream trickled through the glade at the far side. Here he made the only mistake of that kind that he ever made in his entire life. Mayhap he was dizzy from loss of blood and still mazed from the weird happenings of the night; be that as it may, he laid down his rapier and crossed, weaponless, to the stream. There he laved his wounds and bandaged them as best he could, with strips torn from his clothing.

Then he rose and was about to retrace his steps when a motion among the trees on the side of the glade where he first entered, caught his eye. A huge figure stepped out of the jungle, and Kane saw, and recognized, his doom. The man was Gulka, the gorilla-slayer. Kane remembered that he had not seen the black among those doing homage to N'Longa. How could he know the craft and hatred in that dusky, slanting skull that had led the Negro, escaping the vengeance of his tribesmen, to trail down the only man he had ever feared? The Black God had been kind to his neophyte; had led him upon his victim helpless and unarmed. Now Gulka could kill his man openly—and slowly, as a leopard kills, not smiting him down from ambush as he had planned, silently and suddenly.

A wide grin split the Negro's face, and he moistened his lips. Kane, watching him, was coldly and deliberately weighing his chances. Gulka had already spied the rapiers. He was closer to them than was Kane. The Englishman knew that there was no chance of his winning in a sudden race for the swords.

A slow, deadly rage surged in him—the fury of helplessness. The blood churned in his temples and his eyes smoldered with a terrible light as he eyed the Negro. His fingers spread and closed like claws. They were strong, those hands; men had died in their clutch.

Even Gulka's huge black column of a neck might break like a rotten branch between them—a wave of weakness made the futility of these thoughts apparent to an extent that needed not the verification of the moonlight glimmering from the spear in Gulka's black hand. Kane could not even have fled had he wished— and he had never fled from a single foe.

The gorilla-slayer moved out into the glade. Massive, terrible, he was the personification of the primitive, the Stone Age. His mouth yawned in a red cavern of a grin; he bore himself with the haughty arrogance of savage might.

Kane tensed himself for the struggle that could end but one way. He strove to rally his waning forces. Useless; he had lost too much blood. At least he would meet his death on his feet, and somehow he stiffened his buckling knees and held himself erect, though the glade shimmered before him in uncertain waves and the moonlight seemed to have become a red fog through which he dimly glimpsed the approaching black man.

Kane stooped, though the effort nearly pitched him on his face; he dipped water in his cupped hands and dashed it into his face. This revived him, and he straightened, hoping that Gulka would charge and get it over with before his weakness crumpled him to the earth.

Gulka was now about the center of the glade, moving with the slow, easy stride of a great cat stalking a victim. He was not at all in a hurry to consummate his purpose. He wanted to toy with his victim, to see fear come into those grim eyes which had looked him down, even when the possessor of those eyes had been bound to the death stake. He wanted to slay, at last, slowly, glutting his tigerish blood-lust and torture-lust to the fullest extent.

Then suddenly he halted, turned swiftly, facing another side of the glade. Kane, wondering, followed his glance.

At first it seemed like a blacker shadow among the jungle shadows. At first there was no motion, no sound, but Kane instinctively knew that some terrible menace lurked there in the darkness that masked and merged the silent trees. A sullen horror brooded there, and Kane felt as if, from that monstrous shadow, inhuman eyes seared his very soul. Yet simultaneously there came the fantastic sensation that these eyes were not directed on him. He looked at the gorilla-slayer.

The black man had apparently forgotten him; he stood, half-crouching, spear lifted, eyes fixed upon that clump of blackness. Kane looked again. Now there was motion in the shadows; they merged fantastically and moved out into the glade, much as Gulka had done. Kane blinked: was this the illusion that precedes death? The shape he looked upon was such as he had visioned dimly in wild nightmares, when the wings of sleep bore him back through lost ages.

He thought at first it was some blasphemous mockery of a man, for it went erect and was tall as a tall man. But it was inhumanly broad and thick, and its gigantic arms hung nearly to its misshapen feet. Then the moonlight smote full upon its bestial face, and Kane's mazed mind thought that the thing was the

Black God coming out of the shadows, animated and blood-lusting. Then he saw that it was covered with hair, and he remembered the manlike thing dangling from the roof-pole in the native village. He looked at Gulka.

The Negro was facing the gorilla, spear at the charge. He was not afraid, but his sluggish mind was wondering over the miracle that brought this beast so far from his native jungles.

The mighty ape came out into the moonlight and there was a terrible majesty about his movements. He was nearer Kane than Gulka but he did not seem to be aware of the white man. His small, blazing eyes were fixed on the black man with terrible intensity. He advanced with a curious swaying stride.

Far away the drums whispered through the night, like an accompaniment to this grim Stone Age drama. The savage crouched in the middle of the glade, but the primordial came out of the jungle with eyes blood-shot and blood-lusting. The Negro was face to face with a thing more primitive than he. Again ghosts of memories whispered to Kane: you have seen such sights before (they murmured), back in the dim days, the dawn days, when beast and beast-man battled for supremacy.

Gulka moved away from the ape in a half-circle, crouching, spear ready. With all his craft he was seeking to trick the gorilla, to make a swift kill, for he had never before met such a monster as this, and though he did not fear, he had begun to doubt. The ape made no attempt to stalk or circle; he strode straight forward toward Gulka.

The black man who faced him and the white man who watched could not know the brutish love, the brutish hate that had driven the monster down from the low, forest-covered hills of the north to follow for leagues the trail of him who was the scourge of his kind—the slayer of his mate, whose body now hung from the roof-pole of the Negro village.

The end came swiftly, almost like a sudden gesture. They were close, now, beast and beast-man; and suddenly, with an earth-shaking roar, the gorilla charged. A great hairy arm smote aside the thrusting spear, and the ape closed with the Negro. There was a shattering sound as of many branches breaking simultaneously, and Gulka slumped silently to the earth, to lie with arms, legs and body flung in strange, unnatural positions. The ape towered an instant above him, like a statue of the primordial triumphant.

Far away Kane heard the drums murmur. The soul of the jungle, the soul of the jungle: this phrase surged through his mind with monotonous reiteration.

The three who had stood in power before the Black God that night, where were they? Back in the village where the drums rustled lay Songa—King Songa, once lord of life and death, now a shriveled corpse with a face set in a mask of horror. Stretched on his back in the middle of the glade lay he whom Kane had followed many a league by land and sea. And Gulka the gorilla-slayer lay at the feet of his killer, broken at last by the savagery which had made him a true son of this grim land which had at last overwhelmed him.

Yet the Black God still reigned, thought Kane dizzily, brooding back in the shadows of this dark country, bestial, blood-lusting, caring naught who lived or died, so that he drank.

Kane watched the mighty ape, wondering how long it would be before the huge simian spied and charged him. But the gorilla gave no evidence of having even seen him. Some dim impulse of vengeance yet unglutted prompting him, he bent and raised the Negro. Then he slouched toward the jungle, Gulka's limbs trailing limply and grotesquely. As he reached the trees, the ape halted, whirling the giant form high in the air with seemingly no effort, and dashed the dead man up among the branches. There was a rending sound as a broken projecting limb tore through the body hurled so powerfully against it, and the dead gorilla-slayer dangled there hideously.

A moment the clear moon limned the great ape in its glimmer, as he stood silently gazing up at his victim; then like a dark shadow he melted noiselessly into the jungle.

Kane walked slowly to the middle of the glade and took up his rapier. The blood had ceased to flow from his wounds, and some of his strength was returning, enough, at least, for him to reach the coast where his ship awaited him. He halted at the edge of the glade for a backward glance at Le Loup's upturned face and still form, white in the moonlight, and at the dark shadow among the trees that was Gulka, left by some bestial whim, hanging as the she-gorilla hung in the village.

Afar the drums muttered: "The wisdom of our land
is ancient; the wisdom of our land is dark; whom we
serve, we destroy. Flee if you would live, but you will
never forget our chant. Never, never," sang the drums.

Kane turned to the trail which led to the beach and
the ship waiting there.

The Harp of Alfred

Weird Tales, September 1928

I heard the harp of Alfred
As I went o'er the downs,
When thorn-trees stood at even
Like monks in dusky gowns;
I heard the music Guthrum heard
Beside the wasted towns;

When Alfred, like a peasant,
Came harping down the hill,
And the drunken Danes made merry
With the man they sought to kill,
And the Saxon king laughed in their beards
And bent them to his will.

I heard the harp of Alfred
As twilight waned to night;
I heard ghost armies tramping
As the dim stars flamed white;
And Guthrum walked at my left hand,
And Alfred at my right.

Easter Island

Weird Tales, December 1928

How many weary centuries have flown
Since strange-eyed beings walked this ancient
    shore;
Hearing, as we, the green Pacific's roar,
Hewing fantastic gods from sullen stone!
The sands are bare; the idols stand alone.
Impotent 'gainst the years was all their lore:
They are forgot in ages dim and hoar;
Yet still, as then, the long tide-surges drone.

What dreams had they, that shaped these
    uncouth things?
Before these gods what victims bled and died?
What purple galleys swept along the strand
That bore the tribute of what dim sea-kings?
But now they reign o'er a forgotten land,
Gazing forever out beyond the tide.

Skulls in the Stars

Weird Tales, January 1929

> *He told how murderers walk the earth*
> *Beneath the curse of Cain,*
> *With crimson clouds before their eyes*
> *And flames about their brain:*
> *For blood has left upon their souls*
> *Its everlasting stain.*
>
> *—Hood*

1

There are two roads to Torkertown. One, the shorter and more direct route, leads across a barren upland moor, and the other, which is much longer, winds its tortuous way in and out among the hummocks and quagmires of the swamps, skirting the low hills to the east. It was a dangerous and tedious trail; so Solomon Kane halted in amazement when a breathless youth from the village he had just left, overtook him and implored him for God's sake to take the swamp road.

"The swamp road!" Kane stared at the boy.

He was a tall, gaunt man, was Solomon Kane, his darkly pallid face and deep brooding eyes made more somber by the drab Puritanical garb he affected.

"Yes, sir, 'tis far safer," the youngster answered his surprized exclamation.

"Then the moor road must be haunted by Satan himself, for your townsmen warned me against traversing the other."

"Because of the quagmires, sir, that you might not see in the dark. You had better return to the village and continue your journey in the morning, sir."

"Taking the swamp road?"

"Yes, sir."

Kane shrugged his shoulders and shook his head.

"The moon rises almost as soon as twilight dies. By its light I can reach Torkertown in a few hours, across the moor."

"Sir, you had better not. No one ever goes that way. There are no houses at all upon the moor, while in the swamp there is the house of old Ezra who lives there all alone since his maniac cousin, Gideon, wandered off and died in the swamp and was never found—and old Ezra though a miser would not refuse you lodging should you decide to stop until morning. Since you must go, you had better go the swamp road."

Kane eyed the boy piercingly. The lad squirmed and shuffled his feet.

"Since this moor road is so dour to wayfarers," said the Puritan, "why did not the villagers tell me the whole tale, instead of vague mouthings?"

"Men like not to talk of it, sir. We hoped that you

would take the swamp road after the men advised you to, but when we watched and saw that you turned not at the forks, they sent me to run after you and beg you to reconsider."

"Name of the Devil!" exclaimed Kane sharply, the unaccustomed oath showing his irritation; "the swamp road and the moor road—what is it that threatens me and why should I go miles out of my way and risk the bogs and mires?"

"Sir," said the boy, dropping his voice and drawing closer, "we be simple villagers who like not to talk of such things lest foul fortune befall us, but the moor road is a way accurst and hath not been traversed by any of the countryside for a year or more. It is death to walk those moors by night, as hath been found by some score of unfortunates. Some foul horror haunts the way and claims men for his victims."

"So? And what is this thing like?"

"No man knows. Shadow has ever seen it and lived, but late-farers have heard terrible laughter far out on the fen and men have heard the horrid shrieks of its victims. Sir, in God's name return to the village, there pass the night, and tomorrow take the swamp trail to Torkertown."

Far back in Kane's gloomy eyes a scintillant light had begun to glimmer, like a witch's torch glinting under fathoms of cold gray ice. His blood quickened. Adventure! The lure of life-risk and battle! The thrill of breathtaking, touch-and-go drama! Not that Kane recognized his sensations as such. He sincerely considered that he voiced his real feelings when he said:

"These things be deeds of some power of evil. The

lords of darkness have laid a curse upon the country. A strong man is needed to combat Satan and his might. Therefore I go, who have defied him many a time."

"Sir," the boy began, then closed his mouth as he saw the futility of argument. He only added, "The corpses of the victims are bruised and torn, sir."

He stood there at the crossroads, sighing regretfully as he watched the tall, rangy figure swinging up the road that led toward the moors.

The sun was setting as Kane came over the brow of the low hill which debouched into the upland fen. Huge and blood-red it sank down behind the sullen horizon of the moors, seeming to touch the rank grass with fire; so for a moment the watcher seemed to be gazing out across a sea of blood. Then the dark shadows came gliding from the east, the western blaze faded, and Solomon Kane struck out boldly in the gathering darkness.

The road was dim from disuse but was clearly defined. Kane went swiftly but warily, sword and pistols at hand. Stars blinked out and night winds whispered among the grass like weeping specters. The moon began to rise, lean and haggard, like a skull among the stars.

Then suddenly Kane stopped short. From somewhere in front of him sounded a strange and eerie echo—or something like an echo. Again, this time louder. Kane started forward again. Were his senses deceiving him? No!

Far out, there pealed a whisper of frightful laughter. And again, closer this time. No human being ever laughed like that—there was no mirth in it, only hatred and horror and soul-destroying terror. Kane halted. He was not afraid, but for the second he was almost unnerved. Then, stabbing through that awesome laughter, came the sound of a scream that was undoubtedly human. Kane started forward, increasing his gait. He cursed the illusive lights and flickering shadows which veiled the moor in the rising moon and made accurate sight impossible. The laughter continued, growing louder, as did the screams. Then sounded faintly the drum of frantic human feet. Kane broke into a run.

Some human was being hunted to his death out there on the fen, and by what manner of horror God alone knew. The sound of the flying feet halted abruptly and the screaming rose unbearably, mingled with other sounds unnamable and hideous. Evidently the man had been overtaken, and Kane, his flesh crawling, visualized some ghastly fiend of the darkness crouching on the back of its victim—crouching and tearing.

Then the noise of a terrible and short struggle came clearly through the abysmal silence of the fen and the footfalls began again, but stumbling and uneven. The screaming continued, but with a gasping gurgle. The sweat stood cold on Kane's forehead and body. This was heaping horror on horror in an intolerable manner.

God, for a moment's clear light! The frightful drama was being enacted within a very short distance of him, to judge by the ease with which the sounds reached him. But this hellish half-light veiled all in shifting shadows, so that the moors appeared a haze of blurred illusions, and stunted trees and bushes seemed like giants.

Kane shouted, striving to increase the speed of his advance. The shrieks of the unknown broke into a hideous shrill squealing; again there was the sound of a struggle, and then from the shadows of the tall grass a thing came reeling—a thing that had once been a man—a gore-covered, frightful thing that fell at Kane's feet and writhed and groveled and raised its terrible face to the rising moon, and gibbered and yammered, and fell down again and died in its own blood.

The moon was up now and the light was better. Kane bent above the body, which lay stark in its unnamable mutilation, and he shuddered—a rare thing for him, who had seen the deeds of the Spanish Inquisition and the witch-finders.

Some wayfarer, he supposed. Then like a hand of ice on his spine he was aware that he was not alone. He looked up, his cold eyes piercing the shadows whence the dead man had staggered. He saw nothing, but he knew—he felt—that other eyes gave back his stare, terrible eyes not of this earth. He straightened and drew a pistol, waiting. The moonlight spread like a lake of pale blood over the moor, and trees and grasses took on their proper sizes.

The shadows melted, and Kane *saw!* At first he thought it only a shadow of mist, a wisp of moor fog that swayed in the tall grass before him. He gazed. More illusion, he thought. Then the thing began to take on shape, vague and indistinct. Two hideous eyes flamed at him—eyes which held all the stark horror which has been the heritage of man since the fearful dawn ages—eyes frightful and insane, with an insanity transcending earthly insanity. The form of the thing was misty and vague, a brain-shattering travesty on the human form, like, yet horridly unlike. The grass and bushes beyond showed clearly through it.

Kane felt the blood pound in his temples, yet he was as cold as ice. How such an unstable being as that which wavered before him could harm a man in a physical way was more than he could understand, yet the red horror at his feet gave mute testimony that the fiend could act with terrible material effect.

Of one thing Kane was sure: there would be no hunting of him across the dreary moors, no screaming and fleeing to be dragged down again and again. If he must die he would die in his tracks, his wounds in front.

Now a vague and grisly mouth gaped wide and the demoniac laughter again shrieked out, soul-shaking in its nearness. And in the midst of that threat of doom, Kane deliberately leveled his long pistol and fired. A maniacal yell of rage and mockery answered the report, and the thing came at him like a flying sheet of smoke, long shadowy arms stretched to drag him down.

Kane, moving with the dynamic speed of a famished wolf, fired the second pistol with as little effect, snatched his long rapier from its sheath and thrust into the center of the misty attacker. The blade sang as it passed clear through, encountering no solid resistance, and Kane felt icy fingers grip his limbs, bestial talons tear his garments and the skin beneath.

He dropped the useless sword and sought to grapple with his foe. It was like fighting a floating mist, a flying shadow armed with daggerlike claws. His savage blows met empty air, his leanly mighty arms, in whose grasp strong men had died, swept nothingness and clutched emptiness. Naught was solid or real save the flaying, apelike fingers with their crooked talons, and the crazy eyes which burned into the shuddering depths of his soul.

Kane realized that he was in a desperate plight indeed. Already his garments hung in tatters and he bled from a score of deep wounds. But he never flinched, and the thought of flight never entered his mind. He had never fled from a single foe, and had the thought occurred to him he would have flushed with shame.

He saw no help for it now, but that his form should lie there beside the fragments of the other victim, but the thought held no terrors for him. His only wish was to give as good an account of himself as possible before the end came, and if he could, to inflict some damage on his unearthly foe.

There above the dead man's torn body, man fought with demon under the pale light of the rising moon, with all the advantages with the demon, save one. And that one was enough to overcome all the others. For if abstract hate may bring into material substance a ghostly thing, may not courage, equally abstract, form a concrete weapon to combat that ghost?

Kane fought with his arms and his feet and his hands, and he was aware at last that the ghost began to give back before him, that the fearful laughter changed to screams of baffled fury. For man's only weapon is courage that flinches not from the gates of Hell itself, and against such not even the legions of Hell can stand.

Of this Kane knew nothing; he only knew that the talons which tore and rended him seemed to grow weaker and wavering, that a wild light grew and grew in the horrible eyes. And reeling and gasping, he rushed in, grappled the thing at last and threw it, and as they tumbled about on the moor and it writhed and lapped his limbs like a serpent of smoke, his flesh crawled and his hair stood on end, for he began to understand its gibbering.

He did not hear and comprehend as a man hears and comprehends the speech of a man, but the frightful secrets it imparted in whisperings and yammerings and screaming silences sank fingers of ice and flame into his soul, and he *knew*.

2

The hut of old Ezra the miser stood by the road in the midst of the swamp, half-screened by the sullen trees which grew about it. The walls were rotting, the roof crumbling, and great, pallid and green fungus-monsters clung to it and writhed about the doors and windows, as if seeking to peer within. The trees leaned above it and their gray branches intertwined so that it crouched in the semi-darkness like a monstrous dwarf over whose shoulder ogres leer.

The road which wound down into the swamp,

among rotting stumps and rank hummocks and scummy, snake-haunted pools and bogs, crawled past the hut. Many people passed that way these days, but few saw old Ezra, save a glimpse of a yellow face, peering through the fungus-screened windows, itself like an ugly fungus.

Old Ezra the miser partook much of the quality of the swamp, for he was gnarled and bent and sullen; his fingers were like clutching parasitic plants and his locks hung like drab moss above eyes trained to the murk of the swamplands. His eyes were like a dead man's, yet hinted of depths abysmal and loathsome as the dead lakes of the swamplands.

These eyes gleamed now at the man who stood in front of his hut. This man was tall and gaunt and dark, his face was haggard and claw-marked, and he was bandaged of arm and leg. Somewhat behind this man stood a number of villagers.

"You are Ezra of the swamp road?"

"Aye, and what want ye of me?"

"Where is your cousin Gideon, the maniac youth who abode with you?"

"Gideon?"

"Aye."

"He wandered away into the swamp and never came back. No doubt he lost his way and was set upon by wolves or died in a quagmire or was struck by an adder."

"How long ago?"

"Over a year."

"Aye. Hark ye, Ezra the miser. Soon after your cousin's disappearance, a countryman, coming home across the moors, was set upon by some unknown fiend and torn to pieces, and thereafter it became death to cross those moors. First men of the countryside, then strangers who wandered over the fen, fell to the clutches of the thing. Many men have died, since the first one.

"Last night I crossed the moors, and heard the flight and pursuing of another victim, a stranger who knew not the evil of the moors. Ezra the miser, it was a fearful thing, for the wretch twice broke from the fiend, terribly wounded, and each time the demon caught and dragged him down again. And at last he fell dead at my very feet, done to death in a manner that would freeze the statue of a saint."

The villagers moved restlessly and murmured fearfully to each other, and old Ezra's eyes shifted furtively. Yet the somber expression of Solomon Kane never altered, and his condor-like stare seemed to transfix the miser.

"Aye, aye!" muttered old Ezra hurriedly; "a bad thing, a bad thing! Yet why do you tell this thing to me?"

"Aye, a sad thing. Harken further, Ezra. The fiend came out of the shadows and I fought with it, over the body of its victim. Aye, how I overcame it, I know not, for the battle was hard and long, but the powers of good and light were on my side, which are mightier than the powers of Hell.

"At the last I was stronger, and it broke from me and fled, and I followed to no avail. Yet before it fled it whispered to me a monstrous truth."

Old Ezra started, stared wildly, seemed to shrink into himself.

"Nay, why tell me this?" he muttered.

"I returned to the village and told my tale," said Kane, "for I knew that now I had the power to rid the moors of its curse forever. Ezra, come with us!"

"Where?" gasped the miser.

"To the rotting oak on the moors."

Ezra reeled as though struck; he screamed incoherently and turned to flee.

On the instant, at Kane's sharp order, two brawny villagers sprang forward and seized the miser. They twisted the dagger from his withered hand, and pinioned his arms, shuddering as their fingers encountered his clammy flesh.

Kane motioned them to follow, and turning strode up the trail, followed by the villagers, who found their strength taxed to the utmost in their task of bearing their prisoner along. Through the swamp they went and out, taking a little-used trail which led up over the low hills and out on the moors.

The sun was sliding down the horizon and old Ezra stared at it with bulging eyes—stared as if he could not gaze enough. Far out on the moors reared up the great oak tree, like a gibbet, now only a decaying shell. There Solomon Kane halted.

Old Ezra writhed in his captor's grasp and made inarticulate noises.

"Over a year ago," said Solomon Kane, "you, fearing that your insane cousin Gideon would tell men of your cruelties to him, brought him away from the swamp by the very trail by which we came, and murdered him here in the night."

Ezra cringed and snarled.

"You can not prove this lie!"

Kane spoke a few words to an agile villager. The youth clambered up the rotting bole of the tree and from a crevice, high up, dragged something that fell with a clatter at the feet of the miser. Ezra went limp with a terrible shriek.

The object was a man's skeleton, the skull cleft.

"You—how knew you this? You are Satan!" gibbered old Ezra.

Kane folded his arms.

"The thing I fought last night told me this thing as we reeled in battle, and I followed it to this tree. *For the fiend is Gideon's ghost.*"

Ezra shrieked again and fought savagely.

"You knew," said Kane somberly, "you knew what thing did these deeds. You feared the ghost of the maniac, and that is why you chose to leave his body on the fen instead of concealing it in the swamp. For you knew the ghost would haunt the place of his death. He was insane in life, and in death he did not know where to find his slayer; else he had come to you in your hut. He hates no man but you, but his mazed spirit can not tell one man from another, and he slays all, lest he let his killer escape. Yet he will know you and rest in peace forever after. Hate hath made of his ghost a solid thing that can rend and slay, and though he feared you terribly in life, in death he fears you not."

Kane halted. He glanced at the sun.

"All this I had from Gideon's ghost, in his yammer-

ings and his whisperings and his shrieking silences.
Naught but your death will lay that ghost."

Ezra listened in breathless silence and Kane pro-
nounced the words of his doom.

"A hard thing it is," said Kane somberly, "to sentence a man to death in cold blood and in such a
manner as I have in mind, but you must die that others
may live—and God knoweth you deserve death.

"You shall not die by noose, bullet or sword, but at
the talons of him you slew—for naught else will
satiate him."

At these words Ezra's brain shattered, his knees
gave way and he fell groveling and screaming
for death, begging them to burn him at the stake, to
flay him alive. Kane's face was set like death, and the
villagers, the fear rousing their cruelty, bound the
screeching wretch to the oak tree, and one of them
bade him make his peace with God. But Ezra
made no answer, shrieking in a high shrill voice
with unbearable monotony. Then the villager would
have struck the miser across the face, but Kane
stayed him.

"Let him make his peace with Satan, whom he is
more like to meet," said the Puritan grimly. "The sun
is about to set. Loose his cords so that he may work
loose by dark, since it is better to meet death free and
unshackled than bound like a sacrifice."

As they turned to leave him, old Ezra yammered
and gibbered unhuman sounds and then fell silent,
staring at the sun with terrible intensity.

They walked away across the fen, and Kane flung a
last look at the grotesque form bound to the tree,

seeming in the uncertain light like a great fungus growing to the bole. And suddenly the miser screamed hideously:

"Death! Death! There are skulls in the stars!"

"Life was good to him, though he was gnarled and churlish and evil," Kane sighed. "Mayhap God has a place for such souls where fire and sacrifice may cleanse them of their dross as fire cleans the forest of fungous things. Yet my heart is heavy within me."

"Nay, sir," one of the villagers spoke, "you have done but the will of God, and good alone shall come of this night's deed."

"Nay," answered Kane heavily, "I know not—I know not."

The sun had gone down and night spread with amazing swiftness, as if great shadows came rushing down from unknown voids to cloak the world with hurrying darkness. Through the thick night came a weird echo, and the men halted and looked back the way they had come.

Nothing could be seen. The moor was an ocean of shadows and the tall grass about them bent in long waves before the faint wind, breaking the deathly stillness with breathless murmurings.

Then far away the red disk of the moon rose over the fen, and for an instant a grim silhouette was etched blackly against it. A shape came flying across the face of the moon—a bent, grotesque thing whose feet seemed scarcely to touch the earth; and close behind came a thing like a flying shadow—a nameless, shapeless horror.

A moment the racing twain stood out boldly against the moon; then they merged into one unnamable, formless mass, and vanished in the shadows.

Far across the fen sounded a single shriek of terrible laughter.

Crete

Weird Tales, February 1929

The green waves wash above us
Who slumber in the bay
As washed the tide of ages
That swept our race away.

Our cities—dusty ruins;
Our galleys—deep-sea slime;
Our very ghosts, forgotten,
Bow to the sweep of Time.

Our land lies stark before it
As we to alien spears,
But, ah, the love we bore it
Outlasts the crawling years.

Ah, jeweled spires at even—
The lute's soft golden sigh—
The Lion-Gates of Knossos
When dawn was in the sky.

Moon Mockery

Weird Tales, April 1929

I walked in Tara's Wood one summer night,
   And saw, amid the still, star-haunted skies,
   A slender moon in silver mist arise,
And hover on the hill as if in fright.
Burning, I seized her veil and held her tight:
   An instant all her glow was in my eyes;
   Then she was gone, swift as a white bird flies,
And I went down the hill in opal light.

And soon I was aware, as down I came,
   That all was strange and new on every side;
     Strange people went about me to and fro,
And when I spoke with trembling mine own name
   They turned away, but one man said: "He died
     In Tara Wood, a hundred years ago."

Rattle of Bones

Weird Tales, June 1929

"Landlord, ho!" The shout broke the lowering silence and reverberated through the black forest with sinister echoing.

"This place hath a forbidding aspect, meseemeth."

Two men stood in front of the forest tavern. The building was low, long and rambling, built of heavy logs. Its small windows were heavily barred and the door was closed. Above the door its sinister sign showed faintly—a cleft skull.

This door swung slowly open and a bearded face peered out. The owner of the face stepped back and motioned his guests to enter—with a grudging gesture it seemed. A candle gleamed on a table; a flame smoldered in the fireplace.

"Your names?"

"Solomon Kane," said the taller man briefly.

"Gaston l'Armon," the other spoke curtly. "But what is that to you?"

"Strangers are few in the Black Forest," grunted the host, "bandits many. Sit at yonder table and I will bring food."

The two men sat down, with the bearing of men who have traveled far. One was a tall gaunt man, clad in a featherless hat and somber black garments, which set off the dark pallor of his forbidding face. The other was of a different type entirely, bedecked with lace and plumes, although his finery was somewhat stained from travel. He was handsome in a bold way, and his restless eyes shifted from side to side, never still an instant.

The host brought wine and food to the rough-hewn table and then stood back in the shadows, like a somber image. His features, now receding into vagueness, now luridly etched in the firelight as it leaped and flickered, were masked in a beard which seemed almost animal-like in thickness. A great nose curved above this beard and two small red eyes stared unblinkingly at his guests.

"Who are you?" suddenly asked the younger man.

"I am the host of the Cleft Skull Tavern," sullenly replied the other. His tone seemed to challenge his questioner to ask further.

"Do you have many guests?" l'Armon pursued.

"Few come twice," the host grunted.

Kane started and glanced up straight into those small red eyes, as if he sought for some hidden meaning in the host's words. The flaming eyes seemed to dilate, then dropped sullenly before the Englishman's cold stare.

"I'm for bed," said Kane abruptly, bringing his meal to a close. "I must take up my journey by daylight."

"And I," added the Frenchman. "Host, show us to our chambers."

Black shadows wavered on the walls as the two followed their silent host down a long, dark hall. The stocky, broad body of their guide seemed to grow and expand in the light of the small candle which he carried, throwing a long, grim shadow behind him.

At a certain door he halted, indicating that they were to sleep there. They entered; the host lit a candle with the one he carried, then lurched back the way he had come.

In the chamber the two men glanced at each other. The only furnishings of the room were a couple of bunks, a chair or two and a heavy table.

"Let us see if there be any way to make fast the door," said Kane. "I like not the looks of mine host."

"There are racks on door and jamb for a bar," said Gaston, "but no bar."

"We might break up the table and use its pieces for a bar," mused Kane.

"*Mon Dieu*," said l'Armon, "you are timorous, *m'sieu.*"

Kane scowled. "I like not being murdered in my sleep," he answered gruffly.

"My faith!" the Frenchman laughed. "We are chance met—until I overtook you on the forest road an hour before sunset, we had never seen each other."

"I have seen you somewhere before," answered Kane, "though I can not now recall where. As for the other, I assume every man is an honest fellow until he shows me he is a rogue; moreover, I am a light sleeper and slumber with a pistol at hand."

The Frenchman laughed again.

"I was wondering how *m'sieu* could bring himself to sleep in the room with a stranger! Ha! Ha! All right, *m'sieu* Englishman, let us go forth and take a bar from one of the other rooms."

Taking the candle with them, they went into the corridor. Utter silence reigned and the small candle twinkled redly and evilly in the thick darkness.

"Mine host hath neither guests nor servants," muttered Solomon Kane. "A strange tavern! What is the name, now? These German words come not easily to me—the Cleft Skull? A bloody name, i'faith."

They tried the rooms next to theirs, but no bar rewarded their search. At last they came to the last room at the end of the corridor. They entered. It was furnished like the rest, except that the door was provided with a small barred opening, and fastened from the outside with a heavy bolt, which was secured at one end to the door-jamb. They raised the bolt and looked in.

"There should be an outer window, but there is not," muttered Kane. "Look!"

The floor was stained darkly. The walls and the one bunk were hacked in places, great splinters having been torn away.

"Men have died in here," said Kane, somberly. "Is yonder not a bar fixed in the wall?"

"Aye, but 'tis made fast," said the Frenchman, tugging at it. "The—"

A section of the wall swung back and Gaston gave a

quick exclamation. A small, secret room was revealed, and the two men bent over the grisly thing that lay upon its floor.

"The skeleton of a man!" said Gaston. "And behold, how his bony leg is shackled to the floor! He was imprisoned here and died."

"Nay," said Kane, "the skull is cleft—methinks mine host had a grim reason for the name of his hellish tavern. This man, like us, was no doubt a wanderer who fell into the fiend's hands."

"Likely," said Gaston without interest; he was engaged in idly working the great iron ring from the skeleton's leg bones. Failing in this, he drew his sword and with an exhibition of remarkable strength cut the chain which joined the ring on the leg to a ring set deep in the log floor.

"Why should he shackle a skeleton to the floor?" mused the Frenchman. "*Monbleu!* 'Tis a waste of good chain. Now, *m'sieu*," he ironically addressed the white heap of bones, "I have freed you and you may go where you like!"

"Have done!" Kane's voice was deep. "No good will come of mocking the dead."

"The dead should defend themselves," laughed l'Armon. "Somehow, I will slay the man who kills me, though my corpse climb up forty fathoms of ocean to do it."

Kane turned toward the outer door, closing the door of the secret room behind him. He liked not this talk which smacked of demonry and witchcraft; and he was in haste to face the host with the charge of his guilt.

As he turned, with his back to the Frenchman, he felt the touch of cold steel against his neck and knew that a pistol muzzle was pressed close beneath the base of his brain.

"Move not, *m'sieu*!" The voice was low and silky. "Move not, or I will scatter your few brains over the room."

The Puritan, raging inwardly, stood with his hands in air while l'Armon slipped his pistols and sword from their sheaths.

"Now you can turn," said Gaston, stepping back.

Kane bent a grim eye on the dapper fellow, who stood bareheaded now, hat in one hand, the other hand leveling his long pistol.

"Gaston the Butcher!" said the Englishman somberly. "Fool that I was to trust a Frenchman! You range far, murderer! I remember you now, with that cursed great hat off—I saw you in Calais some years agone."

"Aye—and now you will see me never again. What was that?"

"Rats exploring yon skeleton," said Kane, watching the bandit like a hawk, waiting for a single slight wavering of that black gun muzzle. "The sound was of the rattle of bones."

"Like enough," returned the other. "Now, *M'sieu* Kane, I know you carry considerable money on your person. I had thought to wait until you slept and then slay you, but the opportunity presented itself and I took it. You trick easily."

"I had little thought that I should fear a man with whom I had broken bread," said Kane, a deep timbre of slow fury sounding in his voice.

The bandit laughed cynically. His eyes narrowed as he began to back slowly toward the outer door. Kane's sinews tensed involuntarily; he gathered himself like a giant wolf about to launch himself in a death leap, but Gaston's hand was like a rock and the pistol never trembled.

"We will have no death plunges after the shot," said Gaston. "Stand still, *m'sieu*; I have seen men killed by dying men, and I wish to have distance enough between us to preclude that possibility. My faith—I will shoot, you will roar and charge, but you will die before you reach me with your bare hands. And mine host will have another skeleton in his secret niche. That is, if I do not kill him myself. The fool knows me not nor I him, moreover—"

The Frenchman was in the doorway now, sighting along the barrel. The candle, which had been stuck in a niche on the wall, shed a weird and flickering light which did not extend past the doorway. And with the suddenness of death, from the darkness behind Gaston's back, a broad, vague form rose up and a gleaming blade swept down. The Frenchman went to his knees like a butchered ox, his brains spilling from his cleft skull. Above him towered the figure of the host, a wild and terrible spectacle, still holding the hanger with which he had slain the bandit.

"Ho! ho!" he roared. "Back!"

Kane had leaped forward as Gaston fell, but the host thrust into his very face a long pistol which he held in his left hand.

"Back!" he repeated in a tigerish roar, and Kane

retreated from the menacing weapon and the insanity in the red eyes.

The Englishman stood silent, his flesh crawling as he sensed a deeper and more hideous threat than the Frenchman had offered. There was something inhuman about this man, who now swayed to and fro like some great forest beast while his mirthless laughter boomed out again.

"Gaston the Butcher!" he shouted, kicking the corpse at his feet. "Ho! ho! My fine brigand will hunt no more! I had heard of this fool who roamed the Black Forest—he wished gold and he found death! Now your gold shall be mine; and more than gold—vengeance!"

"I am no foe of yours," Kane spoke calmly.

"All men are my foes! Look—the marks on my wrists! See—the marks on my ankles! And deep in my back—the kiss of the knout! And deep in my brain, the wounds of the years of the cold, silent cells where I lay as punishment for a crime I never committed!" The voice broke in a hideous, grotesque sob.

Kane made no answer. This man was not the first he had seen whose brain had shattered amid the horrors of the terrible Continental prisons.

"But I escaped!" the scream rose triumphantly. "And here I make war on all men...What was that?"

Did Kane see a flash of fear in those hideous eyes?

"My sorcerer is rattling his bones!" whispered the host, then laughed wildly. "Dying, he swore his very bones would weave a net of death for me. I shackled his corpse to the floor, and now, deep in the night, I hear his bare skeleton clash and rattle as he seeks to be free, and I laugh, I laugh! Ho! ho! How he yearns to rise and stalk like old King Death along these dark corridors when I sleep, to slay me in my bed!"

Suddenly the insane eyes flared hideously: "You were in that secret room, you and this dead fool! Did he talk to you?"

Kane shuddered in spite of himself. Was it insanity or did he actually hear the faint rattle of bones, as if the skeleton had moved slightly? Kane shrugged his shoulders; rats will even tug at dusty bones.

The host was laughing again. He sidled around Kane, keeping the Englishman always covered, and with his free hand opened the door. All was darkness within, so that Kane could not even see the glimmer of the bones on the floor.

"All men are my foes!" mumbled the host, in the incoherent manner of the insane. "Why should I spare any man? Who lifted a hand to my aid when I lay for years in the vile dungeons of Karlsruhe—and for a deed never proven? Something happened to my brain, then. I became as a wolf—a brother to these of the Black Forest to which I fled when I escaped.

"They have feasted, my brothers, on all who lay in my tavern—all except this one who now clashes his bones, this magician from Russia. Lest he come stalking back through the black shadows when night is over the world, and slay me—for who may slay the dead?—I stripped his bones and shackled him. His sorcery was not powerful enough to save him from me, but all men know that a dead magician is more evil than a living one. Move not, Englishman! Your bones I shall leave in this secret room beside this one, to—"

The maniac was standing partly in the doorway of the secret room, now, his weapon still menacing Kane. Suddenly he seemed to topple backward, and vanished in the darkness; and at the same instant a vagrant gust of wind swept down the outer corridor and slammed the door shut behind him. The candle on the wall flickered and went out. Kane's groping hands, sweeping over the floor, found a pistol, and he straightened, facing the door where the maniac had vanished. He stood in the utter darkness, his blood freezing, while a hideous muffled screaming came from the secret room, intermingled with the dry, grisly rattle of fleshless bones. Then silence fell.

Kane found flint and steel and lighted the candle. Then, holding it in one hand and the pistol in the other, he opened the secret door.

"Great God!" he muttered as cold sweat formed on his body. "This thing is beyond all reason, yet with mine own eyes I see it! Two vows have here been kept, for Gaston the Butcher swore that even in death he would avenge his slaying, and his was the hand which set yon fleshless monster free. And he—"

The host of the Cleft Skull lay lifeless on the floor of the secret room, his bestial face set in lines of terrible fear; and deep in his broken neck were sunk the bare fingerbones of the sorcerer's skeleton.

Forbidden Magic

Weird Tales, July 1929

There came to me a Shape one summer night
   When all the world lay silent in the stars
   And moonlight crossed my room with ghostly bars.
It whispered hints of weird unhallowed sight;
I followed, then in waves of spectral light
   Mounted the shimmery ladders of my soul,
   Where moon-pale spiders, huge as dragons, stole—
Great forms like moths with wings of whispy white.

Then round the world the sighing of the loon
   Shook misty lakes beneath the false dawn's gleams.
     Rose-tinted shone the skyline's minaret.
     I rose in fear and then with blood and sweat
   Beat out the iron fabrics of my dreams
And shaped of them a web to snare the moon.

The Shadow Kingdom

Weird Tales, August 1929

1. A King Comes Riding

The blare of the trumpets grew louder, like a deep golden tide surge, like the soft booming of the evening tides against the silver beaches of Valusia. The throng shouted, women flung roses from the roofs as the rhythmic chiming of silver hoofs came clearer and the first of the mighty array swung into view in the broad white street that curved round the golden-spired Tower of Splendor.

First came the trumpeters, slim youths, clad in scarlet, riding with a flourish of long, slender golden trumpets; next the bowmen, tall men from the mountains; and behind these the heavily armed footmen, their broad shields clashing in unison, their long spears swaying in perfect rhythm to their stride. Behind them came the mightiest soldiery in all the world, the Red Slayers, horsemen, splendidly mounted, armed in red from helmet to spur. Proudly they sat their steeds, looking neither to right nor to left, but aware of the shouting for all that. Like bronze statues they were, and there was never a waver in the forest of spears that reared above them.

Behind those proud and terrible ranks came the motley files of the mercenaries, fierce, wild-looking warriors, men of Mu and of Kaa-u and of the hills of the east and the isles of the west. They bore spears and heavy swords, and a compact group that marched somewhat apart were the bowmen of Lemuria. Then came the light foot of the nation, and more trumpeters brought up the rear.

A brave sight, and a sight which aroused a fierce thrill in the soul of Kull, king of Valusia. Not on the Topaz Throne at the front of the regal Tower of Splendor sat Kull, but in the saddle, mounted on a great stallion, a true warrior king. His mighty arm swung up in reply to the salutes as the hosts passed. His fierce eyes passed the gorgeous trumpeters with a casual glance, rested longer on the following soldiery; they blazed with a ferocious light as the Red Slayers halted in front of him with a clang of arms and a rearing of steeds, and tendered him the crown salute. They narrowed slightly as the mercenaries strode by. They saluted no one, the mercenaries. They walked with shoulders flung back, eyeing Kull boldly and straightly, albeit with a certain appreciation; fierce eyes, unblinking; savage eyes, staring from beneath shaggy manes and heavy brows.

And Kull gave back a like stare. He granted much to brave men, and there were no braver in all the world, not even among the wild tribesmen who now disowned him. But Kull was too much the savage to have any great love for these. There were too many feuds. Many were age-old enemies of Kull's nation, and though the name of Kull was now a word accursed among the mountains and valleys of his people, and though Kull had put them from his mind, yet the old hates, the ancient passions still lingered. For Kull was no Valusian but an Atlantean.

The armies swung out of sight around the gem-blazing shoulders of the Tower of Splendor and Kull reined his stallion about and started toward the palace at an easy gait, discussing the review with the commanders that rode with him, using not many words, but saying much.

"The army is like a sword," said Kull, "and must not be allowed to rust." So down the street they rode, and Kull gave no heed to any of the whispers that reached his hearing from the throngs that still swarmed the streets.

"That is Kull, see! Valka! But what a king! And what a man! Look at his arms! His shoulders!"

And an undertone of more sinister whisperings: "Kull! Ha, accursed usurper from the pagan isles"—"Aye, shame to Valusia that a barbarian sits on the Throne of Kings." . . .

Little did Kull heed. Heavy-handed had he seized the decaying throne of ancient Valusia and with a heavier hand did he hold it, a man against a nation.

After the council chamber, the social palace where Kull replied to the formal and laudatory phrases of the lords and ladies, with carefully hidden, grim amusement at such frivolities; then the lords and ladies took their formal departure and Kull leaned back upon the ermine throne and contemplated matters of state until an attendant requested permission from the great king to speak, and announced an emissary from the Pictish embassy.

Kull brought his mind back from the dim mazes of Valusian statecraft where it had been wandering, and gazed upon the Pict with little favor. The man gave back the gaze of the king without flinching. He was a lean-hipped, massive-chested warrior of middle height, dark, like all his race, and strongly built. From strong, immobile features gazed dauntless and inscrutable eyes.

"The chief of the Councilors, Ka-nu of the tribe, right hand of the king of Pictdom, sends greetings and says: 'There is a throne at the feast of the rising moon for Kull, king of kings, lord of lords, emperor of Valusia.'"

"Good," answered Kull. "Say to Ka-nu the Ancient, ambassador of the western isles, that the king of Valusia will quaff wine with him when the moon floats over the hills of Zalgara."

Still the Pict lingered. "I have a word for the king, not"—with a contemptuous flip of his hand—"for these slaves."

Kull dismissed the attendants with a word, watching the Pict warily.

The man stepped nearer, and lowered his voice: "Come alone to feast tonight, lord king. Such was the word of my chief."

The king's eyes narrowed, gleaming like gray sword steel, coldly.

"Alone?"

"Aye."

They eyed each other silently, their mutual tribal enmity seething beneath their cloak of formality. Their mouths spoke the cultured speech, the conventional court phrases of a highly polished race, a race not their own, but from their eyes gleamed the primal traditions of the elemental savage. Kull might be the king of Valusia and the Pict might be an emissary to her courts, but there in the throne hall of kings, two tribesmen glowered at each other, fierce and wary, while ghosts of wild wars and world-ancient feuds whispered to each.

To the king was the advantage and he enjoyed it to its fullest extent. Jaw resting on hand, he eyed the Pict, who stood like an image of bronze, head flung back, eyes unflinching.

Across Kull's lips stole a smile that was more a sneer.

"And so I am to come—alone?" Civilization had taught him to speak by innuendo and the Pict's dark eyes glittered, though he made no reply. "How am I to know that you come from Ka-nu?"

"I have spoken," was the sullen response.

"And when did a Pict speak truth?" sneered Kull, fully aware that the Picts never lied, but using this means to enrage the man.

"I see your plan, king," the Pict answered imperturbably. "You wish to anger me. By Valka, you need go no further! I am angry enough. And I challenge you to meet me in single battle, spear, sword or dagger, mounted or afoot. Are you king or man?"

Kull's eyes glinted with the grudging admiration a

warrior must needs give a bold foeman, but he did not fail to use the chance of further annoying his antagonist.

"A king does not accept the challenge of a nameless savage," he sneered, "nor does the emperor of Valusia break the Truce of Ambassadors. You have leave to go. Say to Ka-nu I will come alone."

The Pict's eyes flashed murderously. He fairly shook in the grasp of the primitive blood-lust; then, turning his back squarely upon the king of Valusia, he strode across the Hall of Society and vanished through the great door.

Again Kull leaned back upon the ermine throne and meditated.

So the chief of the Council of Picts wished him to come alone? But for what reason? Treachery? Grimly Kull touched the hilt of his great sword. But scarcely. The Picts valued too greatly the alliance with Valusia to break it for any feudal reason. Kull might be a warrior of Atlantis and hereditary enemy of all Picts, but too, he was king of Valusia, the most potent ally of the Men of the West.

Kull reflected long upon the strange state of affairs that made him ally of ancient foes and foe of ancient friends. He rose and paced restlessly across the hall, with the quick, noiseless tread of a lion. Chains of friendship, tribe and tradition had he broken to satisfy his ambition. And, by Valka, god of the sea and the land, he had realized that ambition! He was king of Valusia—a fading, degenerate Valusia, a Valusia living mostly in dreams of bygone glory, but still a mighty land and the greatest of the Seven Empires. Valusia—

Land of Dreams, the tribesmen named it, and sometimes it seemed to Kull that he moved in a dream. Strange to him were the intrigues of court and palace, army and people. All was like a masquerade, where men and women hid their real thoughts with a smooth mask. Yet the seizing of the throne had been easy—a bold snatching of opportunity, the swift whirl of swords, the slaying of a tyrant of whom men had wearied unto death, short, crafty plotting with ambitious statesmen out of favor at court—and Kull, wandering adventurer, Atlantean exile, had swept up to the dizzy heights of his dreams: he was lord of Valusia, king of kings. Yet now it seemed that the seizing was far easier than the keeping. The sight of the Pict had brought back youthful associations to his mind, the free, wild savagery of his boyhood. And now a strange feeling of dim unrest, of unreality, stole over him as of late it had been doing. Who was he, a straightforward man of the seas and the mountain, to rule a race strangely and terribly wise with the mysticisms of antiquity? An ancient race—

"I am Kull!" said he, flinging back his head as a lion flings back his mane. "I am Kull!"

His falcon gaze swept the ancient hall. His self-confidence flowed back....And in a dim nook of the hall a tapestry moved—slightly.

2. Thus Spake the Silent Halls of Valusia

The moon had not risen, and the garden was lighted with torches aglow in silver cressets when Kull sat down in the throne before the table of Ka-nu, ambassador of the western isles. At his right hand sat the ancient Pict, as much unlike an emissary of that fierce race as a man could be. Ancient was Ka-nu and wise in statecraft, grown old in the game. There was no elemental hatred in the eyes that looked at Kull appraisingly; no tribal traditions hindered his judgments. Long associations with the statesmen of the civilized nations had swept away such cobwebs. Not "Who and what is this man?" was the question ever foremost in Ka-nu's mind, but "Can I use this man, and how?" Tribal prejudices he used only to further his own schemes.

And Kull watched Ka-nu, answering his conversation briefly, wondering if civilization would make of him a thing like the Pict. For Ka-nu was soft and paunchy. Many years had stridden across the sky-rim since Ka-nu had wielded a sword. True, he was old, but Kull had seen men older than he in the forefront of battle. The Picts were a long-lived race. A beautiful girl stood at Ka-nu's elbow, refilling his goblet, and she was kept busy. Meanwhile Ka-nu kept up a running fire of jests and comments, and Kull, secretly contemptuous of his garrulity, nevertheless missed none of his shrewd humor.

At the banquet were Pictish chiefs and statesmen, the latter jovial and easy in their manner, the warriors formally courteous, but plainly hampered by their tribal affinities. Yet Kull, with a tinge of envy, was cognizant of the freedom and ease of the affair as contrasted with like affairs of the Valusian court. Such freedom prevailed in the rude camps of Atlantis—Kull shrugged his shoulders. After all, doubtless Ka-nu, who had seemed to have forgotten he was a Pict as far as time-hoary custom and prejudice went, was right and he, Kull, would better become a Valusian in mind as in name.

At last when the moon had reached her zenith, Ka-nu, having eaten and drunk as much as any three men there, leaned back upon his divan with a comfortable sigh and said, "Now, get you gone, friends, for the king and I would converse on such matters as concerns not children. Yes, you too, my pretty; yet first let me kiss those ruby lips—so; now dance away, my rose-bloom."

Ka-nu's eyes twinkled above his white beard as he surveyed Kull, who sat erect, grim and uncompromising.

"You are thinking, Kull," said the old statesman, suddenly, "that Ka-nu is a useless old reprobate, fit for nothing except to guzzle wine and kiss wenches!"

In fact, this remark was so much in line with his actual thoughts, and so plainly put, that Kull was rather startled, though he gave no sign.

Ka-nu gurgled and his paunch shook with his

mirth. "Wine is red and women are soft," he remarked tolerantly. "But—ha-ha!—think not old Ka-nu allows either to interfere with business."

Again he laughed, and Kull moved restlessly. This seemed much like being made sport of, and the king's scintillant eyes began to glow with a feline light.

Ka-nu reached for the wine-pitcher, filled his beaker and glanced questioningly at Kull, who shook his head irritably.

"Aye," said Ka-nu equably, "it takes an old head to stand strong drink. I am growing old, Kull, so why should you young men begrudge me such pleasures as we oldsters must find? Ah me, I grow ancient and withered, friendless and cheerless."

But his looks and expressions failed far of bearing out his words. His rubicund countenance fairly glowed, and his eyes sparkled, so that his white beard seemed incongruous. Indeed, he looked remarkably elfin, reflected Kull, who felt vaguely resentful. The old scoundrel had lost all of the primitive virtues of his race and of Kull's race, yet he seemed more pleased in his aged days than otherwise.

"Hark ye, Kull," said Ka-nu, raising an admonitory finger, "'tis a chancy thing to laud a young man, yet I must speak my true thoughts to gain your confidence."

"If you think to gain it by flattery—"

"Tush. Who spake of flattery? I flatter only to dis-guard."

There was a keen sparkle in Ka-nu's eyes, a cold glimmer that did not match his lazy smile. He knew men, and he knew that to gain his end he must smite straight with this tigerish barbarian, who, like a wolf

scenting a snare, would scent out unerringly any false-
ness in the skein of his word-web.

"You have power, Kull," said he, choosing his
words with more care than he did in the council rooms
of the nation, "to make yourself mightiest of all kings,
and restore some of the lost glories of Valusia. So. I
care little for Valusia—though the women and wine be
excellent—save for the fact that the stronger Valusia
is, the stronger is the Pict nation. More, with an
Atlantean on the throne, eventually Atlantis will
become united—"

Kull laughed in harsh mockery. Ka-nu had touched
an old wound.

"Atlantis made my name accursed when I went to
seek fame and fortune among the cities of the world.
We—they—are age-old foes of the Seven Empires,
greater foes of the allies of the Empires, as you should
know."

Ka-nu tugged his beard and smiled enigmatically.

"Nay, nay. Let it pass. But I know whereof I speak.
And then warfare will cease, wherein there is no gain;
I see a world of peace and prosperity—man loving his
fellow man—the good supreme. All this can you
accomplish—*if you live!*"

"Ha!" Kull's lean hand closed on his hilt and he
half-rose, with a sudden movement of such dynamic
speed that Ka-nu, who fancied men as some men fancy
blooded horses, felt his old blood leap with a sudden
thrill. Valka, what a warrior! Nerves and sinews of
steel and fire, bound together with the perfect coordination, the fighting instinct, that makes the terrible
warrior.

But none of Ka-nu's enthusiasm showed in his mildly sarcastic tone.

"Tush. Be seated. Look about you. The gardens are deserted, the seats empty, save for ourselves. You fear not *me*?"

Kull sank back, gazing about him warily.

"There speaks the savage," mused Ka-nu. "Think you if I planned treachery I would enact it here where suspicion would be sure to fall upon me? Tut. You young tribesmen have much to learn. There were my chiefs who were not at ease because you were born among the hills of Atlantis, and you despise me in your secret mind because I am a Pict. Tush. I see you as Kull, king of Valusia, not as Kull, the reckless Atlantean, leader of the raiders who harried the western isles. So you should see in me, not a Pict but an international man, a figure of the world. Now to that figure, hark! If you were slain tomorrow who would be king?"

"Kaanuub, baron of Blaal."

"Even so. I object to Kaanuub for many reasons, yet most of all for the fact that he is but a figurehead."

"How so? He was my greatest opponent, but I did not know that he championed any cause but his own."

"The night can hear," answered Ka-nu obliquely. "There are worlds within worlds. But you may trust me and you may trust Brule, the Spear-slayer. Look!" He drew from his robes a bracelet of gold representing a winged dragon coiled thrice, with three horns of ruby on the head.

"Examine it closely. Brule will wear it on his arm when he comes to you tomorrow night so that you may know him. Trust Brule as you trust yourself, and do what he tells you to. And in proof of trust, look ye!"

And with the speed of a striking hawk, the ancient snatched something from his robes, something that flung a weird green light over them, and which he replaced in an instant.

"The stolen gem!" exclaimed Kull recoiling. "The green jewel from the Temple of the Serpent! Valka! You! And why do you show it to me?"

"To save your life. To prove my trust. If I betray your trust, deal with me likewise. You hold my life in your hand. Now I could not be false to you if I would, for a word from you would be my doom."

Yet for all his words the old scoundrel beamed merrily and seemed vastly pleased with himself.

"But why do you give me this hold over you?" asked Kull, becoming more bewildered each second.

"As I told you. Now, you see that I do not intend to deal you false, and tomorrow night when Brule comes to you, you will follow his advice without fear of treachery. Enough. An escort waits outside to ride to the palace with you, lord."

Kull rose. "But you have told me nothing."

"Tush. How impatient are youths!" Ka-nu looked more like a mischievous elf than ever. "Go you and dream of thrones and power and kingdoms, while I dream of wine and soft women and roses. And fortune ride with you, King Kull."

As he left the garden, Kull glanced back to see Ka-nu still reclining lazily in his seat, a merry ancient, beaming on all the world with jovial fellowship.

A mounted warrior waited for the king just without the garden and Kull was slightly surprized to see that it was the same that had brought Ka-nu's invitation. No word was spoken as Kull swung into the saddle nor as they clattered along the empty streets.

The color and the gayety of the day had given away to the eerie stillness of night. The city's antiquity was more than ever apparent beneath the bent, silver moon. The huge pillars of the mansions and palaces towered up into the stars. The broad stairways, silent and deserted, seemed to climb endlessly until they vanished in the shadowy darkness of the upper realms. Stairs to the stars, thought Kull, his imaginative mind inspired by the weird grandeur of the scene.

Clang! Clang! Clang! sounded the silver hoofs on the broad, moon-flooded streets, but otherwise there was no sound. The age of the city, its incredible antiquity, was almost oppressive to the king; it was as if the great silent buildings laughed at him, noiselessly, with unguessable mockery. And what secrets did they hold?

"You are young," said the palaces and the temples and the shrines, "but we are old. The world was wild with youth when we were reared. You and your tribe shall pass, but we are invincible, indestructible. We towered above a strange world, ere Atlantis and Lemuria rose from the sea; we still shall reign when the green waters sigh for many a restless fathom above the spires of Lemuria and the hills of Atlantis and when the isles of the Western Men are the mountains of a strange land.

"How many kings have we watched ride down these streets before Kull of Atlantis was even a dream in the mind of Ka, bird of Creation? Ride on, Kull of Atlantis; greater shall follow you; greater came before you. They are dust; they are forgotten; we stand; we know; we are. Ride, ride on, Kull of Atlantis; Kull the king, Kull the fool!"

And it seemed to Kull that the clashing hoofs took up the silent refrain to beat it into the night with hollow re-echoing mockery:

"Kull—the—king! Kull—the—fool!"

Glow, moon; you light a king's way! Gleam, stars; you are torches in the train of an emperor! And clang, silver-shod hoofs; you herald that Kull rides through Valusia.

Ho! Awake, Valusia! It is Kull that rides, Kull the king!

"We have known many kings," said the silent halls of Valusia.

And so in a brooding mood Kull came to the palace, where his bodyguard, men of the Red Slayers, came to take the rein of the great stallion and escort Kull to his rest. There the Pict, still sullenly speechless, wheeled his steed with a savage wrench of the rein and fled away in the dark like a phantom; Kull's heightened imagination pictured him speeding through the silent streets like a goblin out of the Elder World.

There was no sleep for Kull that night, for it was nearly dawn and he spent the rest of the night hours pacing the throne room, and pondering over what had passed. Ka-nu had told him nothing, yet he had put himself in Kull's complete power. At what had he hinted when he had said the baron of Blaal was naught but a figurehead? And who was this Brule who was to come to him by night, wearing the mystic armlet of the dragon? And why? Above all, why had Ka-nu shown him the green gem of terror, stolen long ago from the temple of the Serpent, for which the world would rock in wars were it known to the weird and terrible keepers of that temple, and from whose vengeance not even Ka-nu's ferocious tribesmen might be able to save him? But Ka-nu knew he was safe, reflected Kull, for the statesman was too shrewd to expose himself to risk without profit. But was it to throw the king off his guard and pave the way to treachery? Would Ka-nu dare let him live now? Kull shrugged his shoulders.

3. They That Walk the Night

The moon had not risen when Kull, hand to hilt, stepped to a window. The windows opened upon the great inner gardens of the royal palace, and the breezes of the night, bearing the scents of spice trees, blew the filmy curtains about. The king looked out. The walks and groves were deserted; carefully trimmed trees were bulky shadows; fountains nearby flung their slender sheen of silver in the starlight and distant fountains rippled steadily. No guards walked those gardens, for so closely were the outer walls guarded that it seemed impossible for any invader to gain access to them.

Vines curled up the walls of the palace, and even as Kull mused upon the ease with which they might be climbed, a segment of shadow detached itself from the darkness below the window and a bare, brown arm curved up over the sill. Kull's great sword hissed halfway from the sheath; then the king halted. Upon the muscular forearm gleamed the dragon armlet shown him by Ka-nu the night before.

The possessor of the arm pulled himself up over the sill and into the room with the swift, easy motion of a climbing leopard.

"You are Brule?" asked Kull, and then stopped in surprize not unmingled with annoyance and suspicion; for the man was he whom Kull had taunted in the hall of Society; the same who had escorted him from the Pictish embassy.

"I am Brule, the Spear-slayer," answered the Pict in a guarded voice; then swiftly, gazing closely in Kull's face, he said, barely above a whisper:

"*Ka nama kaa lajerama!*"

Kull started. "Ha! What mean you?"

"Know you not?"

"Nay, the words are unfamiliar; they are of no language I ever heard—and yet, by Valka!—somewhere—I have heard—"

"Aye," was the Pict's only comment. His eyes swept the room, the study room of the palace. Except for a few tables, a divan or two and great shelves of books of parchment, the room was barren compared to the grandeur of the rest of the palace.

"Tell me, king, who guards the door?"

"Eighteen of the Red Slayers. But how come you, stealing through the gardens by night and scaling the walls of the palace?"

Brule sneered. "The guards of Valusia are blind buffaloes. I could steal their girls from under their noses. I stole amid them and they saw me not nor heard me. And the walls—I could scale them without the aid of vines. I have hunted tigers on the foggy beaches when the sharp east breezes blew the mist in from seaward and I have climbed the steeps of the western sea mountain. But come—nay, touch this armlet."

He held out his arm and, as Kull complied wonderingly, gave an apparent sigh of relief.

"So. Now throw off those kingly robes; for there are ahead of you this night such deeds as no Atlantean ever dreamed of."

Brule himself was clad only in a scanty loin-cloth through which was thrust a short, curved sword.

"And who are you to give me orders?" asked Kull, slightly resentful.

"Did not Ka-nu bid you follow me in all things?" asked the Pict irritably, his eyes flashing momentarily. "I have no love for you, lord, but for the moment I have put the thought of feuds from my mind. Do you likewise. But come."

Walking noiselessly, he led the way across the room to the door. A slide in the door allowed a view of the outer corridor, unseen from without, and the Pict bade Kull look.

"What see you?"

"Naught but the eighteen guardsmen."

The Pict nodded, motioned Kull to follow him across the room. At a panel in the opposite wall Brule stopped and fumbled there a moment. Then with a light movement he stepped back, drawing his sword as he did so. Kull gave an exclamation as the panel swung silently open, revealing a dimly lighted passageway.

"A secret passage!" swore Kull softly. "And I knew nothing of it! By Valka, someone shall dance for this!"

"Silence!" hissed the Pict.

Brule was standing like a bronze statue as if straining every nerve for the slightest sound; something about his attitude made Kull's hair prickle slightly, not from fear but from some eerie anticipation. Then beckoning, Brule stepped through the secret doorway which stood open behind them. The passage was bare, but not dust covered as should have been the case with an unused secret corridor. A vague, gray light filtered through somewhere, but the source of it was not apparent. Every few feet Kull saw doors, invisible, as he knew, from the outside, but easily apparent from within.

"The palace is a very honeycomb," he muttered.

"Aye. Night and day you are watched, king, by many eyes."

The king was impressed by Brule's manner. The Pict went forward slowly, warily, half-crouching, blade held low and thrust forward. When he spoke it was in a whisper and he continually flung glances from side to side.

The corridor turned sharply and Brule warily gazed past the turn.

"Look!" he whispered. "But remember! No word! No sound—on your life!"

Kull cautiously gazed past him. The corridor changed just at the bend to a flight of steps. And then Kull recoiled. At the foot of those stairs lay the eigh-

teen Red Slayers who were that night stationed to
watch the king's study room. Brule's grip upon his
mighty arm and Brule's fierce whisper at his shoulder
alone kept Kull from leaping down those stairs.

"Silent, Kull! Silent, in Valka's name!" hissed the
Pict. "These corridors are empty now, but I risked
much in showing you, that you might then believe
what I had to say. Back now to the room of study."
And he retraced his steps, Kull following; his mind in a
turmoil of bewilderment.

"This is treachery," muttered the king, his steel-
gray eyes a-smolder, "foul and swift! Mere minutes
have passed since those men stood at guard."

Again in the room of study Brule carefully closed
the secret panel and motioned Kull to look again
through the slit of the outer door. Kull gasped audibly.
For without stood the eighteen guardsmen!

"This is sorcery!" he whispered, half-drawing his
sword. "Do dead men guard the king?"

"*Aye!*" came Brule's scarcely audible reply; there
was a strange expression in the Pict's scintillant eyes.
They looked squarely into each other's eyes for an
instant, Kull's brow wrinkled in a puzzled scowl as he
strove to read the Pict's inscrutable face. Then Brule's
lips, barely moving, formed the words:

"*The—snake—that—speaks!*"

"Silent!" whispered Kull, laying his hand over
Brule's mouth. "That is death to speak! That is a name
accursed!"

The Pict's fearless eyes regarded him steadily.

"Look again, King Kull. Perchance the guard was
changed."

"Nay, those are the same men. In Valka's name, this is sorcery—this is insanity! I saw with my own eyes the bodies of those men, not eight minutes agone. Yet there they stand."

Brule stepped back, away from the door, Kull mechanically following.

"Kull, what know ye of the traditions of this race ye rule?"

"Much—and yet, little. Valusia is so old—"

"Aye," Brule's eyes lighted strangely, "we are but barbarians—infants compared to the Seven Empires. Not even they themselves know how old they are. Neither the memory of man nor the annals of the historians reach back far enough to tell us when the first men came up from the sea and built cities on the shore. But Kull, *men were not always ruled by men!*"

The king started. Their eyes met.

"Aye, there is a legend of my people—"

"And mine!" broke in Brule. "That was before we of the isles were allied with Valusia. Aye, in the reign of Lion-fang, seventh war chief of the Picts, so many years ago no man remembers how many. Across the sea we came, from the isles of the sunset, skirting the shores of Atlantis, and falling upon the beaches of Valusia with fire and sword. Aye, the long white beaches resounded with the clash of spears, and the night was like day from the flame of the burning castles. And the king, the king of Valusia, who died on the red sea sands that dim day—" His voice trailed off; the two stared at each other, neither speaking; then each nodded.

"Ancient is Valusia!" whispered Kull. "The hills of

Atlantis and Mu were isles of the sea when Valusia was young."

The night breeze whispered through the open window. Not the free, crisp sea air such as Brule and Kull knew and reveled in, in their land, but a breath like a whisper from the past, laden with musk, scents of forgotten things, breathing secrets that were hoary when the world was young.

The tapestries rustled, and suddenly Kull felt like a naked child before the inscrutable wisdom of the mystic past. Again the sense of unreality swept upon him. At the back of his soul stole dim, gigantic phantoms, whispering monstrous things. He sensed that Brule experienced similar thoughts. The Pict's eyes were fixed upon his face with a fierce intensity. Their glances met. Kull felt warmly a sense of comradeship with this member of an enemy tribe. Like rival leopards turning at bay against hunters, these two savages made common cause against the inhuman powers of antiquity.

Brule again led the way back to the secret door. Silently they entered and silently they proceeded down the dim corridor, taking the opposite direction from that in which they had previously traversed it. After a while the Pict stopped and pressed close to one of the secret doors, bidding Kull look with him through the hidden slot.

"This opens upon a little-used stair which leads to a corridor running past the study-room door."

They gazed, and presently, mounting the stair silently, came a silent shape.

"Tu! Chief councilor!" exclaimed Kull. "By night

and with bared dagger! How, what means this, Brule?"

"Murder! And foulest treachery!" hissed Brule. "Nay"—as Kull would have flung the door aside and leaped forth—"we are lost if you meet him here, for more lurk at the foot of those stairs. Come!"

Half-running, they darted back along the passage. Back through the secret door Brule led, shutting it carefully behind them, then across the chamber to an opening into a room seldom used. There he swept aside some tapestries in a dim corner nook and, drawing Kull with him, stepped behind them. Minutes dragged. Kull could hear the breeze in the other room blowing the window curtains about, and it seemed to him like the murmur of ghosts. Then through the door, stealthily, came Tu, chief councilor of the king. Evidently he had come through the study room and, finding it empty, sought his victim where he was most likely to be.

He came with upraised dagger, walking silently. A moment he halted, gazing about the apparently empty room, which was lighted dimly by a single candle. Then he advanced cautiously, apparently at a loss to understand the absence of the king. He stood before the hiding place—and—

"Slay!" hissed the Pict.

Kull with a single mighty leap hurled himself into the room. Tu spun, but the blinding, tigerish speed of the attack gave him no chance for defense or counter-attack. Sword steel flashed in the dim light and grated on bone as Tu toppled backward, Kull's sword standing out between his shoulders.

Kull leaned above him, teeth bared in the killer's snarl, heavy brows a-scowl above eyes that were like the gray ice of the cold sea. Then he released the hilt and recoiled, shaken, dizzy, the hand of death at his spine.

For as he watched, Tu's face became strangely dim and unreal; the features mingled and merged in a seemingly impossible manner. Then, like a fading mask of fog, the face suddenly vanished and in its stead gaped and leered *a monstrous serpent's head!*

"Valka!" gasped Kull, sweat beading his forehead, and again: "Valka!"

Brule leaned forward, face immobile. Yet his glittering eyes mirrored something of Kull's horror.

"Regain your sword, lord king," said he. "There are yet deeds to be done."

Hesitantly Kull set his hand to the hilt. His flesh crawled as he set his foot upon the terror which lay at their feet, and as some jerk of muscular reaction caused the frightful mouth to gape suddenly, he recoiled, weak with nausea. Then, wrathful at himself, he plucked forth his sword and gazed more closely at the nameless thing that had been known as Tu, chief councilor. Save for the reptilian head, the thing was the exact counterpart of a man.

"A man with the head of a snake!" Kull murmured. "This, then, is a priest of the serpent god?"

"Aye. Tu sleeps unknowing. These fiends can take any form they will. That is, they can, by a magic charm or the like, fling a web of sorcery about their faces, as an actor dons a mask, so that they resemble anyone they wish to."

"Then the old legends were true," mused the king; "the grim old tales few dare even whisper, lest they die as blasphemers, are no fantasies. By Valka, I had thought—I had guessed—but it seems beyond the bounds of reality. Ha! The guardsmen outside the door—"

"They too are snake-men. Hold! What would you do?"

"Slay them!" said Kull between his teeth.

"Strike at the skull if at all," said Brule. "Eighteen wait without the door and perhaps a score more in the corridors. Hark ye, king, Ka-nu learned of this plot. His spies have pierced the inmost fastnesses of the snake priests and they brought hints of a plot. Long ago he discovered the secret passageways of the palace, and at his command I studied the map thereof and came here by night to aid you, lest you die as other kings of Valusia have died. I came alone for the reason that to send more would have roused suspicion. Many could not steal into the palace as I did. Some of the foul conspiracy you have seen. Snake-men guard your door, and that one, as Tu, could pass anywhere else in the palace; in the morning, if the priests failed, the real guards would be holding their places again, nothing knowing, nothing remembering; there to take the blame if the priests succeeded. But stay you here while I dispose of this carrion."

So saying, the Pict shouldered the frightful thing stolidly and vanished with it through another secret panel. Kull stood alone, his mind a-whirl. Neophytes of the mighty serpent, how many lurked among his cities? How might he tell the false from the true? Aye, how many of his trusted councilors, his generals, were men? He could be certain—of whom?

The secret panel swung inward and Brule entered.

"You were swift."

"Aye!" The warrior stepped forward, eyeing the floor. "There is gore upon the rug. See?"

Kull bent forward; from the corner of his eye he saw a blur of movement, a glint of steel. Like a loosened bow he whipped erect, thrusting upward. The warrior sagged upon the sword, his own clattering to the floor. Even at that instant Kull reflected grimly that it was appropriate that the traitor should meet his death upon the sliding, upward thrust used so much by his race. Then, as Brule slid from the sword to sprawl motionless on the floor, the face began to merge and fade, and as Kull caught his breath, his hair a-prickle, the human features vanished and there the jaws of a great snake gaped hideously, the terrible beady eyes venomous even in death.

"He was a snake priest all the time!" gasped the king. "Valka! What an elaborate plan to throw me off my guard! Ka-nu there, is he a man? Was it Ka-nu to whom I talked in the gardens? Almighty Valka!" as his flesh crawled with a horrid thought; "are the people of Valusia men or are they *all* serpents?"

Undecided he stood, idly seeing that the thing named Brule no longer wore the dragon armlet. A sound made him wheel.

Brule was coming through the secret door.

"Hold!" upon the arm upthrown to halt the king's hovering sword gleamed the dragon armlet. "Valka!"

The Pict stopped short. Then a grim smile curled his lips.

"By the gods of the seas! These demons are crafty past reckoning. For it must be that that one lurked in the corridors, and seeing me go carrying the carcass of that other, took my appearance. So. I have another to do away with."

"Hold!" there was the menace of death in Kull's voice; "I have seen two men turn to serpents before my eyes. How may I know if you are a true man?"

Brule laughed. "For two reasons, King Kull. No snake-man wears this"—he indicated the dragon armlet—"nor can any say these words," and again Kull heard the strange phrase: *"Ka nama kaa lajerama."*

"Ka nama kaa lajerama," Kull repeated mechanically. "Now where, in Valka's name, have I heard that? I have not! And yet—and yet—"

"Aye, you remember, Kull," said Brule. "Through the dim corridors of memory those words lurk; though you never heard them in this life, yet in the bygone ages they were so terribly impressed upon the soul mind that never dies, that they will always strike dim chords in your memory, though you be reincarnated for a million years to come. For that phrase has come secretly down the grim and bloody eons, since when, uncounted centuries ago, those words were watchwords for the race of men who battled with the grisly beings of the Elder Universe. For none but a real man of men may speak them, whose jaws and mouth are shaped different from any other creature. Their meaning has been forgotten but not the words themselves."

"True," said Kull. "I remember the legends—Valka!" He stopped short, staring, for suddenly, like the silent swinging wide of a mystic door, misty, unfathomed reaches opened in the recesses of his consciousness and for an instant he seemed to gaze back through the vastnesses that spanned life and life; seeing through the vague and ghostly fogs dim shapes reliving dead centuries—men in combat with hideous monsters, vanquishing a planet of frightful terrors. Against a gray, ever-shifting background moved strange nightmare forms, fantasies of lunacy and fear; and man, the jest of the gods, the blind, wisdomless striver from dust to dust, following the long bloody trail of his destiny, knowing not why, bestial, blundering, like a great murderous child, yet feeling somewhere a spark of divine fire. . . . Kull drew a hand across his brow, shaken; these sudden glimpses into the abysses of memory always startled him.

"They are gone," said Brule, as if scanning his secret mind; "the bird-women, the harpies, the bat-men, the flying fiends, the wolf-people, the demons, the goblins—all save such as this being that lies at our feet, and a few of the wolf-men. Long and terrible was the war, lasting through the bloody centuries, since first the first men, risen from the mire of apedom, turned upon those who then ruled the world. And at last mankind conquered, so long ago that naught but dim legends come to us through the ages. The snake-people were the last to go, yet at last men conquered even them and drove them forth into the waste lands of the world, there to mate with true snakes until some day, say the sages, the horrid breed shall vanish utterly. Yet the Things returned in crafty guise as men grew soft and degenerate, forgetting ancient wars. Ah, that was a grim and secret war! Among the men of the Younger Earth stole the frightful monsters of the Elder Planet, safeguarded by their horrid wisdom and mysticisms, taking all forms and shapes, doing deeds of horror secretly. No man knew who was true man and who false. No man could trust any man. Yet by means of their own craft they formed ways by which the false might be known from the true. Men took for a sign and a standard the figure of the flying dragon, the winged dinosaur, a monster of past ages, which was the greatest foe of the serpent. And men used those words which I spoke to you as a sign and symbol, for as I said, none but a true man can repeat them. So mankind triumphed. Yet again the fiends came after the years of forgetfulness had gone by—for man is still an ape in that he forgets what is not ever before his eyes. As priests they came; and for that men in their luxury and might had by then lost faith in the old religions and worships, the snake-men, in the guise of teachers of a new and truer cult, built a monstrous religion about the worship of the serpent god. Such is their power that it is now death to repeat the old legends of the snake-people, and people bow again to the serpent god in new form; and blind fools that they are, the great hosts of men see no connection between this power and the power men overthrew eons ago. As priests the snake-men are content to rule—and yet—" He stopped.

"Go on." Kull felt an unaccountable stirring of the short hair at the base of his scalp.

"Kings have reigned as true men in Valusia," the Pict whispered, "and yet, slain in battle, have died serpents—as died he who fell beneath the spear of Lion-fang on the red beaches when we of the isles harried the Seven Empires. And how can this be, Lord Kull? These kings were born of women and lived as men! This—the true kings died in secret—as you would have died tonight—and priests of the Serpent reigned in their stead, no man knowing."

Kull cursed between his teeth. "Aye, it must be. No one has ever seen a priest of the Serpent and lived, that is known. They live in utmost secrecy."

"The statecraft of the Seven Empires is a mazy, monstrous thing," said Brule. "There the true men know that among them glide the spies of the serpent, and the men who are the Serpent's allies—such as Kaanuub, baron of Blaal—yet no man dares seek to unmask a suspect lest vengeance befall him. No man trusts his fellow and the true statesmen dare not speak to each other what is in the minds of all. Could they be sure, could a snake-man or plot be unmasked before them all, then would the power of the Serpent be more than half-broken; for all would then ally and make common cause, sifting out the traitors. Ka-nu alone is of sufficient shrewdness and courage to cope with them, and even Ka-nu learned only enough of their plot to tell me what would happen—what has happened up to this time. Thus far I was prepared; from now on we must trust to our luck and our craft. Here and now I think we are safe; those snake-men without the door dare not leave their post lest true men come here unexpectedly. But tomorrow they will try something else, you may be sure. Just what they will do, none can say, not even Ka-nu; but we must stay at each other's sides, King Kull, until we conquer or both be dead. Now come with me while I take this carcass to the hiding-place where I took the other being."

Kull followed the Pict with his grisly burden through the secret panel and down the dim corridor. Their feet, trained to the silence of the wilderness, made no noise. Like phantoms they glided through the ghostly light, Kull wondering that the corridors should be deserted; at every turn he expected to run full upon some frightful apparition. Suspicion surged back upon him; was this Pict leading him into ambush? He fell back a pace or two behind Brule, his ready sword hovering at the Pict's unheeding back. Brule should die first if he meant treachery. But if the Pict was aware of the king's suspicion, he showed no sign. Stolidly he tramped along, until they came to a room, dusty and long unused, where moldy tapestries hung heavy. Brule drew aside some of these and concealed the corpse behind them.

Then they turned to retrace their steps, when suddenly Brule halted with such abruptness that he was closer to death than he knew; for Kull's nerves were on edge.

"Something moving in the corridor," hissed the Pict. "Ka-nu said these ways would be empty, yet—"

He drew his sword and stole into the corridor, Kull following warily.

A short way down the corridor a strange, vague

glow appeared that came toward them. Nerves a-leap, they waited, backs to the corridor wall; for what they knew not, but Kull heard Brule's breath hiss through his teeth and was reassured as to Brule's loyalty.

The glow merged into a shadowy form. A shape vaguely like a man it was, but misty and illusive, like a wisp of fog, that grew more tangible as it approached, but never fully material. A face looked at them, a pair of luminous great eyes, that seemed to hold all the tortures of a million centuries. There was no menace in that face, with its dim, worn features, but only a great pity—and that face—that face—

"Almighty gods!" breathed Kull, an icy hand at his soul; "Eallal, king of Valusia, who died a thousand years ago!"

Brule shrank back as far as he could, his narrow eyes widened in a blaze of pure horror, the sword shaking in his grip, unnerved for the first time that weird night. Erect and defiant stood Kull, instinctively holding his useless sword at the ready; flesh a-crawl, hair a-prickle, yet still a king of kings, as ready to challenge the powers of the unknown dead as the powers of the living.

The phantom came straight on, giving them no heed; Kull shrank back as it passed them, feeling an icy breath like a breeze from the arctic snow. Straight on went the shape with slow, silent footsteps, as if the chains of all the ages were upon those vague feet; vanishing about a bend of the corridor.

"Valka!" muttered the Pict, wiping the cold beads from his brow; "That was no man! That was a ghost!"

"Aye!" Kull shook his head wonderingly. "Did you

not recognize the face? That was Eallal, who reigned in Valusia a thousand years ago and who was found hideously murdered in his throne room—the room now known as the Accursed Room. Have you not seen his statue in the Fame Room of Kings?"

"Yes, I remember the tale now. Gods, Kull! That is another sign of the frightful and foul power of the snake priests—that king was slain by snake-people and thus his soul became their slave, to do their bidding throughout eternity! For the sages have ever maintained that if a man is slain by a snake-man his ghost becomes their slave."

A shudder shook Kull's gigantic frame. "Valka! But what a fate! Hark ye"—his fingers closed upon Brule's sinewy arm like steel—"hark ye! If I am wounded unto death by these foul monsters, swear that ye will smite your sword through my breast lest my soul be enslaved."

"I swear," answered Brule, his fierce eyes lighting. "And do ye the same by me, Kull."

Their strong right hands met in a silent sealing of their bloody bargain.

4. Masks

Kull sat upon his throne and gazed broodingly out upon the sea of faces turned toward him. A courtier was speaking in evenly modulated tones, but the king scarcely heard him. Close by, Tu, chief councilor, stood ready at Kull's command, and each time the king looked at him, Kull shuddered inwardly. The surface of court life was as the unrippled surface of the sea between tide and tide. To the musing king the affairs of the night before seemed as a dream, until his eyes dropped to the arm of his throne. A brown, sinewy hand rested there, upon the wrist of which gleamed a dragon armlet; Brule stood beside his throne and ever the Pict's fierce secret whisper brought him back from the realm of unreality in which he moved.

No, that was no dream, that monstrous interlude. As he sat upon his throne in the Hall of Society and gazed upon the courtiers, the ladies, the lords, the statesmen, he seemed to see their faces as things of illusion, things unreal, existent only as shadows and mockeries of substance. Always he had seen their faces as masks, but before he had looked on them with contemptuous tolerance, thinking to see beneath the masks shallow, puny souls, avaricious, lustful, deceitful; now there was a grim undertone, a sinister meaning, a vague horror that lurked beneath the smooth masks. While he exchanged courtesies with some nobleman or councilor he seemed to see the smiling face fade like smoke and the frightful jaws of a serpent gaping there. How many of those he looked upon were horrid, inhuman monsters, plotting his death, beneath the smooth mesmeric illusion of a human face?

Valusia—land of dreams and nightmares—a kingdom of the shadows, ruled by phantoms who glided back and forth behind the painted curtains, mocking the futile king who sat upon the throne— himself a shadow.

And like a comrade shadow Brule stood by his side, dark eyes glittering from immobile face. A real man, Brule! And Kull felt his friendship for the savage become a thing of reality and sensed that Brule felt a friendship for him beyond the mere necessity of state-craft.

And what, mused Kull, were the realities of life? Ambition, power, pride? The friendship of man, the love of women—which Kull had never known—battle, plunder, what? Was it the real Kull who sat upon the throne or was it the real Kull who had scaled the hills of Atlantis, harried the far isles of the sunset, and laughed upon the green roaring tides of the Atlantean sea? How could a man be so many different men in a lifetime? For Kull knew that there were many Kulls and he wondered which was the real Kull. After all, the priests of the Serpent merely went a step further in their magic, for all men wore masks, and many a dif-ferent mask with each different man or woman; and Kull wondered if a serpent did not lurk under every mask.

So he sat and brooded in strange, mazy thought-ways, and the courtiers came and went and the minor affairs of the day were completed, until at last the king and Brule sat alone in the Hall of Society save for the drowsy attendants.

Kull felt a weariness. Neither he nor Brule had slept the night before, nor had Kull slept the night before that, when in the gardens of Ka-nu he had had his first hint of the weird things to be. Last night nothing further had occurred after they had returned to the study room from the secret corridors, but they had neither dared nor cared to sleep. Kull, with the incredible vitality of a wolf, had aforetime gone for days upon days without sleep, in his wild savage days, but now his mind was edged from constant thinking and from the nerve-breaking eeriness of the past night. He needed sleep, but sleep was furthest from his mind.

And he would not have dared sleep if he had thought of it. Another thing that had shaken him was the fact that though he and Brule had kept a close watch to see if, or when, the study-room guard was changed, yet it was changed without their knowledge; for the next morning those who stood on guard were able to repeat the magic words of Brule, but they remembered nothing out of the ordinary. They thought that they had stood at guard all night, as usual, and Kull said nothing to the contrary. He believed them true men, but Brule had advised absolute secrecy, and Kull also thought it best.

Now Brule leaned over the throne, lowering his voice so not even a lazy attendant could hear: "They will strike soon, I think, Kull. A while ago Ka-nu gave me a secret sign. The priests know that we know of their plot, of course, but they know not how much we know. We must be ready for any sort of action. Ka-nu and the Pictish chiefs will remain within hailing distance now until this is settled one way or another. Ha, Kull, if it comes to a pitched battle, the streets and the castles of Valusia will run red!"

Kull smiled grimly. He would greet any sort of action with a ferocious joy. This wandering in a labyrinth of illusion and magic was extremely irksome to his nature. He longed for the leap and clang of swords, for the joyous freedom of battle.

Then into the Hall of Society came Tu again, and the rest of the councilors.

"Lord king, the hour of the council is at hand and we stand ready to escort you to the council room."

Kull rose, and the councilors bent the knee as he passed through the way opened by them for his passage, rising behind him and following. Eyebrows were raised as the Pict strode defiantly behind the king, but no one dissented. Brule's challenging gaze swept the smooth faces of the councilors with the defiance of an intruding savage.

The group passed through the halls and came at last to the council chamber. The door was closed, as usual, and the councilors arranged themselves in the order of their rank before the dais upon which stood the king. Like a bronze statue Brule took up his stand behind Kull.

Kull swept the room with a swift stare. Surely no chance of treachery here. Seventeen councilors there were, all known to him; all of them had espoused his cause when he ascended the throne.

"Men of Valusia—" he began in the conventional manner, then halted, perplexed. The councilors had risen as a man and were moving toward him. There was no hostility in their looks, but their actions were strange for a council room. The foremost was close to him when Brule sprang forward, crouched like a leopard.

"*Ka nama kaa lajerama!*" his voice crackled through the sinister silence of the room and the foremost councilor recoiled, hand flashing to his robes; and like a spring released Brule moved and the man pitched headlong to the glint of his sword—headlong he pitched and lay still while his face faded and became the head of a mighty snake.

"Slay, Kull!" rasped the Pict's voice. "They be all serpent men!"

The rest was a scarlet maze. Kull saw the familiar faces dim like fading fog and in their places gaped horrid reptilian visages as the whole band rushed forward. His mind was dazed but his giant body faltered not.

The singing of his sword filled the room, and the onrushing flood broke in a red wave. But they surged forward again, seemingly willing to fling their lives away in order to drag down the king. Hideous jaws gaped at him; terrible eyes blazed into his unblinkingly; a frightful fetid scent pervaded the atmosphere—the serpent scent that Kull had known in southern jungles. Swords and daggers leaped at him and he was dimly aware that they wounded him. But Kull was in his element; never before had he faced such grim foes but it mattered little; they lived, their veins held blood that could be spilt and they died when his great sword cleft their skulls or drove through their bodies. Slash, thrust, thrust and swing. Yet had Kull died there but for the man who crouched at his side, parrying and thrusting. For the king was clear berserk, fighting in the terrible Atlantean way, that seeks death to deal death; he made no effort to avoid thrusts and slashes, standing straight up and ever plunging forward, no thought in his frenzied mind but to slay. Not often did Kull forget his fighting craft in his primitive fury, but now some chain had broken in his soul, flooding his mind with a red wave of slaughter-lust. He slew a foe at each blow, but they surged about him, and time and again Brule turned a thrust that would have slain, as he crouched beside Kull, parrying and warding with cold skill, slaying not as Kull slew with long slashes and plunges, but with short overhand blows and upward thrusts.

Kull laughed, a laugh of insanity. The frightful faces swirled about him in a scarlet blaze. He felt steel sink into his arm and dropped his sword in a flashing arc that cleft his foe to the breast-bone. Then the mists faded and the king saw that he and Brule stood alone above a sprawl of hideous crimson figures who lay still upon the floor.

"Valka! What a killing!" said Brule, shaking the blood from his eyes. "Kull, had these been warriors who knew how to use the steel, we had died here. These serpent priests know naught of swordcraft and die easier than any men I ever slew. Yet had there been a few more, I think the matter had ended otherwise."

Kull nodded. The wild berserker blaze had passed, leaving a mazed feeling of great weariness. Blood seeped from wounds on breast, shoulder, arm and leg. Brule, himself bleeding from a score of flesh wounds, glanced at him in some concern.

"Lord Kull, let us hasten to have your wounds dressed by the women."

Kull thrust him aside with a drunken sweep of his mighty arm.

"Nay, we'll see this through ere we cease. Go

you, though, and have your wounds seen to—I command it."

The Pict laughed grimly. "Your wounds are more than mine, lord king—" he began, then stopped as a sudden thought struck him. "By Valka, Kull, this is not the council room!"

Kull looked about and suddenly other fogs seemed to fade. "Nay, this is the room where Eallal died a thousand years ago—since unused and named 'Accursed'."

"Then by the gods, they tricked us after all!" exclaimed Brule in a fury, kicking the corpses at their feet. "They caused us to walk like fools into their ambush! By their magic they changed the appearance of all—"

"Then there is further deviltry afoot," said Kull, "for if there be true men in the councils of Valusia they should be in the real council room now. Come swiftly."

And leaving the room with its ghastly keepers they hastened through halls that seemed deserted until they came to the real council room. Then Kull halted with a ghastly shudder. *From the council room sounded a voice speaking, and the voice was his!*

With a hand that shook he parted the tapestries and gazed into the room. There sat the councilors, counterparts of the men he and Brule had just slain, and upon the dais stood Kull, king of Valusia.

He stepped back, his mind reeling.

"This is insanity!" he whispered. "Am I Kull? Do I stand here or is that Kull yonder in very truth and am I but a shadow, a figment of thought?"

Brule's hand clutching his shoulder, shaking him fiercely, brought him to his senses.

"Valka's name, be not a fool! Can you yet be astounded after all we have seen? See you not that those are true men bewitched by a snake-man who has taken your form, as those others took their forms? By now you should have been slain and yon monster reigning in your stead, unknown by those who bowed to you. Leap and slay swiftly or else we are undone. The Red Slayers, true men, stand close on each hand and none but you can reach and slay him. Be swift!"

Kull shook off the onrushing dizziness, flung back his head in the old, defiant gesture. He took a long, deep breath as does a strong swimmer before diving into the sea; then, sweeping back the tapestries, made the dais in a single lion-like bound. Brule had spoken truly. There stood men of the Red Slayers, guardsmen trained to move quick as the striking leopard; any but Kull had died ere he could reach the usurper. But the sight of Kull, identical with the man upon the dais, held them in their tracks, their minds stunned for an instant, and that was long enough. He upon the dais snatched for his sword, but even as his fingers closed upon the hilt, Kull's sword stood out behind his shoulders and the thing that men had thought the king pitched forward from the dais to lie silent upon the floor.

"Hold!" Kull's lifted hand and kingly voice stopped the rush that had started, and while they stood astounded he pointed to the thing which lay before them—whose face was fading into that of a snake.

They recoiled, and from one door came Brule and from another came Ka-nu.

These grasped the king's bloody hand and Ka-nu spoke: "Men of Valusia, you have seen with your own eyes. This is the true Kull, the mightiest king to whom Valusia has ever bowed. The power of the Serpent is broken and ye be all true men. King Kull, have you commands?"

"Lift that carrion," said Kull, and men of the guard took up the thing.

"Now follow me," said the king, and he made his way to the Accursed Room. Brule, with a look of concern, offered the support of his arm but Kull shook him off.

The distance seemed endless to the bleeding king, but at last he stood at the door and laughed fiercely and grimly when he heard the horrified ejaculations of the councilors.

At his orders the guardsmen flung the corpse they carried beside the others, and motioning all from the room Kull stepped out last and closed the door.

A wave of dizziness left him shaken. The faces turned to him, pallid and wonderingly, swirled and mingled in a ghostly fog. He felt the blood from his wound trickling down his limbs and he knew that what he was to do, he must do quickly or not at all.

His sword rasped from its sheath.

"Brule, are you there?"

"Aye!" Brule's face looked at him through the mist, close to his shoulder, but Brule's voice sounded leagues and eons away.

"Remember our vow, Brule. And now, bid them stand back."

His left arm cleared a space as he flung up his sword. Then with all his waning power he drove it through the door into the jamb, driving the great sword to the hilt and sealing the room forever.

Legs braced wide, he swayed drunkenly, facing the horrified councilors. "Let this room be doubly accursed. And let those rotting skeletons lie there forever as a sign of the dying might of the serpent. Here I swear that I shall hunt the serpent-men from land to land, from sea to sea, giving no rest until all be slain, that good triumph and the power of Hell be broken. This thing I swear—I—Kull—king—of—Valusia."

His knees buckled as the faces swayed and swirled. The councilors leaped forward, but ere they could reach him, Kull slumped to the floor, and lay still, face upward.

The councilors surged about the fallen king, chattering and shrieking. Ka-nu beat them back with his clenched fists, cursing savagely.

"Back, you fools! Would you stifle the little life that is yet in him? How, Brule, is he dead or will he live?"—to the warrior who bent above the prostrate Kull.

"Dead?" sneered Brule irritably. "Such a man as this is not so easily killed. Lack of sleep and loss of blood have weakened him—by Valka, he has a score of deep wounds, but none of them mortal. Yet have those gibbering fools bring the court women here at once."

Brule's eyes lighted with a fierce, proud light.

"Valka, Ka-nu, but here is such a man as I knew not existed in these degenerate days. He will be in the saddle in a few scant days and then may the serpent-men of the world beware of Kull of Valusia. Valka! But that will be a rare hunt! Ah, I see long years of prosperity for the world with such a king upon the throne of Valusia."

The Mirrors of Tuzun Thune

Weird Tales, September 1929

"A wild, weird clime that lieth sublime
Out of Space, out of Time."

—*Poe.*

There comes, even to kings, the time of great weariness. Then the gold of the throne is brass, the silk of the palace becomes drab. The gems in the diadem and upon the fingers of the women sparkle drearily like the ice of the white seas; the speech of men is as the empty rattle of a jester's bell and the feel comes of things unreal; even the sun is copper in the sky and the breath of the green ocean is no longer fresh.

Kull sat upon the throne of Valusia and the hour of weariness was upon him. They moved before him in an endless, meaningless panorama, men, women, priests, events and shadows of events; things seen and things to be attained. But like shadows they came and went, leaving no trace upon his consciousness, save that of a great mental fatigue. Yet Kull was not tired.

There was a longing in him for things beyond himself and beyond the Valusian court. An unrest stirred in him and strange, luminous dreams roamed his soul. At his bidding there came to him Brule the Spear-slayer, warrior of Pictland, from the islands beyond the West.

"Lord king, you are tired of the life of the court. Come with me upon my galley and let us roam the tides for a space."

"Nay." Kull rested his chin moodily upon his mighty hand. "I am weary beyond all these things. The cities hold no lure for me—and the borders are quiet. I hear no more the sea-songs I heard when I lay as a boy on the booming crags of Atlantis, and the night was alive with blazing stars. No more do the green woodlands beckon me as of old. There is a strangeness upon me and a longing beyond life's longings. Go!"

Brule went forth in a doubtful mood, leaving the king brooding upon his throne. Then to Kull stole a girl of the court and whispered:

"Great king, seek Tuzun Thune, the wizard. The secrets of life and death are his, and the stars in the sky and the lands beneath the seas."

Kull looked at the girl. Fine gold was her hair and her violet eyes were slanted strangely; she was beautiful, but her beauty meant little to Kull.

"Tuzun Thune," he repeated. "Who is he?"

"A wizard of the Elder Race. He lives here, in Valusia, by the Lake of Visions in the House of a Thousand Mirrors. All things are known to him, lord king; he speaks with the dead and holds converse with the demons of the Lost Lands."

Kull arose.

"I will seek out this mummer; but no word of my going, do you hear?"

"I am your slave, my lord." And she sank to her knees meekly, but the smile of her scarlet mouth was cunning behind Kull's back and the gleam of her narrow eyes was crafty.

Kull came to the house of Tuzun Thune, beside the Lake of Visions. Wide and blue stretched the waters of the lake and many a fine palace rose upon its banks; many swan-winged pleasure boats drifted lazily upon its hazy surface and evermore there came the sound of soft music.

Tall and spacious, but unpretentious, rose the House of a Thousand Mirrors. The great doors stood open and Kull ascended the broad stair and entered, unannounced. There in a great chamber, whose walls were of mirrors, he came upon Tuzun Thune, the wizard. The man was ancient as the hills of Zalgara; like wrinkled leather was his skin, but his cold gray eyes were like sparks of sword steel.

"Kull of Valusia, my house is yours," said he, bowing with old-time courtliness and motioning Kull to a throne-like chair.

"You are a wizard, I have heard," said Kull bluntly, resting his chin upon his hand and fixing his somber eyes upon the man's face. "Can you do wonders?"

The wizard stretched forth his hand; his fingers opened and closed like a bird's claws.

"Is that not a wonder—that this blind flesh obeys the thoughts of my mind? I walk, I breathe, I speak—are they all not wonders?"

Kull meditated awhile, then spoke. "Can you summon up demons?"

"Aye. I can summon up a demon more savage than any in ghostland—by smiting you in the face."

Kull started, then nodded. "But the dead, can you talk to the dead?"

"I talk with the dead always—as I am talking now. Death begins with birth and each man begins to die when he is born; even now you are dead, King Kull, because you were born."

"But you, you are older than men become; do wizards never die?"

"Men die when their time comes. No later, no sooner. Mine has not come."

Kull turned these answers over in his mind.

"Then it would seem that the greatest wizard of Valusia is no more than an ordinary man, and I have been duped in coming here."

Tuzun Thune shook his head. "Men are but men, and the greatest men are they who soonest learn the simpler things. Nay, look into my mirrors, Kull."

The ceiling was a great many mirrors, and the walls were mirrors, perfectly jointed, yet many mirrors of many sizes and shapes.

"Mirrors are the world, Kull," droned the wizard. "Gaze into my mirrors and be wise."

Kull chose one at random and looked into it intently. The mirrors upon the opposite wall were reflected there, reflecting others, so that he seemed to be gazing down a long, luminous corridor, formed by mirror behind mirror; and far down this corridor

moved a tiny figure. Kull looked long ere he saw that
the figure was the reflection of himself. He gazed and
a queer feeling of pettiness came over him; it seemed
that that tiny figure was the true Kull, representing the
real proportions of himself. So he moved away and
stood before another.

"Look closely, Kull. That is the mirror of the past,"
he heard the wizard say.

Gray fogs obscured the vision, great billows of
mist, ever heaving and changing like the ghost of a
great river; through these fogs Kull caught swift
fleeting visions of horror and strangeness; beasts and
men moved there and shapes neither men nor beasts;
great exotic blossoms glowed through the grayness;
tall tropic trees towered high over reeking swamps,
where reptilian monsters wallowed and bellowed; the
sky was ghastly with flying dragons and the restless
seas rocked and roared and beat endlessly along the
muddy beaches. Man was not, yet man was the dream
of the gods and strange were the nightmare forms that
glided through the noisome jungles. Battle and
onslaught were there, and frightful love. Death was
there, for Life and Death go hand in hand. Across the
slimy beaches of the world sounded the bellowing of
the monsters, and incredible shapes loomed through
the steaming curtain of the incessant rain.

"This is of the future."

Kull looked in silence.

"See you—what?"

"A strange world," said Kull heavily. "The Seven
Empires are crumbled to dust and are forgotten. The
restless green waves roar for many a fathom above the

eternal hills of Atlantis; the mountains of Lemuria of the West are the islands of an unknown sea. Strange savages roam the elder lands and new lands flung strangely from the deeps, defiling the elder shrines. Valusia is vanished and all the nations of today; they of tomorrow are strangers. They know us not."

"Time strides onward," said Tuzun Thune calmly. "We live today; what care we for tomorrow—or yesterday? The Wheel turns and nations rise and fall; the world changes, and times return to savagery to rise again through the long ages. Ere Atlantis was, Valusia was, and ere Valusia was, the Elder Nations were. Aye, we, too, trampled the shoulders of lost tribes in our advance. You, who have come from the green sea hills of Atlantis to seize the ancient crown of Valusia, you think my tribe is old, we who held these lands ere the Valusians came out of the East, in the days before there were men in the sea lands. But men were here when the Elder Tribes rode out of the waste lands, and men before men, tribe before tribe. The nations pass and are forgotten, for that is the destiny of man."

"Yes," said Kull. "Yet is it not a pity that the beauty and glory of men should fade like smoke on a summer sea?"

"For what reason, since that is their destiny? I brood not over the lost glories of my race, nor do I labor for races to come. Live now, Kull, live now. The dead are dead; the unborn are not. What matters men's forgetfulness of you when you have forgotten yourself in the silent worlds of death? Gaze in my mirrors and be wise."

Kull chose another mirror and gazed into it.

"That is the mirror of the deepest magic; what see ye, Kull?"

"Naught but myself."

"Look closely, Kull; is it in truth you?"

Kull stared into the great mirror, and the image that was his reflection returned his gaze.

"I come before this mirror," mused Kull, chin on fist, "and I bring this man to life. This is beyond my understanding, since first I saw him in the still waters of the lakes of Atlantis, till I saw him again in the gold-rimmed mirrors of Valusia. He is I, a shadow of myself, part of myself—I can bring him into being or slay him at my will; yet"—he halted, strange thoughts whispering through the vast dim recesses of his mind like shadowy bats flying through a great cavern—"yet where is he when I stand not in front of a mirror? May it be in man's power thus lightly to form and destroy a shadow of life and existence? How do I know that when I step back from the mirror he vanishes into the void of Naught?

"Nay, by Valka, am I the man or is he? Which of us is the ghost of the other? Mayhap these mirrors are but windows through which we look into another world. Does he think the same of me? Am I no more than a shadow, a reflection of himself—to him, as he to me? And if I am the ghost, what sort of a world lives upon the other side of this mirror? What armies ride there and what kings rule? This world is all I know. Knowing naught of any other, how can I judge? Surely there are green hills there and booming seas and wide plains where men ride to battle. Tell me, wizard who are wiser than most men, tell me, are there worlds beyond our worlds?"

"A man has eyes, let him see," answered the wizard. "Who would see must first believe."

The hours drifted by and Kull still sat before the mirrors of Tuzun Thune, gazing into that which depicted himself. Sometimes it seemed that he gazed upon hard shallowness; at other times gigantic depths seemed to loom before him. Like the surface of the sea was the mirror of Tuzun Thune; hard as the sea in the sun's slanting beams, in the darkness of the stars, when no eye can pierce her deeps; vast and mystic as the sea when the sun smites her in such way that the watcher's breath is caught at the glimpse of tremendous abysses. So was the mirror in which Kull gazed.

At last the king rose with a sigh and took his departure still wondering. And Kull came again to the House of a Thousand Mirrors; day after day he came and sat for hours before the mirror. The eyes looked out at him, identical with his, yet Kull seemed to sense a difference—a reality that was not of him. Hour upon hour he would stare with strange intensity into the mirror; hour after hour the image gave back his gaze.

The business of the palace and of the council went neglected. The people murmured; Kull's stallion stamped restlessly in his stable and Kull's warriors diced and argued aimlessly with one another. Kull heeded not. At times he seemed on the point of discovering some vast, unthinkable secret. He no longer thought of the image in the mirror as a shadow of himself; the thing, to him, was an entity, similar in outer appearance, yet basically as far from Kull him-

self as the poles are far apart. The image, it seemed to
Kull, had an individuality apart from Kull's; he was no
more dependent on Kull than Kull was dependent on
him. And day by day Kull doubted in which world he
really lived; was he the shadow, summoned at will by
the other? Did he instead of the other live in a world of
delusion, the shadow of the real world?

Kull began to wish that he might enter the personality beyond the mirror for a space, to see what might
be seen; yet should he manage to go beyond that door
could he ever return? Would he find a world identical
with the one in which he moved? A world, of which
his was but a ghostly reflection? Which was reality
and which illusion?

At times Kull halted to wonder how such thoughts
and dreams had come to enter his mind and at times
he wondered if they came of his own volition or—here
his thoughts would become mazed. His meditations
were his own; no man ruled his thoughts and he would
summon them at his pleasure; yet could he? Were they
not as bats, coming and going, not at his pleasure but
at the bidding or ruling of—of whom? The gods? The
Women who wove the webs of Fate? Kull could come
to no conclusion, for at each mental step he became
more and more bewildered in a hazy gray fog of illusory assertions and refutations. This much he knew:
that strange visions entered his mind, like bats flying
unbidden from the whispering void of non-existence;
never had he thought these thoughts, but now they
ruled his mind, sleeping and waking, so that he
seemed to walk in a daze at times; and his sleep was
fraught with strange, monstrous dreams.

"Tell me, wizard," he said, sitting before the mirror, eyes fixed intently upon his image, "how can I pass yon door? For of a truth, I am not sure that that is the real world and this the shadow; at least, that which I see must exist in some form."

"See and believe," droned the wizard. "Man must believe to accomplish. Form is shadow, substance is illusion, materiality is dream; man is because he believes he is; what is man but a dream of the gods? Yet man can be that which he wishes to be; form and substance, they are but shadows. The mind, the ego, the essence of the god-dream—that is real, that is immortal. See and believe, if you would accomplish, Kull."

The king did not fully understand; he never fully understood the enigmatical utterances of the wizard, yet they struck somewhere in his being a dim responsive chord. So day after day he sat before the mirrors of Tuzun Thune. Ever the wizard lurked behind him like a shadow.

Then came a day when Kull seemed to catch glimpses of strange lands; there flitted across his consciousness dim thoughts and recognitions. Day by day he had seemed to lose touch with the world; all things had seemed each succeeding day more ghostly and unreal; only the man in the mirror seemed like reality. Now Kull seemed to be close to the doors of some mightier worlds; giant vistas gleamed fleetingly; the fogs of unreality thinned, "form is shadow, substance is illusion; they are but shadows" sounded as if from some far country of his consciousness. He remembered the wizard's words and it seemed to him that now he almost understood—form and substance, could not he change himself at will, if he knew the master key that opened this door? What worlds within what worlds awaited the bold explorer?

The man in the mirror seemed smiling at him—closer, closer—a fog enwrapped all and the reflection dimmed suddenly—Kull knew a sensation of fading, of change, of merging—

"Kull!" the yell split the silence into a million vibratory fragments!

Mountains crashed and worlds tottered as Kull, hurled back by that frantic shout, made a superhuman effort, how or why he did not know.

A crash, and Kull stood in the room of Tuzun Thune before a shattered mirror, mazed and half-blind with bewilderment. There before him lay the body of Tuzun Thune, whose time had come at last, and above him stood Brule the Spear-slayer, sword dripping red and eyes wide with a kind of horror.

"Valka!" swore the warrior. "Kull, it was time I came!"

"Aye, yet what happened?" The king groped for words.

"Ask this traitress," answered the Spear-slayer, indicating a girl who crouched in terror before the king; Kull saw that it was she who first sent him to Tuzun Thune. "As I came in I saw you fading into yon mirror as smoke fades into the sky, by Valka! Had I not seen I would not have believed—you had almost vanished when my shout brought you back."

"Aye," muttered Kull, "I had almost gone beyond the door that time."

"This fiend wrought most craftily," said Brule. "Kull, do you not now see how he spun and flung over you a web of magic? Kaanuub of Blaal plotted with this wizard to do away with you, and this wench, a girl of Elder Race, put the thought in your mind so that you would come here. Kananu of the council learned of the plot today; I know not what you saw in that mirror, but with it Tuzun Thune enthralled your soul and almost by his witchery he changed your body to mist—"

"Aye." Kull was still mazed. "But being a wizard, having knowledge of all the ages and despising gold, glory and position, what could Kaanuub offer Tuzun Thune that would make of him a foul traitor?"

"Gold, power and position," grunted Brule. "The sooner you learn that men are men whether wizard, king or thrall, the better you will rule, Kull. Now what of her?"

"Naught, Brule," as the girl whimpered and groveled at Kull's feet. "She was but a tool. Rise, child, and go your ways; none shall harm you."

Alone with Brule, Kull looked for the last time on the mirrors of Tuzun Thune.

"Mayhap he plotted and conjured, Brule; nay, I doubt you not, yet—was it his witchery that was changing me to thin mist, or had I stumbled on a secret? Had you not brought me back, had I faded in dissolution or had I found worlds beyond this?"

Brule stole a glance at the mirrors, and twitched his shoulders as if he shuddered. "Aye. Tuzun Thune stored the wisdom of all the hells here. Let us begone, Kull, ere they bewitch me, too."

"Let us go, then," answered Kull, and side by side they went forth from the House of a Thousand Mirrors—where, mayhap, are prisoned the souls of men.

None look now in the mirrors of Tuzun Thune. The pleasure boats shun the shore where stands the wizard's house and no one goes in the house or to the room where Tuzun Thune's dried and withered carcass lies before the mirrors of illusion. The place is shunned as a place accursed, and though it stands for a thousand years to come, no footsteps shall echo there. Yet Kull upon his throne meditates often upon the strange wisdom and untold secrets hidden there and wonders....

For there are worlds beyond worlds, as Kull knows, and whether the wizard bewitched him by words or by mesmerism, vistas did open to the king's gaze beyond that strange door, and Kull is less sure of reality since he gazed into the mirrors of Tuzun Thune.

The Moor Ghost

Weird Tales, September 1929

They haled him to the crossroads
As day was at its close;
They hung him to the gallows
And left him for the crows.

His hands in life were bloody,
His ghost will not be still;
He haunts the naked moorlands
About the gibbet hill.

And oft a lonely traveler
Is found upon the fen
Whose dead eyes hold a horror
Beyond the world of men.

The villagers then whisper,
With accents grim and dour:
"This man has met at midnight
The phantom of the moor."

Red Thunder

JAPM: The Poetry Weekly,
September 16, 1929

Thunder in the black skies beating down the rain,
Thunder in the black cliffs, looming o'er the main,
Thunder on the black sea and thunder in my brain.

God's on the night wind, Satan's on his throne
By the red lake lurid and great grim stone—
Still through the roofs of Hell the brooding thun-
  ders drone.

Trident for a rapier, Satan thrusts and foins
Crouching on his throne with his great goat loins—
Souls are his footstools and hearts are his coins.

Slave of all the ages, though lord of the air;
Solomon o'ercame him, set him roaring there,
Crouching on the coals where the great flames
  flare.

Thunder from the grim gulfs, out of cosmic deep
Where the red eyes glimmer and the black wings
  sweep,
Thunder down to Satan, wake him from his sleep!

Thunder on the shores of Hell, scattering the coal,
Riding down the mountain on the moon-mare's
    foal,
Blasting out the caves of the gnome and the troll.

Satan, brother Satan, rise and break your chain!
Solomon is dust and his spells grow vain —
Rise through the world in the thunder and the rain.

Rush upon the cities, roaring in your might,
Break down the towers in the moon's pale light,
Build a wall of corpses for God's great sight,
Quench the red thunder in my brain this night.

SKULL-FACE

Weird Tales, October 1929,
November 1929 and December 1929
(3-part serial)

1. The Face in the Mist

*"We are no other than a moving row
Of Magic Shadow-shapes that come and go."*
—Omar Khayyam

The horror first took concrete form amid that most unconcrete of all things—a hashish dream. I was off on a timeless, spaceless journey through the strange lands that belong to this state of being, a million miles away from earth and all things earthly; yet I became cognizant that something was reaching across the unknown voids—something that tore ruthlessly at the separating curtains of my illusions and intruded itself into my visions.

I did not exactly return to ordinary waking life, yet

I was conscious of a seeing and a recognizing that was unpleasant and seemed out of keeping with the dream I was at that time enjoying. To one who has never known the delights of hashish, my explanation must seem chaotic and impossible. Still, I was aware of a rending of mists and then the Face intruded itself into my sight. I though at first it was merely a skull; then I saw that it was a hideous yellow instead of white, and was endowed with some horrid form of life. Eyes glimmered deep in the sockets and the jaws moved as if in speech. The body, except for the high, thin shoulders, was vague and indistinct, but the hands, which floated in the mists before and below the skull, were horribly vivid and filled me with crawling fears. They were like the hands of a mummy, long, lean and yellow, with knobby joints and cruel curving talons.

Then, to complete the vague horror which was swiftly taking possession of me, a voice spoke— imagine a man so long dead that his vocal organ had grown rusty and unaccustomed to speech. This was the thought which struck me and made my flesh crawl as I listened.

"A strong brute and one who might be useful somehow. See that he is given all the hashish he requires."

Then the face began to recede, even as I sensed that I was the subject of conversation, and the mists billowed and began to close again. Yet for a single instant a scene stood out with startling clarity. I gasped—or sought to. For over the high, strange shoulder of the apparition another face stood out clearly for an instant, as if the owner peered at me.

Red lips, half-parted, long dark eyelashes, shading vivid eyes, a shimmery cloud of hair. Over the shoulder of Horror, breathtaking beauty for an instant looked at me.

2. The Hashish Slave

*"Up from Earth's center through the Seventh Gate
I rose, and on the Throne of Saturn sate."*
                                        —*Omar Khayyam*

My dream of the skull-face was borne over that usually uncrossable gap that lies between hashish enchantment and humdrum reality. I sat cross-legged on a mat in Yun Shatu's Temple of Dreams and gathered the fading forces of my decaying brain to the task of remembering events and faces.

This last dream was so entirely different from any I had ever had before, that my waning interest was roused to the point of inquiring as to its origin. When I first began to experiment with hashish, I sought to find a physical or psychic basis for the wild flights of illusion pertaining thereto, but of late I had been content to enjoy without seeking cause and effect.

Whence this unaccountable sensation of familiarity in regard to that vision? I took my throbbing head between my hands and laboriously sought a clue. A living dead man and a girl of rare beauty who had looked over his shoulder. Then I remembered.

Back in the fog of days and nights which veils a

hashish addict's memory, my money had given out. It seemed years or possibly centuries, but my stagnant reason told me that it had probably been only a few days. At any rate, I had presented myself at Yun Shatu's sordid dive as usual and had been thrown out by the great Negro Hassim when it was learned I had no more money.

My universe crashing to pieces about me, and my nerves humming like taut piano wires for the vital need that was mine, I crouched in the gutter and gibbered bestially, till Hassim swaggered out and stilled my yammerings with a blow that felled me, half-stunned.

Then as I presently rose, staggeringly and with no thought save of the river which flowed with cool murmur so near me—as I rose, a light hand was laid like the touch of a rose on my arm. I turned with a frightened start, and stood spellbound before the vision of loveliness which met my gaze. Dark eyes limpid with pity surveyed me and the little hand on my ragged sleeve drew me toward the door of the Dream Temple. I shrank back, but a low voice, soft and musical, urged me, and filled with a trust that was strange, I shambled along with my beautiful guide.

At the door Hassim met us, cruel hands lifted and a dark scowl on his ape-like brow, but as I cowered there, expecting a blow, he halted before the girl's upraised hand and her word of command which had taken on an imperious note.

I did not understand what she said, but I saw dimly, as in a fog, that she gave the black man money, and she led me to a couch where she had me recline and arranged the cushions as if I were king of Egypt instead of a ragged, dirty renegade who lived only for hashish. Her slim hand was cool on my brow for a moment, and then she was gone and Yussef Ali came bearing the stuff for which my very soul shrieked—and soon I was wandering again through those strange and exotic countries that only a hashish slave knows.

Now as I sat on the mat and pondered the dream of the skull-face I wondered more. Since the unknown girl had led me back into the dive, I had come and gone as before, when I had plenty of money to pay Yun Shatu. Someone certainly was paying him for me, and while my subconscious mind had told me it was the girl, my rusty brain had failed to grasp the fact entirely, or to wonder why. What need of wondering? So someone paid and the vivid-hued dreams continued, what cared I? But now I wondered. For the girl who had protected me from Hassim and had brought the hashish for me was the same girl I had seen in the skull-face dream.

Through the soddenness of my degradation the lure of her struck like a knife piercing my heart and strangely revived the memories of the days when I was a man like other men—not yet a sullen, cringing slave of dreams. Far and dim they were, shimmery islands in the mist of years—and what a dark sea lay between!

I looked at my ragged sleeve and the dirty, claw-like hand protruding from it; I gazed through the hanging smoke which fogged the sordid room, at the low bunks along the wall whereon lay the blankly staring dreamers—slaves, like me, of hashish or of opium. I gazed at the slippered Chinamen gliding softly to and fro bearing pipes or roasting balls of concentrated purgatory over tiny flickering fires. I gazed at Hassim standing, arms folded, beside the door like a great statue of black basalt.

And I shuddered and hid my face in my hands because with the faint dawning of returning manhood, I knew that this last and most cruel dream was futile— I had crossed an ocean over which I could never return, had cut myself off from the world of normal men or women. Naught remained now but to drown this dream as I had drowned all my others—swiftly and with hope that I should soon attain that Ultimate Ocean which lies beyond all dreams.

So these fleeting moments of lucidity, of longing, that tear aside the veils of all dope slaves—unexplainable, without hope of attainment.

So I went back to my empty dreams, to my phantasmagoria of illusions; but sometimes, like a sword cleaving a mist, through the high lands and the low lands and seas of my visions floated, like half-forgotten music, the sheen of dark eyes and shimmery hair.

You ask how I, Stephen Costigan, American and a man of some attainments and culture, came to lie in a filthy dive of London's Limehouse? The answer is simple—no jaded debauchee, I, seeking new sensations in the mysteries of the Orient. I answer— Argonne! Heavens, what deeps and heights of horror lurk in that one word alone! Shell-shocked—shell-torn. Endless days and nights without end and roaring red hell over No Man's Land where I lay shot and bayoneted to shreds of gory flesh. My body recovered, how I know not; my mind never did.

And the leaping fires and shifting shadows in my tortured brain drove me down and down, along the stairs of degradation, uncaring until at last I found surcease in Yun Shatu's Temple of Dreams, where I slew my red dreams in other dreams—the dreams of hashish whereby a man may descend to the lower pits of the reddest hells or soar into those unnamable heights where the stars are diamond pinpoints beneath his feet.

Not the visions of the sot, the beast, were mine. I attained the unattainable, stood face to face with the unknown and in cosmic calmness knew the unguessable. And was content after a fashion, until the sight of burnished hair and scarlet lips swept away my dream-built universe and left me shuddering among its ruins.

3. The Master of Doom

*"And He that toss'd you down into the Field,
He knows about it all—He knows! He knows!"*
　　　　　　　　　　　—Omar Khayyam

A hand shook me roughly as I emerged languidly from my latest debauch.

"The Master wishes you! Up, swine!"

Hassim it was who shook me and who spoke.

"To Hell with the Master!" I answered, for I hated Hassim—and feared him.

"Up with you or you get no more hashish," was the brutal response, and I rose in trembling haste.

I followed the huge black man and he led the way to the rear of the building, stepping in and out among the wretched dreamers on the floor.

"Muster all hands on deck!" droned a sailor in a bunk. "All hands!"

Hassim flung open the door at the rear and motioned me to enter. I had never before passed through that door and had supposed it led into Yun Shatu's private quarters. But it was furnished only with a cot, a bronze idol of some sort before which incense burned, and a heavy table.

Hassim gave me a sinister glance and seized the table as if to spin it about. It turned as if it stood on a revolving platform and a section of the floor turned with it, revealing a hidden doorway in the floor. Steps led downward in the darkness.

Hassim lighted a candle and with a brusque gesture invited me to descend. I did so, with the sluggish obedience of the dope addict, and he followed, closing the door above us by means of an iron lever fastened to the underside of the floor. In the semi-darkness we went down the rickety steps, some nine or ten I should say, and then came upon a narrow corridor.

Here Hassim again took the lead, holding the candle high in front of him. I could scarcely see the sides of this cave-like passageway but knew that it was not wide. The flickering light showed it to be bare of any sort of furnishings save for a number of strange-looking chests which lined the walls—receptacles containing opium and other dope, I thought.

A continuous scurrying and the occasional glint of small red eyes haunted the shadows, betraying the presence of vast numbers of the great rats which infest the Thames waterfront of that section.

Then more steps loomed out of the dark in front of us as the corridor came to an abrupt end. Hassim led the way up and at the top knocked four times against what seemed the underside of a floor. A hidden door opened and a flood of soft, illusive light streamed through.

Hassim hustled me up roughly and I stood blinking in such a setting as I had never seen in my wildest flights of vision. I stood in a jungle of palm trees through which wriggled a million vivid-hued dragons! Then, as my startled eyes became accustomed to the light, I saw that I had not been suddenly transferred to some other planet, as I had at first thought. The palm trees were there, and the dragons, but the trees were artificial and stood in great pots and the dragons writhed across heavy tapestries which hid the walls.

The room itself was a monstrous affair—inhumanly large, it seemed to me. A thick smoke, yellowish and tropical in suggestion, seemed to hang over all, veiling the ceiling and baffling upward glances. This smoke, I saw, emanated from an altar in front of the wall to my left. I started. Through the saffron-billowing fog two eyes, hideously large and vivid, glittered at me. The vague outlines of some bestial idol took indistinct shape. I flung an uneasy glance about, marking the oriental divans and couches and the bizarre furnishings, and then my eyes halted and rested on a lacquer screen just in front of me.

I could not pierce it and no sound came from

beyond it, yet I felt eyes searing into my consciousness through it, eyes that burned through my very soul. A strange aura of evil flowed from that strange screen with its weird carvings and unholy decorations.

Hassim salaamed profoundly before it and then, without speaking, stepped back and folded his arms, statue-like.

A voice suddenly broke the heavy and oppressive silence.

"You who are a swine, would you like to be a man again?"

I started. The tone was inhuman, cold—more, there was a suggestion of long disuse of the vocal organs— the voice I had heard in my dream!

"Yes," I replied, trance-like, "I would like to be a man again."

Silence ensued for a space; then the voice came again with a sinister whispering undertone at the back of its sound like bats flying through a cavern.

"I shall make you a man again because I am a friend to all broken men. Not for a price shall I do it, nor for gratitude. And I give you a sign to seal my promise and my vow. Thrust your hand through the screen."

At these strange and almost unintelligible words I stood perplexed, and then, as the unseen voice repeated the last command, I stepped forward and thrust my hand through a slit which opened silently in the screen. I felt my wrist seized in an iron grip and something seven times colder than ice touched the inside of my hand. Then my wrist was released, and drawing forth my hand I saw a strange symbol traced in blue close to the base of my thumb—a thing like a scorpion.

The voice spoke again in a sibilant language I did not understand, and Hassim stepped forward deferentially. He reached about the screen and then turned to me, holding a goblet of some amber-colored liquid which he proffered me with an ironical bow. I took it hesitatingly.

"Drink and fear not," said the unseen voice. "It is only an Egyptian wine with life-giving qualities."

So I raised the goblet and emptied it; the taste was not unpleasant, and even as I handed the beaker to Hassim again, I seemed to feel new life and vigor whip along my jaded veins.

"Remain at Yun Shatu's house," said the voice. "You will be given food and a bed until you are strong enough to work for yourself. You will use no hashish nor will you require any. Go!"

As in a daze, I followed Hassim back through the hidden door, down the steps, along the dark corridor and up through the other door that let us into the Temple of Dreams.

As we stepped from the rear chamber into the main room of the dreamers, I turned to the Negro wonderingly.

"Master? Master of what? Of Life?"

Hassim laughed, fiercely and sardonically.

"Master of Doom!"

4. The Spider and the Fly

"There was the Door to which I found no Key;
There was the Veil through which I might not
see."

—Omar Khayyam

I sat on Yun Shatu's cushions and pondered with a clearness of mind new and strange to me. As for that, all my sensations were new and strange. I felt as if I had wakened from a monstrously long sleep, and though my thoughts were sluggish, I felt as though the cobwebs which had dogged them for so long had been partly brushed away.

I drew my hand across my brow, noting how it trembled. I was weak and shaky and felt the stirrings of hunger—not for dope but for food. What had been in the draft I had quenched in the chamber of mystery? And why had the "Master" chosen me, out of all the other wretches of Yun Shatu's, for regeneration?

And who was this Master? Somehow the word sounded vaguely familiar—I sought laboriously to remember. Yes—I had heard it, lying half-waking in the bunks or on the floor—whispered sibilantly by Yun Shatu or by Hassim or by Yussef Ali, the Moor, muttered in their low-voiced conversations and mingled always with words I could not understand. Was not Yun Shatu, then, master of the Temple of Dreams?

I had thought and the other addicts thought that the withered Chinaman held undisputed sway over this drab kingdom and that Hassim and Yussef Ali were his servants. And the four China boys who roasted opium with Yun Shatu and Yar Khan the Afghan and Santiago the Haitian and Ganra Singh, the renegade Sikh—all in the pay of Yun Shatu, we supposed— bound to the opium lord by bonds of gold or fear.

For Yun Shatu was a power in London's Chinatown and I had heard that his tentacles reached across the seas into high places of mighty and mysterious tongs. Was that Yun Shatu behind the lacquer screen? No; I knew the Chinaman's voice and besides I had seen him puttering about in the front of the Temple just as I went through the back door.

Another thought came to me. Often, lying half-torpid, in the late hours of night or in the early grayness of dawn, I had seen men and women steal into the Temple, whose dress and bearing were strangely out of place and incongruous. Tall, erect men, often in evening dress, with their hats drawn low about their brows, and fine ladies, veiled, in silks and furs. Never two of them came together, but always they came separately and, hiding their features, hurried to the rear door, where they entered and presently came forth again, hours later sometimes. Knowing that the lust for dope finds resting-place in high positions sometimes, I had never wondered overmuch, supposing that these were wealthy men and women of society who had fallen victims to the craving, and that somewhere in the back of the building there was a private chamber for such. Yet now I wondered—sometimes these persons had remained only a few moments—was it always opium for which they came, or did they, too, traverse that strange corridor and converse with the One behind the screen?

My mind dallied with the idea of a great specialist to whom came all classes of people to find surcease from the dope habit. Yet it was strange that such a one should select a dope-joint from which to work—strange, too, that the owner of that house should apparently look on him with so much reverence.

I gave it up as my head began to hurt with the unwonted effort of thinking, and shouted for food. Yussef Ali brought it to me on a tray, with a promptness which was surprizing. More, he salaamed as he departed, leaving me to ruminate on the strange shift of my status in the Temple of Dreams.

I ate, wondering what the One of the screen wanted with me. Not for an instant did I suppose that his actions had been prompted by the reasons he pretended; the life of the underworld had taught me that none of its denizens leaned toward philanthropy. And underworld the chamber of mystery had been, in spite of its elaborate and bizarre nature. And where could it be located? How far had I walked along the corridor? I shrugged my shoulders, wondering if it were not all a hashish-induced dream; then my eye fell upon my hand—and the scorpion traced thereon.

"Muster all hands!" droned the sailor in the bunk. "All hands!"

To tell in detail of the next few days would be boresome to any who have not tasted the dire slavery of dope. I waited for the craving to strike me again—waited with sure sardonic hopelessness. All day, all night—another day—then the miracle was forced upon my doubting brain. Contrary to all theories and supposed facts of science and common sense the craving had left me as suddenly and completely as a bad dream! At first I could not credit my senses but believed myself to be still in the grip of a dope nightmare. But it was true. From the time I quaffed the goblet in the room of mystery, I felt not the slightest desire for the stuff which had been life itself to me. This, I felt vaguely, was somehow unholy and certainly opposed to all rules of nature. If the dread being behind the screen had discovered the secret of breaking hashish's terrible power, what other monstrous secrets had he discovered and what unthinkable dominance was his? The suggestion of evil crawled serpent-like through my mind.

I remained at Yun Shatu's house, lounging in a bunk or on cushions spread upon the floor, eating and drinking at will, but now that I was becoming a normal man again, the atmosphere became most revolting to me and the sight of the wretches writhing in their dreams reminded me unpleasantly of what I myself had been, and it repelled, nauseated me.

So one day, when no one was watching me, I rose and went out on the street and walked along the waterfront. The air, burdened though it was with smoke and foul scents, filled my lungs with strange freshness and aroused new vigor in what had once been a powerful frame. I took new interest in the sounds of men living and working, and the sight of a vessel being unloaded at one of the wharfs actually thrilled me. The force of longshoremen was short, and presently I found myself heaving and lifting and carrying, and though the sweat coursed down my brow and my limbs trembled at the effort, I exulted in the thought that at last I was able to labor for myself again, no matter how low or drab the work might be.

As I returned to the door of Yun Shatu's that evening—hideously weary but with the renewed feeling of manhood that comes of honest toil—Hassim met me at the door.

"You been where?" he demanded roughly.

"I've been working on the docks," I answered shortly.

"You don't need to work on docks," he snarled. "The Master got work for you."

He led the way, and again I traversed the dark stairs and the corridor under the earth. This time my faculties were alert and I decided that the passageway could not be over thirty or forty feet in length. Again I stood before the lacquer screen and again I heard the inhuman voice of living death.

"I can give you work," said the voice. "Are you willing to work for me?"

I quickly assented. After all, in spite of the fear which the voice inspired, I was deeply indebted to the owner.

"Good. Take these."

As I started toward the screen a sharp command halted me and Hassim stepped forward and reaching behind took what was offered. This was a bundle of pictures and papers, apparently.

"Study these," said the One behind the screen, "and learn all you can about the man portrayed thereby. Yun Shatu will give you money; buy yourself such clothes as seamen wear and take a room at the front of the Temple. At the end of two days, Hassim will bring you to me again. Go!"

The last impression I had, as the hidden door closed above me, was that the eyes of the idol, blinking through the everlasting smoke, leered mockingly at me.

The front of the Temple of Dreams consisted of rooms for rent, masking the true purpose of the building under the guise of a waterfront boarding house. The police had made several visits to Yun Shatu but had never got any incriminating evidence against him.

So in one of these rooms I took up my abode and set to work studying the material given me.

The pictures were all of one man, a large man, not unlike me in build and general facial outline, except that he wore a heavy beard and was inclined to blondness whereas I am dark. The name, as written on the accompanying papers, was Major Fairlan Morley, special commissioner to Natal and the Transvaal. This office and title were new to me and I wondered at the connection between an African commissioner and an opium house on the Thames waterfront.

The papers consisted of extensive data evidently copied from authentic sources and all dealing with Major Morley, and a number of private documents considerably illuminating on the major's private life.

An exhaustive description was given of the man's

personal appearance and habits, some of which seemed very trivial to me. I wondered what the purpose could be, and how the One behind the screen had come in possession of papers of such intimate nature.

I could find no clue in answer to this question but bent all my energies to the task set out for me. I owed a deep debt of gratitude to the unknown man who required this of me and I was determined to repay him to the best of my ability. Nothing, at this time, suggested a snare to me.

5. The Man on the Couch

"What dam of lances sent thee forth to jest at dawn with Death?"

—*Kipling*

At the expiration of two days, Hassim beckoned me as I stood in the opium room. I advanced with a springy, resilient tread, secure in the confidence that I had culled the Morley papers of all their worth. I was a new man; my mental swiftness and physical readiness surprised me—sometimes it seemed unnatural.

Hassim eyed me through narrowed lids and motioned me to follow, as usual. As we crossed the room, my gaze fell upon a man who lay on a couch close to the wall, smoking opium. There was nothing at all suspicious about his ragged, unkempt clothes, his dirty, bearded face or the blank stare, but my eyes, sharpened to an abnormal point, seemed to sense a certain incongruity in the clean-cut limbs which not even the slouchy garments could efface.

Hassim spoke impatiently and I turned away. We entered the rear room, and as he shut the door and turned to the table, it moved of itself and a figure bulked up through the hidden doorway. The Sikh, Ganra Singh, a lean sinister-eyed giant, emerged and proceeded to the door opening into the opium room, where he halted until we should have descended and closed the secret doorway.

Again I stood amid the billowing yellow smoke and listened to the hidden voice.

"Do you think you know enough about Major Morley to impersonate him successfully?"

Startled, I answered, "No doubt I could, unless I met someone who was intimate with him."

"I will take care of that. Follow me closely. Tomorrow you sail on the first boat for Calais. There you will meet an agent of mine who will accost you the instant you step upon the wharfs, and give you further instructions. You will sail second class and avoid all conversation with strangers or anyone. Take the papers with you. The agent will aid you in making up and your masquerade will start in Calais. That is all. Go!"

I departed, my wonder growing. All this rigmarole evidently had a meaning, but one which I could not fathom. Back in the opium room Hassim bade me be seated on some cushions to await his return. To my question he snarled that he was going forth as he had been ordered, to buy me a ticket on the Channel boat. He departed and I sat down, leaning my back against the wall. As I ruminated, it seemed suddenly that eyes were fixed on me so intensely as to disturb my sub-mind. I glanced up quickly but no one seemed to be looking at me. The smoke drifted through the hot atmosphere as usual; Yussef Ali and the Chinese glided back and forth tending to the wants of the sleepers.

Suddenly the door to the rear room opened and a strange and hideous figure came haltingly out. Not all of those who found entrance to Yun Shatu's back room were aristocrats and society members. This was one of the exceptions, and one whom I remembered as having often entered and emerged therefrom. A tall, gaunt figure, shapeless and ragged wrappings and nondescript garments, face entirely hidden. Better that the face be hidden, I thought, for without doubt the wrapping concealed a grisly sight. The man was a leper, who had somehow managed to escape the atten-tion of the public guardians and who was occasionally seen haunting the lower and more mysterious regions of East End—a mystery even to the lowest denizens of Limehouse.

Suddenly my supersensitive mind was aware of a swift tension in the air. The leper hobbled out the door, closed it behind him. My eyes instinctively sought the couch whereon lay the man who had aroused my suspicions earlier in the day. I could have sworn that cold steely eyes glared menacingly before they flickered shut. I crossed to the couch in one stride and bent over the prostrate man. Something about his face seemed unnatural—a healthy bronze seemed to underlie the pallor of complexion.

"Yun Shatu!" I shouted. "A spy is in the house!"

Things happened then with bewildering speed. The man on the couch with one tigerish movement leaped erect and a revolver gleamed in his hand. One sinewy arm flung me aside as I sought to grapple with him and a sharp decisive voice sounded over the babble which broke forth.

"You there! Halt! Halt!"

The pistol in the stranger's hand was leveled at the leper, who was making for the door in long strides!

All about was confusion; Yun Shatu was shrieking volubly in Chinese and the four China boys and Yussef Ali were rushing in from all sides, knives glittering in their hands.

All this I saw with unnatural clearness even as I marked the stranger's face. As the fleeing leper gave no evidence of halting, I saw the eyes harden to steely points of determination, sighting along the pistol barrel—the features set with the grim purpose of the slayer. The leper was almost to the outer door, but death would strike him down ere he could reach it.

And then, just as the finger of the stranger tightened on the trigger, I hurled myself forward and my right fist crashed against his chin. He went down as though struck by a trip-hammer, the revolver exploding harmlessly in the air.

In that instant, with the blinding flare of light that sometimes comes to one, I knew that the leper was none other than the Man Behind the Screen!

I bent over the fallen man, who though not entirely senseless had been rendered temporarily helpless by that terrific blow. He was struggling dazedly to rise but I shoved him roughly down again and seizing the false beard he wore, tore it away. A lean bronzed face was revealed, the strong lines of which not even the artificial dirt and grease-paint could alter.

Yussef Ali leaned above him now, dagger in hand, eyes slits of murder. The brown sinewy hand went up—I caught the wrist.

"Not so fast, you black devil! What are you about to do?"

"This is John Gordon," he hissed, "the Master's greatest foe! He must die, curse you!"

John Gordon! The name was familiar somehow, and yet I did not seem to connect it with the London police nor account for the man's presence in Yun Shatu's dope-joint. However, on one point I was determined.

"You don't kill him, at any rate. Up with you!" This last to Gordon, who with my aid staggered up, still very dizzy.

"That punch would have dropped a bull," I said in wonderment; "I didn't know I had it in me."

The false leper had vanished. Yun Shatu stood gazing at me as immobile as an idol, hands in his wide sleeves, and Yussef Ali stood back, muttering murderously and thumbing his dagger edge, as I led Gordon out of the opium room and through the innocent-appearing bar which lay between that room and the street.

Out in the street I said to him: "I have no idea as to who you are or what you are doing here, but you see what an unhealthful place it is for you. Hereafter be advised by me and stay away."

His only answer was a searching glance, and then

be turned and walked swiftly though somewhat
unsteadily up the street.

6. The Dream Girl

*"I have reached these lands but newly
From an ultimate dim Thule."*

—*Poe*

Outside my room sounded a light footstep. The door-
knob turned cautiously and slowly; the door opened. I
sprang erect with a gasp. Red lips, half-parted, dark
eyes like limpid seas of wonder, a mass of shimmering
hair—framed in my drab doorway stood the girl of my
dreams!

She entered, and half-turning with a sinuous
motion, closed the door. I sprang forward, my hands
outstretched, then halted as she put a finger to her lips.

"You must not talk loudly," she almost whispered.
"He did not say I could not come; yet—"

Her voice was soft and musical, with just a touch of
foreign accent which I found delightful. As for the girl
herself, every intonation, every movement proclaimed
the Orient. She was a fragrant breath from the East.
From her night-black hair, piled high above her
alabaster forehead, to her little feet, encased in high-
heeled pointed slippers, she portrayed the highest ideal
of Asiatic loveliness—an effect which was heightened
rather than lessened by the English blouse and skirt
which she wore.

"You are beautiful!" I said dazedly. "Who are you?"

"I am Zuleika," she answered with a shy smile. "I—I am glad you like me. I am glad you no longer dream hashish dreams."

Strange that so small a thing should set my heart to leaping wildly!

"I owe it all to you, Zuleika," I said huskily. "Had not I dreamed of you every hour since you first lifted me from the gutter, I had lacked the power of even hoping to be freed from my curse."

She blushed prettily and intertwined her white fingers as if in nervousness.

"You leave England tomorrow?" she said suddenly.

"Yes. Hassim has not returned with my ticket—" I hesitated suddenly, remembering the command of silence.

"Yes, I know, I know!" she whispered swiftly, her eyes widening. "And John Gordon has been here! He saw you!"

"Yes!"

She came close to me with a quick lithe movement.

"You are to impersonate some man! Listen, while you are doing this, you must not ever let Gordon see you! He would know you, no matter what your disguise! He is a terrible man!"

"I don't understand," I said, completely bewildered. "How did the Master break me of my hashish craving? Who is this Gordon and why did he come here? Why does the Master go disguised as a leper—and who is he? Above all, why am I to impersonate a man I never saw or heard of?"

"I cannot—I dare not tell you!" she whispered, her face paling. "I —"

Somewhere in the house sounded the faint tones of a Chinese gong. The girl started like a frightened gazelle.

"I must go! *He* summons me!"

She opened the door, darted through, halted a moment to electrify me with her passionate exclamation: "Oh, be careful, be very careful, sahib!"

Then she was gone.

7. The Man of the Skull

"What the hammer? What the chain?
In what furnace was thy brain?
What the anvil? What dread grasp
Dare its deadly terrors clasp?"

—*Blake*

A while after my beautiful and mysterious visitor had left, I sat in meditation. I believed that I had at last stumbled onto an explanation of a part of the enigma, at any rate. This was the conclusion I had reached: Yun Shatu, the opium lord, was simply the agent or servant of some organization or individual whose work was on a far larger scale than merely supplying dope addicts in the Temple of Dreams. This man or these men needed co-workers among all classes of people; in other words, I was being let in with a group of opium smugglers on a gigantic scale. Gordon no doubt had been investigating the case, and his presence alone showed that it was no ordinary one, for I knew that he held a high position with the English government, though just what, I did not know.

Opium or not, I determined to carry out my obligation to the Master. My moral sense had been blunted by the dark ways I had traveled, and the thought of despicable crime did not enter my head. I was indeed hardened. More, the mere debt of gratitude was increased a thousand-fold by the thought of the girl. To the Master I owed it that I was able to stand up on my feet and look into her clear eyes as a man should. So if he wished my services as a smuggler of dope, he should have them. No doubt I was to impersonate some man so high in governmental esteem that the usual actions of the customs officers would be deemed unnecessary; was I to bring some rare dream-producer into England?

These thoughts were in my mind as I went downstairs, but ever back of them hovered other and more alluring suppositions—what was the reason for the girl, here in this vile dive—a rose in a garbage-heap—and who was she?

As I entered the outer bar, Hassim came in, his brows set in a dark scowl of anger, and, I believed, fear. He carried a newspaper in his hand, folded.

"I told you to wait in opium room," he snarled.

"You were gone so long that I went up to my room. Have you the ticket?"

He merely grunted and pushed on past me into the opium room, and standing at the door I saw him cross the floor and disappear into the rear room. I stood there, my bewilderment increasing. For as Hassim had brushed past me, I had noted an item on the face of the paper, against which his black thumb was tightly pressed as if to mark that special column of news.

And with the unnatural celerity of action and judgment which seemed to be mine those days, I had in that fleeting instant read:

African Special Commissioner Found Murdered!
The body of Major Fairlan Morley was yesterday discovered in a rotting ship's hold at Bordeaux...

No more I saw of the details, but that alone was enough to make me think! The affair seemed to be taking on an ugly aspect. Yet—

Another day passed. To my inquiries, Hassim snarled that the plans had been changed and I was not to go to France. Then, late in the evening, he came to bid me once more to the room of mystery.

I stood before the lacquer screen, the yellow smoke acrid in my nostrils, the woven dragons writhing along the tapestries, the palm trees rearing thick and oppressive.

"A change has come in our plans," said the hidden voice. "You will not sail as was decided before. But I have other work that you may do. Mayhap this will be more to your type of usefulness, for I admit you have somewhat disappointed me in regard to subtlety. You interfered the other day in such manner as will no doubt cause me great inconvenience in the future."

I said nothing, but a feeling of resentment began to stir in me.

"Even after the assurance of one of my most trusted servants," the toneless voice continued, with no mark of any emotion save a slightly rising note, "you insisted on releasing my most deadly enemy. Be more circumspect in the future."

"I saved your life!" I said angrily.

"And for that reason alone I overlook your mistake—this time!"

A slow fury suddenly surged up in me.

"This time! Make the best of it this time, for I assure you there will be no next time. I owe you a greater debt than I can ever hope to pay, but that does not make me your slave. I have saved your life—the debt is as near paid as a man can pay it. Go your way and I go mine!"

A low, hideous laugh answered me, like a reptilian hiss.

"You fool! You will pay with your whole life's toil! You say you are not my slave? I say you are—just as black Hassim there beside you is my slave—just as the girl Zuleika is my slave, who has bewitched you with her beauty."

These words sent a wave of hot blood to my brain and I was conscious of a flood of fury which completely engulfed my reason for a second. Just as all my moods and senses seemed sharpened and exaggerated those days, so now this burst of rage transcended every moment of anger I had ever had before.

"Hell's fiends!" I shrieked. "You devil—who are you and what is your hold on me? I'll see you or die!"

Hassim sprang at me, but I hurled him backward and with one stride reached the screen and flung it aside with an incredible effort of strength. Then I shrank back, hands outflung, shrieking. A tall, gaunt figure stood before me, a figure arrayed grotesquely in a silk brocaded gown which fell to the floor.

From the sleeves of this gown protruded hands which filled me with crawling horror—long, predatory hands, with thin bony fingers and curved talons—withered skin of a parchment brownish-yellow, like the hands of a man long dead.

The hands—but, oh God, the face! A skull to which no vestige of flesh seemed to remain but on which taut brownish-yellow skin grew fast, etching out every detail of that terrible death's-head. The forehead was high and in a way magnificent, but the head was curiously narrow through the temples, and from under penthouse brows great eyes glimmered like pools of yellow fire. The nose was high-bridged and very thin; the mouth was a mere colorless gash between thin, cruel lips. A long, bony neck supported this frightful vision and completed the effect of a reptilian demon from some medieval hell.

I was face to face with the skull-faced man of my dreams!

8. Black Wisdom

"By thought a crawling ruin,
By life a leaping mire,
By a broken heart in the breast of the world
And the end of the world's desire."

—Chesterton

The terrible spectacle drove for the instant all thought
of rebellion from my mind. My very blood froze in my
veins and I stood motionless. I heard Hassim laugh
grimly behind me. The eyes in the cadaverous face
blazed fiendishly at me and I blanched from the concentrated satanic fury in them.

Then the horror laughed sibilantly.

"I do you a great honor, Mr. Costigan; among a
very few, even of my own servants, you may say that
you saw my face and lived. I think you will be more
useful to me living than dead."

I was silent, completely unnerved. It was difficult to
believe that this man lived, for his appearance certainly belied the thought. He seemed horribly like a
mummy. Yet his lips moved when he spoke and his
eyes flamed with hideous life.

"You will do as I say," he said abruptly, and his
voice had taken on a note of command. "You doubtless know, or know of, Sir Haldred Frenton?"

"Yes."

Every man of culture in Europe and America was familiar with the travel books of Sir Haldred Frenton, author and soldier of fortune.

"You will go to Sir Haldred's estate tonight—"

"Yes?"

"And kill him!"

I staggered, literally. This order was incredible—unspeakable! I had sunk low, low enough to smuggle opium, but to deliberately murder a man I had never seen, a man noted for his kindly deeds! That was too monstrous even to contemplate.

"You do not refuse?"

The tone was as loathly and as mocking as the hiss of a serpent.

"Refuse?" I screamed, finding my voice at last. "Refuse? You incarnate devil! Of course I refuse! You—"

Something in the cold assurance of his manner halted me—froze me into apprehensive silence.

"You fool!" he said calmly. "I broke the hashish chains—do you know how? Four minutes from now you will know and curse the day you were born! Have you not thought it strange, the swiftness of brain, the resilience of body—the brain that should be rusty and slow, the body that should be weak and sluggish from years of abuse? That blow that felled John Gordon—have you not wondered at its might? The ease with which you mastered Major Morley's records—have you not wondered at that? You fool, you are bound to me by chains of steel and blood and fire! I have kept you alive and sane—I alone. Each day the life-saving elixir has been given you in your wine. You could not

live and keep your reason without it. And I and only I
know its secret!"

He glanced at a queer timepiece which stood on a
table at his elbow.

"This time I had Yun Shatu leave the elixir out—I
anticipated rebellion. The time is near—ha, it strikes!"

Something else he said, but I did not hear. I did not
see, nor did I feel in the human sense of the word. I
was writhing at his feet, screaming and gibbering in
the flames of such hells as men have never dreamed of.

Aye, I knew now! He had simply given me a dope so
much stronger that it drowned the hashish. My unnatural ability was explainable now—I had simply been
acting under the stimulus of something which combined all the hells in its makeup, which stimulated,
something like heroin, but whose effect was unnoticed
by the victim. What it was, I had no idea, nor did I
believe anyone knew save that hellish being who stood
watching me with grim amusement. But it had held my
brain together, instilling into my system a need for it,
and now my frightful craving tore my soul asunder.

Never, in my moments of worst shell-shock or my
moments of hashish-craving, have I ever experienced
anything like that. I burned with the heat of a thousand hells and froze with an iciness that was colder
than any ice, a hundred times. I swept down to the
deepest pits of torture and up to the highest crags of
torment—a million yelling devils hemmed me in,
shrieking and stabbing. Bone by bone, vein by vein,
cell by cell I felt my body disintegrate and fly in bloody
atoms all over the universe—and each separate cell
was an entire system of quivering, screaming nerves.

And they gathered from far voids and reunited with a greater torment.

Through the fiery bloody mists I heard my own voice screaming, a monotonous yammering. Then with distended eyes I saw a golden goblet, held by a claw-like hand, swim into view—a goblet filled with an amber liquid.

With a bestial screech, I seized it with both hands, being dimly aware that the metal stem gave beneath my fingers, and brought the brim to my lips. I drank in frenzied haste, the liquid slopping down onto my breast.

9. Kathulos of Egypt

*"Night shall be thrice night over you,
And Heaven an iron cope."*

—*Chesterton*

The Skull-faced One stood watching me critically as I sat panting on a couch, completely exhausted. He held in his hand the goblet and surveyed the golden stem, which was crushed out of all shape. This my maniac fingers had done in the instant of drinking.

"Superhuman strength, even for a man in your condition," he said with a sort of creaky pedantry. "I doubt if even Hassim here could equal it. Are you ready for your instructions now?"

I nodded, wordless. Already the hellish strength of

the elixir was flowing through my veins, renewing my burnt-out force. I wondered how long a man could live as I lived being constantly burned out and artificially rebuilt.

"You will be given a disguise and will go alone to the Frenton estate. No one suspects any design against Sir Haldred and your entrance into the estate and the house itself should be a matter of comparative ease. You will not don the disguise—which will be of unique nature—until you are ready to enter the estate. You will then proceed to Sir Haldred's room and kill him, breaking his neck with your bare hands—this is essential—"

The voice droned on, giving the ghastly orders in a frightfully casual and matter-of-fact way. The cold sweat beaded my brow.

"You will then leave the estate, taking care to leave the imprint of your hand somewhere plainly visible, and the automobile, which will be waiting for you at some safe place nearby, will bring you back here, you having first removed the disguise. I have, in case of complications, any amount of men who will swear that you spent the entire night in the Temple of Dreams and never left it. But here must be no detection! Go warily and perform your task surely, for you know the alternative."

I did not return to the opium house but was taken through winding corridors, hung with heavy tapestries, to a small room containing only an oriental couch. Hassim gave me to understand that I was to remain here until after nightfall and then left me. The door was closed but I made no effort to discover if it was locked. The Skull-faced Master held me with stronger shackles than locks and bolts.

Seated upon the couch in the bizarre setting of a chamber which might have been a room in an Indian zenana, I faced fact squarely and fought out my battle. There was still in me some trace of manhood left— more than the fiend had reckoned, and added to this were black despair and desperation. I chose and determined on my only course.

Suddenly the door opened softly. Some intuition told me whom to expect, nor was I disappointed. Zuleika stood, a glorious vision before me—a vision which mocked me, made blacker my despair and yet thrilled me with wild yearning and reasonless joy.

She bore a tray of food which she set beside me, and then she seated herself on the couch, her large eyes fixed upon my face. A flower in a serpent den she was, and the beauty of her took hold of my heart.

"Steephen!" she whispered, and I thrilled as she spoke my name for the first time.

Her luminous eyes suddenly shone with tears and she laid her little hand on my arm. I seized it in both my rough hands.

"They have set you a task which you fear and hate!" she faltered.

"Aye," I almost laughed, "but I'll fool them yet! Zuleika, tell me—what is the meaning of all this?"

She glanced fearfully around her.

"I do not know all"—she hesitated—"your plight is all my fault but I—I hoped—Steephen, I have watched you every time you came to Yun Shatu's for months. You did not see me but I saw you, and I saw in you, not the broken sot your rags proclaimed, but a wounded soul, a soul bruised terribly on the ramparts of life. And from my heart I pitied you. Then when Hassim abused you that day"—again tears started to her eyes—"I could not bear it and I knew how you suffered for want of hashish. So I paid Yun Shatu, and going to the Master I—I—oh, you will hate me for this!" she sobbed.

"No—no—never—"

"I told him that you were a man who might be of use to him and begged him to have Yun Shatu supply you with what you needed. He had already noticed you, for his is the eye of the slaver and all the world is his slave market! So he bade Yun Shatu do as I asked; and now—better if you had remained as you were, my friend."

"No! No!" I exclaimed. "I have known a few days of regeneration, even if it was false! I have stood before you as a man, and that is worth all else!"

And all that I felt for her must have looked forth from my eyes, for she dropped hers and flushed. Ask me not how love comes to a man; but I knew that I loved Zuleika—had loved this mysterious oriental girl since first I saw her—and somehow I felt that she, in a measure, returned my affection. This realization made blacker and more barren the road I had chosen; yet—for pure love must ever strengthen a man—it nerved me to what I must do.

"Zuleika," I said, speaking hurriedly, "time flies and there are things I must learn; tell me—who are you and why do you remain in this den of Hades?"

"I am Zuleika—that is all I know. I am Circassian

by blood and birth; when I was very little I was captured in a Turkish raid and raised in a Stamboul
harem; while I was yet too young to marry, my master
gave me as a present to—to *Him*."

"And who is he—this skull-faced man?"

"He is Kathulos of Egypt—that is all I know. My
master."

"An Egyptian? Then what is he doing in London—
why all this mystery?"

She intertwined her fingers nervously.

"Steephen, please speak lower; always there is
someone listening everywhere. I do not know who the
Master is or why he is here or why he does these
things. I swear by Allah! If I knew I would tell you.
Sometimes distinguished-looking men come here to
the room where the Master receives them—not the
room where you saw him—and he makes me dance
before them and afterward flirt with them a little. And
always I must repeat exactly what they say to me.
That is what I must always do—in Turkey, in the
Barbary States, in Egypt, in France and in England.
The Master taught me French and English and edu-
cated me in many ways himself. He is the greatest sorcerer in all the world and knows all ancient magic and
everything."

"Zuleika," I said, "my race is soon run, but let me
get you out of this—come with me and I swear I'll get
you away from this fiend!"

She shuddered and hid her face.

"No, no, I cannot!"

"Zuleika," I asked gently, "what hold has he over
you, child—dope also?"

"No, no!" she whimpered. "I do not know—I do not know—but I cannot—I never can escape him!"

I sat, baffled for a few moments; then I asked, "Zuleika, where are we right now?"

"This building is a deserted storehouse back of the Temple of Silence."

"I thought so. What is in the chests in the tunnel?"

"I do not know."

Then suddenly she began weeping softly. "You too, a slave, like me—you who are so strong and kind—oh Steephen, I cannot bear it!"

I smiled. "Lean closer, Zuleika, and I will tell you how I am going to fool this Kathulos."

She glanced apprehensively at the door.

"You must speak low. I will lie in your arms and while you pretend to caress me, whisper your words to me."

She glided into my embrace, and there on the dragon-worked couch in that house of horror I first knew the glory of Zuleika's slender form nestling in my arms—of Zuleika's soft cheek pressing my breast. The fragrance of her was in my nostrils, her hair in my eyes, and my senses reeled; then with my lips hidden by her silky hair I whispered, swiftly:

"I am going first to warn Sir Haldred Frenton—then to find John Gordon and tell him of this den. I will lead the police here and you must watch closely and be ready to hide from *Him*—until we can break through and kill or capture him. Then you will be free."

"But you!" she gasped, paling. "You must have the elixir, and only he—"

"I have a way of outdoing him, child," I answered.

She went pitifully white and her woman's intuition sprang at the right conclusion.

"You are going to kill yourself!"

And much as it hurt me to see her emotion, I yet felt a torturing thrill that she should feel so on my account. Her arms tightened about my neck.

"Don't, Steephen!" she begged. "It is better to live, even—"

"No, not at that price. Better to go out clean while I have the manhood left."

She stared at me wildly for an instant; then, pressing her red lips suddenly to mine, she sprang up and fled from the room. Strange, strange are the ways of love. Two stranded ships on the shores of life, we had drifted inevitably together, and though no word of love had passed between us, we knew each other's heart—through grime and rags, and through accouterments of the slave, we knew each other's heart and from the first loved as naturally and as purely as it was intended from the beginning of Time.

The beginning of life now and the end for me, for as soon as I had completed my task, ere I felt again the torments of my curse, love and life and beauty and torture should be blotted out together in the stark finality of a pistol ball scattering my rotting brain. Better a clean death than—

The door opened again and Yussef Ali entered.

"The hour arrives for departure," he said briefly. "Rise and follow."

I had no idea, of course, as to the time. No window opened from the room I occupied—I had seen no outer window whatever. The rooms were lighted by tapers in censers swinging from the ceiling. As I rose the slim young Moor slanted a sinister glance in my direction.

"This lies between you and me," he said sibilantly. "Servants of the same Master we—but this concerns ourselves alone. Keep your distance from Zuleika— the Master has promised her to me in the days of the empire."

My eyes narrowed to slits as I looked into the frowning, handsome face of the Oriental, and such hate surged up in me as I have seldom known. My fingers involuntarily opened and closed, and the Moor, marking the action, stepped back, hand in his girdle.

"Not now—there is work for us both—later perhaps." Then in a sudden cold gust of hatred, "Swine! Ape-man! When the Master is finished with you I shall quench my dagger in your heart!"

I laughed grimly.

"Make it soon, desert-snake, or I'll crush your spine between my hands."

10. The Dark House

"Against all man-made shackles and a man-made hell—
Alone—at last—unaided—I rebel!"

—*Mundy*

I followed Yussef Ali along the winding hallways, down the steps—Kathulos was not in the idol room—

and along the tunnel, then through the rooms of the
Temple of Dreams and out into the street, where the
street lamps gleamed drearily through the fogs and a
slight drizzle. Across the street stood an automobile,
curtains closely drawn.

"That is yours," said Hassim, who had joined us.
"Saunter across natural-like. Don't act suspicious. The
place may be watched. The driver knows what to do."

Then he and Yussef Ali drifted back into the bar
and I took a single step toward the curb.

"Steephen!"

A voice that made my heart leap spoke my name! A
white hand beckoned from the shadows of a doorway.
I stepped quickly there.

"Zuleika!"

"Shhh!"

She clutched my arm, slipped something into my
hand; I made out vaguely a small flask of gold.

"Hide this, quick!" came her urgent whisper.
"Don't come back but go away and hide. This is full of
elixir—I will try to get you some more before that is
all gone. You must find a way of communicating
with me."

"Yes, but how did you get this?" I asked amazedly.

"I stole it from the Master! Now please, I must go
before he misses me."

And she sprang back into the doorway and vanished. I stood undecided. I was sure that she had
risked nothing less than her life in doing this and I was
torn by the fear of what Kathulos might do to her,
were the theft discovered. But to return to the house of
mystery would certainly invite suspicion, and I might

carry out my plan and strike back before the Skull-faced One learned of his slave's duplicity.

So I crossed the street to the waiting automobile. The driver was a Negro whom I had never seen before, a lanky man of medium height. I stared hard at him, wondering how much he had seen. He gave no evidence of having seen anything, and I decided that even if he had noticed me step back into the shadows he could not have seen what passed there nor have been able to recognize the girl.

He merely nodded as I climbed in the back seat, and a moment later we were speeding away down the deserted and fog-haunted streets. A bundle beside me I concluded to be the disguise mentioned by the Egyptian.

To recapture the sensations I experienced as I rode through the rainy, misty night would be impossible. I felt as if I were already dead and the bare and dreary streets about me were the roads of death over which my ghost had been doomed to roam forever. A torturing joy was in my heart, and bleak despair—the despair of a doomed man. Not that death itself was so repellent—a dope victim dies too many deaths to shrink from the last—but it was hard to go out just as love had entered my barren life. And I was still young.

A sardonic smile crossed my lips—they were young, too, the men who died beside me in No Man's Land. I drew back my sleeve and clenched my fists, tensing my muscles. There was no surplus weight on my frame, and much of the firm flesh had wasted away, but the cords of the great biceps still stood out like knots of iron, seeming to indicate massive strength. But I knew my might was false, that in reality I was a broken hulk of a man, animated only by the artificial fire of the elixir, without which a frail girl might topple me over.

The automobile came to a halt among some trees. We were on the outskirts of an exclusive suburb and the hour was past midnight. Through the trees I saw a large house looming darkly against the distant flares of nighttime London.

"This is where I wait," said the Negro. "No one can see the automobile from the road or from the house."

Holding a match so that its light could not be detected outside the car, I examined the "disguise" and was hard put to restrain an insane laugh. The disguise was the complete hide of a gorilla! Gathering the bundle under my arm I trudged toward the wall which surrounded the Frenton estate. A few steps and the trees where the Negro hid with the car merged into one dark mass. I did not believe he could see me, but for safety's sake I made, not for the high iron gate at the front, but for the wall at the side where there was no gate.

No light showed in the house. Sir Haldred was a bachelor and I was sure that the servants were all in bed long ago. I negotiated the wall with ease and stole across the dark lawn to a side door, still carrying the grisly "disguise" under my arm. The door was locked, as I had anticipated, and I did not wish to arouse anyone until I was safely in the house, where the sound of voices would not carry to one who might have followed me. I took hold of the knob with both hands, and, exerting slowly the inhuman strength that was mine, began to twist. The shaft turned in my hands and the lock within shattered suddenly, with a noise that was like the crash of a cannon in the stillness. An instant more and I was inside and had closed the door behind me.

I took a single stride in the darkness in the direction I believed the stair to be, then halted as a beam of light flashed into my face. At the side of the beam I caught the glimmer of a pistol muzzle. Beyond a lean shadowy face floated.

"Stand where you are and put up your hands!"

I lifted my hands, allowing the bundle to slip to the floor. I had heard that voice only once but I recognized it—knew instantly that the man who held that light was John Gordon.

"How many are with you?"

His voice was sharp, commanding.

"I am alone," I answered. "Take me into a room where a light cannot be seen from the outside and I'll tell you some things you want to know."

He was silent; then, bidding me take up the bundle I had dropped, he stepped to one side and motioned me to precede him into the next room. There he directed me to a stairway and at the top landing opened a door and switched on lights.

I found myself in a room whose curtains were closely drawn. During this journey Gordon's alertness had not relaxed, and now he stood, still covering me with his revolver. Clad in conventional garments, he stood revealed a tall, leanly but powerfully built man, taller than I but not so heavy—with steel-gray eyes and clean-cut features. Something about the man attracted me, even as I noted a bruise on his jawbone where my fist had struck in our last meeting.

"I cannot believe," he said crisply, "that this apparent clumsiness and lack of subtlety is real. Doubtless you have your own reasons for wishing me to be in a secluded room at this time, but Sir Haldred is efficiently protected even now. Stand still."

Muzzle pressed against my chest, he ran his hand over my garments for concealed weapons, seeming slightly surprized when he found none.

"Still," he murmured as if to himself, "a man who can burst an iron lock with his bare hands has scant need of weapons."

"You are wasting valuable time," I said impatiently. "I was sent here tonight to kill Sir Haldred Frenton—"

"By whom?" the question was shot at me.

"By the man who sometimes goes disguised as a leper."

He nodded, a gleam in his scintillant eyes.

"My suspicions were correct, then."

"Doubtless. Listen to me closely—do you desire the death or arrest of that man?"

Gordon laughed grimly.

"To one who wears the mark of the scorpion on his hand, my answer would be superfluous."

"Then follow my directions and your wish shall be granted."

His eyes narrowed suspiciously.

"So that was the meaning of this open entry and non-resistance," he said slowly. "Does the dope which dilates your eyeballs so warp your mind that you think to lead me into ambush?"

I pressed my hands against my temples. Time was racing and every moment was precious—how could I convince this man of my honesty?

"Listen; my name is Stephen Costigan of America. I was a frequenter of Yun Shatu's dive and a hashish addict—as you have guessed, but just now a slave of stronger dope. By virtue of this slavery, the man you know as a false leper, whom Yun Shatu and his friends call 'Master,' gained dominance over me and sent me here to murder Sir Haldred—why, God only knows. But I have gained a space of respite by coming into possession of some of this dope which I must have in order to live, and I fear and hate this Master. Listen to me and I swear, by all things holy and unholy, that before the sun rises the false leper shall be in your power!"

I could tell that Gordon was impressed in spite of himself.

"Speak fast!" he rapped.

Still I could sense his disbelief and a wave of futility swept over me.

"If you will not act with me," I said, "let me go and somehow I'll find a way to get to the Master and kill him. My time is short—my hours are numbered and my vengeance is yet to be realized."

"Let me hear your plan, and talk fast," Gordon answered.

"It is simple enough. I will return to the Masters lair and tell him I have accomplished that which he sent me to do. You must follow closely with your men and while I engage the Master in conversation, surround the house. Then, at the signal, break in and kill or seize him."

Gordon frowned. "Where is this house?"

"The warehouse back of Yun Shatu's has been converted into a veritable oriental palace."

"The warehouse!" he exclaimed. "How can that be? I had thought of that first, but I have carefully examined it from without. The windows are closely barred and spiders have built webs across them. The doors are nailed fast on the outside and the seals that mark the warehouse as deserted have never been broken or disturbed in any way."

"They tunneled up from beneath," I answered. "The Temple of Dreams is directly connected with the warehouse."

"I have traversed the alley between the two buildings," said Gordon, "and the doors of the warehouse opening into that alley are, as I have said, nailed shut from without just as the owners left them. There is apparently no rear exit of any kind from the Temple of Dreams."

"A tunnel connects the buildings, with one door in the rear room of Yun Shatu's and the other in the idol room of the warehouse."

"I have been in Yun Shatu's back room and found no such door."

"The table rests upon it. You noted the heavy table in the center of the room? Had you turned it around the secret door would have opened in the floor. Now this is my plan: I will go in through the Temple of Dreams and meet the Master in the idol room. You will have men secretly stationed in front of the warehouse and others upon the other street, in front of the Temple of Dreams. Yun Shatu's building, as you know, faces the waterfront, while the warehouse, fronting the opposite direction, faces a narrow street running parallel with the river. At the signal let the men in this street break open the front of the warehouse and rush in, while simultaneously those in front of Yun Shatu's make an invasion through the Temple of Dreams. Let these make for the rear room, shooting without mercy any who may seek to deter them, and there open the secret door as I have said. There being, to the best of my knowledge, no other exit from the Master's lair, he and his servants will necessarily seek to make their escape through the tunnel. Thus we will have them on both sides."

Gordon ruminated while I studied his face with breathless interest.

"This may be a snare," he muttered, "or an attempt to draw me away from Sir Haldred, but—"

I held my breath.

"I am a gambler by nature," he said slowly. "I am going to follow what you Americans call a hunch— but God help you if you are lying to me!"

I sprang erect.

"Thank God! Now aid me with this suit, for I must be wearing it when I return to the automobile waiting for me."

His eyes narrowed as I shook out the horrible masquerade and prepared to don it.

"This shows, as always, the touch of the master hand. You were doubtless instructed to leave marks of your hands, encased in those hideous gauntlets?"

"Yes, though I have no idea why."

"I think I have—the Master is famed for leaving no

real clues to mark his crimes—a great ape escaped from a neighboring zoo earlier in the evening and it seems too obvious for mere chance, in the light of this disguise. The ape would have gotten the blame of Sir Haldred's death."

The thing was easily gotten into and the illusion of reality it created was so perfect as to draw a shudder from me as I viewed myself in a mirror.

"It is now two o'clock," said Gordon. "Allowing for the time it will take you to get back to Limehouse and the time it will take me to get my men stationed, I promise you that at half-past four the house will be closely surrounded. Give me a start—wait here until I have left this house, so I will arrive at least as soon as you."

"Good!" I impulsively grasped his hand. "There will doubtless be a girl there who is in no way implicated with the Master's evil doings, but only a victim of circumstances such as I have been. Deal gently with her."

"It shall be done. What signal shall I look for?"

"I have no way of signaling for you and I doubt if any sound in the house could be heard on the street. Let your men make their raid on the stroke of five."

I turned to go.

"A man is waiting for you with a car, I take it? Is he likely to suspect anything?"

"I have a way of finding out, and if he does," I replied grimly, "I will return alone to the Temple of Dreams."

11. Four Thirty-Four

"Doubting, dreaming dreams no mortal ever dared to dream before."

—*Poe*

The door closed softly behind me, the great dark house looming up more starkly than ever. Stooping, I crossed the wet lawn at a run, a grotesque and unholy figure, I doubt not, since any man had at a glance sworn me to be not a man but a giant ape. So craftily had the Master devised!

I clambered the wall, dropped to the earth beyond and made my way through the darkness and the drizzle to the group of trees which masked the automobile.

The Negro driver leaned out of the front seat. I was breathing hard and sought in various ways to simulate the actions of a man who has just murdered in cold blood and fled the scene of his crime.

"You heard nothing, no sound, no scream?" I hissed, gripping his arm.

"No noise except a slight crash when you first went in," he answered. "You did a good job—nobody passing along the road could have suspected anything."

"Have you remained in the car all the time?" I asked. And when he replied that he had, I seized his ankle and ran my hand over the soles of his shoe; it was perfectly dry, as was the cuff of his trouser leg. Satisfied, I climbed into the back seat. Had he taken a step on the earth, shoe and garment would have showed it by the telltale dampness.

I ordered him to refrain from starting the engine until I had removed the apeskin, and then we sped through the night and I fell victim to doubts and uncertainties. Why should Gordon put any trust in the word of a stranger and a former ally of the Master's? Would he not put my tale down as the ravings of a dope-crazed addict, or a lie to ensnare or befool him? Still, if he had not believed me, why had he let me go?

I could but trust. At any rate, what Gordon did or did not do would scarcely affect my fortunes ultimately, even though Zuleika had furnished me with that which would merely extend the number of my days. My thought centered on her, and more than my hope of vengeance on Kathulos was the hope that Gordon might be able to save her from the clutches of the fiend. At any rate, I thought grimly, if Gordon failed me, I still had my hands and if I might lay them upon the bony frame of the Skull-faced One—

Abruptly I found myself thinking of Yussef Ali and his strange words, the import of which just occurred to me, *"The Master has promised her to me in the days of the empire!"*

The days of the empire—what could that mean?

The automobile at last drew up in front of the building which hid the Temple of Silence—now dark and still. The ride had seemed interminable and as I dismounted I glanced at the timepiece on the dashboard of the car. My heart leaped—it was four thirty-four, and unless my eyes tricked me I saw a movement in the shadows across the street, out of the flare of the street lamp. At this time of night it could mean only one of two things—some menial of the Master watching for my return or else Gordon had kept his word. The Negro drove away and I opened the door, crossed the deserted bar and entered the opium room. The bunks and the floor were littered with the dreamers, for such places as these know nothing of day or night as normal people know, but all lay deep in sottish slumber.

The lamps glimmered through the smoke and a silence hung mist-like over all.

12. The Stroke of Five

"He saw gigantic tracks of death,
And many a shape of doom."

—Chesterton

Two of the China-boys squatted among the smudge fires, staring at me unwinkingly as I threaded my way among the recumbent bodies and made my way to the rear door. For the first time I traversed the corridor alone and found time to wonder again as to the contents of the strange chests which lined the walls.

Four raps on the underside of the floor, and a moment later I stood in the idol room. I gasped in amazement—the fact that across a table from me sat

Kathulos in all his horror was not the cause of my
exclamation. Except for the table, the chair on which
the Skull-faced One sat and the altar—now bare of
incense—the room was perfectly bare! Drab, unlovely
walls of the unused warehouse met my gaze instead of
the costly tapestries I had become accustomed to. The
palms, the idol, the lacquered screen—all were gone.

"Ah, Mr. Costigan, you wonder, no doubt."

The dead voice of the Master broke in on my
thoughts. His serpent eyes glittered balefully. The long
yellow fingers twined sinuously upon the table.

"You thought me to be a trusting fool, no doubt!"
he rapped suddenly. "Did you think I would not have
you followed? You fool, Yussef Ali was at your heels
every moment!"

An instant I stood speechless, frozen by the crash of
these words against my brain; then as their import
sank home, I launched myself forward with a roar. At
the same instant, before my clutching fingers could
close on the mocking horror on the other side of the
table, men rushed from every side. I whirled, and with
the clarity of hate, from the swirl of savage faces I sin-
gled out Yussef Ali, and crashed my right fist against
his temple with every ounce of my strength. Even as he
dropped, Hassim struck me to my knees and a
Chinaman flung a man-net over my shoulders. I
heaved erect, bursting the stout cords as if they were
strings, and then a blackjack in the hands of Ganra
Singh stretched me stunned and bleeding on the floor.

Lean sinewy hands seized and bound me with cords
that cut cruelly into my flesh. Emerging from the mists
of semi-unconsciousness, I found myself lying on the

altar with the masked Kathulos towering over me like a gaunt ivory tower. About in a semicircle stood Ganra Singh, Yar Khan, Yun Shatu and several others whom I knew as frequenters of the Temple of Dreams. Beyond them—and the sight cut me to the heart—I saw Zuleika crouching in a doorway, her face white and her hands pressed against her cheeks, in an attitude of abject terror.

"I did not fully trust you," said Kathulos sibilantly, "so I sent Yussef Ali to follow you. He reached the group of trees before you and following you into the estate heard your very interesting conversation with John Gordon—for he scaled the house-wall like a cat and clung to the window ledge! Your driver delayed purposely so as to give Yussef Ali plenty of time to get back—I have decided to change my abode anyway. My furnishings are already on their way to another house, and as soon as we have disposed of the traitor—you!—we shall depart also, leaving a little surprise for your friend Gordon when he arrives at five-thirty."

My heart gave a sudden leap of hope. Yussef Ali had misunderstood, and Kathulos lingered here in false security while the London detective force had already silently surrounded the house. Over my shoulder I saw Zuleika vanish from the door.

I eyed Kathulos, absolutely unaware of what he was saying. It was not long until five—if he dallied longer—then I froze as the Egyptian spoke a word and Li Kung, a gaunt, cadaverous Chinaman, stepped from the silent semicircle and drew from his sleeve a long thin dagger. My eyes sought the timepiece that still rested on the table and my heart sank. It was still ten minutes until five. My death did not matter so much, since it simply hastened the inevitable, but in my mind's eye I could see Kathulos and his murderers escaping while the police awaited the stroke of five.

The Skull-face halted in some harangue, and stood in a listening attitude. I believe his uncanny intuition warned him of danger. He spoke a quick staccato command to Li Kung and the Chinaman sprang forward, dagger lifted above my breast.

The air was suddenly supercharged with dynamic tension. The keen dagger-point hovered high above me—loud and clear sounded the skirl of a police whistle and on the heels of the sound there came a terrific crash from the front of the warehouse!

Kathulos leaped into frenzied activity. Hissing orders like a cat spitting, he sprang for the hidden door and the rest followed him. Things happened with the speed of a nightmare. Li Kung had followed the rest, but Kathulos flung a command over his shoulder and the Chinaman turned back and came rushing toward the altar where I lay, dagger high, desperation in his countenance.

A scream broke through the clamor and as I twisted desperately about to avoid the descending dagger, I caught a glimpse of Kathulos dragging Zuleika away. Then with a frenzied wrench I toppled from the altar just as Li Kung's dagger, grazing my breast, sank inches deep into the dark-stained surface and quivered there.

I had fallen on the side next to the wall and what was taking place in the room I could not see, but it seemed as if far away I could hear men screaming faintly and hideously. Then Li Kung wrenched his blade free and sprang, tigerishly, around the end of the altar. Simultaneously a revolver cracked from the doorway—the Chinaman spun clear around, the dagger flying from his hand—he slumped to the floor.

Gordon came running from the doorway where a few moments earlier Zuleika had stood, his pistol still smoking in his hand. At his heels were three rangy, clean-cut men in plain clothes. He cut my bonds and dragged me upright.

"Quick! Where have they gone?"

The room was empty of life save for myself, Gordon and his men, though two dead men lay on the floor.

I found the secret door and after a few seconds' search located the lever which opened it. Revolvers drawn, the men grouped about me and peered nervously into the dark stairway. Not a sound came up from the total darkness.

"This is uncanny!" muttered Gordon. "I suppose the Master and his servants went this way when they left the building—as they are certainly not here now!—and Leary and his men should have stopped them either in the tunnel itself or in the rear room of Yun Shatu's. At any rate, in either event they should have communicated with us by this time."

"Look out, sir!" one of the men exclaimed suddenly, and Gordon, with an ejaculation, struck out with his pistol barrel and crushed the life from a huge snake which had crawled silently up the steps from the blackness beneath.

"Let us see into this matter," said he, straightening.

But before he could step onto the first stair, I halted him; for, flesh crawling, I began dimly to understand something of what had happened—I began to understand the silence in the tunnel, the absence of the detectives, the screams I had heard some minutes previously while I lay on the altar. Examining the lever which opened the door, I found another smaller lever—I began to believe I knew what those mysterious chests in the tunnel contained.

"Gordon," I said hoarsely, "have you an electric torch?"

One of the men produced a large one.

"Direct the light into the tunnel, but as you value your life, do not put a foot upon the steps."

The beam of light struck through the shadows, lighting the tunnel, etching out boldly a scene that will haunt my brain all the rest of my life. On the floor of the tunnel, between the chests which now gaped open, lay two men who were members of London's finest secret service. Limbs twisted and faces horribly distorted they lay, and above and about them writhed, in long glittering scaly shimmerings, scores of hideous reptiles.

The clock struck five.

13. The Blind Beggar Who Rode

"He seemed a beggar such as lags
Looking for crusts and ale."

—Chesterton

The cold gray dawn was stealing over the river as we stood in the deserted bar of the Temple of Dreams. Gordon was questioning the two men who had remained on guard outside the building while their unfortunate companion, went in to explore the tunnel.

"As soon as we heard the whistle, sir, Leary and Murken rushed the bar and broke into the opium room, while we waited here at the bar door according to orders. Right away several ragged dopers came tumbling out and we grabbed them. But no one else came out and we heard nothing from Leary and Murken; so we just waited until you came, sir."

"You saw nothing of a giant Negro, or of the Chinaman Yun Shatu?"

"No, sir. After a while the patrolmen arrived and we threw a cordon around the house, but no one was seen."

Gordon shrugged his shoulders; a few cursory questions had satisfied him that the captives were harmless addicts and he had them released.

"You are sure no one else came out?"

"Yes, sir—no, wait a moment. A wretched old blind

beggar did come out, all rags and dirt and with a
ragged girl leading him. We stopped him but didn't
hold him—a wretch like that couldn't be harmful."

"No?" Gordon jerked out. "Which way did he go?"

"The girl led him down the street to the next block
and then an automobile stopped and they got in and
drove off, sir."

Gordon glared at him.

"The stupidity of the London detective has right-
fully become an international jest," he said acidly.
"No doubt it never occurred to you as being strange
that a Limehouse beggar should ride about in his own
automobile."

Then impatiently waving aside the man, who
sought to speak further, he turned to me and I saw the
lines of weariness beneath his eyes.

"Mr. Costigan, if you will come to my apartment
we may be able to clear up some new things."

14. The Black Empire

*"Oh the new spears dipped in life-blood as the
woman shrieked in vain!*

*Oh the days before the English! When will those
days come again?"*

—*Mundy*

Gordon struck a match and absently allowed it to
flicker and go out in his hand. His Turkish cigarette
hung unlighted between his fingers.

"This is the most logical conclusion to be reached," he was saying. "The weak link in our chain was lack of men. But curse it, one cannot round up an army at two o'clock in the morning, even with the aid of Scotland Yard. I went on to Limehouse, leaving orders for a number of patrolmen to follow me as quickly as they could be got together, and to throw a cordon about the house.

"They arrived too late to prevent the Master's servants slipping out of the side doors and windows, no doubt, as they could easily do with only Finnegan and Hansen on guard at the front of the building. However, they arrived in time to prevent the Master himself from slipping out in that way—no doubt he lingered to effect his disguise and was caught in that manner. He owes his escape to his craft and boldness and to the carelessness of Finnegan and Hansen. The girl who accompanied him—"

"She was Zuleika, without doubt."

I answered listlessly, wondering anew what shackles bound her to the Egyptian sorcerer.

"You owe your life to her," Gordon rapped, lighting another match. "We were standing in the shadows in front of the warehouse, waiting for the hour to strike, and of course ignorant as to what was going on in the house, when a girl appeared at one of the barred windows and begged us for God's sake to do something, that a man was being murdered. So we broke in at once. However, she was not to be seen when we entered."

"She returned to the room, no doubt," I muttered, "and was forced to accompany the Master. God grant he knows nothing of her trickery."

"I do not know," said Gordon, dropping the charred match stem, "whether she guessed at our true identity or whether she just made the appeal in desperation.

"However, the main point is this: evidence points to the fact that, on hearing the whistle, Leary and Murken invaded Yun Shatu's from the front at the same instant my three men and I made our attack on the warehouse front. As it took us some seconds to batter down the door, it is logical to suppose that they found the secret door and entered the tunnel before we affected an entrance into the warehouse.

"The Master, knowing our plans beforehand, and being aware that an invasion would be made through the tunnel and having long ago made preparations for such an exigency—"

An involuntary shudder shook me.

"—the Master worked the lever that opened the chest—the screams you heard as you lay upon the altar were the death shrieks of Leary and Murken. Then, leaving the Chinaman behind to finish you, the Master and the rest descended into the tunnel—incredible as it seems—and threading their way unharmed among the serpents, entered Yun Shatu's house and escaped therefrom as I have said."

"That seems impossible. Why should not the snakes turn on them?"

Gordon finally ignited his cigarette and puffed a few seconds before replying.

"The reptiles might still have been giving their full and hideous attention to the dying men, or else—I have on previous occasions been confronted with indisputable proof of the Master's dominance over beasts and reptiles of even the lowest or most dangerous orders. How he and his slaves passed unhurt among those scaly fiends must remain, at present, one of the many unsolved mysteries pertaining to that strange man."

I stirred restlessly in my chair. This brought up a point for the purpose of clearing up which I had come to Gordon's neat but bizarre apartments.

"You have not yet told me," I said abruptly, "who this man is and what is his mission."

"As to who he is, I can only say that he is known as you name him—the Master. I have never seen him unmasked, nor do I know his real name nor his nationality."

"I can enlighten you to an extent there," I broke in. "I have seen him unmasked and have heard the name his slaves call him."

Gordon's eyes blazed and he leaned forward.

"His name," I continued, "is Kathulos and he claims to be an Egyptian."

"Kathulos!" Gordon repeated. "You say he claims to be an Egyptian—have you any reason for doubting his claim of that nationality?"

"He may be of Egypt," I answered slowly, "but he is different, somehow, from any human I ever saw or hope to see. Great age might account for some of his peculiarities, but there are certain lineal differences that my anthropological studies tell me have been present since birth—features which would be abnormal to any other man but which are perfectly normal in Kathulos. That sounds paradoxical, I admit, but to appreciate fully the horrid inhumanness of the man, you would have to see him yourself."

Gordon sat at attention while I swiftly sketched the appearance of the Egyptian as I remembered him— and that appearance was indelibly etched on my brain forever.

As I finished he nodded.

"As I have said, I never saw Kathulos except when disguised as a beggar, a leper or some such thing— when he was fairly swathed in rags. Still, I too have been impressed with a strange difference about him— something that is not present in other men."

Gordon tapped his knee with his fingers—a habit of his when deeply engrossed by a problem of some sort.

"You have asked as to the mission of this man," he began slowly. "I will tell you all I know."

"My position with the British government is a unique and peculiar one. I hold what might be called a roving commission—an office created solely for the purpose of suiting my special needs. As a secret service official during the war, I convinced the powers of a need of such office and of my ability to fill it.

"Somewhat over seventeen months ago I was sent to South Africa to investigate the unrest which has been growing among the natives of the interior ever since the World War and which has of late assumed alarming proportions. There I first got on the track of this man Kathulos. I found, in roundabout ways, that Africa was a seething cauldron of rebellion from Morocco to Cape Town. The old, old vow had been made again—the Negroes and the Mohammedans, banded together, should drive the white men into the sea.

"This pact has been made before but always, hitherto, broken. Now, however, I sensed a giant intellect and a monstrous genius behind the veil, a genius powerful enough to accomplish this union and hold it together. Working entirely on hints and vague whispered clues, I followed the trail up through Central Africa and into Egypt. There, at last, I came upon definite evidence that such a man existed. The whispers hinted of a living dead man—a *skull-faced* man. I learned that this man was the high priest of the mysterious Scorpion society of northern Africa. He was spoken of variously as Skull-face, the Master, and the Scorpion.

"Following a trail of bribed officials and filched state secrets, I at last trailed him to Alexandria, where I had my first sight of him in a dive in the native quarter—disguised as a leper. I heard him distinctly addressed as 'Mighty Scorpion' by the natives, but he escaped me.

"All trace vanished then; the trail ran out entirely until rumors of strange happenings in London reached me and I came back to England to investigate an apparent leak in the war office.

"As I thought, the Scorpion had preceded me. This man, whose education and craft transcend anything I ever met with, is simply the leader and instigator of a world-wide movement such as the world has never seen before. He plots, in a word, the overthrow of the white races!

"His ultimate aim is a black empire, with himself as emperor of the world! And to that end he has banded together in one monstrous conspiracy the black, the brown and the yellow."

"I understand now what Yussef Ali meant when he said 'the days of the empire,'" I muttered.

"Exactly," Gordon rapped with suppressed excitement. "Kathulos' power is unlimited and unguessed. Like an octopus his tentacles stretch to the high places of civilization and the far corners of the world. And his main weapon is—dope! He has flooded Europe and no doubt America with opium and hashish, and in spite of all effort it has been impossible to discover the break in the barriers through which the hellish stuff is coming. With this he ensnares and enslaves men and women.

"You have told me of the aristocratic men and women you saw coming to Yun Shatu's dive. Without doubt they were dope addicts—for, as I said, the habit lurks in high places—holders of governmental positions, no doubt, coming to trade for the stuff they craved and giving in return state secrets, inside information and promise of protection for the Master's crimes.

"Oh, he does not work haphazardly! Before ever the black flood breaks, he will be prepared; if he has his way, the governments of the white races will be honeycombs of corruption—the strongest men of the white races will be dead. The white men's secrets of war will be his. When it comes, I look for a simultaneous uprising against white supremacy, of all the colored races—races who, in the last war, learned the white men's ways of battle, and who, led by such a man as Kathulos and armed with white men's finest weapons, will be almost invincible.

"A steady stream of rifles and ammunition has been

pouring into East Africa and it was not until I discovered the source that it was stopped. I found that a staid and reliable Scotch firm was smuggling these arms among the natives and I found more: the manager of this firm was an opium slave. That was enough. I saw Kathulos' hand in the matter. The manager was arrested and committed suicide in his cell— that is only one of the many situations with which I am called upon to deal.

"Again, the case of Major Fairlan Morley. He, like myself, held a very flexible commission and had been sent to the Transvaal to work upon the same case. He sent to London a number of secret papers for safe-keeping. They arrived some weeks ago and were put in a bank vault. The letter accompanying them gave explicit instructions that they were to be delivered to no one but the major himself, when he called for them in person, or in event of his death, to myself.

"As soon as I learned that he had sailed from Africa I sent trusted men to Bordeaux, where he intended to make his first landing in Europe. They did not succeed in saving the major's life, but they certified his death, for they found his body in a deserted ship whose hulk was stranded on the beach. Efforts were made to keep the affair a secret but somehow it leaked into the papers with the result—"

"I begin to understand why I was to impersonate the unfortunate major," I interrupted.

"Exactly. A false beard furnished you, and your black hair dyed blond, you would have presented yourself at the bank, received the papers from the banker, who knew Major Morley just intimately enough to be deceived by your appearance, and the papers would have then fallen into the hands of the Master.

"I can only guess at the contents of those papers, for events have been taking place too swiftly for me to call for and obtain them. But they must deal with subjects closely connected with the activities of Kathulos. How he learned of them and of the provisions of the letter accompanying them, I have no idea, but as I said, London is honeycombed with his spies.

"In my search for clues, I often frequented Limehouse disguised as you first saw me. I went often to the Temple of Dreams and even once managed to enter the back room, for I suspected some sort of rendezvous in the rear of the building. The absence of any exit baffled me and I had no time to search for secret doors before I was ejected by the giant black man Hassim, who had no suspicion of my true identity. I noticed that very often the leper entered or left Yun Shatu's, and finally it was borne on me that past a shadow of doubt this supposed leper was the Scorpion himself.

"That night you discovered me on the couch in the opium room, I had come there with no especial plan in mind. Seeing Kathulos leaving, I determined to rise and follow him, but you spoiled that."

He fingered his chin and laughed grimly.

"I was an amateur boxing champion in Oxford," said he, "but Tom Cribb himself could not have withstood that blow—or have dealt it."

"I regret it as I regret few things."

"No need to apologize. You saved my life immedi-

ately afterward—I was stunned, but not too much to
know that that brown devil Yussef Ali was burning to
cut out my heart."

"How did you come to be at Sir Haldred Frenton's
estate? And how is it that you did not raid Yun Shatu's
dive?"

"I did not have the place raided because I knew
somehow Kathulos would be warned and our efforts
would come to naught. I was at Sir Haldred's that
night because I have contrived to spend at least part of
each night with him since he returned from the Congo.
I anticipated an attempt upon his life when I learned
from his own lips that he was preparing, from the
studies he made on this trip, a treatise on the secret
native societies of West Africa. He hinted that the dis-
closures he intended to make therein might prove sen-
sational, to say the least. Since it is to Kathulos'
advantage to destroy such men as might be able to
arouse the Western world to its danger, I knew that Sir
Haldred was a marked man. Indeed, two distinct
attempts were made upon his life on his journey to the
coast from the African interior. So I put two trusted
men on guard and they are at their post even now.

"Roaming about the darkened house, I heard the
noise of your entry, and, warning my men, I stole
down to intercept you. At the time of our conversation, Sir Haldred was sitting in his unlighted study, a
Scotland Yard man with drawn pistol on each side of
him. Their vigilance no doubt accounts for Yussef Ali's
failure to attempt what you were sent to do.

"Something in your manner convinced me in spite
of yourself," he meditated. "I will admit I had some

bad moments of doubt as I waited in the darkness that precedes dawn, outside the warehouse."

Gordon rose suddenly and going to a strong box which stood in a corner of the room, drew thence a thick envelope.

"Although Kathulos has checkmated me at almost every move," he said, "I have not been entirely idle. Noting the frequenters of Yun Shatu's, I have compiled a partial list of the Egyptian's right-hand men, and their records. What you have told me has enabled me to complete that list. As we know, his henchmen are scattered all over the world, and there are possibly hundreds of them here in London. However, this is a list of those I believe to be in his closest council, now with him in England. He told you himself that few even of his followers ever saw him unmasked."

We bent together over the list, which contained the following names: "Yun Shatu, Hongkong Chinese, suspected opium smuggler—keeper of Temple of Dreams—resident of Limehouse seven years. Hassim, ex-Senegalese Chief—wanted in French Congo for murder. Santiago, Negro—fled from Haiti under suspicion of voodoo worship atrocities. Yar Khan, Afridi, record unknown. Yussef Ali, Moor, slave-dealer in Morocco—suspected of being a German spy in the World War—an instigator of the Fellaheen Rebellion on the upper Nile. Ganra Singh, Lahore, India, Sikh— smuggler of arms into Afghanistan—took an active part in the Lahore and Delhi riots—suspected of murder on two occasions—a dangerous man. Stephen Costigan, American—resident in England since the war—hashish addict—man of remarkable strength. Li Kung, northern China, opium smuggler."

Lines were drawn significantly through three names—mine, Li Kung's and Yussef Ali's. Nothing was written next to mine, but following Li Kung's name was scrawled briefly in Gordon's rambling characters: "Shot by John Gordon during the raid on Yun Shatu's." And following the name of Yussef Ali: "Killed by Stephen Costigan during the Yun Shatu raid."

I laughed mirthlessly. Black empire or not, Yussef Ali would never hold Zuleika in his arms, for he had never risen from where I felled him.

"I know not," said Gordon somberly as he folded the list and replaced it in the envelope, "what power Kathulos has that draws together black men and yellow men to serve him—that unites world-old foes. Hindu, Moslem and pagan are among his followers. And back in the mists of the East where mysterious and gigantic forces are at work, this uniting is culminating on a monstrous scale."

He glanced at his watch.

"It is nearly ten. Make yourself at home here, Mr. Costigan, while I visit Scotland Yard and see if any clue has been found as to Kathulos' new quarters. I believe that the webs are closing on him, and with your aid I promise you we will have the gang located within a week at most."

15. The Mark of the Tulwar

*"The fed wolf curls by his drowsy mate
In a tight-trod earth; but the lean wolves wait."*
—*Mundy*

I sat alone in John Gordon's apartments and laughed mirthlessly. In spite of the elixir's stimulus, the strain of the previous night, with its loss of sleep and its heartrending actions, was telling on me. My mind was a chaotic whirl wherein the faces of Gordon, Kathulos and Zuleika shifted with numbing swiftness. All the mass of information Gordon had given to me seemed jumbled and incoherent.

Through this state of being, one fact stood out boldly. I must find the latest hiding-place of the Egyptian and get Zuleika out of his hands—if indeed she still lived.

A week, Gordon had said—I laughed again—a week and I would be beyond aiding anyone. I had found the proper amount of elixir to use—knew the minimum amount my system required—and knew that I could make the flask last me four days at most. Four days! Four days in which to comb the rat-holes of Limehouse and Chinatown—four days in which to ferret out, somewhere in the mazes of East End, the lair of Kathulos.

I burned with impatience to begin, but nature

rebelled, and staggering to a couch, I fell upon it and was asleep instantly.

Then someone was shaking me.

"Wake up, Mr. Costigan!"

I sat up, blinking. Gordon stood over me, his face haggard.

"There's devil's work done, Costigan! The Scorpion has struck again!"

I sprang up, still half-asleep and only partly realizing what he was saying. He helped me into my coat, thrust my hat at me, and then his firm grip on my arm was propelling me out of his door and down the stairs. The street lights were blazing; I had slept an incredible time.

"A logical victim!" I was aware that my companion was saying. "He should have notified me the instant of his arrival!"

"I don't understand—" I began dazedly.

We were at the curb now and Gordon hailed a taxi, giving the address of a small and unassuming hotel in a staid and prim section of the city.

"The Baron Rokoff," he rapped as we whirled along at reckless speed, "a Russian free-lance, connected with the war office. He returned from Mongolia yesterday and apparently went into hiding. Undoubtedly he had learned something vital in regard to the slow waking of the East. He had not yet communicated with us, and I had no idea that he was in England until just now."

"And you learned—"

"The baron was found in his room, his dead body mutilated in a frightful manner!"

The respectable and conventional hotel which the doomed baron had chosen for his hiding-place was in a state of mild uproar, suppressed by the police. The management had attempted to keep the matter quiet, but somehow the guests had learned of the atrocity and many were leaving in haste—or preparing to, as the police were holding all for investigation.

The baron's room, which was on the top floor, was in a state to defy description. Not even in the Great War have I seen a more complete shambles. Nothing had been touched; all remained just as the chambermaid had found it a half-hour since. Tables and chairs lay shattered on the floor, and the furniture, floor and walls were spattered with blood. The baron, a tall, muscular man in life, lay in the middle of the room, a fearful spectacle. His skull had been cleft to the brows, a deep gash under his left armpit had shorn through his ribs, and his left arm hung by a shred of flesh. The cold bearded face was set in a look of indescribable horror.

"Some heavy, curved weapon must have been used," said Gordon, "something like a saber, wielded with terrific force. See where a chance blow sank inches deep into the windowsill. And again, the thick back of this heavy chair has been split like a shingle. A saber, surely."

"A tulwar," I muttered, somberly. "Do you not recognize the handiwork of the Central Asian butcher? Yar Khan has been here."

"The Afghan! He came across the roofs, of course, and descended to the window-ledge by means of a knotted rope made fast to something on the edge of the roof. About one-thirty the maid, passing through the corridor, heard a terrific commotion in the baron's room—smashing of chairs and a sudden short shriek which died abruptly into a ghastly gurgle and then ceased—to the sound of heavy blows, curiously muffled, such as a sword might make when driven deep into human flesh. Then all noises stopped suddenly.

"She called the manager and they tried the door and, finding it locked, and receiving no answer to their shouts, opened it with the desk key. Only the corpse was there, but the window was open. This is strangely unlike Kathulos' usual procedure. It lacks subtlety. Often his victims have appeared to have died from natural causes. I scarcely understand."

"I see little difference in the outcome," I answered. "There is nothing that can be done to apprehend the murderer as it is."

"True," Gordon scowled. "We know who did it but there is no proof—not even a fingerprint. Even if we knew where the Afghan is hiding and arrested him, we could prove nothing—there would be a score of men to swear alibis for him. The baron returned only yesterday. Kathulos probably did not know of his arrival until tonight. He knew that on the morrow Rokoff would make known his presence to me and impart what he learned in northern Asia. The Egyptian knew he must strike quickly, and lacking time to prepare a safer and more elaborate form of murder, he sent the Afridi with his tulwar. There is nothing we can do, at least not until we discover the Scorpion's hiding-place; what the baron had learned in Mongolia, we shall never know, but that it dealt with the plans and aspirations of Kathulos, we may be sure."

We went down the stairs again and out on the street, accompanied by one of the Scotland Yard men, Hansen. Gordon suggested that we walk back to his apartment and I greeted the opportunity to let the cool night air blow some of the cobwebs out of my mazed brain.

As we walked along the deserted streets, Gordon suddenly cursed savagely.

"This is a veritable labyrinth we are following, leading nowhere! Here, in the very heart of civilization's metropolis, the direct enemy of that civilization commits crimes of the most outrageous nature and goes free! We are children, wandering in the night, struggling with an unseen evil—dealing with an incarnate devil, of whose true identity we know nothing and whose true ambitions we can only guess.

"Never have we managed to arrest one of the Egyptian's direct henchmen, and the few dupes and tools of his we have apprehended have died mysteriously before they could tell us anything. Again I repeat: what strange power has Kathulos that dominates these men of different creeds and races? The men in London with him are, of course, mostly renegades, slaves of dope, but his tentacles stretch all over the East. Some dominance is his: the power that sent the Chinaman, Li Kung, back to kill you, in the face of certain death; that sent Yar Khan the Moslem over the roofs of London to do murder; that holds Zuleika the Circassian in unseen bonds of slavery.

"Of course we know," he continued after a brooding silence, "that the East has secret societies which are behind and above all considerations of creeds. There are cults in Africa and the Orient whose origin dates back to Ophir and the fall of Atlantis. This man must be a power in some or possibly all of these societies. Why, outside the Jews, I know of no oriental race which is so cordially despised by the other Eastern races, as the Egyptians! Yet here we have a man, an Egyptian by his own word, controlling the lives and destinies of orthodox Moslems, Hindus, Shintos and devil-worshippers. It's unnatural.

"Have you ever"—he turned to me abruptly—"heard the ocean mentioned in connection with Kathulos?"

"Never."

"There is a widespread superstition in northern Africa, based on a very ancient legend, that the great leader of the colored races would come out of the sea! And I once heard a Berber speak of the Scorpion as 'The Son of the Ocean.'"

"That is a term of respect among that tribe, is it not?"

"Yes; still I wonder sometimes."

16. The Mummy Who Laughed

"Laughing as littered skulls that lie
After lost battles turn to the sky
An everlasting laugh."

—*Chesterton*

"A shop open this late," Gordon remarked suddenly.

A fog had descended on London and along the

quiet street we were traversing the lights glimmered with the peculiar reddish haze characteristic of such atmospheric conditions. Our footfalls echoed drearily. Even in the heart of a great city there are always sections which seem overlooked and forgotten. Such a street was this. Not even a policeman was in sight.

The shop which had attracted Gordon's attention was just in front of us, on the same side of the street. There was no sign over the door, merely some sort of emblem, something like a dragon. Light flowed from the open doorway and the small show windows on each side. As it was neither a café nor the entrance to a hotel we found ourselves idly speculating over its reason for being open. Ordinarily, I suppose, neither of us would have given the matter a thought, but our nerves were so keyed up that we found ourselves instinctively suspicious of anything out of the ordinary. Then something occurred which was distinctly out of the ordinary.

A very tall, very thin man, considerably stooped, suddenly loomed up out of the fog in front of us, and beyond the shop. I had only a glance of him—an impression of incredible gauntness, of worn, wrinkled garments, a high silk hat drawn close over the brows, a face entirely hidden by a muffler; then he turned aside and entered the shop. A cold wind whispered down the street, twisting the fog into wispy ghosts, but the coldness that came upon me transcended the wind's.

"Gordon!" I exclaimed in a fierce, low voice; "my senses are no longer reliable or else Kathulos himself has just gone into that house!"

Gordon's eyes blazed. We were now close to the shop, and lengthening his strides into a run he hurled himself into the door, the detective and I close upon his heels.

A weird assortment of merchandise met our eyes. Antique weapons covered the walls, and the floor was piled high with curious things. Maori idols shouldered Chinese josses, and suits of medieval armor bulked darkly against stacks of rare oriental rugs and Latin-make shawls. The place was an antique shop. Of the figure who had aroused our interest we saw nothing.

An old man clad bizarrely in red fez, brocaded jacket and Turkish slippers came from the back of the shop; he was a Levantine of some sort.

"You wish something, sirs?"

"You keep open rather late," Gordon said abruptly, his eyes traveling swiftly over the shop for some secret hiding-place that might conceal the object of our search.

"Yes, sir. My customers number many eccentric professors and students who keep very irregular hours. Often the night boats unload special pieces for me and very often I have customers later than this. I remain open all night, sir."

"We are merely looking around," Gordon returned, and in an aside to Hansen: "Go to the back and stop anyone who tries to leave that way."

Hansen nodded and strolled casually to the rear of the shop. The back door was clearly visible to our view, through a vista of antique furniture and tarnished hangings strung up for exhibition. We had followed the Scorpion—if he it was—so closely that I did not believe he would have had time to traverse the full length of the shop and make his exit without our having seen him as we came in. For our eyes had been on the rear door ever since we had entered.

Gordon and I browsed around casually among the curios, handling and discussing some of them but I have no idea as to their nature. The Levantine had seated himself cross-legged on a Moorish mat close to the center of the shop and apparently took only a polite interest in our explorations.

After a time Gordon whispered to me: "There is no advantage in keeping up this pretense. We have looked everywhere the Scorpion might be hiding, in the ordinary manner. I will make known my identity and authority and we will search the entire building openly."

Even as he spoke a truck drew up outside the door and two burly Negroes entered. The Levantine seemed to have expected them, for he merely waved them toward the back of the shop and they responded with a grunt of understanding.

Gordon and I watched them closely as they made their way to a large mummy-case which stood upright against the wall not far from the back. They lowered this to a level position and then started for the door, carrying it carefully between them.

"Halt!" Gordon stepped forward, raising his hand authoritatively.

"I represent Scotland Yard," he said swiftly, "and have sanction for anything I choose to do. Set that mummy down; nothing leaves this shop until we have thoroughly searched it."

The Negroes obeyed without a word and my friend turned to the Levantine, who, apparently not perturbed or even interested, sat smoking a Turkish water-pipe.

"Who was that tall man who entered just before we did, and where did he go?"

"No one entered before you, sir. Or, if anyone did, I was at the back of the shop and did not see him. You are certainly at liberty to search my shop, sir."

And search it we did, with the combined craft of a secret service expert and a denizen of the underworld—while Hansen stood stolidly at his post, the two Negroes standing over the carved mummy-case watched us impassively and the Levantine sitting like a sphinx on his mat, puffing a fog of smoke into the air. The whole thing had a distinct effect of unreality.

At last, baffled, we returned to the mummy-case, which was certainly long enough to conceal even a man of Kathulos' height. The thing did not appear to be sealed as is the usual custom, and Gordon opened it without difficulty. A formless shape, swathed in moldering wrappings, met our eyes. Gordon parted some of the wrappings and revealed an inch or so of withered, brownish, leathery arm. He shuddered involuntarily as he touched it, as a man will do at the touch of a reptile or some inhumanly cold thing. Taking a small metal idol from a stand nearby, he rapped on the shrunken breast and the arm. Each gave out a solid thumping, like some sort of wood.

Gordon shrugged his shoulders. "Dead for two thousand years anyway and I don't suppose I should risk destroying a valuable mummy simply to prove what we know to be true."

He closed the case again.

"The mummy may have crumbled some, even from this much exposure, but perhaps it did not."

This last was addressed to the Levantine who replied merely by a courteous gesture of his hand, and the Negroes once more lifted the case and carried it to the truck, where they loaded it on, and a moment later mummy, truck and Negroes had vanished in the fog.

Gordon still nosed about the shop, but I stood stock-still in the center of the floor. To my chaotic and dope-ridden brain I attribute it, but the sensation had been mine, that through the wrappings of the mummy's face, great eyes had burned into mine, eyes like pools of yellow fire, that seared my soul and froze me where I stood. And as the case had been carried through the door, I knew that the lifeless thing in it, dead, God only knows how many centuries, was laughing, hideously and silently.

17. The Dead Man from the Sea

"The blind gods roar and rave and dream
  Of all cities under the sea."
                                    —*Chesterton*

Gordon puffed savagely at his Turkish cigarette, staring abstractedly and unseeingly at Hansen, who sat opposite him.

"I suppose we must chalk up another failure against ourselves. That Levantine, Kamonos, is evidently a creature of the Egyptian's and the walls and floors of his shop are probably honeycombed with secret panels and doors which would baffle a magician."

Hansen made some answer but I said nothing. Since our return to Gordon's apartment, I had been conscious of a feeling of intense languor and sluggishness which not even my condition could account for. I knew that my system was full of the elixir—but my mind seemed strangely slow and hard of comprehension in direct contrast with the average state of my mentality when stimulated by the hellish dope.

This condition was slowly leaving me, like mist floating from the surface of a lake, and I felt as if I were waking gradually from a long and unnaturally sound sleep.

Gordon was saying: "I would give a good deal to know if Kamonos is really one of Kathulos' slaves or if the Scorpion managed to make his escape through some natural exit as we entered."

"Kamonos is his servant, true enough," I found myself saying slowly, as if searching for the proper words. "As we left, I saw his gaze light upon the scorpion which is traced on my hand. His eyes narrowed, and as we were leaving he contrived to brush close against me—and to whisper in a quick low voice: 'Soho, 48.'"

Gordon came erect like a loosened steel bow.

"Indeed!" he rapped. "Why did you not tell me at the time?"

"I don't know."

My friend eyed me sharply.

"I noticed you seemed like a man intoxicated all the way from the shop," said he. "I attributed it to some aftermath of hashish. But no. Kathulos is undoubtedly a masterful disciple of Mesmer—his power over venomous reptiles shows that, and I am beginning to believe it is the real source of his power over humans.

"Somehow, the Master caught you off your guard in that shop and partly asserted his dominance over your mind. From what hidden nook he sent his thought waves to shatter your brain, I do not know, but Kathulos was somewhere in that shop, I am sure."

"He was. He was in the mummy-case."

"The mummy-case!" Gordon exclaimed rather impatiently. "That is impossible! The mummy quite filled it and not even such a thin being as the Master could have found room there."

I shrugged my shoulders, unable to argue the point but somehow sure of the truth of my statement.

"Kamonos," Gordon continued, "doubtless is not a member of the inner circle and does not know of your change of allegiance. Seeing the mark of the scorpion, he undoubtedly supposed you to be a spy of the Master's. The whole thing may be a plot to ensnare us, but I feel that the man was sincere—Soho 48 can be nothing less than the Scorpion's new rendezvous."

I too felt that Gordon was right, though a suspicion lurked in my mind.

"I secured the papers of Major Morley yesterday," be continued, "and while you slept, I went over them. Mostly they but corroborated what I already knew—touched on the unrest of the natives and repeated the theory that one vast genius was behind all. But there was one matter which interested me greatly and which I think will interest you also."

From his strong box he took a manuscript written in the close, neat characters of the unfortunate major, and in a monotonous droning voice which betrayed little of his intense excitement he read the following nightmarish narrative:

"This matter I consider worth jotting down—as to whether it has any bearing on the case at hand, further developments will show. At Alexandria, where I spent some weeks seeking further clues as to the identity of the man known as the Scorpion, I made the acquaintance, through my friend Ahmed Shah, of the noted Egyptologist Professor Ezra Schuyler of New York. He verified the statement made by various laymen, concerning the legend of the 'ocean-man.' This myth, handed down from generation to generation, stretches back into the very mists of antiquity and is, briefly, that someday a man shall come up out of the sea and shall lead the people of Egypt to victory over all others. This legend has spread over the continent so that now all black races consider that it deals with the coming of a universal emperor. Professor Schuyler gave it as his opinion that the myth was somehow connected with the lost Atlantis, which, he maintains, was located between the African and South American continents and to whose inhabitants the ancestors of the Egyptians were tributary. The reasons for his connection are too lengthy and vague to note here, but following the line of his theory he told me a strange and fantastic tale. He said that a close friend of his, Von

Lorfmon of Germany, a sort of free-lance scientist, now dead, was sailing off the coast of Senegal some years ago, for the purpose of investigating and classifying the rare specimens of sea life found there. He was using for his purpose a small trading-vessel, manned by a crew of Moors, Greeks and Negroes.

"Some days out of sight of land, something floating was sighted, and this object, being grappled and brought aboard, proved to be a mummy-case of a most curious kind. Professor Schuyler explained to me the features whereby it differed from the ordinary Egyptian style, but from his rather technical account I merely got the impression that it was a strangely shaped affair carved with characters neither cuneiform nor hieroglyphic. The case was heavily lacquered, being watertight and airtight, and Von Lorfmon had considerable difficulty in opening it. However, he managed to do so without damaging the case, and a most unusual mummy was revealed. Schuyler said that he never saw either the mummy or the case, but that from descriptions given him by the Greek skipper who was present at the opening of the case, the mummy differed as much from the ordinary man as the case differed from the conventional type.

"Examination proved that the subject had not undergone the usual procedure of mummification. All parts were intact just as in life, but the whole form was shrunk and hardened to a wood-like consistency. Cloth wrappings swathed the thing and they crumbled to dust and vanished the instant air was let in upon them.

"Von Lorfmon was impressed by the effect upon

the crew. The Greeks showed no interest beyond that which would ordinarily be shown by any man, but the Moors, and even more the Negroes, seemed to be rendered temporarily insane! As the case was hoisted on board, they all fell prostrate on the deck and raised a sort of worshipful chant, and it was necessary to use force in order to exclude them from the cabin wherein the mummy was exposed. A number of fights broke out between them and the Greek element of the crew, and the skipper and Von Lorfmon thought best to put back to the nearest port in all haste. The skipper attributed it to the natural aversion of seamen toward having a corpse on board, but Von Lorfmon seemed to sense a deeper meaning.

"They made port in Lagos, and that very night Von Lorfmon was murdered in his stateroom and the mummy and its case vanished. All the Moor and Negro sailors deserted ship the same night. Schuyler said—and here the matter took on a most sinister and mysterious aspect—that immediately afterward this widespread unrest among the natives began to smolder and take tangible form; he connected it in some manner with the old legend.

"An aura of mystery, also, hung over Von Lorfmon's death. He had taken the mummy into his stateroom, and anticipating an attack from the fanatical crew, had carefully barred and bolted door and portholes. The skipper, a reliable man, swore that it was virtually impossible to affect an entrance from without. And what signs were present pointed to the fact that the locks had been worked from within. The scientist was killed by a dagger which formed part of his collection and which was left in his breast.

"As I have said, immediately afterward the African cauldron began to seethe. Schuyler said that in his opinion the natives considered the ancient prophecy fulfilled. The mummy was the man from the sea.

"Schuyler gave as his opinion that the thing was the work of Atlanteans and that the man in the mummy-case was a native of lost Atlantis. How the case came to float up through the fathoms of water which cover the forgotten land, he does not venture to offer a theory. He is sure that somewhere in the ghost-ridden mazes of the African jungles the mummy has been enthroned as a god, and, inspired by the dead thing, the black warriors are gathering for a wholesale massacre. He believes, also, that some crafty Moslem is the direct moving power of the threatened rebellion."

Gordon ceased and looked up at me.

"Mummies seem to weave a weird dance through the warp of the tale," he said. "The German scientist took several pictures of the mummy with his camera, and it was after seeing these—which strangely enough were not stolen along with the thing—that Major Morley began to think himself on the brink of some monstrous discovery. His diary reflects his state of mind and becomes incoherent—his condition seems to have bordered on insanity. What did he learn to unbalance him so? Do you suppose that the mesmeric spells of Kathulos were used against him?"

"These pictures—" I began.

"They fell into Schuyler's hands and he gave one to Morley. I found it among the manuscripts."

He handed the thing to me, watching me narrowly.

I stared, then rose unsteadily and poured myself a tumbler of wine.

"'Not a dead idol in a voodoo hut," I said shakily, "but a monster animated by fearsome life, roaming the world for victims. Morley had seen the Master— that is why his brain crumbled. Gordon, as I hope to live again, *that face is the face of Kathulos*!"

Gordon stared wordlessly at me.

"The Master hand, Gordon," I laughed. A certain grim enjoyment penetrated the mists of my horror, at the sight of the steel-nerved Englishman struck speechless, doubtless for the first time in his life.

He moistened his lips and said in a scarcely recognizable voice, "Then, in God's name, Costigan, nothing is stable or certain, and mankind hovers at the brink of untold abysses of nameless horror. If that dead monster found by Von Lorfmon be in truth the Scorpion, brought to life in some hideous fashion, what can mortal effort do against him?"

"The mummy at Kamonos'—" I began.

"Aye, the man whose flesh, hardened by a thousand years of non-existence—that must have been Kathulos himself! He would have just had time to strip, wrap himself in the linens and step into the case before we entered. You remember that the case, leaning upright against the wall, stood partly concealed by a large Burmese idol, which obstructed our view and doubtless gave him time to accomplish his purpose. My God, Costigan, with what horror of the prehistoric world are we dealing?"

"I have heard of Hindu fakirs who could induce a condition closely resembling death," I began. "Is it not possible that Kathulos, a shrewd and crafty Oriental, could have placed himself in this state and his followers have placed the case in the ocean where it was sure to be found? And might not he have been in this shape tonight at Kamonos'?"

Gordon shook his head.

"No, I have seen these fakirs. None of them ever feigned death to the extent of becoming shriveled and hard—in a word, dried up. Morley, narrating in another place the description of the mummy-case as jotted down by Von Lorfmon and passed on to Schuyler, mentions the fact that large portions of seaweed adhered to it—seaweed of a kind found only at great depths, on the bottom of the ocean. The wood, too, was of a kind which Von Lorfmon failed to recognize or to classify, in spite of the fact that he was one of the greatest living authorities on flora. And his notes again and again emphasize the enormous age of the thing. He admitted that there was no way of telling how old the mummy was, but his hints intimate that he believed it to be, not thousands of years old, but millions of years!

"No. We must face the facts. Since you are positive that the picture of the mummy is the picture of Kathulos—and there is little room for fraud—one of two things is practically certain: the Scorpion was never dead but ages ago was placed in that mummy-case and his life preserved in some manner, or else—he was dead and has been brought to life! Either of these theories, viewed in the cold light of reason, is absolutely untenable. Are we all insane?"

"Had you ever walked the road to hashish land," I

said somberly, "you could believe anything to be true. Had you ever gazed into the terrible reptilian eyes of Kathulos the sorcerer, you would not doubt that he was both dead and alive."

Gordon gazed out the window, his fine face haggard in the gray light which had begun to steal through them.

"At any rate," said he, "there are two places which I intend exploring thoroughly before the sun rises again—Kamonos' antique shop and Soho 48."

18. The Grip of the Scorpion

"While from a proud tower in the town
Death looks gigantically down."

—*Poe*

Hansen snored on the bed as I paced the room. Another day had passed over London and again the street lamps glimmered through the fog. Their lights affected me strangely. They seemed to beat, solid waves of energy, against my brain. They twisted the fog into strange sinister shapes. Footlights of the stage that is the streets of London, how many grisly scenes had they lighted? I pressed my hands hard against my throbbing temples, striving to bring my thoughts back from the chaotic labyrinth where they wandered.

Gordon I had not seen since dawn. Following the clue of "Soho 48" he had gone forth to arrange a raid upon the place and he thought it best that I should remain under cover. He anticipated an attempt upon my life, and again he feared that if I went searching among the dives I formerly frequented it would arouse suspicion.

Hansen snored on. I seated myself and began to study the Turkish shoes which clothed my feet. Zuleika had worn Turkish slippers—how she floated through my waking dreams, gilding prosaic things with her witchery! Her face smiled at me from the fog; her eyes shone from the flickering lamps; her phantom footfalls re-echoed through the misty chambers of my skull.

They beat an endless tattoo, luring and haunting till it seemed that these echoes found echoes in the hallway outside the room where I stood, soft and stealthy. A sudden rap at the door and I started.

Hansen slept on as I crossed the room and flung the door swiftly open. A swirling wisp of fog had invaded the corridor, and through it, like a silver veil, I saw her—Zuleika stood before me with her shimmering hair and her red lips parted and her great dark eyes.

Like a speechless fool I stood and she glanced quickly down the hallway and then stepped inside and closed the door.

"Gordon!" she whispered in a thrilling undertone. "Your friend! The Scorpion has him!"

Hansen had awakened and now sat gaping stupidly at the strange scene which met his eyes.

Zuleika did not heed him.

"And oh, Steephen!" she cried, and tears shone in her eyes, "I have tried so hard to secure some more elixir but I could not."

"Never mind that," I finally found my speech. "Tell me about Gordon."

"He went back to Kamonos' alone, and Hassim and Ganra Singh took him captive and brought him to the Master's house. Tonight assemble a great host of the people of the Scorpion for the sacrifice."

"Sacrifice!" A grisly thrill of horror coursed down my spine. Was there no limit to the ghastliness of this business?

"Quick, Zuleika, where is this house of the Master's?"

"Soho, 48. You must summon the police and send many men to surround it, but you must not go yourself—"

Hansen sprang up quivering for action, but I turned to him. My brain was clear now, or seemed to be, and racing unnaturally.

"Wait!" I turned back to Zuleika. "When is this sacrifice to take place?"

"At the rising of the moon."

"That is only a few hours before dawn. Time to save him, but if we raid the house they'll kill him before we can reach them. And God only knows how many diabolical things guard all approaches."

"I do not know," Zuleika whimpered. "I must go now, or the Master will kill me."

Something gave way in my brain at that; something like a flood of wild and terrible exultation swept over me.

"The Master will kill no one!" I shouted, flinging my arms on high. "Before ever the east turns red for dawn, the Master dies! By all things holy and unholy I swear it!"

Hansen stared wildly at me and Zuleika shrank back as I turned on her. To my dope-inspired brain had come a sudden burst of light, true and unerring. I knew Kathulos was a mesmerist—that he understood fully the secret of dominating another's mind and soul. And I knew that at last I had hit upon the reason of his power over the girl. Mesmerism! As a snake fascinates and draws to him a bird, so the Master held Zuleika to him with unseen shackles. So absolute was his rule over her that it held even when she was out of his sight, working over great distances.

There was but one thing which would break that hold: the magnetic power of some other person whose control was stronger with her than Kathulos'. I laid my hands on her slim little shoulders and made her face me.

"Zuleika," I said commandingly, "here you are safe; you shall not return to Kathulos. There is no need of it. Now you are free."

But I knew I had failed before I ever started. Her eyes held a look of amazed, unreasoning fear and she twisted timidly in my grasp.

"Steephen, please let me go!" she begged. "I must— I must!"

I drew her over to the bed and asked Hansen for his handcuffs. He handed them to me, wonderingly, and I fastened one cuff to the bedpost and the other to her slim wrist. The girl whimpered but made no resistance, her limpid eyes seeking mine in mute appeal.

It cut me to the quick to enforce my will upon her in this apparently brutal manner but I steeled myself.

"Zuleika," I said tenderly, "you are now my prisoner. The Scorpion cannot blame you for not returning to him when you are unable to do so—and before dawn you shall be free of his rule entirely."

I turned to Hansen and spoke in a tone which admitted of no argument.

"Remain here, just without the door, until I return. On no account allow any strangers to enter—that is, anyone whom you do not personally know. And I charge you, on your honor as a man, do not release this girl, no matter what she may say. If neither I nor Gordon have returned by ten o'clock tomorrow, take her to this address—that family once was friends of mine and will take care of a homeless girl. I am going to Scotland Yard."

"Steephen," Zuleika wailed, "you are going to the Master's lair! You will be killed. Send the police, do not go!"

I bent, drew her into my arms, felt her lips against mine, then tore myself away.

The fog plucked at me with ghostly fingers, cold as the hands of dead men, as I raced down the street. I had no plan, but one was forming in my mind, beginning to seethe in the stimulated cauldron that was my brain. I halted at the sight of a policeman pacing his beat, and beckoning him to me, scribbled a terse note on a piece of paper torn from a notebook and handed it to him.

"Get this to Scotland Yard; it's a matter of life and death and it has to do with the business of John Gordon."

At that name, a gloved hand came up in swift assent, but his assurance of haste died out behind me as I renewed my flight. The note stated briefly that Gordon was a prisoner at Soho 48 and advised an immediate raid in force—advised, nay, in Gordon's name, commanded it.

My reason for my actions was simple; I knew that the first noise of the raid sealed John Gordon's doom. Somehow I first must reach him and protect or free him before the police arrived.

The time seemed endless, but at last the grim gaunt outlines of the house that was Soho 48 rose up before me, a giant ghost in the fog. The hour grew late; few people dared the mists and the dampness as I came to a halt in the street before this forbidding building. No lights showed from the windows, either upstairs or down. It seemed deserted. But the lair of the scorpion often seems deserted until the silent death strikes suddenly.

Here I halted and a wild thought struck me. One way or another, the drama would be over by dawn. Tonight was the climax of my career, the ultimate top of life. Tonight I was the strongest link in the strange chain of events. Tomorrow it would not matter whether I lived or died. I drew the flask of elixir from my pocket and gazed at it. Enough for two more days if properly eked out. Two more days of life! Or—I needed stimulation as I never needed it before; the task in front of me was one no mere human could hope to accomplish. If I drank the entire remainder of the elixir, I had no idea as to the duration of its effect, but it would last the night through. And my legs were shaky; my mind had curious periods of utter vacuity;

weakness of brain and body assailed me. I raised the flask and with one draft drained it.

For an instant I thought it was death. Never had I taken such an amount.

Sky and world reeled and I felt as if I would fly into a million vibrating fragments, like the bursting of a globe of brittle steel. Like fire, like hell-fire the elixir raced along my veins and I was a giant! A monster! A superman!

Turning, I strode to the menacing, shadowy doorway. I had no plan; I felt the need of none. As a drunken man walks blithely into danger, I strode to the lair of the Scorpion, magnificently aware of my superiority, imperially confident of my stimulation and sure as the unchanging stars that the way would open before me.

Oh, there never was a superman like that who knocked commandingly on the door of Soho 48 that night in the rain and the fog!

I knocked four times, the old signal that we slaves had used to be admitted into the idol room at Yun Shatu's. An aperture opened in the center of the door and slanted eyes looked warily out. They slightly widened as the owner recognized me, then narrowed wickedly.

"You fool!" I said angrily. "Don't you see the mark?"

I held my hand to the aperture.

"Don't you recognize me? Let me in, curse you."

I think the very boldness of the trick made for its success. Surely by now all the Scorpion's slaves knew of Stephen Costigan's rebellion, knew that he was marked for death. And the very fact that I came there, inviting doom, confused the doorman.

The door opened and I entered. The man who had admitted me was a tall, lank Chinaman I had known as a servant at Kathulos. He closed the door behind me and I saw we stood in a sort of vestibule, lighted by a dim lamp whose glow could not be seen from the street for the reason that the windows were heavily curtained. The Chinaman glowered at me undecided. I looked at him, tensed. Then suspicion flared in his eyes and his hand flew to his sleeve. But at the instant I was on him and his lean neck broke like a rotten bough between my hands.

I eased his corpse to the thickly carpeted floor and listened. No sound broke the silence. Stepping as stealthily as a wolf, fingers spread like talons, I stole into the next room. This was furnished in oriental style, with couches and rugs and gold-worked drapery, but was empty of human life. I crossed it and went into the next one. Light flowed softly from the censers which were swung from the ceiling, and the Eastern rugs deadened the sound of my footfalls; I seemed to be moving through a castle of enchantment.

Every moment I expected a rush of silent assassins from the doorways or from behind the curtains or screen with their writhing dragons. Utter silence reigned. Room after room I explored and at last halted at the foot of the stairs. The inevitable censer shed an uncertain light, but most of the stairs were veiled in shadows. What horrors awaited me above?

But fear and the elixir are strangers and I mounted

that stair of lurking terror as boldly as I had entered that house of terror. The upper rooms I found to be much like those below and with them they had this fact in common: they were empty of human life. I sought an attic but there seemed no door letting into one. Returning to the first floor, I made a search for an entrance into the basement, but again my efforts were fruitless. The amazing truth was borne in upon me: except for myself and that dead man who lay sprawled so grotesquely in the outer vestibule, there were no men in that house, dead or living.

I could not understand it. Had the house been bare of furniture I should have reached the natural conclusion that Kathulos had fled—but no signs of flight met my eye. This was unnatural, uncanny. I stood in the great shadowy library and pondered. No, I had made no mistake in the house. Even if the broken corpse in the vestibule were not there to furnish mute testimony, everything in the room pointed toward the presence of the Master. There were the artificial palms, the lacquered screens, the tapestries, even the idol, though now no incense smoke rose before it. About the walls were ranged long shelves of books, bound in strange and costly fashion—books in every language in the world, I found from a swift examination, and on every subject—outré and bizarre, most of them.

Remembering the secret passage in the Temple of Dreams, I investigated the heavy mahogany table which stood in the center of the room. Bur nothing resulted. A sudden blaze of fury surged up in me, primitive and unreasoning. I snatched a statuette from the table and dashed it against the shelf-covered wall.

The noise of its breaking would surely bring the gang from their hiding- place. But the result was much more startling than that!

The statuette struck the edge of a shelf and instantly the whole section of shelves with their load of books swung silently outward, revealing a narrow doorway! As in the other secret door, a row of steps led downward. At another time I would have shuddered at the thought of descending, with the horrors of the other tunnel fresh in my mind, but inflamed as I was by the elixir, I strode forward without an instant's hesitancy.

Since there was no one in the house, they must be somewhere in the tunnel or in whatever lair to which the tunnel led. I stepped through the doorway, leaving the door open; the police might find it that way and follow me, though somehow I felt as if mine would be a lone hand from start to grim finish.

I went down a considerable distance and then the stair debouched into a level corridor some twenty feet wide—a remarkable thing. In spite of the width, the ceiling was rather low and from it hung small, curiously shaped lamps which flung a dim light. I stalked hurriedly along the corridor like old Death seeking victims, and as I went I noted the work of the thing. The floor was of great broad flags and the walls seemed to be of huge blocks of evenly set stone. This passage was clearly no work of modern days; the slaves of Kathulos never tunneled there. Some secret way of medieval times, I thought—and after all, who knows what catacombs lie below London, whose secrets are greater and darker than those of Babylon and Rome?

On and on I went, and now I knew that I must be far below the earth. The air was dank and heavy, and cold moisture dripped from the stones of walls and ceiling. From time to time I saw smaller passages leading away in the darkness but I determined to keep to the larger main one.

A ferocious impatience gripped me. I seemed to have been walking for hours and still only dank damp walls and bare flags and guttering lamps met my eyes. I kept a close watch for sinister-appearing chests or the like—saw no such things.

Then as I was about to burst into savage curses, another stair loomed up in the shadows in front of me.

19. Dark Fury

"The ringed wolf glared the circle round
Through baleful, blue-lit eye,
Not unforgetful of his debt.
Quoth he, 'I'll do some damage yet
Or ere my turn to die!'"

—*Mundy*

Like a lean wolf I glided up the stairs. Some twenty feet up there was a sort of landing from which other corridors diverged, much like the lower one by which I had come. The thought came to me that the earth below London must be honeycombed with such secret passages, one above the other.

Some feet above this landing the steps halted at a

door, and here I hesitated, uncertain as to whether I should chance knocking or not. Even as I meditated, the door began to open. I shrank back against the wall, flattening myself out as much as possible. The door swung wide and a Moor came through. Only a glimpse I had of the room beyond, out of the corner of my eye, but my unnaturally alert senses registered the fact that the room was empty.

And on the instant, before be could turn, I smote the Moor a single deathly blow behind the angle of the jawbone and be toppled headlong down the stairs, to lie in a crumpled heap on the landing, his limbs tossed grotesquely about.

My left hand caught the door as it started to slam shut and in an instant I was through and standing in the room beyond. As I had thought, there was no occupant of this room. I crossed it swiftly and entered the next. These rooms were furnished in a manner before which the furnishings of the Soho house paled into insignificance. Barbaric, terrible, unholy—these words alone convey some slight idea of the ghastly sights which met my eyes. Skulls, bones and complete skeletons formed much of the decorations, if such they were. Mummies leered from their cases and mounted reptiles ranged the walls. Between these sinister relics hung African shields of hide and bamboo, crossed with assagais and war daggers. Here and there reared obscene idols, black and horrible.

And in between and scattered about among these evidences of savagery and barbarism were vases, screens, rugs and hangings of the highest oriental workmanship; a strange and incongruous effect.

I had passed through two of these rooms without seeing a human being, when I came to stairs leading upward. Up these I went, several flights, until I came to a door in a ceiling. I wondered if I was still under the earth. Surely the first stairs had let into a house of some sort. I raised the door cautiously. Starlight met my eyes and I drew myself warily up and out. There I halted. A broad flat roof stretched away on all sides and beyond its rim on all sides glimmered the lights of London. Just what building I was on, I had no idea, but that it was a tall one I could tell, for I seemed to be above most of the lights I saw. Then I saw that I was not alone.

Over against the shadows of the ledge that ran around the roof's edge, a great menacing form bulked in starlight. A pair of eyes glinted at me with a light not wholly sane; the starlight glanced silver from a curving length of steel. Yar Khan the Afghan killer fronted me in the silent shadows.

A fierce wild exultation surged over me. Now I could begin to pay the debt I owed Kathulos and all his hellish band! The dope fired my veins and sent waves of inhuman power and dark fury through me. A spring and I was on my feet in a silent, deathly rush.

Yar Khan was a giant, taller and bulkier than I. He held a tulwar, and from the instant I saw him I knew that he was full of the dope to the use of which he was addicted—heroin.

As I came in he swung his heavy weapon high in the air, but ere he could strike I seized his sword wrist in an iron grip and with my free hand drove smashing blows into his midriff.

Of that hideous battle, fought in silence above the sleeping city with only the stars to see, I remember little. I remember tumbling back and forth, locked in a death embrace. I remember the stiff beard rasping my flesh as his dope-fired eyes gazed wildly into mine. I remember the taste of hot blood in my mouth, the tang of fearful exultation in my soul, the onrushing and upsurging of inhuman strength and fury.

God, what a sight for a human eye, had anyone looked upon that grim roof where two human leopards, dope maniacs, tore each other to pieces!

I remember his arm breaking like rotten wood in my grip and the tulwar falling from his useless hand. Handicapped by a broken arm, the end was inevitable, and with one wild uproaring flood of might, I rushed him to the edge of the roof and bent him backward far out over the ledge. An instant we struggled there; then I tore loose his hold and hurled him over, and one single shriek came up as he hurtled into the darkness below.

I stood upright, arms hurled up toward the stars, a terrible statue of primordial triumph. And down my breast trickled streams of blood from the long wounds left by the Afghan's frantic nails, on neck and face.

Then I turned with the craft of the maniac. Had no one heard the sound of that battle? My eyes were on the door through which I had come, but a noise made me turn, and for the first time I noticed a small affair like a tower jutting up from the roof. There was no window there, but there was a door, and even as I looked that door opened and a huge black form framed itself in the light that streamed from within. Hassim!

He stepped out on the roof and closed the door, his shoulders hunched and neck outthrust as he glanced this way and that. I struck him senseless to the roof with one hate-driven smash. I crouched over him, waiting some sign of returning consciousness; then away in the sky close to the horizon, I saw a faint red tint. The rising of the moon!

Where in God's name was Gordon? Even as I stood undecided, a strange noise reached me. It was curiously like the droning of many bees.

Striding in the direction from which it seemed to come, I crossed the roof and leaned over the ledge. A sight nightmarish and incredible met my eyes.

Some twenty feet below the level of the roof on which I stood, there was another roof, of the same size and clearly a part of the same building. On one side it was bounded by the wall; on the other three sides a parapet several feet high took the place of a ledge.

A great throng of people stood, sat and squatted, close-packed on the roof—and without exception they were Negroes! There were hundreds of them, and it was their low-voiced conversation which I had heard. But what held my gaze was that upon which their eyes were fixed.

About the center of the roof rose a sort of teocalli some ten feet high, almost exactly like those found in Mexico and on which the priests of the Aztecs sacrificed human victims. This, allowing for its infinitely smaller scale, was an exact type of those sacrificial pyramids. On the flat top of it was a curiously carved altar, and beside it stood a lank, dusky form whom even the ghastly mask he wore could not disguise to my gaze—Santiago, the Haiti voodoo fetish man. On the altar lay John Gordon, stripped to the waist and bound hand and foot, but conscious.

I reeled back from the roof edge, rent in twain by indecision. Even the stimulus of the elixir was not equal to this. Then a sound brought me about to see Hassim struggling dizzily to his knees. I reached him with two long strides and ruthlessly smashed him down again. Then I noticed a queer sort of contrivance dangling from his girdle. I bent and examined it. It was a mask similar to that worn by Santiago. Then my mind leaped swift and sudden to a wild desperate plan, which to my dope-ridden brain seemed not at all wild or desperate. I stepped softly to the tower and, opening the door, peered inward. I saw no one who might need to be silenced, but I saw a long silken robe hanging upon a peg in the wall. The luck of the dope fiend! I snatched it and closed the door again. Hassim showed no signs of consciousness but I gave him another smash on the chin to make sure and, seizing his mask, hurried to the ledge.

A low guttural chant floated up to me, jangling, barbaric, with an undertone of maniacal blood-lust. The Negroes, men and women, were swaying back and forth to the wild rhythm of their death chant. On the teocalli Santiago stood like a statue of black basalt, facing the east, dagger held high—a wild and terrible sight, naked as he was save for a wide silken girdle and that inhuman mask on his face. The moon thrust a red rim above the eastern horizon and a faint breeze stirred the great black plumes which nodded above the voodoo man's mask. The chant of the worshipers dropped to a low, sinister whisper.

I hurriedly slipped on the death mask, gathered the robe close about me and prepared for the descent. I was prepared to drop the full distance, being sure in the superb confidence of my insanity that I would land unhurt, but as I climbed over the ledge I found a steel ladder leading down. Evidently Hassim, one of the voodoo priests, intended descending this way. So down I went, and in haste, for I knew that the instant the moon's lower rim cleared the city's skyline, that motionless dagger would descend into Gordon's breast.

Gathering the robe close about me so as to conceal my white skin, I stepped down upon the roof and strode forward through rows of black worshipers who shrank aside to let me through. To the foot of the teocalli I stalked and up the stair that ran about it, until I stood beside the death altar and marked the dark red stains upon it. Gordon lay on his back, his eyes open, his face drawn and haggard, but his gaze dauntless and unflinching.

Santiago's eyes blazed at me through the slits of his mask, but I read no suspicion in his gaze until I reached forward and took the dagger from his hand. He was too much astonished to resist, and the black throng fell suddenly silent. That he saw my hand was not that of a Negro it is certain, but he was simply struck speechless with astonishment. Moving swiftly I cut Gordon's bonds and hauled him erect. Then Santiago with a shriek leaped upon me—shrieked again and, arms flung high, pitched headlong from the teocalli with his own dagger buried to the hilt in his breast.

Then the black worshipers were on us with a screech and a roar—leaping on the steps of the teocalli like black leopards in the moonlight, knives flashing, eyes gleaming whitely.

I tore mask and robe from me and answered Gordon's exclamation with a wild laugh. I had hoped that by virtue of my disguise I might get us both safely away but now I was content to die there at his side.

He tore a great metal ornament from the altar, and as the attackers came he wielded this. A moment we held them at bay and then they flowed over us like a black wave. This to me was Valhalla! Knives stung me and blackjacks smashed against me, but I laughed and drove my iron fists in straight, steam-hammer smashes that shattered flesh and bone. I saw Gordon's crude weapon rise and fall, and each time a man went down. Skulls shattered and blood splashed and the dark fury swept over me. Nightmare faces swirled about me and I was on my knees; up again and the faces crumpled before my blows. Through far mists I seemed to hear a hideous familiar voice raised in imperious command.

Gordon was swept away from me but from the sounds I knew that the work of death still went on. The stars reeled through fogs of blood, but Hell's exaltation was on me and I reveled in the dark tides of fury until a darker, deeper tide swept over me and I knew no more.

20. Ancient Horror

"Here now in his triumph where all things falter,
Stretched out on the spoils that his own
hand spread,
As a God self-slain on his own strange altar,
Death lies dead."

—*Swinburne*

Slowly I drifted back into life—slowly, slowly. A mist held me and in the mist I saw a Skull—

I lay in a steel cage like a captive wolf, and the bars were too strong, I saw, even for my strength. The cage seemed to be set in a sort of niche in the wall and I was looking into a large room. This room was under the earth, for the floor was of stone flags and the walls and ceiling were composed of gigantic block of the same material. Shelves ranged the walls, covered with weird appliances, apparently of a scientific nature, and more were on the great table that stood in the center of the room. Beside this sat Kathulos.

The sorcerer was clad in a snaky yellow robe, and those hideous hands and that terrible head were more pronouncedly reptilian than ever. He turned his great yellow eyes toward me, like pools of livid fire, and his parchment-thin lips moved in what probably passed for a smile.

I staggered erect and gripped the bars, cursing.

"Gordon, curse you, where is Gordon?"

Kathulos took a test-tube from the table, eyed it closely and emptied it into another.

"Ah, my friend awakes," he murmured in his voice—the voice of a living dead man.

He thrust his hands into his long sleeves and turned fully to me.

"I think in you," he said distinctly, "I have created a Frankenstein monster. I made of you a superhuman creature to serve my wishes and you broke from me. You are the bane of my might, worse than Gordon even. You have killed valuable servants and interfered with my plans. However, your evil comes to an end tonight. Your friend Gordon broke away but he is being hunted through the tunnels and cannot escape.

"You," he continued with the sincere interest of the scientist, "are a most interesting subject. Your brain must be formed differently from any other man that ever lived. I will make a close study of it and add it to my laboratory. How a man, with the apparent need of the elixir in his system, has managed to go on for two days still stimulated by the last draft is more than I can understand."

My heart leaped. With all his wisdom, little Zuleika had tricked him and he evidently did not know that she had filched a flask of the life-giving stuff from him.

"The last draft you had from me," he went on, "was sufficient only for some eight hours. I repeat, it has me puzzled. Can you offer any suggestion?"

I snarled wordlessly. He sighed.

"As always the barbarian. Truly the proverb speaks: 'Jest with the wounded tiger and warm the adder in your bosom before you seek to lift the savage from his savagery.'"

He meditated awhile in silence. I watched him uneasily. There was about him a vague and curious difference—his long fingers emerging from the sleeves drummed on the chair arms and some hidden exultation strummed at the back of his voice, lending it unaccustomed vibrancy.

"And you might have been a king of the new regime," he said suddenly. "Aye, the new—new and inhumanly old!"

I shuddered as his dry cackling laugh rasped out.

He bent his head as if listening. From far off seemed to come a hum of guttural voices. His lips writhed in a smile.

"My black children," he murmured. "They tear my enemy Gordon to pieces in the tunnels. They, Mr. Costigan, are my real henchmen and it was for their edification tonight that I laid John Gordon on the sacrificial stone. I would have preferred to have made some experiments with him, based on certain scientific theories, but my children must be humored. Later under my tutelage they will outgrow their childish superstitions and throw aside their foolish customs, but now they must be led gently by the hand.

"How do you like these under-the-earth corridors, Mr. Costigan?" he switched suddenly. "You thought of them—what? No doubt that the white savages of your Middle Ages built them? Faugh! These tunnels are older than your world! They were brought into being by mighty kings, too many eons ago for your mind to grasp, when an imperial city towered where this crude village of London stands. All trace of that metropolis has crumbled to dust and vanished, but these corridors were built by more than human skill— ha ha! Of all the teeming thousands who move daily above them, none knows of their existence save my servants—and not all of them. Zuleika, for instance, does not know of them, for of late I have begun to doubt her loyalty and shall doubtless soon make of her an example."

At that I hurled myself blindly against the side of the cage, a red wave of hate and fury tossing me in its grip. I seized the bars and strained until the veins stood out on my forehead and the muscles bulged and crackled in my arms and shoulders. And the bars bent before my onslaught—a little but no more, and finally the power flowed from my limbs and I sank down trembling and weakened. Kathulos watched me imperturbably.

"The bars hold," be announced with something almost like relief in his tone. "Frankly, I prefer to be on the opposite side of them. You are a human ape if there was ever one."

He laughed suddenly and wildly.

"But why do you seek to oppose me?" he shrieked unexpectedly. "Why defy me, who am Kathulos, the Sorcerer, great even in the days of the old empire? Today, invincible! A magician, a scientist, among igno- rant savages! Ha ha!"

I shuddered, and sudden blinding light broke in on me. Kathulos himself was an addict, and was fired by the stuff of his choice! What hellish concoction was strong enough, terrible enough to thrill the Master and inflame him, I do not know, nor do I wish to know. Of all the uncanny knowledge that was his, I, knowing the man as I did, count this the most weird and grisly.

"You, you paltry fool!" he was ranting, his face lit supernaturally.

"Know you who I am? Kathulos of Egypt! Bah! They knew me in the old days! I reigned in the dim misty sea lands ages and ages before the sea rose and engulfed the land. I died, not as men die; the magic draft of life everlasting was ours! I drank deep and slept. Long I slept in my lacquered case! My flesh withered and grew hard; my blood dried in my veins. I became as one dead. But still within me burned the spirit of life, sleeping but anticipating the awakening. The great cities crumbled to dust. The sea drank the land. The tall shrines and the lofty spires sank beneath the green waves. All this I knew as I slept, as a man knows in dreams. Kathulos of Egypt? Faugh! *Kathulos of Atlantis!*"

I uttered a sudden involuntary cry. This was too grisly for sanity.

"Aye, the magician, the sorcerer.

"And down the long years of savagery, through which the barbaric races struggled to rise without their masters, the legend came of the day of empire, when one of the Old Race would rise up from the sea. Aye, and lead to victory the black people who were our slaves in the old days.

"These brown and yellow people, what care I for them? The blacks were the slaves of my race, and I am their god today. They will obey me. The yellow and

the brown peoples are fools—I make them my tools
and the day will come when my black warriors will
turn on them and slay at my word. And you, you
white barbarians, whose ape-ancestors forever defied
my race and me, your doom is at hand! And when I
mount my universal throne, the only whites shall be
white slaves!

"The day came as prophesied, when my case,
breaking free from the halls where it lay—where it had
lain when Atlantis was still sovereign of the world—
where since her empery it had sunk into the green
fathoms—when my case, I say, was smitten by the
deep sea tides and moved and stirred, and thrust aside
the clinging seaweed that masks temples and minarets,
and came floating up past the lofty sapphire and
golden spires, up through the green waters, to float
upon the lazy waves of the sea.

"Then came a white fool carrying out the destiny of
which he was not aware. The men on his ship, true
believers, knew that the time had come. And I—the air
entered my nostrils and I awoke from the long, long
sleep. I stirred and moved and lived. And rising in the
night, I slew the fool that had lifted me from the
ocean, and my servants made obeisance to me and
took me into Africa, where I abode awhile and learned
new languages and new ways of a new world and
became strong.

"The wisdom of your dreary world—ha ha! I who
delved deeper in the mysteries of the old than any man
dared go! All that men know today, I know, and the
knowledge beside that which I have brought down the
centuries is as a grain of sand beside a mountain! You

should know something of that knowledge! By it I lifted you from one hell to plunge you into a greater! You fool, here at my hand is that which would lift you from this! Aye, would strike from you the chains whereby I have bound you!"

He snatched up a golden vial and shook it before my gaze. I eyed it as men dying in the desert must eye the distant mirages. Kathulos fingered it meditatively. His unnatural excitement seemed to have passed suddenly, and when he spoke again it was in the passionless, measured tones of the scientist.

"That would indeed be an experiment worthwhile—to free you of the elixir habit and see if your dope-riddled body would sustain life. Nine times out of ten the victim, with the need and stimulus removed, would die—but you are such a giant of a brute—"

He sighed and set the vial down.

"The dreamer opposes the man of destiny. My time is not my own or I should choose to spend my life pent in my laboratories, carrying out my experiments. But now, as in the days of the old empire when kings sought my counsel, I must work and labor for the good of the race at large. Aye, I must toil and sow the seed of glory against the full coming of the imperial days when the seas give up all their living dead."

I shuddered. Kathulos laughed wildly again. His fingers began to drum his chair arms and his face gleamed with the unnatural light once more. The red visions had begun to seethe in his skull again.

"Under the green seas they lie, the ancient masters, in their lacquered cases, dead as men reckon death, but only sleeping. Sleeping through the long ages as hours, awaiting the day of awakening! The old masters, the wise men, who foresaw the day when the sea would gulp the land, and who made ready. Made ready that they might rise again in the barbaric days to come. As did I. Sleeping they lie, ancient kings and grim wizards, who died as men die, before Atlantis sank. Who, sleeping, sank with her but who shall arise again!

"Mine the glory! I rose first. And I sought out the site of old cities, on shores that did not sink. Vanished, long vanished. The barbarian tide swept over them thousands of years ago as the green waters swept over their elder sister of the deeps. On some, the deserts stretch bare. Over some, as here, young barbarian cities rise."

He halted suddenly. His eyes sought one of the dark openings that marked a corridor. I think his strange intuition warned him of some impending danger but I do not believe that he had any inkling of how dramatically our scene would be interrupted.

As he looked, swift footsteps sounded and a man appeared suddenly in the doorway—a man disheveled, tattered and bloody. John Gordon! Kathulos sprang erect with a cry, and Gordon, gasping as from superhuman exertion, brought down the revolver he held in his hand and fired point-blank. Kathulos staggered, clapping his hand to his breast, and then, groping wildly, reeled to the wall and fell against it. A doorway opened and he reeled through, but as Gordon leaped fiercely across the chamber, a blank stone surface met his gaze, which yielded not to his savage hammerings.

He whirled and ran drunkenly to the table where lay a bunch of keys the Master had dropped there.

"The vial!" I shrieked. "Take the vial!" And he thrust it into his pocket.

Back along the corridor through which he had come sounded a faint clamor growing swiftly like a wolf-pack in full cry. A few precious seconds spent with fumbling for the right key, then the cage door swung open and I sprang out. A sight for the gods we were, the two of us! Slashed, bruised and cut, our garments hanging in tatters—my wounds had ceased to bleed, but now as I moved they began again, and from the stiffness of my hands I knew that my knuckles were shattered. As for Gordon, he was fairly drenched in blood from crown to foot.

We made off down a passage in the opposite direction from the menacing noise, which I knew to be the black servants of the Master in full pursuit of us. Neither of us was in good shape for running, but we did our best. Where we were going I had no idea. My superhuman strength had deserted me and I was going now on willpower alone. We switched off into another corridor and we had not gone twenty steps until, looking back, I saw the first of the black devils round the corner.

A desperate effort increased our lead a trifle. But they had seen us, were in full view now, and a yell of fury broke from them to be succeeded by a more sinister silence as they bent all efforts to overhauling us.

There a short distance in front of us we saw a stair loom suddenly in the gloom. If we might reach that— but we saw something else.

Against the ceiling, between us and the stairs, hung a huge thing like an iron grille, with great spikes along the bottom—a portcullis. And even as we looked, without halting in our panting strides, it began to move.

"They're lowering the portcullis!" Gordon croaked, his blood-streaked face a mask of exhaustion and will.

Now the blacks were only ten feet behind us—now the huge grate, gaining momentum, with a creak of rusty, unused mechanism, rushed downward. A final spurt, a gasping straining nightmare of effort—and Gordon, sweeping us both along in a wild burst of pure nerve-strength, hurled us under and through, and the grate crashed behind us!

A moment we lay gasping, not heeding the frenzied horde who raved and screamed on the other side of the grate. So close had that final leap been, that the great spikes in their descent had torn shreds from our clothing.

The blacks were thrusting at us with daggers through the bars, but we were out of reach and it seemed to me that I was content to lie there and die of exhaustion. But Gordon weaved unsteadily erect and hauled me with him.

"Got to get out," he croaked; "go to warn—Scotland Yard—honeycombs in heart of London—high explosives—arms—ammunition."

We blundered up the steps, and in front of us I seemed to hear a sound of metal grating against metal. The stairs ended abruptly, on a landing that terminated in a blank wall. Gordon hammered against this and the inevitable secret doorway opened. Light streamed in, through the bars of a sort of grille. Men in the uniform of London police were sawing at these with hacksaws, and even as they greeted us, an opening was made through which we crawled.

"You're hurt, sir!" One of the men took Gordon's arm.

My companion shook him off.

"There's no time to lose! Out of here, as quick as we can go!"

I saw that we were in a basement of some sort. We hastened up the steps and out into the early dawn which was turning the east scarlet. Over the tops of smaller houses I saw in the distance a great gaunt building on the roof of which, I felt instinctively, that wild drama had been enacted the night before.

"That building was leased some months ago by a mysterious Chinaman," said Gordon, following my gaze. "Office building originally—the neighborhood deteriorated and the building stood vacant for some time. The new tenant added several stories to it but left it apparently empty. Had my eye on it for some time."

This was told in Gordon's jerky swift manner as we started hurriedly along the sidewalk. I listened mechanically, like a man in a trance. My vitality was ebbing fast and I knew that I was going to crumple at any moment.

"The people living in the vicinity had been reporting strange sights and noises. The man who owned the basement we just left heard queer sounds emanating from the wall of the basement and called the police. About that time I was racing back and forth among those cursed corridors like a hunted rat and I heard the police banging on the wall. I found the secret door and opened it but found it barred by a grating. It was while I was telling the astounded policemen to procure a hacksaw that the pursuing Negroes, whom I had eluded for the moment, came into sight and I was forced to shut the door and run for it again. By pure luck I found you and by pure luck managed to find the way back to the door.

"Now we must get to Scotland Yard. If we strike swiftly, we may capture the entire band of devils. Whether I killed Kathulos or not I do not know, or if he can be killed by mortal weapons. But to the best of my knowledge all of them are now in those subterranean corridors and—"

At that moment the world shook! A brain-shattering roar seemed to break the sky with its incredible detonation; houses tottered and crashed to ruins; a mighty pillar of smoke and flame burst from the earth and on its wings great masses of debris soared skyward. A black fog of smoke and dust and falling timbers enveloped the world, a prolonged thunder seemed to rumble up from the center of the earth as of walls and ceilings falling, and amid the uproar and the screaming I sank down and knew no more.

21. The Breaking of the Chain

"And like a soul belated,
In heaven and hell unmated;
By cloud and mist abated;
Come out of darkness morn."

—Swinburne

There is little need to linger on the scenes of horror of that terrible London morning. The world is familiar with and knows most of the details attendant to the great explosion which wiped out a tenth of that great city with a resultant loss of lives and property. For such a happening some reason must needs be given; the tale of the deserted building got out, and many wild stories were circulated. Finally, to still the rumors, the report was unofficially given out that this building had been the rendezvous and secret stronghold of a gang of international anarchists, who had stored its basement full of high explosives and who had supposedly ignited these accidentally. In a way there was a good deal to this tale, as you know, but the threat that had lurked there far transcended any anarchist.

All this was told to me, for when I sank unconscious, Gordon, attributing my condition to exhaustion and a need of the hashish to the use of which he thought I was addicted, lifted me and with the aid of the stunned policemen got me to his rooms before returning to the scene of the explosion. At his rooms he found Hansen, and Zuleika handcuffed to the bed as I had left her. He released her and left her to tend to me, for all London was in a terrible turmoil and he was needed elsewhere.

When I came to myself at last, I looked up into her starry eyes and lay quiet, smiling up at her. She sank down upon my bosom, nestling my head in her arms and covering my face with her kisses.

"Steephen!" she sobbed over and over, as her tears splashed hot on my face.

I was scarcely strong enough to put my arms about her but I managed it, and we lay there for a space, in silence, except for the girl's hard, racking sobs.

"Zuleika, I love you," I murmured.

"And I love you, Steephen," she sobbed. "Oh, it is so hard to part now—but I'm going with you, Steephen; I can't live without you!"

"My dear child," said John Gordon, entering the room suddenly, "Costigan's not going to die. We will let him have enough hashish to tide him along, and when he is stronger we will take him off the habit slowly."

"You don't understand, sahib; it is not hashish Steephen must have. It is something which only the Master knew, and now that he is dead or is fled, Steephen cannot get it and must die."

Gordon shot a quick, uncertain glance at me. His fine face was drawn and haggard, his clothes sooty and torn from his work among the debris of the explosion.

"She's right, Gordon," I said languidly. "I'm dying. Kathulos killed the hashish-craving with a concoction he called the elixir. I've been keeping myself alive on some of the stuff that Zuleika stole from him and gave me, but I drank it all last night."

I was aware of no craving of any kind, no physical or mental discomfort even. All my mechanism was slowing down fast; I had passed the stage where the need of the elixir would tear and rend me. I felt only a great lassitude and a desire to sleep. And I knew that the moment I closed my eyes, I would die.

"A strange dope, that elixir," I said with growing languor. "It burns and freezes and then at last the craving kills easily and without torment."

"Costigan, curse it," said Gordon desperately, "you can't go like this! That vial I took from the Egyptian's table—what is in it?"

"The Master swore it would free me of my curse and probably kill me also," I muttered. "I'd forgotten about it. Let me have it; it can no more than kill me and I'm dying now."

"Yes, quick, let me have it!" exclaimed Zuleika fiercely, springing to Gordon's side, her hands passionately outstretched. She returned with the vial which he had taken from his pocket, and knelt beside me, holding it to my lips, while she murmured to me gently and soothingly in her own language.

I drank, draining the vial, but feeling little interest in the whole matter. My outlook was purely impersonal, at such a low ebb was my life, and I cannot even remember how the stuff tasted. I only remember feeling a curious sluggish fire burn faintly along my veins, and the last thing I saw was Zuleika crouching over me, her great eyes fixed with a burning intensity on me. Her tense little hand rested inside her blouse, and remembering her vow to take her own life if I died I tried to lift a hand and disarm her, tried to tell Gordon to take away the dagger she had hidden in her garments. But speech and action failed me and I drifted away into a curious sea of unconsciousness.

Of that period I remember nothing. No sensation fired my sleeping brain to such an extent as to bridge the gulf over which I drifted. They say I lay like a dead man for hours, scarcely breathing, while Zuleika hovered over me, never leaving my side an instant, and fighting like a tigress when anyone tried to coax her away to rest. Her chain was broken.

As I had carried the vision of her into that dim land of nothingness, so her dear eyes were the first thing which greeted my returning consciousness. I was aware of a greater weakness than I thought possible for a man to feel, as if I had been an invalid for months, but the life in me, faint though it was, was sound and normal, caused by no artificial stimulation. I smiled up at my girl and murmured weakly:

"Throw away your dagger, little Zuleika; I'm going to live."

She screamed and fell on her knees beside me, weeping and laughing at the same time. Women are strange beings, of mixed and powerful emotions, truly.

Gordon entered and grasped the hand which I could not lift from the bed.

"You're a case for an ordinary human physician now, Costigan," he said. "Even a layman like myself can tell that. For the first time since I've known you, the look in your eyes is entirely sane. You look like a man who has had a complete nervous breakdown, and needs about a year of rest and quiet. Great heavens, man, you've been through enough, outside your dope experience, to last you a lifetime."

"Tell me first," said I, "was Kathulos killed in the explosion?"

"I don't know," answered Gordon somberly. "Apparently the entire system of subterranean passages was destroyed. I know my last bullet—the last bullet that was in the revolver which I wrested from one of my attackers—found its mark in the Master's body, but whether he died from the wound, or whether a bullet can hurt him, I do not know. And whether in his death agonies he ignited the tons and tons of high explosives which were stored in the corridors, or whether the Negroes did it unintentionally, we shall never know.

"My God, Costigan, did you ever see such a honeycomb? And we know not how many miles in either direction the passages reached. Even now Scotland Yard men are combing the subways and basements of the town for secret openings. All known openings, such as the one through which we came and the one in Soho 48, were blocked by falling walls. The office building was simply blown to atoms."

"What about the men who raided Soho 48?"

"The door in the library wall had been closed. They found the Chinaman you killed, but searched the house without avail. Lucky for them, too, else they had doubtless been in the tunnels when the explosion came, and perished with the hundreds of Negroes who must have died then."

"Every Negro in London must have been there."

"I dare say. Most of them are voodoo worshipers at heart and the power the Master wielded was incredible. They died, but what of him? Was he blown to atoms by the stuff which he had secretly stored, or crushed when the stone walls crumbled and the ceilings came thundering down?"

"There is no way to search among those subterranean ruins, I suppose?"

"None whatever. When the walls caved in, the tons of earth upheld by the ceilings also came crashing down, filling the corridors with dirt and broken stone, blocking them forever. And on the surface of the earth, the houses which the vibration shook down were heaped high in utter ruins. What happened in those terrible corridors must remain forever a mystery."

My tale draws to a close. The months that followed passed uneventfully, except for the growing happiness which to me was paradise, but which would bore you were I to relate it. But one day Gordon and I again discussed the mysterious happenings that had had their being under the grim hand of the Master.

"Since that day," said Gordon, "the world has been quiet. Africa has subsided and the East seems to have returned to her ancient sleep. There can be but one answer—living or dead, Kathulos was destroyed that morning when his world crashed about him."

"Gordon," said I, "what is the answer to that greatest of all mysteries?"

My friend shrugged his shoulders.

"I have come to believe that mankind eternally hovers on the brinks of secret oceans of which it knows nothing. Races have lived and vanished before our race rose out of the slime of the primitive, and it is likely still others will live upon the earth after ours has vanished. Scientists have long upheld the theory that the Atlanteans possessed a higher civilization than our own, and on very different lines. Certainly Kathulos himself was proof that our boasted culture and knowledge were nothing beside that of whatever fearful civilization produced him.

"His dealings with you alone have puzzled all the scientific world, for none of them has been able to explain how he could remove the hashish craving, stimulate you with a drug so infinitely more powerful, and then produce another drug which entirely effaced the effects of the other."

"I have him to thank for two things," I said slowly; "the regaining of my lost manhood—and Zuleika. Kathulos, then, is dead, as far as any mortal thing can die. But what of those others—those 'ancient masters' who still sleep in the sea?"

Gordon shuddered.

"As I said, perhaps mankind loiters on the brink of unthinkable chasms of horror. But a fleet of gunboats is even now patrolling the oceans unobtrusively, with orders to destroy instantly any strange case that may be found floating—to destroy it and its contents. And if my word has any weight with the English government and the nations of the world, the seas will be so patrolled until doomsday shall let down the curtain on the races of today."

"At night I dream of them, sometimes," I muttered, "sleeping in their lacquered cases, which drip with strange seaweed, far down among the green surges— where unholy spires and strange towers rise in the dark ocean."

"We have been face to face with an ancient horror," said Gordon somberly, "with a fear too dark and mysterious for the human brain to cope with. Fortune has been with us; she may not again favor the sons of men. It is best that we be ever on our guard. The universe was not made for humanity alone; life takes strange phases and it is the first instinct of nature for the different species to destroy each other. No doubt we seemed as horrible to the Master as he did to us. We have scarcely tapped the chest of secrets which nature has stored, and I shudder to think of what that chest may hold for the human race."

"That's true," said I, inwardly rejoicing at the vigor which was beginning to course through my wasted veins, "but men will meet obstacles as they come, as men have always risen to meet them. Now, I am beginning to know the full worth of life and love, and not all the devils from all the abysses can hold me."

Gordon smiled.

"You have it coming to you, old comrade. The best thing is to forget all that dark interlude, for in that course lies light and happiness."

DEAD MAN'S HATE

Weird Tales, January 1930

They hanged John Farrel in the dawn amid the
    market-place;
At dusk came Adam Brand to him and spat upon
    his face.
"Ho, neighbors all," spake Adam Brand, "see ye
    John Farrel's fate!
"Tis proven here a hempen noose is stronger
    than man's hate!

"For heard ye not John Farrel's vow to be
    avenged on me
Come life or death? See how he hangs high on
    the gallows tree!"
Yet never a word the people spake, in fear and
    wild surprize—
For the grisly corpse raised up its head and
    stared with sightless eyes,

And with strange motions, slow and stiff,
    pointed at Adam Brand
And clambered down the gibbet tree, the noose
    within its hand.

With gaping mouth stood Adam Brand like a
    statue carved of stone,
Till the dead man laid a clammy hand hard on
    his shoulder-bone.

Then Adam shrieked like a soul in hell; the red
    blood left his face
And he reeled away in a drunken run through
    the screaming market-place;
And close behind, the dead man came with face
    like a mummy's mask,
And the dead joints cracked and the stiff legs
    creaked with their unwanted task.

Men fled before the flying twain or shrank with
    bated breath,
And they saw on the face of Adam Brand the seal
    set there by death.
He reeled on buckling legs that failed, yet on and
    on he fled;
So through the shuddering market-place, the
    dying fled the dead.

At the riverside fell Adam Brand with a scream
    that rent the skies;
Across him fell John Farrel's corpse, nor ever the
    twain did rise.
There was no wound on Adam Brand but his
    brow was cold and damp,
For the fear of death had blown out his life as a
    witch blows out a lamp.

*His lips writhed in a horrid grin like a fiend's on
　　Satan's coals,
And the men that looked on his face that day, his
　　stare still haunts their souls.
Such was the fate of Adam Brand, a strange,
　　unearthly fate;
For stronger than death or hempen noose are the
　　fires of a dead man's hate.*

THE FEARSOME TOUCH OF DEATH

Weird Tales, February 1930

As long as midnight cloaks the earth
With shadows grim and stark,
God save us from the Judas kiss
Of a dead man in the dark.

Old Adam Farrel lay dead in the house wherein he had lived alone for the last twenty years. A silent, churlish recluse, in his life he had known no friends, and only two men had watched his passing.

Dr. Stein rose and glanced out the window into the gathering dusk.

"You think you can spend the night here, then?" he asked his companion.

This man, Falred by name, assented.

"Yes, certainly. I guess it's up to me."

"Rather a useless and primitive custom, sitting up with the dead," commented the doctor, preparing to depart, "but I suppose in common decency we will have to bow to precedence. Maybe I can find someone who'll come over here and help you with your vigil."

Falred shrugged his shoulders. "I doubt it. Farrel wasn't liked—wasn't known by many people. I scarcely knew him myself, but I don't mind sitting up with the corpse."

Dr. Stein was removing his rubber gloves and Falred watched the process with an interest that almost amounted to fascination. A slight, involuntary shudder shook him at the memory of touching these gloves—slick, cold, clammy things, like the touch of death.

"You may get lonely tonight, if I don't find anyone," the doctor remarked as he opened the door. "Not superstitious, are you?"

Falred laughed. "Scarcely. To tell the truth, from what I hear of Farrel's disposition, I'd rather be watching his corpse than have been his guest in life."

The door closed and Falred took up his vigil. He seated himself in the only chair the room boasted, glanced casually at the formless, sheeted bulk on the bed opposite him, and began to read by the light of the dim lamp which stood on the rough table.

Outside, the darkness gathered swiftly, and finally Falred laid down his magazine to rest his eyes. He looked again at the shape which had, in life, been the form of Adam Farrel, wondering what quirk in the human nature made the sight of a corpse not so unpleasant, but such an object of fear to man. Unthinking ignorance, seeing in dead things a reminder of death to come, he decided lazily, and began idly contemplating as to what life had held for this grim and crabbed old man, who had neither relatives nor friends, and who had seldom left the house wherein he had died. The usual tales of miser-hoarded wealth had accumulated, but Falred felt so little interest in the whole matter that it was not even necessary for him to overcome any temptation to prey about the house for possible hidden treasure.

He returned to his reading with a shrug. The task was more boresome than he had thought for. After a while he was aware that every time he looked up from his magazine and his eyes fell upon the bed with its grim occupant, he started involuntarily as if he had, for an instant, forgotten the presence of the dead man and was unpleasantly reminded of the fact. The start was slight and instinctive, but he felt almost angered at himself. He realized, for the first time, the utter and deadening silence which enwrapped the house—a silence apparently shared by the night, for no sound came through the window. Adam Farrel lived as far apart from his neighbors as possible, and there was no other house within hearing distance.

Falred shook himself as if to rid his mind of unsavory speculations, and went back to his reading. A sudden vagrant gust of wind whipped through the window, in which the light in the lamp flickered and went out suddenly. Falred, cursing softly, groped in the darkness for matches, burning his fingers on the lamp chimney. He struck a match, relighted the lamp, and glancing over at the bed, got a horrible mental jolt. Adam Farrel's face stared blindly at him, the dead eyes wide and blank, framed in the gnarled gray features. Even as Falred instinctively shuddered, his reason explained the apparent phenomenon: the sheet that covered the corpse had been carelessly thrown across the face and the sudden puff of wind had disarranged and flung it aside.

Yet there was something grisly about the thing, something fearsomely suggestive—as if, in the cloaking dark, a dead hand had flung aside the sheet, just as if the corpse were about to rise. . . .

Falred, an imaginative man, shrugged his shoulders at these ghastly thoughts and crossed the room to replace the sheet. The dead eyes seemed to stare malevolently, with an evilness that transcended the dead man's churlishness in life. The workings of a vivid imagination, Falred knew, and he re-covered the gray face, shrinking as his hand chanced to touch the cold flesh—slick and clammy, the touch of death. He shuddered with the natural revulsion of the living for the dead, and went back to his chair and magazine.

At last, growing sleepy, he lay down upon a couch which, by some strange whim of the original owner, formed part of the room's scant furnishings, and composed himself for slumber. He decided to leave the light burning, telling himself that it was in accordance with the usual custom of leaving lights burning for the dead; for he was not willing to admit to himself that already he was conscious of a dislike for lying in the darkness with the corpse. He dozed, awoke with a start and looked at the sheeted form of the bed. Silence reigned over the house, and outside it was very dark.

The hour was approaching midnight, with its accompanying eerie domination over the human mind. Falred glanced again at the bed where the body lay and found the sight of the sheeted object most repellent. A fantastic idea had birth in his mind, and grew, that beneath the sheet, the mere lifeless body had become a strange, monstrous thing, a hideous, conscious being, that watched him with eyes which burned through the fabric of the cloth. This thought— a mere fantasy, of course—he explained to himself by the legends of vampires, undead ghosts and such like—the fearsome attributes with which the living have cloaked the dead for countless ages, since primitive man first recognized in death something horrid and apart from life. Man feared death, thought Falred, and some of this fear of death took hold on the dead so that they, too, were feared. And the sight of the dead engendered grisly thoughts, gave rise to dim fears of hereditary memory, lurking back in the dark corners of the brain.

At any rate, that silent, hidden thing was getting on his nerves. He thought of uncovering the face, on the principle that familiarity breeds contempt. The sight of the features, calm and still in death, would banish, he thought, all such wild conjectures as were haunting him in spite of himself. But the thought of those dead eyes staring in the lamplight was intolerable; so at last he blew out the light and lay down. This fear had been stealing upon him so insidiously and gradually that he had not been aware of its growth.

With the extinguishing of the light, however, and the blotting out of the sight of the corpse, things assumed their true character and proportions, and Falred fell asleep almost instantly, on his lips a faint smile for his previous folly.

He awakened suddenly. How long he had been asleep he did not know. He sat up, his pulse pounding frantically, the cold sweat beading his forehead. He knew instantly where he was, remembered the other occupant of the room. But what had awakened him? A dream—yes, now he remembered—a hideous dream in which the dead man had risen from the bed and stalked stiffly across the room with eyes of fire and a horrid leer frozen on his gray lips. Falred had seemed to lie motionless, helpless; then as the corpses reached a gnarled and horrible hand, he had awakened.

He strove to pierce the gloom, but the room was all blackness and all without was so dark that no gleam of light came through the window. He reached a shaking hand toward the lamp, then recoiled as if from a hidden serpent. Sitting here in the dark with a fiendish corpse was bad enough, but he dared not light the lamp, for fear that his reason would be snuffed out like a candle at what he might see. Horror, stark and unreasoning, had full possession of his soul; he no longer questioned the instinctive fears that rose in him. All those legends he had heard came back to him and brought a belief in them. Death was a hideous thing, a brain-shattering horror, imbuing lifeless men with a horrid malevolence. Adam Farrel in his life had been simply a churlish but harmless man; now he was a terror, a monster, a fiend lurking in the shadows of fear, ready to leap on mankind with talons dipped deep in death and insanity.

Falred sat there, his blood freezing, and fought out his silent battle. Faint glimmerings of reason had begun to touch his fright when a soft, stealthy sound again froze him. He did not recognize it as the whisper of the night wind across the windowsill. His frenzied

fancy knew it only as the tread of death and horror.
He sprang from the couch, then stood undecided.
Escape was in his mind but he was too dazed to even
try to formulate a plan of escape. Even his sense of
direction was gone. Fear had so stultified his mind
that he was not able to think consciously. The blackness spread in long waves about him and its darkness
and void entered into his brain. His motions, such as
they were, were instinctive. He seemed shackled with
mighty chains and his limbs responded sluggishly, like
an imbecile's.

A terrible horror grew up in him and reared its
grisly shape, that the dead man was behind him, was
stealing upon him from the rear. He no longer thought
of lighting the lamp; he no longer thought of anything.
Fear filled his whole being; there was room for
nothing else.

He backed slowly away in the darkness, hands
behind him, instinctively feeling the way. With a terrific effort he partly shook the clinging mists of horror
from him, and, the cold sweat clammy upon his body,
strove to orient himself. He could see nothing, but the
bed was across the room, in front of him. He was
backing away from it. There was where the dead man
was lying, according to all rules of nature; if the thing
were, as he felt, behind him, then the old tales were
true: death did implant in lifeless bodies an unearthly
animation, and dead men did roam the shadows to
work their ghastly and evil will upon the sons of men.
Then—great God!—what was man but a wailing
infant, lost in the night and beset by frightful things
from the black abysses and the terrible unknown voids

of space and time? These conclusions he did not reach by any reasoning process; they leaped full-grown into his terror-dazed brain. He worked his way slowly backward, groping, clinging to the thought that the dead man must be in front of him.

Then his back-flung hands encountered something—something slick, cold and clammy—like the touch of death. A scream shook the echoes, followed by the crash of a falling body.

The next morning they who came to the house of death found two corpses in the room. Adam Farrel's sheeted body lay motionless upon the bed, and across the room lay the body of Falred, beneath the shelf where Dr. Stein had absent-mindedly left his gloves—rubber gloves, slick and clammy to the touch of a hand groping in the dark—a hand of one fleeing his own fear—rubber gloves, slick and clammy and cold, like the touch of death.

THE VOICE OF EL-LIL

Oriental Stories,
October–November 1930

Maskat, like many another port, is a haven for the drifters of many nations who bring their tribal customs and peculiarities with them. Turk rubs shoulders with Greek and Arab squabbles with Hindoo. The tongues of half the Orient resound in the loud smelly bazaar. Therefore it did not seem particularly incongruous to hear, as I leaned on a bar tended by a smirking Eurasian, the musical notes of a Chinese gong sound clearly through the lazy hum of native traffic. There was certainly nothing so startling in those mellow tones that the big Englishman next me should start and swear and spill his whisky-and-soda on my sleeve.

He apologized and berated his clumsiness with honest profanity, but I saw he was shaken. He interested me as his type always does—a fine upstanding fellow he was; over six feet tall, broad-shouldered, narrow-hipped, heavy-limbed, the perfect fighting man, brown-faced, blue-eyed and tawny-haired. His breed is old as Europe, and the man himself brought to mind vague legendary characters—Hengist, Hereward, Cerdic—born rovers and fighters of the original Anglo-Saxon stock.

I saw, furthermore, that he was in a mood to talk. I introduced myself, ordered drinks and waited. My specimen thanked me, muttered to himself, quaffed his liquor hastily and spoke abruptly:

"You're wondering why a grown man should be so suddenly upset by such a small thing—well, I admit that damned gong gave me a start. It's that fool Yotai Lao, bringing his nasty joss sticks and Buddhas into a decent town—for a half-penny I'd bribe some Moslem fanatic to cut his yellow throat and sink his confounded gong into the gulf. And I'll tell you why I hate the thing.

"My name," said my Saxon, "is Bill Kirby. It was in Jibuti on the Gulf of Aden that I met John Conrad. A slim, keen-eyed young New Englander he was—professor too, for all his youth. Victim of obsession also, like most of his kind. He was a student of bugs, and it was a particular bug that had brought him to the East Coast; or rather, the hope of the blooming beast, for he never found it. It was almost uncanny to see the chap work himself into a blaze of enthusiasm when speaking on his favorite subject. No doubt he could have taught me much I should know, but insects are not among my enthusiasms, and he talked, dreamed and thought of little else at first. . . .

"Well, we paired off well from the start. He had money and ambitions and I had a bit of experience and a roving foot. We got together a small, modest but efficient safari and wandered down into the back country of Somaliland. Now you'll hear it spoken today that this country has been exhaustively explored and I can prove that statement to be a lie. We found things that no white man has ever dreamed of.

"We had trekked for the best part of a month and had gotten into a part of the country I knew was unknown to the average explorer. The veldt and thorn forests gave way to what approached real jungle and what natives we saw were a thick-lipped, low-browed, dog-toothed breed—not like the Somali at all. We wandered on though, and our porters and askari began muttering among themselves. Some of the black fellows had been hobnobbing with them and telling them tales that frightened them from going on. Our men wouldn't talk to me or Conrad about it, but we had a camp servant, a half-caste named Selim, and I told him to see what he could learn. That night he came to my tent. We had pitched camp in a sort of big glade and had built a thorn boma; for the lions were raising merry Cain in the bush.

"'Master,' said he in the mongrel English he was so proud of, 'them black fella he is scaring the porters and askari with bad ju-ju talk. They be tell about a mighty ju-ju curse on the country in which we go to, and—'

"He stopped short, turned ashy, and my head jerked up. Out of the dim, jungle-haunted mazes of the south whispered a haunting voice. Like the echo of an echo it was, yet strangely distinct, deep, vibrant, melodious. I stepped from my tent and saw Conrad standing before a fire, taut and tense as a hunting hound.

"'Did you hear that?' he asked. 'What was it?'

"'A native drum,' I answered—but we both knew I lied. The noise and chatter of our natives about their cooking-fires had ceased as if they had all died suddenly.

"We heard nothing more of it that night, but the next morning we found ourselves deserted. The black boys had decamped with all the luggage they could lay hand to. We held a council of war, Conrad, Selim and I. The half-caste was scared pink, but the pride of his white blood kept him carrying on.

"'What now?' I asked Conrad. 'We've our guns and enough supplies to give us a sporting chance of reaching the coast.'

"'Listen!' he raised his hand. Out across the bush-country throbbed again that haunting whisper. 'We'll go on. I'll never rest until I know what makes that sound. I never heard anything like it in the world before.'

"'The jungle will pick our bally bones,' I said. He shook his head.

"'Listen!' said he.

"It was like a call. It got into your blood. It drew you as a fakir's music draws a cobra. I knew it was madness. But I didn't argue. We cached most of our duffle and started on. Each night we built a thorn boma and sat inside it while the big cats yowled and grunted outside. And ever clearer as we worked deeper and deeper in the jungle mazes, we heard that voice. It was deep, mellow, musical. It made you dream strange things; it was pregnant with vast age. The lost glories of antiquity whispered in its booming. It centered in its resonance all the yearning and mystery of life; all the magic soul of the East. I awoke in the middle of the night to listen to its whispering echoes, and slept to dream of sky-towering minarets, of long ranks of bowing, brown-skinned worshippers, of purple-canopied peacock thrones and thundering golden chariots.

"Conrad had found something at last that rivaled his infernal bugs in his interest. He didn't talk much; he hunted insects in an absent-minded way. All day he would seem to be in an attitude of listening, and when the deep golden notes would roll out across the jungle, he would tense like a hunting dog on the scent, while into his eyes would steal a look strange for a civilized professor. By Jove, it's curious to see some ancient primal influence steal through the veneer of a cold-blooded scientist's soul and touch the red flow of life beneath! It was new and strange to Conrad; here was something he couldn't explain away with his new-fangled, bloodless psychology.

"Well, we wandered on in that mad search—for it's the white man's curse to go into Hell to satisfy his curiosity. Then in the gray light of an early dawn the camp was rushed. There was no fight. We were simply flooded and submerged by numbers. They must have stolen up and surrounded us on all sides; for the first thing I knew, the camp was full of fantastic figures and there were half a dozen spears at my throat. It rasped me terribly to give up without a shot fired, but there was no bettering it, and I cursed myself for not having kept a better lookout. We should have expected something of the kind, with that devilish chiming in the south.

"There were at least a hundred of them, and I got a chill when I looked at them closely. They weren't black boys and they weren't Arabs. They were lean men of middle height, light yellowish brown, with dark eyes and big noses. They wore no beards and their heads were close-shaven. They were clad in a sort of tunic, belted at the waist with a wide leather girdle, and sandals. They also wore a queer kind of iron helmet, peaked at the top, open in front and coming down nearly to their shoulders behind and at the sides. They carried big metal-braced shields, nearly square, and were armed with narrow-bladed spears, strangely made bows and arrows, and short straight swords such as I had never seen before—or since.

"They bound Conrad and me hand and foot and they butchered Selim then and there—cut his throat like a pig while he kicked and howled. A sickening sight—Conrad nearly fainted and I dare say I looked a bit pale myself. Then they set out in the direction we had been heading, making us walk between them, with our hands tied behind our backs and their spears threatening us. They brought along our scanty dunnage, but from the way they carried the guns I didn't believe they knew what those were for. Scarcely a word had been spoken between them and when I essayed various dialects I only got the prod of a spearpoint. Their silence was a bit ghostly and altogether ghastly. I felt as if we'd been captured by a band of spooks.

"I didn't know what to make of them. They had the look of the Orient about them but not the Orient with which I was familiar, if you understand me. Africa is of the East but not one with it. They looked no more African than a Chinaman does. This is hard to explain. But I'll say this: Tokyo is Eastern, and Benares is equally so, but Benares symbolizes a different, older phase of the Orient, while Peking represents still another, and older one. These men were of an Orient I had never known; they were part of an East older than Persia—older than Assyria—older than Babylon! I felt it about them like an aura and I shuddered from the gulfs of Time they symbolized. Yet it fascinated me, too. Beneath the Gothic arches of an age-old jungle, speared along by silent Orientals whose type has been forgotten for God knows how many eons, a man can have fantastic thoughts. I almost wondered if these fellows were real, or but the ghosts of warriors dead four thousand years!

"The trees began to thin and the ground sloped upward. At last we came out upon a sort of cliff and saw a sight that made us gasp. We were looking into a big valley surrounded entirely by high, steep cliffs, through which various streams had cut narrow canyons to feed a good-sized lake in the center of the valley. In the center of that lake was an island and on that island was a temple and at the farther end of the lake was a city! No native village of mud and bamboo, either. This seemed to be of stone, yellowish-brown in color.

"The city was walled and consisted of square-built, flat-topped houses, some apparently three or four stories high. All the shores of the lake were in cultivation and the fields were green and flourishing, fed by artificial ditches. They had a system of irrigation that amazed me. But the most astonishing thing was the temple on the island.

"I gasped, gaped and blinked. It was the tower of Babel true to life! Not as tall or as big as I'd imagined it, but some ten tiers high and sullen and massive just like the pictures, with that same intangible impression of evil hovering over it.

"Then as we stood there, from that vast pile of masonry there floated out across the lake that deep resonant booming—close and clear now—and the very cliffs seemed to quiver with the vibrations of that music-laden air. I stole a glance at Conrad; he looked all at sea. He was of that class of scientists who have the universe classified and pigeon-holed and everything in its proper little nook. By Jove! It knocks them in a heap to be confronted with the paradoxical-unexplainable-shouldn't-be more than it does common chaps like you and me, who haven't much preconceived ideas of things in general.

"The soldiers took us down a stairway cut into the solid rock of the cliffs and we went through irrigated fields where shaven-headed men and dark-eyed women paused in their work to stare curiously at us. They took us to a big, iron-braced gate where a small body of soldiers equipped like our captors challenged them, and after a short parley we were escorted into the city. It was much like any other Eastern city—men, women and children going to and fro, arguing, buying and selling. But all in all, it had that same effect of apartness—of vast antiquity. I couldn't classify the architecture any more than I could understand the language. The only thing I could think of as I stared at those squat, square buildings was the huts certain low-caste, mongrel peoples still build in the valley of the Euphrates in Mesopotamia. Those huts might be a degraded evolution from the architecture in that strange African city.

"Our captors took us straight to the largest building in the city, and while we marched along the streets, we discovered that the houses and walls were not of stone after all, but a sort of brick. We were taken into a huge-columned hall before which stood ranks of silent soldiery, and taken before a dais up which led broad steps. Armed warriors stood behind and on either side of a throne, a scribe stood beside it, girls clad in ostrich-plumes lounged on the broad steps, and on the throne sat a grim-eyed devil who alone of all the men of that fantastic city wore his hair long. He was black-bearded, wore a sort of crown and had the haughtiest, cruelest face I ever saw on any man. An Arab sheikh or Turkish shah was a lamb beside him. He reminded me of some artist's conception of Belshazzar or the Pharaohs—a king who was more than a king in his own mind and the eyes of his people—a king who was at once king and high priest and god.

"Our escort promptly prostrated themselves before him and knocked their heads on the matting until he spoke a languid word to the scribe and this personage signed for them to rise. They rose, and the leader began a long rigmarole to the king, while the scribe

scratched away like mad on a clay tablet and Conrad
and I stood there like a pair of blooming gaping jack-
asses, wondering what it was all about. Then I heard a
word repeated continually, and each time he spoke it,
he indicated us. The word sounded like 'Akkaddian,'
and suddenly my brain reeled with the possibilities it
betokened. It couldn't be—yet it had to be!

"Not wanting to break in on the conversation and
maybe lose my bally head, I said nothing, and at last
the king gestured and spoke, the soldiers bowed again
and seizing us, hustled us roughly from the royal presence into a columned corridor, across a huge chamber
and into a small cell where they thrust us and locked
the door. There was only a heavy bench and one
window, closely barred.

"'My heavens, Bill,' exclaimed Conrad, 'who could
have imagined anything equal to this? It's like a nightmare—or a tale from The Arabian Nights! Where are
we? Who are these people?'

"'You won't believe me,' I said, 'but—you've read
of the ancient empire of Sumeria?'

"'Certainly; it flourished in Mesopotamia some
four thousand years ago. But what—by Jove!' he
broke off, staring at me wide-eyed as the connection
struck him.

"'I leave it to you what the descendants of an Asia-
Minor kingdom are doing in East Africa,' I said,
feeling for my pipe, 'but it must be—the Sumerians
built their cities of sun-dried brick. I saw men making
bricks and stacking them up to dry along the lake
shore. The mud is remarkably like that you find in the
Tigris and Euphrates valley. Likely that's why these

chaps settled here. The Sumerians wrote on clay tablets by scratching the surface with a sharp point just as the chap was doing in the throne room.

"'Then look at their arms, dress and physiognomy. I've seen their art carved on stone and pottery and wondered if those big noses were part of their faces or part of their helmets. And look at that temple in the lake! A small counterpart of the temple reared to the god El-lil in Nippur—which probably started the myth of the tower of Babel.

"'But the thing that clinches it is the fact that they referred to us as Akkaddians. Their empire was conquered and subjugated by Sargon of Akkad in 2750 B.C. If these are descendants of a band who fled their conqueror, it's natural that, pent in these hinterlands and separated from the rest of the world, they'd come to call all outlanders Akkaddians, much as secluded oriental nations call all Europeans Franks in memory of Martel's warriors who scuttled them at Tours.'

"'Why do you suppose they haven't been discovered before now?'

"'Well, if any white man's been here before, they took good care he didn't get out to tell his tale. I doubt if they wander much; probably think the outside world's overrun with bloodthirsty Akkaddians.'

"At this moment the door of our cell opened to admit a slim young girl, clad only in a girdle of silk and golden breast-plates. She brought us food and wine, and I noted how lingeringly she gazed at Conrad. And to my surprize she spoke to us in fair Somali.

"'Where are we?' I asked her. 'What are they going

to do with us? Who are you?'

"'I am Naluna, the dancer of El-lil,' she answered—
and she looked it—lithe as a she-panther she was. 'I
am sorry to see you in this place; no Akkaddian goes
forth from here alive.'

"'Nice friendly sort of chaps,' I grunted, but glad to
find someone I could talk to and understand. 'And
what's the name of this city?'

"'This is Eridu,' said she. 'Our ancestors came here
many ages ago from ancient Sumer, many moons to
the East. They were driven by a great and cruel king,
Sargon of the Akkaddians—desert people. But our
ancestors would not be slaves like their kin, so they
fled, thousands of them in one great band, and traversed many strange, savage countries before they
came to this land.'

"Beyond that her knowledge was very vague and
mixed up with myths and improbable legends. Conrad
and I discussed it afterward, wondering if the old
Sumerians came down the west coast of Arabia and
crossed the Red Sea about where Mocha is now, or if
they went over the Isthmus of Suez and came down on
the African side. I'm inclined to the last opinion.
Likely the Egyptians met them as they came out of
Asia Minor and chased them south. Conrad thought
they might have made most of the trip by water,
because, as he said, the Persian Gulf ran up something
like a hundred and thirty miles farther than it does
now, and Old Eridu was a seaport town. But just at
the moment something else was on my mind.

"'Where did you learn to speak Somali?' I asked
Naluna.

"'When I was little,' she answered, 'I wandered out of the valley and into the jungle where a band of raiding black men caught me. They sold me to a tribe who lived near the coast and I spent my childhood among them. But when I had grown into girlhood I remembered Eridu and one day I stole a camel and rode across many leagues of veldt and jungle and so came again to the city of my birth. In all Eridu I alone can speak a tongue not mine own, except for the black slaves—and they speak not at all, for we cut out their tongues when we capture them. The people of Eridu go not forth beyond the jungles and they traffic not with the black peoples who sometimes come against us, except as they take a few slaves.'

"I asked her why they killed our camp servant and she said that it was forbidden for blacks and whites to mate in Eridu and the offspring of such union was not allowed to live. They didn't like the poor beggar's color.

"Naluna could tell us little of the history of the city since its founding, outside the events that had happened in her own memory—which dealt mainly with scattered raids by a cannibalistic tribe living in the jungles to the south, petty intrigues of court and temple, crop failures and the like—the scope of a woman's life in the East is much the same, whether in the palace of Akbar, Cyrus or Asshurbanipal. But I learned that the ruler's name was Sostoras and that he was both high priest and king—just as the rulers were in old Sumer, four thousand years ago. El-lil was their god, who abode in the temple in the lake, and the deep booming we had heard was, Naluna said, the voice of the god.

"At last she rose to go, casting a wistful look at Conrad, who sat like a man in a trance—for once his confounded bugs were clean out of his mind.

"'Well,' said I, 'what d'you think of it, young fella-me-lad?'

"'It's incredible,' said he, shaking his head. 'It's absurd—an intelligent tribe living here four thousand years and never advancing beyond their ancestors.'

"'You're stung with the bug of progress,' I told him cynically, cramming my pipe bowl full of weed. 'You're thinking of the mushroom growth of your own country. You can't generalize on an Oriental from a Western viewpoint. What about China's famous long sleep? As for these chaps, you forget they're no tribe but the tag-end of a civilization that lasted longer than any has lasted since. They passed the peak of their progress thousands of years ago. With no intercourse with the outside world and no new blood to stir them up, these people are slowly sinking in the scale. I'd wager their culture and art are far inferior to that of their ancestors.'

"'Then why haven't they lapsed into complete barbarism?'

"'Maybe they have, to all practical purposes,' I answered, beginning to draw on my old pipe. 'They don't strike me as being quite the proper thing for off-springs of an ancient and honorable civilization. But remember they grew slowly and their retrogression is bound to be equally slow. Sumerian culture was unusually virile. Its influence is felt in Asia Minor today. The Sumerians had their civilization when our bloomin' ancestors were scrapping with cave bears and sabertooth tigers, so to speak. At least the Aryans hadn't passed the first milestones on the road to progress, whoever their animal neighbors were. Old Eridu was a seaport of consequence as early as 6500 B.C. From then to 2750 B.C. is a bit of time for any empire. What other empire stood as long as the Sumerian? The Akkaddian dynasty established by Sargon stood two hundred years before it was overthrown by another Semitic people, the Babylonians, who borrowed their culture from Akkaddian Sumer just as Rome later stole hers from Greece; the Elamitish Kassite dynasty supplanted the original Babylonian, the Assyrian and the Chaldean followed—well, you know the rapid succession of dynasty on dynasty in Asia Minor, one Semitic people overthrowing another, until the real conquerors hove in view on the Eastern horizon—the Aryan Medes and Persians—who were destined to last scarcely longer than their victims.

"'Compare each fleeting kingdom with the long dreamy reign of the ancient pre-Semitic Sumerians! We think the Minoan Age of Crete is a long time back, but the Sumerian empire of Erech was already beginning to decay before the rising power of Sumerian Nippur, before the ancestors of the Cretans had emerged from the Neolithic Age. The Sumerians had something the succeeding Hamites, Semites and Aryans lacked. They were stable. They grew slowly and if left alone would have decayed as slowly as these fellows are decaying. Still and all, I note these chaps have made one advancement—notice their weapons?

"'Old Sumer was in the Bronze Age. The Assyrians were the first to use iron for anything besides ornaments. But these lads have learned to work iron— probably a matter of necessity. No copper hereabouts but plenty of iron ore, I daresay.'

"'But the mystery of Sumer still remains,' Conrad broke in. 'Who are they? Whence did they come? Some authorities maintain they were of Dravidian origin, akin to the Basques—'

"'It won't stick, me lad,' said I. 'Even allowing for possible admixture of Aryan or Turanian blood in the Dravidian descendants, you can see at a glance these people are not of the same race.'

"'But their language—' Conrad began arguing, which is a fair way to pass the time while you're waiting to be put in the cooking-pot, but doesn't prove much except to strengthen your own original ideas.

"Naluna came again about sunset with food, and this time she sat down by Conrad and watched him eat. Seeing her sitting thus, elbows on knees and chin on hands, devouring him with her large, lustrous dark eyes, I said to the professor in English, so she wouldn't understand: 'The girl's badly smitten with you; play up to her. She's our only chance.'

"He blushed like a blooming school girl. 'I've a fiancée back in the States.'

"'Blow your fiancée,' I said. 'Is it she that's going to keep the bally heads on our blightin' shoulders? I tell you this girl's silly over you. Ask her what they're going to do with us.'

"He did so and Naluna said: 'Your fate lies in the lap of El-lil.'

"'And the brain of Sostoras,' I muttered. 'Naluna, what was done with the guns that were taken from us?'

"She replied that they were hung in the temple of El-lil as trophies of victory. None of the Sumerians was aware of their purpose. I asked her if the natives they sometimes fought had never used guns and she said no. I could easily believe that, seeing that there are many wild tribes in those hinterlands who've scarcely seen a single white man. But it seemed incredible that some of the Arabs who've raided back and forth across Somaliland for a thousand years hadn't stumbled onto Eridu and shot it up. But it turned out to be true—just one of those peculiar quirks and back-eddies in events like the wolves and wildcats you still find in New York state, or those queer pre-Aryan peoples you come onto in small communities in the hills of Connaught and Galway. I'm certain that big slave raids had passed within a few miles of Eridu, yet the Arabs had never found it and impressed on them the meaning of firearms.

"So I told Conrad: 'Play up to her, you chump! If you can persuade her to slip us a gun, we've a sporting chance.'

"So Conrad took heart and began talking to Naluna in a nervous sort of manner. Just how he'd have come out, I can't say, for he was little of the Don Juan, but Naluna snuggled up to him, much to his embarrassment, listening to his stumbling Somali with her soul in her eyes. Love blossoms suddenly and unexpectedly in the East.

"However, a peremptory voice outside our cell made Naluna jump half out of her skin and sent her scurrying, but as she went she pressed Conrad's hand and whispered something in his ear that we couldn't understand, but it sounded highly passionate.

"Shortly after she had left, the cell opened again and there stood a file of silent dark-skinned warriors. A sort of chief, whom the rest addressed as Gorat, motioned us to come out. Then down a long, dim, colonnaded corridor we went, in perfect silence except for the soft scruff of their sandals and the tramp of our boots on the tiling. An occasional torch flaring on the walls or in a niche of the columns lighted the way vaguely. At last we came out into the empty streets of the silent city. No sentry paced the streets or the walls, no lights showed from inside the flat-topped houses. It was like walking a street in a ghost city. Whether every night in Eridu was like that or whether the people kept indoors because it was a special and awesome occasion, I haven't an idea.

"We went on down the streets toward the lake side of the town. There we passed through a small gate in the wall—over which, I noted with a slight shudder, a grinning skull was carved—and found ourselves outside the city. A broad flight of steps led down to the water's edge and the spears at our backs guided us down them. There a boat waited, a strange high-prowed affair whose prototype must have plied the Persian Gulf in the days of Old Eridu.

"Four black men rested on their oars, and when they opened their mouths I saw their tongues had been cut out. We were taken into the boat, our guards got in and we started a strange journey. Out on the silent lake we moved like a dream, whose silence was broken only by the low rippling of the long, slim, golden-worked oars through the water. The stars flecked the deep blue gulf of the lake with silver points. I looked back and saw the silent city of Eridu sleeping beneath the stars. I looked ahead and saw the great dark bulk of the temple loom against the stars. The naked black mutes pulled the shining oars and the silent warriors sat before and behind us with their spears, helms and shields. It was like the dream of some fabulous city of Haroun-al-Raschid's time, or of Sulieman-ben-Daoud's, and I thought how blooming incongruous Conrad and I looked in that setting, with our boots and dingy, tattered khakis.

"We landed on the island and I saw it was girdled with masonry—built up from the water's edge in broad flights of steps which circled the entire island. The whole seemed older, even, than the city—the Sumerians must have built it when they first found the valley, before they began on the city itself.

"We went up the steps, that were worn deep by countless feet, to a huge set of iron doors in the temple, and here Gorat laid down his spear and shield, dropped on his belly and knocked his helmed head on the great sill. Some one must have been watching from a loophole, for from the top of the tower sounded one deep golden note and the doors swung silently open to disclose a dim, torch-lighted entrance. Gorat rose and led the way, we following with those confounded spears pricking our backs.

"We mounted a flight of stairs and came onto a

series of galleries built on the inside of each tier and winding around and up. Looking up, it seemed much higher and bigger than it had seemed from without, and the vague, half-lighted gloom, the silence and the mystery gave me the shudders. Conrad's face gleamed white in the semi-darkness. The shadows of past ages crowded in upon us, chaotic and horrific, and I felt as though the ghosts of all the priests and victims who had walked those galleries for four thousand years were keeping pace with us. The vast wings of dark, forgotten gods hovered over that hideous pile of antiquity.

"We came out on the highest tier. There were three circles of tall columns, one inside the other—and I want to say that for columns built of sun-dried brick, these were curiously symmetrical. But there was none of the grace and open beauty of, say, Greek architecture. This was grim, sullen, monstrous—something like the Egyptian, not quite so massive but even more formidable in starkness—an architecture symbolizing an age when men were still in the dawn-shadows of Creation and dreamed of monstrous gods.

"Over the inner circle of columns was a curving roof—almost a dome. How they built it, or how they came to anticipate the Roman builders by so many ages, I can't say, for it was a startling departure from the rest of their architectural style, but there it was. And from this dome-like roof hung a great round shining thing that caught the starlight in a silver net. I knew then what we had been following for so many mad miles! It was a great gong—the Voice of El-lil. It looked like jade but I'm not sure to this day. But

whatever it was, it was the symbol on which the faith
and cult of the Sumerians hung—the symbol of the
god-head itself. And I know Naluna was right when
she told us that her ancestors brought it with them on
that long, grueling trek, ages ago, when they fled
before Sargon's wild riders. And how many eons
before that dim time must it have hung in El-lil's
temple in Nippur, Erech or Old Eridu, booming out
its mellow threat or promise over the dreamy valley
of the Euphrates, or across the green foam of the
Persian Gulf!

"They stood us just within the first ring of columns,
and out of the shadows somewhere, looking like a
shadow from the past himself, came old Sostoras, the
priest-king of Eridu. He was clad in a long robe of
green, covered with scales like a snake's hide, and it
rippled and shimmered with every step he took. On his
head he wore a head-piece of waving plumes and in his
hand he held a long-shafted golden mallet.

"He tapped the gong lightly and golden waves of
sound flowed over us like a wave, suffocating us in its
exotic sweetness. And then Naluna came. I never
knew if she came from behind the columns or up
through some trap floor. One instant the space before
the gong was bare, the next she was dancing like a
moonbeam on a pool. She was clad in some light,
shimmery stuff that barely veiled her sinuous body
and lithe limbs. And she danced before Sostoras and
the Voice of El-lil as women of her breed had danced
in old Sumer four thousand years ago.

"I can't begin to describe that dance. It made me
freeze and tremble and burn inside. I heard Conrad's

breath come in gasps and he shivered like a reed in the wind. From somewhere sounded music, that was old when Babylon was young, music as elemental as the fire in a tigress' eyes, and as soulless as an African midnight. And Naluna danced. Her dancing was a whirl of fire and wind and passion and all elemental forces. From all basic, primal fundamentals she drew underlying principles and combined them in one spin-wheel of motion. She narrowed the universe to a dagger-point of meaning and her flying feet and shimmering body wove out the mazes of that one central Thought. Her dancing stunned, exalted, maddened and hypnotized.

"As she whirled and spun, she was the elemental Essence, one and a part of all powerful impulses and moving or sleeping powers—the sun, the moon, the stars, the blind groping of hidden roots to light, the fire from the furnace, the sparks from the anvil, the breath of the fawn, the talons of the eagle. Naluna danced, and her dancing was Time and Eternity, the urge of Creation and the urge of Death; birth and dissolution in one, age and infancy combined.

"My dazed mind refused to retain more impressions; the girl merged into a whirling flicker of white fire before my dizzy eyes; then Sostoras struck one light note on the Voice and she fell at his feet, a quivering white shadow. The moon was just beginning to glow over the cliffs to the East.

"The warriors seized Conrad and me, and bound me to one of the outer columns. Him they dragged to the inner circle and bound to a column directly in front of the great gong. And I saw Naluna, white in the growing glow, gaze drawnly at him, then shoot a glance full of meaning at me, as she faded from sight among the dark sullen columns.

"Old Sostoras made a motion and from the shadows came a wizened black slave who looked incredibly old. He had the withered features and vacant stare of a deaf-mute, and the priest-king handed the golden mallet to him. Then Sostoras fell back and stood beside me, while Gorat bowed and stepped back a pace and the warriors likewise bowed and backed still farther away. In fact they seemed most blooming anxious to get as far away from that sinister ring of columns as they could.

"There was a tense moment of waiting. I looked out across the lake at the high, sullen cliffs that girt the valley, at the silent city lying beneath the rising moon. It was like a dead city.

The whole scene was most unreal, as if Conrad and I had been transported to another planet or back into a dead and forgotten age. Then the black mute struck the gong.

"At first it was a low, mellow whisper that flowed out from under the black man's steady mallet. But it swiftly grew in intensity. The sustained, increasing sound became nerve-racking—it grew unbearable. It was more than mere sound. The mute evoked a quality of vibration that entered into every nerve and racked it apart. It grew louder and louder until I felt that the most desirable thing in the world was complete deafness, to be like that blank-eyed mute who neither heard nor felt the perdition of sound he was creating. And yet I saw sweat beading his ape-like brow. Surely some thunder of that brain-shattering cataclysm re-echoed in his own soul. El-lil spoke to us and death was in his voice. Surely, if one of the terrible, black gods of past ages could speak, he would speak in just such tongue! There was neither mercy, pity nor weakness in its roar. It was the assurance of a cannibal god to whom mankind was but a plaything and a puppet to dance on his string.

"Sound can grow too deep, too shrill or too loud for the human ear to record. Not so with the Voice of El-lil, which had its creation in some inhuman age when dark wizards knew how to rack brain, body and soul apart. Its depth was unbearable, its volume was unbearable, yet ear and soul were keenly alive to its resonance and did not grow mercifully numb and dulled. And its terrible sweetness was beyond human endurance; it suffocated us in a smothering wave of sound that yet was barbed with golden fangs. I gasped and struggled in physical agony. Behind me I was aware that even old Sostoras had his hands over his ears, and Gorat groveled on the floor, grinding his face into the bricks.

"And if it so affected me, who was just within the magic circle of columns, and those Sumerians who were outside the circle, what was it doing to Conrad, who was inside the inner ring and beneath that domed roof that intensified every note?

"Till the day he dies Conrad will never be closer to madness and death than he was then. He writhed in his bonds like a snake with a broken back; his face was horribly contorted, his eyes distended, and foam flecked his livid lips. But in that hell of golden, agonizing sound I could hear nothing—I could only see his gaping mouth and his frothy, flaccid lips, loose and writhing like an imbecile's. But I sensed he was howling like a dying dog.

"Oh, the sacrificial dagger of the Semites was merciful. Even Moloch's lurid furnace was easier than the death promised by this rending and ripping vibration that armed sound waves with venomed talons. I felt my own brain was brittle as frozen glass. I knew that a few seconds more of that torture and Conrad's brain would shatter like a crystal goblet and he would die in the black raving of utter madness. And then something snapped me back from the mazes I'd gotten into. It was the fierce grasp of a small hand on mine, behind the column to which I was bound. I felt a tug at my cords as if a knife edge was being passed along them, and my hands were free. I felt something pressed into my hand and a fierce exultation surged through me. I'd recognize the familiar checkered grip of my Webley .44 in a thousand!

"I acted in a flash that took the whole gang off guard. I lunged away from the column and dropped the black mute with a bullet through his brain, wheeled and shot old Sostoras through the belly. He went down, spewing blood, and I crashed a volley square into the stunned ranks of the soldiers. At that range I couldn't miss. Three of them dropped and the rest woke up and scattered like a flock of birds. In a second the place was empty except for Conrad, Naluna and me, and the men on the floor. It was like a dream, the echoes from the shots still crashing, and the acrid scent of powder and blood knifing the air.

"The girl cut Conrad loose and he fell on the floor and yammered like a dying imbecile. I shook him but he had a wild glare in his eyes and was frothing like a mad dog, so I dragged him up, shoved an arm under him and started for the stair. We weren't out of the mess yet, by a long shot. Down those wide, winding, dark galleries we went, expecting any minute to be ambushed, but the chaps must have still been in a bad funk, because we got out of that hellish temple without any interference. Outside the iron portals Conrad collapsed and I tried to talk to him, but he could neither hear nor speak. I turned to Naluna.

"'Can you do anything for him?'

"Her eyes flashed in the moonlight. 'I have not defied my people and my god and betrayed my cult and my race for naught! I stole the weapon of smoke and flame, and freed you, did I not? I love him and I will not lose him now!'

"She darted into the temple and was out almost instantly with a jug of wine. She claimed it had magical powers. I don't believe it. I think Conrad simply was suffering from a sort of shell-shock from close proximity to that fearful noise and that lake water would have done as well as the wine. But Naluna poured some wine between his lips and emptied some over his head, and soon he groaned and cursed.

"'See!' she cried triumphantly, 'the magic wine has lifted the spell El-lil put on him!' And she flung her arms around his neck and kissed him vigorously.

"'My God, Bill,' he groaned, sitting up and holding his head, 'what kind of a nightmare is this?'

"'Can you walk, old chap?' I asked. 'I think we've

stirred up a bloomin' hornet's nest and we'd best leg it out of here.'

"'I'll try.' He staggered up, Naluna helping him. I heard a sinister rustle and whispering in the black mouth of the temple and I judged the warriors and priests inside were working up their nerve to rush us. We made it down the steps in a great hurry to where lay the boat that had brought us to the island. Not even the black rowers were there. An ax and shield lay in it and I seized the ax and knocked holes in the bottoms of the other boats which were tied near it.

"Meanwhile the big gong had begun to boom out again and Conrad groaned and writhed as every intonation rasped his raw nerves. It was a warning note this time and I saw lights flare up in the city and heard a sudden hum of shouts float out across the lake. Something hissed softly by my head and slashed into the water. A quick look showed me Gorat standing in the door of the temple bending his heavy bow. I leaped in, Naluna helped Conrad in, and we shoved off in a hurry to the accompaniment of several more shafts from the charming Gorat, one of which took a lock of hair from Naluna's pretty head.

"I laid to the oars while Naluna steered and Conrad lay on the bottom of the boat and was violently sick. We saw a fleet of boats put out from the city, and as they saw us by the gleam of the moon, a yell of concentrated rage went up that froze the blood in my veins. We were heading for the opposite end of the lake and had a long start on them, but in this way we were forced to round the island and we'd scarcely left it astern when out of some nook leaped a long boat with six warriors—I saw Gorat in the bows with that confounded bow of his.

"I had no spare cartridges so I laid to it with all my might, and Conrad, somewhat green in the face, took the shield and rigged it up in the stern, which was the saving of us, because Gorat hung within bowshot of us all the way across the lake and he filled that shield so full of arrows it resembled a blooming porcupine. You'd have thought they'd had plenty after the slaughter I made among them on the roof, but they were after us like hounds after a hare.

"We'd a fair start on them but Gorat's five rowers shot his boat through the water like a racehorse, and when we grounded on the shore, they weren't half a dozen jumps behind us. As we scrambled out I saw it was either make a fight of it there and be cut down from the front, or else be shot like rabbits as we ran. I called to Naluna to run but she laughed and drew a dagger—she was a man's woman, that girl!

"Gorat and his merry men came surging up to the landing with a clamor of yells and a swirl of oars—they swarmed over the side like a gang of bloody pirates and the battle was on! Luck was with Gorat at the first pass, for I missed him and killed the man behind him. The hammer snapped on an empty shell and I dropped the Webley and snatched up the ax just as they closed with us. By Jove! It stirs my blood now to think of the touch-and-go fury of that fight! Knee-deep in water we met them, hand to hand, chest to chest!

"Conrad brained one with a stone he picked from the water, and out of the tail of my eye, as I swung for

Gorat's head, I saw Naluna spring like a she-panther on another, and they went down together in a swirl of limbs and a flash of steel. Gorat's sword was thrusting for my life, but I knocked it aside with the ax and he lost his footing and went down—for the lake bottom was solid stone there, and treacherous as sin.

"One of the warriors lunged in with a spear, but he tripped over the fellow Conrad had killed, his helmet fell off and I crushed his skull before he could recover his balance. Gorat was up and coming for me, and the other was swinging his sword in both hands for a death blow, but he never struck, for Conrad caught up the spear that had been dropped, and spitted him from behind, neat as a whistle.

"Gorat's point raked my ribs as he thrust for my heart and I twisted to one side, and his up-flung arm broke like a rotten stick beneath my stroke but saved his life. He was game—they were all game or they'd never have rushed my gun. He sprang in like a blood-mad tiger, hacking for my head. I ducked and avoided the full force of the blow but couldn't get away from it altogether and it laid my scalp open in a three-inch gash, clear to the bone—here's the scar to prove it. Blood blinded me and I struck back like a wounded lion, blind and terrible, and by sheer chance I landed squarely. I felt the ax crunch through metal and bone, the haft splintered in my hand, and there was Gorat dead at my feet in a horrid welter of blood and brains.

"I shook the blood out of my eyes and looked about for my companions. Conrad was helping Naluna up and it seemed to me she swayed a little. There was blood on her bosom but it might have come from the red dagger she gripped in a hand stained to the wrist. God! It was a bit sickening, to think of it now. The water we stood in was choked with corpses and ghastly red. Naluna pointed out across the lake and we saw Eridu's boats sweeping down on us—a good way off as yet, but coming swiftly. She led us at a run away from the lake's edge. My wound was bleeding as only a scalp wound can bleed, but I wasn't weakened as yet. I shook the blood out of my eyes, saw Naluna stagger as she ran and tried to put my arm about her to steady her, but she shook me off.

"She was making for the cliffs and we reached them out of breath. Naluna leaned against Conrad and pointed upward with a shaky hand, breathing in great, sobbing gasps. I caught her meaning. A rope ladder led upward. I made her go first with Conrad following. I came after him, drawing the ladder up behind me. We'd gotten some halfway up when the boats landed and the warriors raced up the shore, loosing their arrows as they ran. But we were in the shadow of the cliffs, which made aim uncertain, and most of the shafts fell short or broke on the face of the cliff. One stuck in my left arm, but I shook it out and didn't stop to congratulate the marksman on his eye.

"Once over the cliff's edge, I jerked the ladder up and tore it loose, and then turned to see Naluna sway and collapse in Conrad's arms. We laid her gently on the grass, but a man with half an eye could tell she was going fast. I wiped the blood from her bosom and stared aghast. Only a woman with a great love could have made that run and that climb with such a wound as that girl had under her heart.

"Conrad cradled her head in his lap and tried to falter a few words, but she weakly put her arms around his neck and drew his face down to hers.

"'Weep not for me, my lover,' she said, as her voice weakened to a whisper. 'Thou hast been mine aforetime, as thou shalt be again. In the mud huts of the Old River, before Sumer was, when we tended the flocks, we were as one. In the palaces of Old Eridu, before the barbarians came out of the East, we loved each other. Aye, on this very lake have we floated in past ages, living and loving, thou and I. So weep not, my lover, for what is one little life when we have known so many and shall know so many more? And in each of them, thou art mine and I am thine.

"'But thou must not linger. Hark! They clamor for thy blood below. But since the ladder is destroyed there is but one other way by which they may come upon the cliffs—the place by which they brought thee into the valley. Haste! They will return across the lake, scale the cliffs there and pursue thee, but thou may'st escape them if thou be'st swift. And when thou hearest the Voice of El-lil, remember, living or dead, Naluna loves thee with a love greater than any god.

"'But one boon I beg of thee,' she whispered, her heavy lids drooping like a sleepy child's. 'Press, I beg thee, thy lips on mine, my master, before the shadows utterly enfold me; then leave me here and go, and weep not, oh my lover, for what is—one—little—life—to—us—who—have—loved—in—so—many—'

"Conrad wept like a blithering baby, and so did I, by Judas, and I'll stamp the lousy brains out of the jackass who twits me for it! We left her with her arms folded on her bosom and a smile on her lovely face, and if there's a heaven for Christian folk, she's there with the best of them, on my oath.

"Well, we reeled away in the moonlight and my wounds were still bleeding and I was about done in. All that kept me going was a sort of wild beast instinct to live, I fancy, for if I was ever near to lying down and dying, it was then. We'd gone perhaps a mile when the Sumerians played their last ace. I think they'd realized we'd slipped out of their grasp and had too much start to be caught.

"At any rate, all at once that damnable gong began booming. I felt like howling like a dog with rabies. This time it was a different sound. I never saw or heard of a gong before or since whose notes could convey so many different meanings. This was an insidious call—a luring urge, yet a peremptory command for us to return. It threatened and promised; if its attraction had been great before we stood on the tower of El-lil and felt its full power, now it was almost irresistible. It was hypnotic. I know now how a bird feels when charmed by a snake and how the snake himself feels when the fakirs play on their pipes. I can't begin to make you understand the overpowering magnetism of that call. It made you want to writhe and tear at the air and run back, blind and screaming, as a hare runs into a python's jaws. I had to fight it as a man fights for his soul.

"As for Conrad, it had him in its grip. He halted and rocked like a drunken man.

"'It's no use,' he mumbled thickly. 'It drags at my heart-strings; it's fettered my brain and my soul; it embraces all the evil lure of all the universes. I must go back.'

"And he started staggering back the way we had come—toward that golden lie floating to us over the jungle. But I thought of the girl Naluna that had given up her life to save us from that abomination, and a strange fury gripped me.

"'See here!' I shouted. 'This won't do, you bloody fool! You're off your bally bean! I won't have it, d'you hear?'

"But he paid no heed, shoving by me with eyes like a man in a trance, so I let him have it—an honest right hook to the jaw that stretched him out dead to the world. I slung him over my shoulder and reeled on my way, and it was nearly an hour before he came to, quite sane and grateful to me.

"Well, we saw no more of the people of Eridu. Whether they trailed us at all or not, I haven't an idea. We could have fled no faster than we did, for we were fleeing the haunting, horrible mellow whisper that dogged us from the south. We finally made it back to the spot where we'd cached our dunnage, and then, armed and scantily equipped, we started the long trek for the coast. Maybe you read or heard something about two emaciated wanderers being picked up by an elephant-hunting expedition in the Somaliland back country, dazed and incoherent from suffering. Well, we were about done for, I'll admit, but we were perfectly sane. The incoherent part was when we tried to tell our tale and the blasted idiots wouldn't believe it. They patted our backs and talked in a soothing tone and poured whisky-and-sodas down us. We soon shut up, seeing we'd only be branded as liars or lunatics. They got us back to Jibuti, and both of us had had enough of Africa for a spell. I took ship for India and Conrad went the other way—couldn't get back to New England quick enough, where I hope he married that little American girl and is living happily. A wonderful chap, for all his damnable bugs.

"As for me, I can't hear any sort of a gong today without starting. On that long, grueling trek I never breathed easily until we were beyond the sound of that ghastly Voice. You can't tell what a thing like that may do to your mind. It plays the very deuce with all rational ideas.

"I still hear that hellish gong in my dreams, sometimes, and see that silent, hideously ancient city in that nightmare valley. Sometimes I wonder if it's still calling to me across the years. But that's nonsense. Anyway, there's the yarn as it stands and if you don't believe me, I won't blame you at all."

But I prefer to believe Bill Kirby, for I know his breed from Hengist down, and know him to be like all the rest—truthful, aggressive, profane, restless, sentimental and straightforward, a true brother of the roving, fighting, adventuring Sons of Aryan.

INTERACT WITH DORCHESTER ONLINE!

Want to learn more about your favorite books and authors?
Want to talk with other readers that like to read the same books as you?
Want to see up-to-the-minute Dorchester news?

VISIT DORCHESTER AT:
DorchesterPub.com
Twitter.com/DorchesterPub
Facebook.com (Search Pages)

DISCUSS DORCHESTER'S NOVELS AT:
Dorchester Forums at DorchesterPub.com
GoodReads.com
LibraryThing.com
Myspace.com/books
Shelfari.com
WeRead.com